A NOVEL

MEGAN LISA JONES

ISBN: 0692023348
ISBN 13: 9780692023341

Library of Congress Control Number: 2014906531
Laernn, Los Angeles, CA

To my two kids with love, Lauren & Jason
And to my parents, Handel & Christina

CONTENTS

If I am not for myself, then who will be for me? And if I am only for myself, what am I? And if not now, when?
Rabbi Hillel

I hate war as only a soldier who has lived it can, only as one who has seen its brutality, its futility, and its stupidity.
Dwight D. Eisenhower

Literature has been the salvation of the damned, literature has inspired and guided lovers, routed despair and can perhaps in this case save the world.
John Cheever

BEGIN

Flames of Northern Africa

The lone orange flame, pointing up at God, stuck in George's mind. To God? Who's God? Was there a God? Men really did ask those questions when facing death. At least George did. But first there was the smoke. Why?

The boom that followed seconds later was like the thunder that came after lightening only in that it just did. This noise sent debris flying through the air and a large piece of concrete almost rammed into George's torso, luckily missing by an inch and denting the green car next to him. Clouds of dark smoke mingled with chunks of building materials replaced the outline of the former apartment house.

A gurgling sound caught George's attention, despite his state of shock. A soldier? Him? Hardly. A therapist and professor moonlighting as an interrogator of men who were counted among the world's most dangerous. He turned to see his recent detainee, Khalil, drop the limp body of his guard, Sean. Khalil was holding Sean's gun, pointing straight at George's heart.

"Stop."

Think? What do you say when a murderer, and the man responsible for the mayhem around you, turns his attention to you. Please for mercy? What if you know he has none? Humanity? Khalil believed that killing in the name of his Allah was the right moral choice.

George's eyes were watering and he tasted tears. His nostrils burned with the stench of exploded buildings and human flesh. Khalil's dark eyes were unblinking in the fiery atmosphere and he was quiet.

Another loud bang punctuated the air and George sensed a tearing pain as his lung collapsed. His legs followed suit and George felt the hard pavement connect with his shoulder. A searing rip-like sound made no sense to him but the resulting pain did. Another shot.

George heard more sirens and hoped these were from the authorities arriving and not just more car alarms. Would they reach him in time?

He felt a warm breath on his face and tried to focus his eyes. He saw the cold coal-black eyes of the man who had shot him and smelled the acridness of his sweat. Khalil was studying him. Emotions? George couldn't sense any but he wasn't all that alert anymore. Suddenly his adversary reached out and caressed his cheek. The touch was soft, gentle.

Shouldn't Khalil be running away to escape recapture? The rims of George's vision blurred into utter darkness and the narrow circle in which he could see got smaller and smaller. Imagined or not, George would never be sure, as he felt the soft sweep of lips brushing what must have been the blood of his bullet hole. Then the blackness became absolute.

Fire burned nearby, consuming half the apartment building before firefighters got it under control. Toxic chemicals mixed with sarin dusted the Westwood, California, neighborhood full of UCLA students and other young people, though they wouldn't feel its effects for years.

Khalil walked away like a devil re-entering the burning inferno he'd conjured. Such a different religion, really. Khalil was a mujahedeen and had just taken his first steps into paradise. Where was George headed?

Drifting, his consciousness faltering, George heard the crackling flames. Dying down now? Well, the smoke was intensifying. A siren throbbed in the distance – yet again. How many people had Khalil killed here today in securing his own release? Would the morning papers say?

He tried to yell, to get someone's attention for help.

George felt an arm shaking him back into consciousness and life.

"George, George, stop, wake up…!" Karen's voice was anxious but why was she here at the bombsite? She hadn't come to defuse the terrorist plot.

He tried to focus his eyes in the darkness. The moon was visible through the open curtains blowing in the silvery light. Karen's eyes looked black but her white blonde hair glowed like an angel's. He was home? In his bed?

"I'm sorry," he stammered. "The dream, I can't stop it from coming over and over again." So much for the expertise of a psychology professor. "I can't even cure myself." He felt helpless and vulnerable. Not a man but a child haunted by nightmares in his safe bed and stable world.

Karen's delicate arms were around him and he felt the wetness of her tears against his neck. He didn't try to control the situation, unusual for him, but just gave in to her warmth. What frightened him more? The fact that he'd almost died or that, after close to thirty years of marriage, he was letting his wife take charge?

She pulled back and he felt that familiar tug at his heart. They kept fighting, but every time he looked at her the world stopped and all that existed was her slight and now aged beauty. She smiled and her tears glistened in the moonlight.

"Let's go back to sleep," was all he could say. Where was Khalil tonight?

Guns

More violence.

A gunshot crackled through the night streets and then a burst of more rang out, echoing in the darkness of a barely visible moon. Men were shouting, but words had little meaning in the midst of chaos. Spotlights highlighted the crowds of men yelling anti-government slogans and the masses ebbed and flowed instinctively in unison. Revolution, religious experience or rock concert, they were so similar.

Cairo.

Tall dirty white buildings rose up around the cavernous square, shelter-ing it from the outside world. Tanks lined the many streets that fed into its circular go around. The soldiers that usually patrolled traffic from the center point were huddled together on the fringe instead. The city looked ghostly as the buildings themselves stayed dark. Would the next day find the ruined square bustling again with honking cars, yelling merchants and the choking exhaust of motorbikes?

The fires of northern Africa were burning again, in yet another round of protests. But a lot had changed since the years of Khalil's boyhood in the dusty battles of Algeria's civil war. Algeria was but a trial run for the chang-es that the Islamists were bringing to this world. Allah's reign was about to begin anew and the continued protests throughout the streets of Cairo were yet another requisite step. A power void is filled by the most determined and Al Qaeda fit that bill. Like all evolving organisms determined to survive, they'd emerged from past mistakes leaner, hungrier and more determined. And the chaos just wasn't ending.

Solitude. Khalil felt the loneliness of being in a crowd whose objective wasn't his own. But as with the spider of his nickname he's need to spin his ideology like a web – person to person. Man can't be allowed to decide for himself; hence the importance of propaganda.

Desert nights can be cold, but the heat from the men clustered around Khalil masked that possibility. They were shouting and singing in Arabic, a language he loved and revered, calling for the beginning of a new and better world. The people were being heard? One could hope. Khalil huddled at the outskirts of the mass, knowing that the snipers perched on the tanks would be shooting into the most densely populated parts of the crowd. The army was in control.

Hearing a bullet hit flesh he turned to the resulting panic and whirl of people around the victim. While the night should have been dark, the spotlights brightened Tahrir Square. Carrying the wounded man, a huddled mass groped through the night toward him. As they came close Khalil saw that the body they held was not male but female and he felt a stab of panic. Blonde hair hung limply against the dark pavement beneath. She didn't?

While the people of northern Africa and the Middle East had rebelled against repressive regimes, Khalil fought to bring a new Islamic renaissance into society's ideological void. But he'd also found love. Jennifer, his girlfriend from college in San Diego, had left her empty American life and joined his jihad. Now he saw the blood on her neck as her limp form seemed to seep through the arms of the men holding her, searching for help. He ran to them. Why had she left their room? Couldn't she see that she was the only woman here? Stupid, arrogant Americans. They thought that their nationality immunized them from the dangers of the world. Hadn't they already fought their own civil war? Why did she feel compelled to enter the Egyptians'?

"Follow me," he shouted at the men holding his lover aloft. "I know where to find help." And indeed he did. Any Islamist had a network within any location in the Arab world. No questions asked. He gestured to them and they followed.

Jennifer lifted her head at the sound of his voice. He saw the blankness in her eyes and began to really worry, knowing the look of death. Khalil heard another round of bullets, then cries from the crowd. Smoke filled the air and he saw a car on fire, but only from the corner of his eye.

"Khalil," Jennifer whispered, "you had an important call and I came to find you." Her energy spent, she melted back into the now bloody arms of the men carrying her.

He grasped her wrist felt for a pulse. The last thing he cared about was a stupid call. Everything seems important until you face the dead. For a second he pondered the oddity that the call had come through to their room and not his cell but noted that she was still breathing. She needed a doctor.

"Your cover is blown but you still must carry forth on the plan," she said in a calm voice, her eyes un-focused and her body inert.

"Hurry, over here, to my car," he stated and then let the jolt of her words hit him. Not only was her life now hanging by a thread but his colleagues had just thrown him into a similar fate. Disappearing for over a year into American custody, even though he'd subsequently escaped, had put his loyalty in doubt.

Khalil could barely see Jennifer being loaded into the backseat of his Fiat. They were away from the lights of the crowd and in a humble alley. He saw a few men seated around a candlelit shop, but most of the buildings around them were dark. He heard the door shut and saw her limp body as its blood stained his back seat. Her mules disappeared into darkness without a word, doubtless heading back to the protest in the square. One way to be great in life is to join a cause. And Egypt, rife with corruption and repression was ripe for monumental heroism; he just wouldn't be a part of it tonight. Khalil got behind the wheel and headed away from the trouble.

"Khalil, I'm bleeding," he heard Jennifer say weakly from behind.

"We'll be at a doctor momentarily," he said with authority, "I saw where you were hit. You'll be fine." Of course he was lying. She should never have left their room. Women were so stupid, never listening and always thinking they had the right to interfere. Still, he loved her and hoped she'd live. A simple bullet. Only one bullet. Like the one that had killed his brother, Hassan, so many years before, in the dust of Algeria. That bullet had sent him on the path of jihad and now into the revolution in North Africa. What effect would this one have?

The drive was short.

He pulled into a driveway on a quiet street in the more residential area of Cairo. A bulky man came from the shadows and approached, a large gun visible. Egypt was a land of guns, the way to keep people quiet.

"Brother, why do you come?" a deep voice asked.

"The doctor must care for my passenger. I'm Khalil."

"Ah, Khalil, In'sa Allah," the man responded, his tone reverential. For when Khalil had escaped the Americans he'd also caused the death of many American Special Forces and the explosion of an apartment building. Trusted or not, he was a hero. Many hands came to lift Jennifer and carry her into the doctor's house, hidden behind a wire fence and illuminated brightly within. Her blonde hair spilled down when she was lifted out of the car and Khalil saw that her azure eyes were closed. A good sign or not? Her skin looked ashen, even in the dark light.

The moon didn't do its part as Khalil lingered in the cobblestone court-yard. His cover was blown but he was still responsible for an important assassination. How was that supposed to work?

But wasn't such a paradox always the case? *A wise ruler ought never to keep faith when by doing so it would be against his interests.* So said Machiavelli, his secondary spiritual guide. "Allah bless my mission," he whispered to the night. He then heard Jennifer scream and prayed for her. We are all alone, he thought, and wondered at his loyalties. Mission and Allah first. Himself and Jennifer next.

Kicking a stone he looked at the mansion before him. A man benefiting as much from serving jihad as was possible. The home was three stories and well built. Deep rich curtains sheltered its windows and the desert sands of the region had been kept from the stone steps that led to a wondrous alcove with deep cushioned seats and a round table. Another scream from within and Khalil hurried to check on Jennifer. An explosion from a few miles away wrecked the mansion's calm. The protestors. "What next will the night bring?" he whispered, then felt his cell phone vibrate in his pocket. One part of him was surprised. Hadn't the government shut off most forms of communication earlier that day? Perhaps phones were still allowed in this cauldron of repression. He ignored it anyway. People's rights were as transitory as Allah's moods. For now he was more concerned with whether or not Jennifer would survive until morning.

He headed for the stairs and braced himself for whatever news his God would allow him. Still, he whispered a prayer for her, knowing that Allah was all good and merciful, most of the time.

Start

An assassin's life is lonely.

Radwan glanced around the riverbank, smelling the murky water, the hot dogs and the exhaust fumes of Manhattan. Horns and sirens were blaring and the crowds almost shoved him aside as he wandered slowly past the clusters of tall steel buildings. He clutched his notebook tightly. The air was heavy with rotting garbage and an odd smokiness, distinctive but hard to articulate.

Staring at the United Nations Headquarters he studied for weaknesses in security or, indeed, any other vulnerability. With its circular driveway, row of flags and compound of buildings by the water, it would be hard to defend. But the building itself wasn't his target; rather he was looking for a way to shoot someone entering or leaving. And the ideal way always became apparent if you looked hard enough.

The river behind him was a mess of noise and commotion from boats, people and the water itself. He heard a horn blowing but didn't flinch or let his gaze waver. This racket could easily mask a gunshot, though he'd use a silencer, and it also provided an excellent escape route. He'd be gone before the Coast Guard could mobilize.

High buildings towered around him and he marveled at the multitude of possibilities for a clean shot. Windows, doorways, even rooftops: how would he decide? From a boat, a building or even a straight close up shot to the heart? If he died in the process he'd only meet paradise sooner.

Earlier, Radwan had been at the Four Seasons Hotel on 57th street and would walk back and forth between here and the hotel until he found the right spot to make his kill. KK – his target – liked the Four Seasons and would be staying there for his UN Assembly address during the upcoming global peace conference. Radwan liked the hotel's land-based escape options almost as much as those here by water.

KK was the favored candidate in the forthcoming Egyptian presidential elections. A long standing dissident and ex-soccer player with a foreign university post to avoid domestic incarceration, KK re-entered Egypt when Mubarak fell. Since then, the country had spiraled first into anarchy and then into simmering military repression. Birthing a new democracy in a country with a 30 percent illiteracy rate isn't easy. How do you vote wisely when you can't read? The poor don't understand that democracy doesn't buy food and jobs, money does. KK, the voice of the people, would be dead before the election results could be counted.

Radwan laughed as he saw a few white women looking at him suspiciously. They huddled together and whispered, dressed in that sloppy western basic of trousers and t-shirts. If they only realized. Sometimes the threat you fear really is only a few feet away.

He stared back at them, arrogant he knew. Radwan studied himself as much as his prey. His own personal weaknesses were the only things he had to fear; all other possible risks he could correct for. This detailed planning created a structure into which the actual assassination would fall. No one else's reality would matter on that fateful day; only the one he'd created in advance.

Loneliness or solitude? He'd stopped needing people years ago when his parents had been gunned down before him. Four years old at the time, he and his two sisters had gone to live with an uncle. The girls were married now and Radwan was in New York planning his next shot.

The women waddled away, clutching each other and still murmuring. He laughed again, louder this time. Dark, foreign men were allowed to walk the streets of New York and no one could touch him. He watched as the women started to feed pigeons by the water's edge. Bending, rising, and bending down again with birds swarming in a circle on the grey cement. The bright sun cast stark shadows around him.

Radwan sat on a bench and studied his shoes before looking toward the river, murky and complex in its depth. The wafting smells were salty but also pure. His dark bangs fell into his eyes and he brushed them away. He'd need a haircut.

Killing a man wasn't easy. First, you had to study your target: his environs, his movements and habits, quirks, locales, even his thoughts. Pictures, videos, news articles and the Internet. Was he left-handed or right? Inside his head – not yours – you visualized the day. His missteps, habits and preferences were his vulnerability. The plan had to be perfect and precise. By the time you took aim no possible surprises could be left unexplored.

You could only count on getting one shot.

Assassins were accused of being cold, but why? Killing shouldn't be considered inhuman or an anomaly. Indeed, it happened every day in the civilized world under the guise of war or the death penalty. Hypocrisy.

Radwan pondered his next few weeks. He had so much to do.

The sun was glaring, even with the sunglasses he wore. Light intruded through the corners of his flimsy dark lenses and he stood unsure of where to go next. Should he head to his cheap room on 44th Street and perhaps eat en route? Food held little interest, but he did need sustenance. Perhaps he'd find one of those take-out, self-serve production lines so popular here. He liked the salads and their never-ending variety.

But first he took one more look around at the hustle and commotion. People too rarely paid attention in a busy city like this, did they? How to use that factor to his advantage? As he'd enjoyed complicated math puzzles in university, he now pondered real world problems; where to shoot and how.

Life was so easy in America. He planned to stay.

Time for Allah to cleanse the sin from this decadent and powerful country. Radwan knew his role: a catalyst to bring the war to the United States. Walking quickly now that he was intent on finding food, he was surprised to feel a push from behind and saw the pavement reeling up.

Inhale, Exhale

Inhale, Exhale

Hold up

Wait a minute

Let me put some kush up in it

Rhythmic and tribal, the angry hip-hop song throbbed from somewhere as his ear hit cement.

The physical blow was a surprise. Radwan tasted dirt but had fallen wisely. He twisted his body and saw two teenage boys hovering above him. They wore baggy clothes and baseball caps; the smaller one held a knife.

"Give us your wallet," said the other one, his eyes shifting in all directions, "and you won't get hurt." He needn't have bothered as no one was watching. A fight between angry young hoodlums? Not something in which anyone wanted to get involved.

These two boys thought they would mug him? Radwan evaluated their details, kicked the knife into the air and felt his heel crush ribs. The kid was down and he tripped the other one before he had time to run. He kicked a crushing blow to the throat and didn't wait to see the boy hit the pavement on his own well-deserved trip down, then Radwan hurried away. No one would report the scuffle to the police, and the two broken boys weren't likely to risk a gun or chase after him.

Idiot Americans. Soft like women. They were trained on the streets while he'd slogged through the brutal jihad camps of harsh weather, little food and real wars. He liked America, he really did. So comfortable.

A few shops ahead he saw a food bar restaurant and hurried toward its entrance, suddenly aware of his hunger. Wandering inside, he headed to the cold section first. The salads! He grabbed a container and pondered his choices. Caesar and some of the pasta salad with what looked like chicken? He piled up his dish, then headed to the warmer pasta main dishes. Who could find reason to complain in a city with food like this!

Perhaps his bosses would let him stay here in New York after the assassination. He could get a job and maybe scope out future targets. He hated the snow in winter, but it beat the desperation of the immigrants in Britain or the hatred in the Parisian suburbs. Algeria, his homeland, was a police state always bordering on revolt. So many kept dying there. Here in America Radwan might even eventually afford a car.

He paid for his food and hurried to his room, dodging the crowds that filled the city's sidewalks. He looked forward to enjoying his meal, then coming back to perfecting his plot. Each step had to be perfect. Perfection. Always.

A raindrop hit his eye, and he realized that the clouds had moved in without his even noticing. What if it rained on his fateful day?

Alone

mine had a glass of burgundy, then another. What the fuck, she had a third. Should she go for the bottle? Did she care one way or another? It tasted so good and that giddy light-headedness numbed the world's realities for a kiss of an instant. We take the escapes we can find, fleeting though they may be.

Stretching herself across the high-thread-count white sheets, she reached for the rest of the bottle. As she poured the last maroon liquid into her wine glass her wrist shook and she spilled a few drops on the comforter.

"Red on white," she muttered to herself. "Like blood on snow." Her eyes lingered for a second or so. The staff would clean it up. Hotels. The room was large and decorated tastefully in a range of neutrals. The hotel was only a couple of years old and part of the colorless void that currently seemed the trend on both US coasts. She was in California, just south of San Francisco and waiting to catch a flight to New York in the morning. She'd break whatever hangover she had with a Bloody Mary breakfast and long sleep on board.

Her room service tray was expansively cluttered with the remnants of Steak Béarnaise, mashed potatoes, a frissee salad, assorted rolls, Crème Brule and iced water. Most of it lay untouched, as she'd focused her attention on the wine. The bottle was now as empty as her mind. How had her life come to this?

And the tray. Should she call to have the meal removed or just dump it into the hallway?

Emine grabbed her stack of manila envelopes and decided to get serious, drunk or not. Work was another form of escape and one she'd inevitably face soon. Tomorrow? Who gave a shit? But she'd actually focus on it for a while tonight; ultimately a professional, right? And her bottle was already empty anyway. She took a swig from her thin glass, reassured that while the bottle was empty the glass wasn't.

Glancing at the television, she felt a pang of guilt. Oh, she should watch the evening news but wouldn't. While news was her profession – serious war journalist and all that – knowing what was happening today in the Islamic world, her beat, was key. Well fuck that. She'd done the failed state/civil war thing over and over again and knew that what made it on the news had little bearing on the local reality, which was utter chaos. So another bomb blew? Soldiers called in to kill protestors across the Arab world. Facebook and

Twitter disabled. Yawn. What was she going to do? Quit? Refuse to catch her morning flight and fly home to Mom instead? Oh, no, she needed to call her mom! Emine looked at the time and realized it was close to 4:00 a.m. in Istanbul. Perfect, Mom would just be coming home.

Dialing, she thought about her ongoing assignment.

George, her celebrity interview, was thankfully still alive and healthy after taking a few bullets eighteen months before. After Charles Taylor and a selection of Burmese generals George was a pussycat in that he was neither psychotic nor packing a gun. But George was a book and not an article, which was a first for her, and she was still unsure she could do it. How did she end up committing to following him around and writing a book about the results? Oh, yeah, she had harassed him until he said yes; that self-destructive streak in her that always took on new challenges.

She usually wrote about evil – her legacy from a relationship with an idealistic and now dead doctor turned journalist; so now she'd decided to write the story of a man chasing evil and succeeding. No one really cared about the negative stuff anyway. Perhaps she'd get their attention with an inspiring piece of work.

She heard the phone ring.

"Allo," a voice said from the other end. Clara, her mother's maid.

"Hi, it's Emine. My mom?"

The phone was quiet. A game they played, among many others. Emine and Clara had always competed for Mom's attention. Everyone did, and Mom wouldn't have had it any other way.

"You'll die my love, chasing a dead man into the grave," her mother, the ever-glamorous Liz said, slurring her words.

"Nice to speak to you too, Mom," Emine responded as she pulled her legs close. Slim and encased in black leggings, they almost disappeared into the men's extra-large red t-shirt she was wearing. She listened, comforted, as her mother changed topics and chattered on the phone line, something about a party and too much champagne. A bet and then a jump into a swimming pool. Some dogs. Emine inhaled long and hard on a Camel and marveled at the thrill of hearing her mother's buoyant voice, so carefree and full of joy. She'd find something fun and amusing with a paper bag. Liz was a mess, but artfully so, and Emine always got so caught up in the spectacle.

"Don't smoke, doll. You're so self destructive," Liz finished; her monologue paused for a mother moment. Emine heard her take a deep drag on her own cigarette. Who wouldn't adore her mother, so childlike, well meaning and utterly lost herself? They were so different, with Emine going off to save the world and Liz wallowing in its excesses. Or were they really? Perhaps each just played the role she wanted to see herself in irrespective of the reality

"I'll send you some photos of the war so you can have them framed," Emine said, knowing she could distract Liz. "You can show your friends what I do. Get them to fund a charity."

"E, please, don't treat me like a child," Liz said and Emine smiled to herself. No, they were too busy betting over champagne and diving in a pool to fund a charity, rich through they were. Asking Liz to be socially conscious was the best way to deflate a conversation.

"Tell me about your assignment, the therapist and interrogator? The hero," Liz's soft tone whispered. A harsh, masculine voice echoed in the background and Emine recognized that it wasn't her father. Where had he gotten to, again?

"Oh Mom, he's wonderful." Emine heard herself start to talk about George. He was so smart and insightful, as befit a psychology professor from Stanford who now hosted a celebrity interview show as a fallout from his earlier interrogation success. An expert on the terrorist mind, he understood the sorts of monsters she'd risked her life to interview in the past. And yet, he also displayed unusual compassion. Those flawed men who killed so many often truly believed, shockingly, that they were doing what was right.

"He knows everything about this world of terrorism," Emine said.

"Oh, I'm so proud of you," Liz replied then stayed quiet, allowing Emine to talk on. Liz was so flawed but she listened and that interest could enthrall anyone. Why do the deeply broken seem to redeem themselves with such truly wonderful qualities such that we can't stay mad at them for their thoughtless shallowness?

Emine moved her files to the side and let herself talk. Even if no one else would listen her mother always would.

"George saved so many people by cracking Khalil, a high ranking terrorist boss. Now, George is part of the mass media and spreading his message across the world."

"Saving lives?' Liz asked, always the supporter. You couldn't pay for better.

Emine, raw from whatever demons seemed to haunt her, felt tears welling in her eyes. So much for being a hardened journalist. "Yes, Mom, he is saving lives."

"Well don't forget your camera." Liz inhaled once more. "You win prizes for a reason. That mother in the Sudan, cradling her baby with the crushed skull was lovely."

"Her father took a gunshot at me for that photo." Emine remembered her close escape.

"The picture was wonderful, my doll. Oh, your father is calling and needs me. Kisses." And the phone went dead. Only the man waiting wasn't her father. How we complicate our lives.

Liz was a parody of womanly goodness from an era long past. She wore dressing gowns and worshiped her husband, who scarcely deserved the focus. But he relished it and gave Liz whatever jewels, yachts and other things she wanted, just not his attention. But who wouldn't adore a woman who yielded so thoroughly, who believed, accepted and encouraged. So they both found in lovers their other pleasures. Decadent and card-carrying members of the new gilded age, they symbolized values Emine had difficulty reconciling with what she saw in her daily reality. Such a different world.

Emine turned to the pictures of George that she'd collected. At Stanford. In Washington D.C., Iraq and Afghanistan. Younger, from aging yearbooks. She needed those pictures to better understand him, going into their project. She'd write and photograph this time, in New York. They'd jointly publish a book about the terrorist mind and how he'd made a career out of it. No one wanted a harsh message and he made the issue so accessible with his interviews and analysis.

A Muslim herself, but from Turkey which had traditionally been more modern, Emine kept seeking the answer for peace. Still, her homeland was falling back into the dark ages and so she felt somewhat responsible for providing an alternative mindset. Her father was, after all, a progressive politician fighting an uphill battle. Why did the world have to be so complicated?

Standing, reeling, she checked her bags: cameras, computer, phone, a few clothes, lots of photos, too many photos, and the written ideas of a book meant to change the world. At 26 she had nothing better to do. Recheck and double check. Oh, it was a control move entirely, but she needed it to feel somewhat balanced heading into the instability of her worlds. The planet was a big and bad place but with enough illusions anyone could take it on.

And Liz would always accept her back to the big house overlooking the Bosporus with its hidden garden full of roses. Emine drank from her glass of crimson wine and savored the last few drops.

Parties

George took a glass of white wine from the silver tray and watched Karen do the same. Her face brightened as she surveyed the softly lit, spacious living room with glistening Manhattan visible through floor length windows. How she loved meeting with the famous and rich now that he had haphazardly fallen into those categories.

"Karen, George," their hostess, Gail, swooped down on them with a double kiss to both cheeks and a squeeze on the elbow. "I want you to meet the Sloans. He writes editorials for the *New York Times* and adores addressing terrorism. Normally I don't allow reporters at my parties, but this one is just too important."

She pushed them into the large room, crowded with too many well-dressed people and that one expensive painting extra. George felt a surge of panic as he surveyed the expensive reddish furniture, faded oriental carpets and whiff of gilt and prestige. Around him he saw the faces of *Business Week* and *The Hollywood Reporter*. God, he hated New York and being a celebrity.

Why had Karen talked him into this? How had a Stanford professor turned into an interrogator and then a personality?

"Joe, you must meet George and Karen Harris," Gail puffed, proud, obviously, of making the connection. She was a harmless and not too deep southern girl who had married an ambitious and cunning Jewish lawyer. Now she promoted his brand as a mover and shaker among the well connected. George saw a slight man in a rumpled suit and slightly crooked glasses turn his way.

"Joe Sloan," he said, holding out his hand.

George felt a whiff of relief as he saw Gail guide Karen and Sloan's wife off in the other direction. No more pressure for him to perform? Karen could go to hell.

"George," he said hesitantly and held out his hand.

"I read a lot about you," Joe stated and George felt his comfort zone dissolve. Of course, the reporter had done his homework and was now going to grill him, probably for a story. He took a sip of his wine and glanced around, looking for an escape. Joe grabbed his hand and drew his attention.

"Don't worry, I write an editorial column – opinion – I'm not a real reporter. I was fascinated by the events of last year." Joe smiled and sipped from what looked like a vodka drink of some sort. Perhaps George should switch over. The room hummed with conversation but was devoid of a music soundtrack. Thankfully. A waiter wandered by with a tray of lamb chops, but both George and Joe nodded him on.

Everyone was dressed impeccably and the laughs sounded almost comfortable. George studied Joe and sized him up. Talk or walk away? Well, honestly, he liked the rumpled suit in the palace of perfection.

"The bomb?" George asked and gulped from his wine glass. The liquid was smooth, rich and expensive. How he hated these parties. Karen, meanwhile, was glowing across the room as she spoke to a famous actress. When had she gotten so shallow?

"The fact that you foiled a larger plot, to blow up a series of McDonalds across the nation. Had it succeeded, that plot would have killed many more."

"Yes," was the only response George could muster, other than rolling his eyes? Hadn't he discussed this topic enough? He'd moved on; why couldn't everyone else?

"It bores you," Joe asked and George noted alert brown eyes hidden behind those wire-rimmed glasses. He reassessed the man and realized that someone who wrote an editorial at the NYT wasn't a mere journalist but rather a thought leader and celebrity in his own right. Joe had to know something to reach the pinnacle of his own profession.

Two years earlier George would have started asking Joe questions related to his past, how he'd had achieved his success and influence and what he aimed to do with it. That was before he'd entered this new world, down the rabbit hole and where everyone had an angle and an agenda.

"I read your recent piece on revolution being the new genocide," George stated, took another gulp of his wine and started to feel its effects. The soft lights and steady hum were beginning to feel more comfortable, though he still wished he were home with a good book.

"The poor always seem to find ways of dying." Joe smiled as he spoke. "But don't patronize me," he said, gesturing around him. "These people don't get it. The world is a powder keg exploding. We can't keep supporting repressive regimes that torture their own citizens."

"It's like in *Gone with the Wind*," George began, quick with a literary reference. "Our own people are saying "enough" and those in power keep ignoring the increasing urgency. The world as we know it is slipping away." George sipped as Joe gulped and nodded.

"Change comes slowly until it drowns the world in a torrent. Then we all see the signs we ignored, even though they were in our face each and every day for years," He winked. "The gilded age always ends."

George studied Joe, red faced and intellectual at a polite society party. "You remind me of myself," he stated. "No one listens to me either."

"Wrong! You listen. Those people in northern Africa listen. And..., " Gail was back.

"Bill Clinton is here," she whispered. "You both must meet him. None of that serious political talk at my party!" That hand on the elbow again, pushing them both to the center of the room.

"Will you be on my show?" George asked, not sure why, but knowing that it was the right question to ask.

"Absolutely," Joe shouted, caring not, obviously, about the correctness of his tone. "You should write an op-ed for my paper."

George tried to respond but was pushed into the melee that surrounded the former president. Karen, pretty with her short blonde hair and impeccable beige outfit, was in the center. Her face was lit with a smile as she basked in the aura of the elite. No wonder they'd grown apart. He'd become important, the man who'd foiled a larger terrorist plot and morphed into a media darling with his own show. She, meanwhile, forgot that they were really just two academics who cared more about doing good in the world than being celebrities. How had he let this happen?

Yet part of him acknowledged that by going to these events they strengthened his brand. And she was such a great ambassador with her perfect conversation and impeccable manner. As a team they could find allies that would help them address the terrorist problem now, while it was still solvable. Why did he feel so empty?

George heard music in the background as the entertainment started. *Isn't it Romantic*, a song he'd always loved. No one in this room cared about his mission. Why couldn't he just enjoy his position and engage with others on a lighter level? Why did the world weigh so heavily on his shoulders?

A sharp look from Karen made George realize that he was standing alone and not socializing. She could go to hell, he thought as he turned his back on her. Surrendering his now empty glass to a waiter, he took another and headed to talk to a government official who worked with those in national security. They could discuss bombs.

"We'd like an interview on the chaos in northern Africa," he said, aware of his wife's harsh gaze and that he was interrupting a conversation about golf.

"Call my secretary Monday and we'll set it up," was the man's response. "And where is your favorite course, George?" Sinking, George started to discuss golf, still wondering how he'd ended up here and why he couldn't just be content making small talk like everyone else. Was something wrong with him?

Hours later, after dinner and in a taxi on the way home, they'd fought. Of course. Passing Times Square with its bright lights, theatre signs and throngs of pedestrians the heavy ammunition came out.

"I hate it here. I feel like a fraud," he'd stated.

"You're famous now. Really important. Accept it!" she hissed.

"You just like being married to a famous man. You don't care about me," George said, saw the cabdriver squirm and realized that he'd finally come out with what he'd been too scared to say.

The glow of her angry eyes suddenly seemed brighter than the lights of the city outside the taxi windows. They were stopped at a traffic light underneath Morgan Stanley's ever-present ticker tape showing news stories now that the market was closed.

Karen sat there and stewed. She was so slight and meticulous, with her ash blonde hair, pale blue eyes and sharp cheekbones. Like ice, her voice always jolted him out of his reverie and into the realities he was no longer interested in seeing. Did he love her still?

"Deal with it, George."

So the night ended. At another impasse.

Breathe

Although Jennifer lay on a cot across the room, bandaged and pale, her labored breathing was loud in Khalil's ears. The basement was large and stocked with the best medical equipment available. A mini-trauma unit hidden in the foot of the doctor's home, it had provided many of his fellow rebels with emergency care as the government fought back against their efforts to bring Islamic control. Thick plush velvet curtains covered the doors, which led to other secret rooms full of guns, ammunition and even, sometimes, prisoners. This war, like many others, was being waged from secret bunkers deep underground, just as the Pyramids held their treasures beneath the earth's surface.

Jennifer's bed was small but adequate. Tubes sprouted from various parts of her and the doctor was busy cutting and sewing.

Tired and overworked as always, Khalil slumped against the wall, feeling drowsy. His thoughts drifted and suddenly before his eyes was no longer the darkness of a hidden basement at night but the softer brightness of dawn in San Diego during his visit there a few months ago.

The day replayed as he slept.

Khalil woke up in that soft dawn of her arms. Jennifer not of his dreams but somehow, impossibly, of his reality. An instant in time that might not last but felt all the more real because of how fleeting it felt and was.

"It is better to be feared than loved if you cannot be both," Khalil whispered to the slumbering Jennifer. "Machiavelli wouldn't approve of you." Nor did he. Was he a complete fool for risking his own life to find Jennifer then visit her in San Diego, where he was a wanted man? Probably. But he'd lost her twice already and felt he couldn't survive a third time. "In'sa Allah," he whispered. His fate would have to rest in Allah's hands.

And Khalil was weary so perhaps he'd earned this reward. The travel was getting to him but how could he send someone in his stead when the stakes were so high? He'd learned that no man could operate alone, but the current planning was complex, and thus far he hadn't found a competent associate to share the responsibility. His group could win this war, but they needed a big victory and Khalil was the only one who could deliver it. The world was in flames.

His mind followed the thread to the next stage of his plan. Survival, his own, which wasn't helped by this trip to San Diego and his occasional lover. He knew that his fear, bordering on paranoia, was real. He'd have to leave her soon. Again.

Jennifer's body was soft and warm, the length of her touching him. She stirred slightly under hideous pink sheets. They never did like the same colors but pink sheets? Her blonde hair was spread out beneath her and, much as he disdained the bedding, everything else about her was perfect. She was still thin and pretty, a classic California blonde. Time was showing in the corner of her eyes and the sun marks on her fair skin. He wondered what she thought about the changes in him: the bullet holes, the plastic surgery and the marks of deprivation. He willed away such thoughts and tried to embrace the warmth of the fleeting moment.

He hadn't succeeded in leaving her behind emotionally after he'd asked her to physically leave his jail cell the year before. His American captors couldn't be allowed to see her importance, nor could he admit it to himself then. He hoped she wasn't being watched as a result of that earlier meeting. This was the first time he'd dared visit her apartment, and it would have to be the last.

"Go," he'd told her then, and saw a tear form in her eye, as he'd hurt her yet again. That tear would haunt him until the day he died. He'd loved her so many years before when they attended college in San Diego together. Back then he'd been there on a scholarship from a terrorist organization. After he graduated he'd left her and she'd stayed in San Diego to become a lawyer. More than twenty years had passed since they graduated, but, miraculously, his feelings for her remained.

After his escape he'd called her from Algeria, unsure if she'd speak to him. The country was safer for him but that didn't make it safe. He kept his voice low as he spoke.

"Jennifer?"

"Who is this?" she replied, and he heard acceptance and fear in her voice. She knew who it was but wasn't perhaps ready to admit it. Sitting, clasping the phone tightly, he was in a fairly nice hotel room, for this country outside its capital. In other words, the kind of dump he was used to, with thin walls and ears everywhere. Filth, bugs and heat.

"It's me." He squirmed as he spoke, feeling the chair back digging into his spine. *In'sa Allah*, he whispered, sweating. The walls were grimy but less so than the small window.

"Why are you calling?" she asked and he wished he could see her face. He imagined it instead, and visualized her eyes lighting up on his behalf, since the dream was all his own.

"To talk, to hear your voice," he said. Someone was knocking on his door and he knew he had to face whoever it was. Jihad was like that. "I have to go. Can I call you again?" The knock came again louder the next time.

"Yes, I'd like that." He felt a thrill, unexpected but welcome. She was going to let him call again even after all he'd put her through. Now, more than six months later and after many calls and a few dangerous meetings in Mexico, he was going to make her decide. As he watched her wake she turned to him, her eyes still only half open. The sun touched all corners of the room and his heart warmed.

But the lurch in his stomach reminded him that the real world hadn't been replaced by a dream. That couldn't happen. How long could their affair last? Perhaps if he counted each moment he needed to survive, then he could find the strength to get through them all.

But how would he survive after that?

Khalil reached out for her; once she was awake, he couldn't keep his hands off her. Her body was firm and she held little back. He kissed her hard on the mouth, then felt for the wetness between her legs. She was ready. Last night he'd been gentle and caring, but this morning he wanted to take her hard and fast, to make her yield. She gasped as he entered her but moved with him and came quickly; she'd always liked rough sex and he was more than willing to oblige. He wasn't ready for his own climax yet. Nothing on earth could cheat him out of extending this pleasure, since he got to taste it so rarely.

Jennifer pulled Khalil deeper into her, greedy and grasping. He loved it as he loved her.

Finally, he came inside her, so warm and welcoming. Eventually he'd look into her eyes. Not yet. Intimacy could only proceed so quickly.

Jennifer sighed and he drew her even closer.

"Come with me," he said

"I just did." She laughed and pulled away enough so that he could see those questioning eyes. They were so blue, like the sea of his home.

"I have a passport for you," he continued, fearful she would say no but perhaps even more that she would say yes.

Jennifer's skin was flushed and her shoulders cushioned by the fluffy pillows. Her breasts, starting to sag with age but still beautiful, stuck out above the down comforter. Khalil willed himself to stay calm.

"Come with me," he repeated, reaching out to take her hand. He stroked her palm and waited.

Jennifer opened her mouth but for an instant nothing came out.

"I can't," was all she said.

"I need to go," he said softly and started to dress. He didn't really have time to wash. Then again, he'd prefer to smell like her than like soap. Even her soap.

"Khalil, you chose to leave me years ago." She dropped the words as she stared at him. "I don't, and didn't, want to be with someone who does what you do. You can't just come back here and surprise me."

Khalil felt his rage building but willed it away. *Because fortune is a woman and if she is to be submissive it is necessary to beat and coerce her. Experience shows that she is more often subdued by men who do this than by those who act coldly,* as Machiavelli had whispered to his prince centuries ago. Control.

The morning was getting brighter and Khalil felt the need to move on. He had to catch another flight, one out of this country, a place where he was most certainly not safe. He was risking his life for this woman. She had to yield.

"I fight for Allah and his will," Khalil told her. He could kill her, but he loved her. "That's why I left you before. I knew that you wouldn't understand." He still wanted her and he fought for what he wanted. She was brainwashed; so he needed to be patient. Over time he could teach her.

But for now he had to be disciplined.

Jennifer curled into him, the last thing he expected.

"I love you. I do understand. But I'm not the same as you," she said. She was crying, tears pouring down her cheeks wetting his bare skin, so dark against hers.

"Come with me. Give it a chance," he said, trying. Would she survive or would she be the death of them both? His weakness. Khalil wrapped the comforter tightly around her. Could he protect her – or had he lost his mind?

"You know I can't," Jennifer said, her voice nasal from crying. "I have a life."

"Which you could leave at any moment and not look back," he said, knowing that he spoke the truth. No one was truly satisfied; she just tried to pretend otherwise, like everyone else. Allah provided the only answer, a refuge in a world spinning out of control.

"You think about it," Khalil said, keeping his tone tough. She needed guidance. Inside himself he heard 'please' but ignored it. He wasn't changing, but he loved her and so she had to join him. He was part of a jihad and there was no going back. His brothers would kill him if he tried. And he believed. Better to jump on the change as the world progressed than get crushed in the process. Jennifer grabbed a pillow and hit him with it and he let her.

"I'm leaving," he said and stood up

"Okay." It was a whisper but signified assent. Life is rough.

He wrote out his cell number on a piece of paper and handed it to her, deliberately avoiding those eyes. "Call if you change your mind," Khalil said, then paused. Was she listening as her eyes pooled up with tears? He looked away and finished dressing. "Don't leave your name. I'll recognize your voice. Keep the message brief so they don't have time to track it and I'll call you back with instructions."

He gave her a kiss, breathing in her essence. Then he left for the airport, having already arranged for a taxi.

"Khalil!" she yelled as he shut the door behind him.

The taxi smelled of incense and the driver was a turbaned Sikh.

A light flashed behind them, and Khalil turned to see a car pull out from the curb. Hadn't he noticed it on his way from the airport? But he'd been too intoxicated at the idea of Jennifer to give it more than a passing thought and it had been dark. None of which was an excuse. This was his mistake since he was obviously being followed but by whom?

Did his pursuer's identity matter? The hunt was clearly on. Now what?

Momentarily Khalil considered skipping his flight and crossing the border into Mexico instead. He was so close, and a little cash went a long way greasing palms there. He decided to risk the airport. He wouldn't be back here for a while – better for Jennifer to come to him. Life was full of risks so time for her to take one.

The car behind him pulled ever closer as the traffic tightened up.

How could he have known that Jennifer would call.

A scream shattered his revisit to that time and Khalil looked up to see a nurse moving frantically to assist the doctor. He was back in the reality of Cairo now. The nurse's gown was dark but he could still see the wetness that must have been blood. The doctor's face was pale and his forehead creased.

Jennifer had called him and he'd taken her into his life of serving Allah.

Now, as a result, she was fighting for her life and Khalil felt strangely detached. He watched the chaos then drifted back into a half sleep. Her fate was in Allah's hands, so Khalil began to pray. Stupid woman, for being so disobedient.

Cameras

eorge sat in his chair, before the cameras and waiting for his cue. He wore the right makeup and a well-cut suit, his thinning hair combed neatly across bald areas he was reluctant to acknowledge. For the first few seconds of his television career he'd been nervous, aware that millions of people were watching. But now he was used to hearing himself talk on a brightly lit soundstage and he never seemed to be talking to anyone besides his co-host and guests. How nervous could you be staring into a machine (that didn't contain any form of explosives)?

The job quickly became rote; the guests were fascinating and he did get some input about who was invited on the show.

"I want to question and discuss power," he'd insisted. His former studies had been centered on the minutiae of emotions and psyche, and their relationship to power and control. In class, he'd always been in charge since he was the professor. With his prisoners, the power dynamics were more nuanced; he'd held the key to the door but only they knew their hidden secrets. At this point in his career he wanted a larger framework. Power mattered little in theory, being more dependent on the subtle nuances of practice and very few people got these vital details right. Many of his guests did and George wanted to tap their insights into influence.

Reluctantly, he was finally acknowledging that public images, when built wisely, started with people's assumptions and stereotypes and then reinforced them, often consciously. The masters used those prejudices to their advantage as his detainees had tried to trick him with their pre-planned stories. Consistency of message worked. Getting people to expose another personality dimension was difficult at best and often impossible.

Even the shocking confessions and provocative slips were too-often scripted. So much for being the man behind the curtain. So he kept using what he knew about how people's minds worked to elicit the truth better, knowing that the optimum was to guide them gently. His ratings kept rising.

George's production manager shook the list of names under his nose. Glen always seemed too scared to speak yet had mastered passive aggression. He also drank. Too much repressed emotion.

"Yes, yes, yes and no," George felt the power of his position as he looked through the list of prospective interviewees. The media dictated what people heard and, more importantly, what they believed.

Today he was thrilled. George O'Brien, an Irish version of his namesake and one of the country's most important emerging politicians, was on for the first time. Why did the Irish seemingly make the most inspirational leaders? Each and every one had some sort of sordid secret in his past from Kennedy(s) to Reagan to Daley(s) to Riordan to McCarthy to McNamara to O'Neill. If you added in business leaders with influence you threw in Getty, Welch, Hearst, Ford, Disney, Morse and Huston. They wrapped up the Supreme Court and then there was always George Clooney.

Messy but authentic, and fun, the people loved them all.

O'Brien could have come from central casting, with his twinkling blue eyes and black-brown hair. His suit was rumpled but his tie was impeccable. O'Brien was sitting up straight as a choir boy, hands clasped.

Laura, his co-host, was on vacation so George had O'Brien to himself. Laura would have flirted with O'Brien and plied him with coy compliments. She was nominally in the Bahamas but rumor had it that she was detoxing privately in Malibu. George, who saw the flaws in her fragile psyche almost daily, hoped she'd be okay. Fucked up world, the whole celebrity thing. Drove him almost nuts too.

George asked his next question.

"So you stood up to a number of forces and called for a cut in all public pensions. That was brave. Why did you decide to do it?" George asked and saw the twinkle in the other George's eyes. They both loved the spotlight, didn't they?

O'Brien was leaning back on the tan couch. George saw his eyes dart off to a corner and expected a lie. But on national television you didn't directly call people on their lies but smiled indulgently and hit them with a follow up question later. He gulped his coffee.

"This isn't a nation of handouts!" O'Brien exclaimed, then gave a sly smile. "We're better than that. Our people deserve a great country. We're inspired people, and buying off some politicians to let the elite pillage the country isn't what makes America the best country on earth." George smiled back, conceding. Everyone recognized a showman but at least O'Brien actually followed through on his promises.

A camera swung around for a better angle and George noticed the crew behind the lights and equipment, watching expectant and obedient. They were live and the country was waiting; it felt surreal.

"Are you running for president in the next election?" George asked, knowing his role and adding in as much verve as he could muster. The questions were easy; he worried that he lacked charisma. Still, the ratings held strong even as his insecurities plagued every show. How did O'Brien do it?

With another flash of his blue eyes, his guest spoke, smiling. "George, I will do what the people want." He held his right hand over his shoulder blade and shook his head as he did so. "I only aspire to lead if the people want me to."

The commercial light was flickering, so George announced a break and the machinery stopped spinning.

"How do you do it?" he asked O'Brien directly.

"I really believe," the man said without a blink, "that power and influence is bullshit unless you use it to help your fellow man." Power being the defining word.

"A bleeding heart?" George asked, seeing something he'd seen in his detainees – fanaticism. Too often his interviews were full of sound bites so that he had to follow up with a zinger. Always listening and thinking ahead in case the interview stalled, but that was not the case here with O'Brien and those twinkling eyes.

"No! Fuck heart. Discipline, a defined objective and the will to see it through." O'Brien gulped his water thirstily and looked around the studio. "I hate this dog and pony show but need to sell my message; otherwise I let everyone down," he said. Then his voice softened. "I'm going home after this to watch the game and drink some whisky. Want to come?"

George smiled back, warming at the invitation. He didn't get them often from his guests. They were usually too self involved to see beyond the end of their own personal monologue. O'Brien was a skilled engager; he asked his own questions and got past his selling message.

George decided that he'd vote for this guy; O'Brien convinced you that he cared. No, it was more sophisticated: you just believed and thought it was your idea.

"I'd like that, but my wife would probably leave me," George said, with a half smile, trying to joke but the pain was real. Karen. "I think she has me at some party," he said, facing down O'Brien's frank eyes.

"She won't leave," was all O'Brien said, returning the smile. "She wouldn't dare go, and you could use some good whisky."

The commercial break was over.

Sunlight

The first few rays of dawn were only beginning to spear the darkness as Khalil wandered the banks of the Nile. The moon was a fading flicker, and he could hear the noises of those camped out in Tahrir Square or the streets lining the river. The water's hum and rush were the same now as in antiquity.

The chants sounded like a rock concert. First, came the speaker, eloquent in advocating change, echoed by the crowd, haunting in their unity and force. Back and forth they went, so tribal in their common bonding around noise. A chant. A chorus.

Khalil wandered along Corniche Al-Nil, with the Nile on his right and stark unlit buildings on his left. How had he ended up back in Cairo, his bad luck charm? Last time he'd breathed this air he'd been in a dark jail cell enduring torture. He hated Egypt, yet it was now the hub of a new world order and Khalil was needed to direct that spirit. Oh, he'd spent time here earlier, after leaving Algeria with a price on his head, and now he sometimes questioned whether things ever really changed. The people could now congregate outside of the mosques, but who was in charge?

Hesitating by the river, Khalil gazed into its murky waters. Filthy really, but it still kept Egypt alive as always. Carrying dinghy, tour boats and rickety rowboats along its broad banks this section wasn't as active as other parts. Now, at night, it was quiet, but what would happen if his group blew the Aswan Dam and flooded the countryside?

A man was bathing naked in the dark brown liquid and Khalil turned away from him, aiming for mutual privacy.

Was a nighttime walk by the river the only escape in this crowded city? Could he find any place to hide from his own thoughts? Spiraling through uncertainty and doubt, he could only throw a random rock into the water and wait for the splash before the next thought hit.

The protests had started over a few years ago, and then died down for a while after Mubarak resigned. But democracy didn't come so easily; revolutions were complex and the most dangerous time was after that initial hope crashed into the letdown reality that a country didn't change overnight. Violence and anarchy were always hovering, searching for an opening into which they could explode. A cascading waterfall of opportunity for the group that could seize the people's dreams.

"Allah, please guide me," he prayed.

Dust swirled around Khalil's ankles. He looked up.

"Allah, be with you," murmured an old man, wrapped in a large shawl and limping, as he passed Khalil. Allah, the merciful, never left his side.

"In'sa Allah," Khalil responded to the departing figure and watched dust settle on his black Nikes. Dust, dirt, sand and grime seemed emblematic of the Muslim world. When would men be free of it and living in the castles of Cadiz, as Mohammed had proclaimed?

No matter. Khalil's thoughts returned to his revolution.

The moon was fading now but he hadn't noticed the emerging brighter rays of the sun. Soon. All things in time.

Revolution was simple and control was all that mattered. The army's support set the stage for who would win because guns spoke louder than any man. The starving angry mobs followed those that promised to fill their hungry bellies. Joblessness and education then added kerosene. The uneducated and desperate, easy to lead and risking nothing for change, were the spark itself and the elite power structure was what burned. In this case, decadence, corruption and a tin ear at the top of the region's leadership structure had left them vulnerable and exposed. Hence, violence. And the people here were hungrier now.

Khalil noticed a small teashop and headed toward it. Nearby was the Ramses Hilton with its café and pastries, but he preferred tea on the street. Ordering, he heard excitement in the early morning voices. The street was brightening by now and the locals were men ranging from young to old. A cluster of three youths were telling stories to each other of bravery and valor but what did they really know about battle? When was the last time Egypt fought a real war? They were in jeans with loose and colorful t-shirts, and like him, they wore American shoes. Unlike him they had a newspaper in hand and were sharing its contents.

"Look, the tank, right there…" a boy shouted, waving his arm. "We slept next to it last night."

Khalil cradled his cup of tea in its tiny clear glass. It was sweet and dark, just what he needed to keep his brain focused and calculating. How to organize the protests and seize control? He pulled out his iPhone and began to check recent Facebook activity. The site, for now, was up. Twitter too. How much information had he missed as he wandered the banks of the Nile – people talking to people and someone listening? Did no one else sleep, or was the recent organization from abroad?

New York

Heading for the taxi line outside the JFK terminal, Emine pondered the day ahead or her. She loved the pretzels in New York, so she'd get one of those. But other than that, did she have a purpose? She was supposed to be working on the book with George but too much of it had become about her working and George being absent. Not that she minded so much since he was the star of her show while she as the writer and photographer preferred to fade into the background. Her trip was a gentle shove for him to re-focus. Hosting a political talk show was great, but he'd committed to her book, no – their book – and she was going to ensure that he finished it.

A taxi pulled up and Emine slipped inside, settling her small black roller bag on the seat beside her. She traveled light.

"The Four Seasons," she told the driver and heard her cell ring. "Hello," she said into the phone, tired.

"Emine, it's Ed," a voice said, husky and breaking up over the weak line.

"Well, this is a surprise." She felt a nervousness that she wouldn't have predicted. Ed, her on-again, off-again boyfriend in Paris. The international lawyer sent from New York (here!) to add sophistication to the French office. Ed of the kinky dress up sex and too many boxes of chocolates sent to her apartment. She hated chocolate.

"Emine, we had a date for lunch today…" he started to say, clearly angry. Shit.

"Oh, yes, well, I forgot." She saw the dark brown cab driver staring at her in the rearview mirror, his eyes alert and probing. Why was everyone so nosy? "I just landed in New York and forgot to call you," she sputtered, knowing that she was talking to a corporate lawyer, the most responsible form of humanity on earth unless they wanted to fuck with you. And he liked to fuck with her. Though, yes, she could have called and cancelled the date, knowing she was leaving the country. Why hadn't she?

"You love the drama, Emine," he said, as if reading her mind.

The airport was disappearing behind her and she breathed that distinctive New York air. What were the components? Smog, sea, the trees? Airplane fuel? It smelled so familiar but she couldn't fathom what the essence was. Her driver was fiddling with the radio and driving much too fast. She curled into her seat and contemplated possible responses to Ed. That they both loved the drama because it made them feel alive?

"What's the weather there like?" she asked, yearning for his response. Was arguing ever a worthwhile use of one's time? Why not just enjoy? But she argued anyway. The trees whizzing by outside the cab's windows looked green and the traffic was only moderately filled with other cars. The day was lovely with its blue sky and few clouds.

"Eme, don't distract me," Ed breathed into the phone. Angry. Unsure, because he wasn't quite ready to break up with her? And, with her travels his job was too predictable so he probably got bored. But since he hadn't proposed marriage he really had no right to tie her down and make her conform to his life.

"Distract? Oh, but if you were here I'd be so busy distracting you. Apron or boots?" she tried to turn the conversation to sex because it was more interesting than an argument. Not that either discussion held her in thrall, as both were better in person. Her driver was suddenly less interested in his radio and more in her conversation.

"If you were here I'd strip your clothes from your body and have you take me from behind..." she said, not so quietly, and watched the cabbie's eyes widen.

"In a public place?" Ed asked, suddenly interested.

"You're so juvenile," she responded.

Still, she liked Ed. He was big and muscular, one of those overachieving, gym-going American types and he treated her well. She'd almost marry him, really. If...? Just if.

"Come home, Emine," he said. "I love you."

"Oh, but I can't," she stammered, surprised. He'd never said he loved her before. They were both busy and supposed to be keeping things light. The Queensboro Bridge loomed in front of her amidst the cars and she saw Manhattan with its tall buildings stretching out endlessly.

"That's your answer?" Ed said. He was a lawyer making his point.

Emine felt confused. Answer? What was the question? She tried. "Answer what?" Cars were whizzing by, her driver was still watching her more than the road and her legs were stiff in the black jeans against the car seat.

"Do you love me?" he asked and she felt her eyes open wide. She glanced at the door and wondered if she should jump. Wasn't this why she kept running and writing and taking pictures? To avoid commitment? How many people did she have to lose before God would just leave her alone?

Love? What the fuck?

"Yes," she answered, surprised at herself. Now what?

Calls

eorge watched Karen as she spoke on the phone. Muffy or Buffy or Puffy. She always had a new list of names with parties attached. She'd taken to New York society like nothing he'd ever seen. His kids had been at Columbia, but now they'd graduated and headed on a backpacking trip through Southeast Asia and perhaps Europe. And he was stuck in Manhattan. Damn, it was a small amount of space.

"Do tell." Karen was sitting on the green velvet couch she'd chosen for their tasteful apartment, talking into her phone. She liked green velvet. He watched his wife, huddled over the receiver and dressed in trim jeans and a black silk blouse. She was so joyful and he felt guilty begrudging her that emotion. He went to their liquor stash and poured himself a scotch. It wasn't her fault that she was happy.

Outside their tall windows he saw dusk descending on Manhattan. Their rented apartment was on Central Park South and he could see the lights brightening up the park below. Clusters of bushy trees stretched past the Jacqueline Kennedy Onassis Reservoir and into Harlem.

"She didn't!" Karen hissed into the phone – more a judgment than a question. She was lovely still but as they'd gotten older, he understood her less. With his success, greater every day it seemed, he'd become lonelier and emptier. He was tired of interviewing celebrities and politicians, even more tired of being interviewed and providing insights into world affairs and the horrors of terrorism. Since when did professors become famous? McDonald's had even offered him an advertising contract, but that he'd turned down. Irony of irony, Khalil loved McDonald's and had almost succeeded in bombing a string of them. You'd need a psychiatrist to figure that out.

"George," Karen called and he jumped, gulping some scotch quickly to offset his recoil. Next he'd become a damned alcoholic trying to escape his success. Now that was crazy.

"The phone keeps clicking, and it seems to be for you," she said, looking annoyed that her gossip was being interrupted. Okay, now he knew for sure that her priorities were all messed up. How could someone calling for him dare interrupt her gossip session?

"Yes, dear," he almost said but didn't want to get in a fight by slugging her with a cliché. Dumb move when dealing with a literature professor, tenured. Smarter to stay quiet and alienated. Yes, he knew better, but he was ultimately as lazy as any man.

"Thanks." He forced a smile and watched Karen roll her eyes yet again. Was their reconciliation really such an obvious farce? Divorce wasn't the worst option; people did it all the time.

"George, this is Bill Bright," a deep, nasal voice said, husky and with noticeable authority. Karen skulked off and George took possession of the couch she'd abandoned. He felt the old pain in his knee as he reclined.

"Bright Media," George responded, "You own the studio that makes my show." He swigged his scotch one more time and felt the burning rush as it went down his throat. The velvet nuzzled against his neck as he slumped deeper into the couch. Why would Bill Bright call him? They'd never spoken before so why now? "I'm your new boss," the voice said and George felt a flash of confusion.

"Well, really, you've been my boss indirectly for a while now, right?" he asked. He took another gulp of scotch and felt more relaxed. Bright would make his purpose known.

"I want you to go to Cairo to do some live shows, in the streets," Bright said. "The situation there continues to deteriorate. How many years of insanity can these people take? Damn, I want footage."

George shook his head. He'd almost died the year before, and still people seemed to think that he was some crazy daredevil. Almost out of his periphery he saw Karen watching, back from wherever she'd been brooding. Was there any concern in her eyes? Did he care?

"And so," Bright's voice continued, "we need you to leave on a flight to Cairo at 9:35 tomorrow morning out of JFK…"

"No!" George exclaimed before thinking. Now the scotch was a liability and not an escape. He was not about to hop onto a plane and into an unstable country in the midst of finding itself. Repression, violence or free and fair elections? George wasn't about to find out firsthand; the papers and Internet covered them just fine.

"I'm not going. I'm not a war journalist just a professor turned TV monkey. Very different," George stated, not caring if he lost his cushy celebrity job. He'd be happy to go back to teaching.

"George, I need your help. None of my other 'journalists' will go. What kind of a station have I built? You'll report directly to me, I'll hire bodyguards, a villa or the Mena House Oberoi Hotel with a view of the Pyramids. I'll raise your salary and you'll probably win some fucking prize at the end of the year."

Karen walked out of the room with nary a glance in his direction. She didn't even know what the conversation was about. The scotch couldn't mask his anger.

"Emine will go with you," Bright went on. "I hired her to up your game with that damn book. She's a war journalist by training and skilled with controversial issues." Bright paused and George could sense his tension.

Bright was more than that, he was brilliant. The company he'd built had started with a newspaper in the Midwest then kept adding assets until it now rivaled the top networks. George's show was on a channel that catered to the disenfranchised of the country, a large and growing crowd in the increasingly partisan United States. But Bright had started upping the rhetoric and focusing on violence and conflict. Thus far George's show had stayed pretty tempered. He calculated for an instant, and then acknowledged his past year had been a deviation from his true mission. Bright was wisely staying quiet. He'd presented his deal, and what was the saying – *he who speaks first loses.*

George looked out at Central Park's lights and saw the buildings at the other end. Just one more city, one more place in time. History kept on moving forward even as George did his best to stay hidden in this new life that had somehow created itself. Now he was becoming a war journalist? What had happened to tenure and teaching?

"I want a raise, two bodyguards and a very public residence. The camera has to be trained on me whenever I'm in a crowd so it looks like shooting me will get caught on film," George stated, hearing the calm and certainty in his own voice now. "I'll only commit to a month, then we'll renegotiate." He put his feet on the table and crossed his ankles, still staring at the park. This was the last time he'd see it at night for at least a month.

"I'll double your salary and I want footage after you land. Your first impressions," Bright said, speaking rapidly. "I'm buying you ten million in life insurance and sending Ben, my favorite camera man. That boy is a tank and afraid of nothing. Already called Emine and she is packing."

Listening to these words, George realized he hadn't even begun to think through the reality.

Bright continued talking, leaving little room for George to respond. "Contract is being emailed by my lawyers to you now, signed by me. Sign it and send it back. We pick up all costs related to the risks you take. Bodyguards will meet you at the airport tomorrow and they both speak Arabic. You report directly to me only. The email has my contact information so call me any time. I'm sending your wife a diamond necklace in the morning," Bright concluded and George heard a dial tone on the line.

Diamond necklace or not, Karen was going to kill him. Or would she?

Must be nice to be Bright, rich enough to buy anyone. Just appeal to their hidden desires and offer a lot of money to fulfill them. George couldn't help but wonder about his own hidden desire: helping an ailing world or facing down danger?

He was aware that Karen had walked back into the room. Her cheeks were burning and he saw the pucker on her forehead that signified anger. She must have been listening in on the extension. Conflict number one. Next would be the mobs on the streets of Cairo.

Smoke

The streets looked very different in the mornings. Smoldering debris and what was left of a burnt out car were the first things Khalil saw. Bottles and rocks that had been thrown in the night rested in dark stains of drying blood. While the protestors were generally peaceful the government forces often weren't. Yet many of the police and army had stood politely off to the side and refused to get involved when all hell broke loose.

The women in their scarves and hebeyas came out in the daytime, holding signs and chanting slogans. They nestled amidst the thousands of men who also shouted and moved in unison, that wave of crowds. Khalil and his brothers were the infiltrators, whispering words to the men who, in their pent up rage, were waiting only for the right phrase to fuel their anger. Violence was the simmering disease that affected those with few rights and no prospects.

Revolutions were all the same and patterns repeated. That predictability had to be channeled to ensure that you shaped the winning ideology. Khalil was obsessed with winning this fight. Machiavelli had said, *There is nothing more difficult to take in hand, more perilous to conduct, or more uncertain in its success, than to take the lead in the introduction of a new order of things.* Chaos, anarchy and the rootlessness of an anger unleashed made the outcome uncertain.

"Allah be with you, brother," he whispered to a man throwing rocks at the tanks assembled in the midst of Tahrir Square. The square itself was vastly expansive and bordered with dirty white buildings, shabby in their attempt at dignity. People thronged through the streets, pressed together as the mobs overfilled the area. Motorbikes went whizzing by, gasping and spitting smoke. Many people wore western clothes but a few wore the traditional baggy tunics and hegabs.

A woman in western clothes walked by and Khalil spit at the ground behind her. Whore. Women should be shrouded as was Allah's will and not parading around, boastful of their sex.

"Were there gunshots last night?" he asked a young man beside him. The boy looked to be about eighteen and was also dressed in jeans. His t-shirt said Guns & Roses but he probably had no idea what that meant.

"Yes, a lot. So many, too many," the boy said and looked to the ground. Khalil noted that the pavement was thick with dust and debris, as befit the cast offs in the third world.

"Who?" Khalil asked.

"We don't know," was the response.

The sun was hot now. Thirty degrees Celsius or higher and Khalil felt his sweat blinding him. He wanted water but continued his questioning instead.

"Military?'

"I don't know?"

"Foreigners?"

The boy shook his head. "I don't know," he said softly and Khalil watched him walk away. A vendor came by with water and a meal of mixed lentils, beans and pasta. Khalil bought some and started to eat. The water was surprisingly cold and the food warm in the middle of a desert city. He watched the vendor walk away and wondered how he did it. People always surprised you.

Who was shooting bullets in the night air, and why didn't he know? No one else seemed to know, but Khalil was better connected than most. Either no one was brave enough to tell him or the answer eluded them all; neither a good sign. Khalil sat in the dust, watching the crowd mill around him under their hot sun. He ate and pondered what to do.

The answer would come.

Dust

 mine didn't sleep much the night before her flight with George back to Cairo, a city she knew well. Thinking about what the morning would bring, she was less concerned with her physical

well being than with her mental state. She always bordered on being unstable anyway. That disconnect was what being a war journalist did to you, not to mention her past.

How do we cope when solitary for too long? Sometimes we're even more alone when with others yet that wasn't her situation now. She was flying into a revolution and had to start drawing on internal resources. Certainly, finding someone to counsel her wouldn't be easy now that Egypt was actually burning.

Emine studied her room service menu. She loved the Four Seasons amenities but even this lifestyle did get old eventually. The wine was easy – she'd just order lots. Then what? More tenderloin or lamb chops? Pasta, chicken or should she just brave the streets and get another pretzel?

Fish.

What time was it in Istanbul?

Bright had called her.

"You, again?" she'd exclaimed.

"Nice speaking with you too," her billionaire boss had replied. Luckily he had a sense of humor and tolerated talent, even if it was cranky. She'd actually taken a liking to him momentarily when they were dating. It was walking in on him in intimate company with twins that had ended their affair. Oh, yes, and the wife who cut off her credit at Agent Provocateur.

"Yes, doll?" she'd drawled, knowing he'd dangle a prize that she couldn't resist. That was how the bastard kept people's loyalty. Bought it. And she was wearing a $500 red lace bra and panties he'd funded. Thankfully, she had a real boyfriend now..

"I'm getting you a Pulitzer this time," he stated, and she laughed. Okay, she still liked him, truth be told. Someone with no limits and a thick wallet.

"Thank you," she replied, prim and proper. "What will it cost me?" Night had darkened her Four Seasons view and she was getting hungry. Her bra wasn't enough in the air conditioning so she added a grey cashmere sweater and sweats.

"You and George are on a flight to Cairo tomorrow. I want shots and chaos."

"They attack women reporters there," she replied and heard no response on the line. Fuck him. He just didn't give a shit if she got raped so long as she got a Pulitzer for it.

"Fine," she said, breaking the silence since he wouldn't. "I want a raise," she added, then turned up the thermostat and closed her drapes halfway. He made her ill.

"Double your salary."

"I want a vacation too. Four weeks, paid." She started studying the menu again. Let the bastard stew; he only respected strength. She knew him well enough to know that he was calling her before George because the professor would never go to a war zone alone, so for tonight she held the cards. Tomorrow he'd sell them.

"Emine..." he said.

"What time is the flight and what airline?" she asked and decided on fish with capers and a lemon butter sauce. Did they have soup? Dutifully, she wrote down the information as he read it.

"Emine..." he said again and she listened for the rest. It didn't come. Figured. Phony.

"Bye, doll," she said. "See you." And she heard his phone line click dead. Men.

Emine grabbed her cigarettes and lit one, ignoring the hotel's no smoking policy. Let them sue her...wasn't that what New Yorkers did? She curled up by the window and stared at the small shapes walking so quickly on the still busy streets. Car's headlights darted here and there, adding to what looked like mayhem but what was actually order in a big city.

Shit. Now she had a revolution to face.

Flight

tepping onto the British Airways 747, George felt relief rush through him like the earlier jolt from his morning coffee. Who sanely felt such an emotion heading to a failed state and war zone?

A wave of red caught his eye, causing him to glance down the First Class aisle of the narrow airplane, with its winding carpet and wide upright chairs. A girl was curled up in a seat, intent on the magazine before her. Her arm flashed color as she turned another page. Emine.

She was clad in faded jeans and had heaps of coppery beige hair cascading around her delicate face, which was turned down to read and barely moving. The sheer red drapery of her blouse exposed embroidery at the top of her bra and then billowed down her arms. One leg was tucked under the other and he saw the toe of a boot.

He'd first spoken to Emine after a mutual lawyer friend made an introduction. "Just listen," the man begged, but George had hesitated. His minor celebrity status had brought with it the casual hangers-on, wanting something, anything, to rub off on them. Even his classes had gotten more crowded, and the students were either more reverential or more flippant. It got worse when he began hosting the television show.

But George had tuned in to Emine's siren call because she appealed to his sense of duty. Foolishly he still wanted to do something for his country by fighting terrorists, and she'd promised a larger audience and mission. She had the resume to back up her words, along with a credible lawyer's introduction. The prestigious publisher didn't hurt.

And then had come the half whispered promise of, "You'll make the final cuts. Whatever you want goes." It came in a late night phone call, after another fight with Karen.

George headed down the aisle toward Emine, knowing that Bright would have arranged for adjoining seats. He had so much to read and learn before the landing in Cairo and felt tense about juggling her with his other workload. But their book, and now this Cairo coverage, was important so he'd spend whatever time necessary to get things headed in the right direction.

Excuses.

"Hi, Emine," he said, deliberately casual, as he stood across the aisle from her and extended his hand.

She looked up from her magazine, gazing at him dispassionately with shocking eyes, flashes of a brown rainbow dancing across them as light streamed in the window. She didn't speak. Suddenly, she leapt up, hugged him, then fell back into her seat, laughing.

George twisted to deposit his bag on a nearby seat and slid into his seat across the aisle. They both traveled light.

Her small hands were tightly grasping *The Economist.* "Trying to catch up," she said and waved the magazine. Her voice was soft and carried a strong lilting accent, impossible to place geographically. A mutt accent, she'd probably lived in a mix of locales during her childhood. That part of her he recognized, along with the throaty way the tones caught a syllable here and there.

He shrugged.

"Cat got your tongue?" she said, her voice now strong. George laughed. He pushed his bag under the seat in front of him. Clearly, Emine wasn't so gentle and passive, and that shrouded backbone probably served her well with the soldiers, rebels and warlords she met professionally on a daily basis.

"Looking forward to the flight?" He reached for his seatbelt and studied her from a side-glance. Light conversation could tell you so much about someone, from their openness to their defensiveness.

"Sure," Emine responded, her expression shifting yet again as sadness melted into her features. The girl's moods were like her eyes, reflecting back surprises and change. Odd girl.

"Ready for the revolution? Any thoughts on how we'll concoct a book? George decided to lead her and see if she what she did. He didn't much care what she said as to whether she could adapt quickly and be responsive. They would face days of intense pressure. In the midst of quickly emerging events and even violence he'd need to know that he could rely on her.

Emine wiped a thick lock of hair out of her eyes. Only then did she speak, and slowly, the loose red fabric of her arms waving like Buddhist flags on a windy hillside.

"Remember, I live in war zones; though I haven't been to Cairo lately. Still, it's a city I know well." She gave him a shy half smile. "The book will write itself because we're documenting history as it happens." Her tone was free of irony, and her small frame was tense, bursting with effervescent energy.

"Omar, who you saw blow up, was an old friend," she continued. "We, you and I, are writing on the conflict inherent in these troubled lands and how the people respond. Their choice... You're the expert and I'm the scribe." Emine leaned back into her stained seat.

"Omar almost blew me up. Let's correct that fact," George replied then realized he was shutting down the conversation. In questioning it was important to give a person every encouragement to finish their story. She was also achingly idealistic and such a willing slate. The world would continue writing on her if she stayed so open. Well, judgments were a luxury.

"So, no thesis?" he asked, watching. George always understood the dynamics of power yet felt no pressure to exert his own. Her reputation was stellar but so was his and he was much older. He didn't have time to write books and she was willing to do so; thus the partnership was working so far, but only because he felt he could trust her. He hoped that Cairo wouldn't change that balance but he'd survive regardless. She'd asked for his help and not the other way around, so ultimately, he held the important cards.

"I've been all over interviewing and photographing," she said, deflecting the question. "Gaza, indeed most of the Middle East, Africa and yes, Cairo. I get tired when I think about it." Emine paused and flashed her magazine at him again. "Why don't you write more, George? The bomb...."

He held his breath as she asked about the bomb. Khalil.

He sensed that Emine was a bit naïve, in spite of her job and experience. No way to beat idealism out of those subject to that disease. But why did she assume the world really cared? Mostly, in his experience, only a few people carried the global responsibilities for the rest. Terror itself was a game built around people, not ideals.

"I feel guilty for not writing more," George replied but suddenly the memories of his past year, usually suppressed, came flooding back. That was why he didn't write more. The bomb and the bullet. Better to escape.

Emine was silent as the plane's engine began to whirl, filling the void. The plane lurched, and glancing out the window George saw the airport move away. He wouldn't see home again for a while. His eyes moved from the window back to Emine. She was utterly lovely: her skin smooth and clear, a tranquil Madonna-like expression now holding her delicate features. They both knew where they were headed but what control did they have over events once they arrived? Coming or going, life ultimately takes charge.

"Together we can do more." she said, her tone breathless, her presence still. She smiled and George couldn't help contrasting her with his wife also so slight yet much harder than Emine. But he blocked the memory, his preferred response to Karen, and indeed his favored response to many things.

"Yes," was all he said.

"We're airborne! Look!" Emine said, sounding as gleeful as a child, pointing out the window. George watched Manhattan's tall buildings disappear behind them. The Statue of Liberty seemed to be waving goodbye.

George was happy to escape into his reading as Emine gazed out the window. He needed time to adjust to the world they were entering.

Mirrors

mine already enjoyed watching George. As a professional observer and an artist she'd learned to identify what made a subject engaging, and he had the right qualities. He could disarm people with his easy charm. His eyes were that odd grey which reflected no light and hid emotion in their depths. He'd aged just enough to start losing his colors, his skin displaying a mottled, ashen undertone, sprinkled with the bluish flush of veins under thinning skin. He wasn't scared of connecting, his eyes opening into hers and flashing the occasional understanding. Probably an illusion he'd learned to project, when doing so suited his purpose.

But he talked above her.

"Writing, but with a purpose?" she replied, trying to continue their conversation but noticing that she was losing his interest. Damn, she was usually pretty compelling with her wide eyes and broad statements but he was smarter than that. George was more detached. An intellectual?

"I only document, George. You'll need to add the insight and color," she said, hearing the slight catch in her own voice and not caring. Yes, while

George operated on intellect, she felt only emotion. And George was calm, just like Piers.

Momentarily she caught a flash from the past of gentle green eyes but willed it away, focusing on George instead. Dealing with lost loves in the midst of conversation with a psychologist could only get her into trouble.

"Why do you think the world wants change?" he asked, curiosity shining in his eyes. Had she not known his profession she would have trusted him more. But she'd met enough warlords, crooks and politicians to know that for some men acting was a basic job requirement.

George was leaning back, elegant, using open body language and smiling just enough. He was wearing a navy polo shirt and khaki pants. The silver of his belt buckle matched the silver of his watch. She sighed, remembering that not only was he an American, but also a practiced blank slate.

"I didn't ask the world," she said, smiling back at him. "I'm working to achieve my goals." A strand of hair fell into her eyes, as it always seemed to do. She brushed it away and noticed George's eyes following her hand.

Then he formed a steeple with his two index fingers and touched the tip with his lips. She stared, mesmerized, as he took his time answering.

"Have you defined your goals? Going after violent warlords and terrorists seems a dangerous road to walk. Are you sure you're willing to risk your life? I try to minimize the dangers I confront head on."

"But you're flying into the chaos of Cairo," she replied.

"That I am."

"I like Cairo, even if it's in the process of imploding," she said.

George shook his head but his eyes were gentle. "You're too young to know what you're saying. How old are you?"

Emine felt the tears coming but wouldn't let them burst free in the daytime. She only allowed that flow at night when she couldn't sleep. She'd loved Piers with a passion and desperation she'd never imagined possible, but his absence was absolute and God's will. Who could argue with a deity? And now she was "in love" with another man.

"It's complicated," was all she could say.

Then after a pause, she added, "the world is at a crisis point," unsure of how much he could understand, but wanted to turn the conversation from the personal to the universal. As a politician's daughter she could discuss the state of the world either intelligently or without saying anything of substance. The personal however, was, a quagmire.

"I don't disagree," George responded, and she heard the question in his tone as he put his book down on the adjacent seat. She saw a rabbit and a girl on the cover.

Never feel pressured to say anything or answer anyone's question; you don't owe them anything. She heard Mehmet's words from years ago, echoing in her head. Dad.

She turned her eyes up to George and felt a sudden connection with him. He was a humane man, right? Trying to save the world as she was. Were they both fools, or just incapable of doing anything else?

"I'm Turkish," she said. "We escaped the oppression of Islam with Ataturk in the 1920s as he brought us into the modern age and abandoned the barbaric customs better suited to the Middle Ages."

"Like honor killings and amputations as a punishment for theft?" George asked, his eyes still bright and alert. "You do know that Islam doesn't support the so called jihad going on now. Only a legitimate Koranic authority can declare jihad, and even then the targeting of innocent women and children isn't allowed."

"Yes, and Mohammed refused to bless the body of a suicide," Emine added. "Still, my religion is increasingly being practiced otherwise around the world."

"Ataturk tried to show another way," she continued. "He gave us democracy and a separation of church and state. But now Turkey is increasingly infected with the same Islamic fervor that has destroyed many of our neighbors. They want to do the same to us."

"I can't see you in a chador," George said but his attempt at humor failed to lighten her mood.

Should she trust him? They were partnered on a big project, after all. "God took away some people very dear to me. Before their time."

"I'm sorry."

Emine waited for his questions. They didn't come. She rarely opened up, too frightened of facing the intrusions that invariably followed. But George obviously wasn't going to force anything.

"I love it when silence cloaks a conversation," she responded, addressing the issue head on. "I like you; you don't force noise into an environment," she felt emotion as her words took shape and she looked down at her hands, again avoiding his eyes.

"You're an odd girl. I didn't remember that," he replied in a gentle voice and Emine glanced up, falling into the depth of his eyes. She wasn't quite ready to relax, but perhaps one day, with him, she might.

Emine realized that George was staring at her again and she should talk. He'd soon learn that she often didn't. What was the point of talking if you had nothing to say?

"I'm an artist," she began, searching for the words but not sure where they'd take her. "And it's usually the creative visionaries who articulate what everyone else is too frightened to say." She whispered the last word.

"Perhaps, together, we'll manage to get a message out."

Emine smiled. He understood, perhaps just a little bit, what no one else seemed to grasp. Life was ultimately so simple, wasn't it? We try to survive despite our pain.

"You like to tempt fate?" George asked, surprising her. "Get that adrenaline rush when you scrape through one more close call?" Emine was puzzled by his question and wanted time to figure out why he was shifting the conversation.

Emine heard the two younger men seated in the row in front of hers, talking. She gestured with raised eyebrows for George to do the same.

"The company's new iPhone games will be coming out next month." One of them said.

"They look cool," the other replied.

"Yes," Emine said slowly, once she was ready to answer. Obviously she liked to live dangerously – it was the only way she could feel alive and the only way she knew how to help people. "I document atrocities. I'm very damaged emotionally and only someone like me can do it, but I also have the resources to spread my message. My brand is global now."

"God bless you, my dear," was all he said in response and then turned back to his book. She watched him open it and begin to read. She picked up her magazine, mirroring him, for isn't that what interrogators did? Glancing at the article she saw yet another celebrity entering rehab, dark roots and all, before her gaze wandered back to George, so still and self possessed. "You're okay with having me along, aren't you?" she asked. Once again he gazed back at her, his eyes still kind.

"Of course. I agreed, didn't I? But don't expect me to protect you. I can't." He returned to his book. But she didn't want his refuge. Emine knew the game well enough to understand that a magic spell or Coke can was as good a safeguard as any other when it was your turn to go. God, not man, controlled fate.

Emine had seen what she needed: George could bluff all he wanted, yet he wouldn't be on this plane if he weren't as committed as she was to changing things. She didn't answer him, just smiled back then picked up her magazine and looked at fashion faux pas. George could keep his protective armor of indifference but he was going to help her. She winked at him and liked that he rewarded her with a smile.

The clouds moved closer, brushing against the plane's windows. Emine felt the sheltering comfort of the moment, knowing enough to enjoy it because it couldn't, and wouldn't, last. George had better enjoy his book, *Alice in Wonderland*; she'd seen the cover and knew that, in any failed state, chances were that they'd find a rabbit hole to fall down. Had he chosen the book himself? Apt choice.

Sleep

halil watched Jennifer sleep. She still had tubes sticking in and out of her but luckily the wound wasn't going to be fatal. She'd been moved into one of house's many small bedrooms, scattered

around the various bathrooms and linen closets. The upstairs area was a dim garret, with winding hallways that had been broken up into tiny rooms as befit its makeshift hospital status. The doctor himself lived here only as a front; his children were grown now, so he and his wife really needed very little living space. Those wounded on Allah's mission mattered more than a lifestyle of luxury and excess.

Jennifer's breathing was measured but soft, more a whisper than a resolute fight to live. That was why he'd left her the first time, after they both graduated from the University of San Diego, more than twenty years ago. They'd dated for years, even living together at the end. She'd always been so American, firm in her belief that she had rights and could do as she liked. Arrogant and indifferent to the consequences and resentments that developed in others trampled over in the exercise of her privilege. But bullets were immune to ideology and flesh always caved to pressure. He'd left her to graduate school and the emptiness of western decadence because he feared she lacked the will and discipline for his jihad. Looking at her now, blond hair spread across the white pillow, he knew his earlier decision had been right. And now he'd been a fool and risked both their lives. More importantly, he'd endangered his mission.

Americans no longer understood power, which was why they were using their strength so ineptly these days. They didn't comprehend that, while people might think they wanted free will and human rights, they actually couldn't live with such ambiguity. Wasn't it the American's God who took away man's free will? The heathens should read their own holy books – Jew or Christian. Had the Americans used their full strength Khalil's jihad would have no chance of winning. But this bullshit of compassion? Forget that misguided path. He with the most guns would win, in the long run, except when he opted not to use them. Jennifer, with her law degree and sunny smile, was just as naive. Facing a mob and an army to bring him a stupid message!

Khalil sensed the light diminishing in the frame of the open window. Exhaust and burning dinner fires, along with refuse and human smells, dominated the wafting evening air. Khalil heard a call to prayer but ignored it. The rich, dark rust curtains hung heavily across the window's frames and hid the arc of the sun as it descended for the day. The hotness of Cairo hadn't yet tempered and Khalil felt his own sweat. Jennifer, under her thin sheet and wearing only a cotton tunic looked dry and almost as white as the bedding.

Khalil went to the small mirror perched above the room's porcelain sink and studied his face. Clean-shaven, it was even darker than normal from his time in Cairo's sun. His eyes hadn't changed: dark brown almost to the point of blackness, almond shaped and fringed with thick lashes. His nose, softened by his surgeon in Brazil, no longer had its hawk-like bump. While his cheekbones were still gaunt and his jaw as strong, the basic shape of his face was less angular. Flying to Brazil, Khalil had been distraught at the sudden death of his mother, so his instructions to the surgeon had been vague. "Give me a new identity," he'd had said and it had been done.

After the bomb and the surgeries he'd returned to his brothers and their jihad.

"Are you still loyal?" they'd demanded.

And "what did you tell them?", asked over and over again. His answers hadn't been truthful and his comrades hadn't believed them. Trust is a mirage and Khalil's position was even now more tenuous. Still, he answered only to Allah.

Trust, what a concept. Men, so base and weak, wavering in front of temptation and danger, favoring themselves above others. Theft, greed, avarice, malice, lust and gluttony knew no borders between religions, nations or ideologies. Nor did stupidity.

If man held the ultimate answers there would be no need for God.

Khalil had been deeply lonely, which was why he'd begged Jennifer to leave her decadent Western life and join him. Surprised when she accepted, grateful but still greedy, he was only now realizing the magnitude of his decision. She stood out like a sore thumb and wandered like a child through the world's minefields.

Yet his crushing loneliness was gone.

Revolution brought out the fanatics and opportunists. Romantic and idealistic, it was fueled by hope and this one was about to confront a harsher reality. We all so love a dream don't we?

Khalil studied his lips in the mirror. Their reddish-pink color had faded and now wrinkles marked their borders. His few whiskers were now showing flecks of white amidst the black and the age lines were creasing his forehead and the corners of his eyes. Meanwhile, the room itself was quickly darkening but hadn't reached the duskiness of anonymity. Time was ever passing.

Sensing motion, Khalil whipped around and saw Jennifer trying to sit up. She winced and blinked her large cornflower eyes. Giving him a half smile she settled against her pillows, a bandage peeking out at her collarbone. Without make-up she looked younger than her more made-up and protected self.

Against his will, Khalil felt the surge of calm that always rose like an angel in her presence.

"I'm feeling a little better," she said with an American smile, meant to be reassuring but artificial here. "I'm sorry," she said, grimacing. Khalil walked over and turned on her bedside lamp. He took her hand.

"It was Allah's will," he whispered, bringing her palm to his lips and kissing it.

"We're so different," she said, her eyes so trusting, looking deeply into his. For a second he considered telling her not to trust him but decided against it. We all have our fate; better not to interfere with Allah's will.

The wallpaper was a baroque pattern of deep rusts, peaches and beige. It contrasted with the white sheets the doctor's wife preferred because they were easily bleached of blood.

Khalil started to update Jennifer about the day's events. Unconscious, she'd missed them all. And he worried for them both. Love amidst a war was a vibrant plot for a novel but in real life a recipe for tragedy lived. He wouldn't give her up easily. One of them would have to die for that to happen.

Flying

Emine scribbled on her note pad, pondering the luggage compartments above and the fuzz called a carpet under her feet, wondering how she'd ever agreed to board a flight to Cairo. Breathe, just inhale and exhale. She was landing into chaos and needed to be centered since survival depended on calm. People were sleeping on the plane and the cabin dark.

Dealing with hell was always an emotional adjustment.

The revolution had come and gone, but there were still no jobs for the Egyptian people. She'd need to report on the stories, but most of the obvious ones had already been played and replayed globally. If she asked her dad, the politician she'd consulted in the past on similar stories, he'd focus on the trends brewing beneath the surface.

"Power," he'd say, and she'd worry yet again about the high stakes in life that he liked to play. Answers were never simple but we all still believed in miracles. Mehmet sounded so sure when he spouted ideology, but why did it so often lead to sound bites and platitudes? And what would she find on the ground in the morning?

The air in the plane was cold and she pulled her cashmere blanket closer. That, a notepad, pen and camera were all she really needed on any trip. Well, also her phone and notebook. A pair of jeans.

But what about her life?

Ed had come into her being at a moment of intense pain. First, her brother Selim had died of a heroin overdose then the man she'd thought was the love of her life was gunned down before her eyes. Ed had brought the first smile to her face afterwards and somehow he'd stayed around.

"Always give your heart," Piers had advised her but he'd died before she'd summoned the courage to inform him she wasn't sure she had a heart. Could you really love someone to whom you couldn't confess? But was it fair to define love by your own deficiencies?

Emine pulled out a picture from the pages of her notebook and studied the green eyes and wide face. Was she leaving him finally for a chance at life? She could love Ed too now, right?

"I love you, Piers. I still do," she whispered to the picture before replacing it between the leaves of paper.

Emine wasn't obsessed any longer. No, she was letting go of that love, and holding the memory, nothing more. She shut her eyes and conjured up his presence, feeling the deep peace that brought.

Emine yearned for a cigarette, but that was a no no on airplanes these days.

Piers had taught her everything. How to hold a camera in spite of the gunfire coming their way. How to love and make love, not just fuck, though they did that too. How to develop a picture and add her own effects. Lighting a fire, comforting a widow, getting a story in on time and sleeping under the stars. Being human and feeling again.

Like a lot of war journalists, he'd gotten shot and Emine had caught it on film. "The incoming missiles are increasing, both in frequency and, I think, in size," Piers had said. His misty eyes had darkened as smoke obscured the sun. He was slim, which made him look better on television, and just over her height. She had stopped wearing heels.

"Civilians are cowering in whatever makeshift shelters they can find," he'd said. The sandy walls of an apartment building shook behind him at the moment of impact. But Piers was a journalist out of compassion, not personal ambition and his voice had never wavered regardless of what horrors its owner witnessed. In contrast, some of Emine's pictures had been blurred by her shaky hands.

That night they'd first met, in a bar on a side street in Paris.

"I'm Belgian, and a doctor," he'd said, glass of red wine in hand, brown hair slightly too long.

Perhaps she'd fallen in love then, as he pulled her close and she rested her back on his chest as they continued talking.

55

"I tried Doctors Without Borders first," he said, his deep voice melodious with a lilting accent. "The lack of medication, sanitation and multitude of bodies frustrated me." The pause. He did pauses so well. "I decided I needed to speak out and inform the world so I turned to journalism." Another pause. She'd felt his breath against her body, and curled in closer against the scratchiness of his wool sweater. "What do you do?" he'd asked.

The café was small; with the dim lighting that's called romantic. It was a tourist spot so Edith Piaf sang in the background, proclaiming that she had no regrets. Emine had no regrets.

"I don't do anything." She'd whispered the truth. For she really did nothing except spend her parents' money and waste her life.

"Sometimes I do nothing also," he'd responded and she'd felt his arms encircle her. Even now she felt the tears of that moment when someone forgave her. Lord knows, she never forgave herself.

Piers of the principles. Her of no morals. To her surprise, he embraced her anyway and they became lovers. He gave her an ideology and a cause. Like him, she now aimed to help the poor and oppressed in a world that had forgotten them. What was it the Christian God had said about the meek inheriting the earth? Piers might be dead but what had been his mission would now be her obsession until eternity since she had nothing else left.

Emine stretched and noted how quiet the cabin was. She could use a vodka.

"I love you," he'd whispered to her. It was always a whisper, passing through her and she'd laughed. Nestling into him, they'd talked so much and he'd taught her a whole new world. Then, just twenty-two months ago, in an instant, her life had crumpled into sand along with Piers' body, blood pouring into the hot day and soaking her Timberlands. The day he took the bullet she'd thrown away the last of her Chanel bags.

"And I'll love you all the while," Emine whispered to his ghost. "But perhaps I'm in love with someone else now. I want you and miss you so. I feel you, but you aren't here." Her decision was the right one. With that she saw the Pyramids out her windows.

Landing

George viewed the country below him, the plane lurching hazardously as he gazed at the deep blue Mediterranean Sea brushing up against the desert sands below. The dunes had been there for centuries, surviving all that man had created and destroyed. Buildings cascaded everywhere, forming modern Cairo. He saw the rows of landing lanes and the airport next to them. The sun was bright and the air smoky.

Back to a battle zone. Maybe Karen was right and he was too old for this turmoil. Then again, why the hell not? George thought back to his tour of duty in Iraq. He could almost hear the thump of an outgoing missile and the crunch when it landed. He could visualize the prisoners who'd spit at him and how hatred or fear had been the only emotions he'd seen for days on end. He remembered the words of a young man, late one night, as he disclosed the safe house of a Taliban leader, leading to his capture. While George had left the official life of interrogations and government work he now recognized that neither a classroom nor television studio could keep him fulfilled. He was as addicted to action as Emine; she was just honest enough to admit it.

He glanced over at the girl, alternating between her stack of spiral notebooks and the window. She was in a world of her own.

"I need a beer, let's get a beer," the two achingly young...what were they...men seated in front of George said. They looked tired, poor and thin yet had managed to play cards non-stop for hours. Why here, Cairo and a revolution?

Maybe Karen was right seeing him as a lost cause, but George loved the thrill of being involved in world events as they happened. The problems and solutions. Complexities. The challenges of figuring out the key to unlock a man or situation. He felt alive and challenged in a way his real life couldn't mimic. And someone had better fixing the problems because they sure weren't fixing themselves.

Looking down through the airplane window, he wondered what he'd find on the ground after months of protests and a fallen government. From this vantage the world was pristine.

Egypt was the land of Pharaohs and ancient civilization. The idea of an obedient populace had blown up, as most preconceived notions did, and now all bets were off. What did people really want? Messy free will or another parent? There was no Pharaoh now just the omnipresent army (aching for Mubarak) and a bevy of Islamists.

George was still wondering.

"I brought cards, my iPad and M&Ms," one of the young men said to the other.

"Cool," was the response, a word which seemingly made up fully 10% of their vocabulary. How had they ended up in first class?

Returning to chaos wasn't going to be easy. His bodyguards had introduced themselves prior to the flight and he felt somewhat heartened talking to them. They were smart, articulate and big enough to intimidate but not obvious targets. Still, life somehow surprises us: nice at an ice cream parlor - less so in a revolution.

So George had chosen to read on the flight, after finishing Bright's briefing books, figuring that being relaxed was the best preparation. He'd demolished *Alice in Wonderland*, that Karen had handed him as he walked out their apartment doors. Time to bring a lack of reality into his world through a children's book? But which country was more real, his home or his destination of the day? If Karen had a message for him, why couldn't she just be direct?

She was so perfect: blonde, slim, organized and always right. But she lacked compassion, the bones in her face like ice, shifting more than moving, like icebergs on an open sea. Worst of all, she liked to win and forgot that sometimes so did he.

He was, however, a truly horrible husband.

"Enjoy your trip, George," she'd drawled the night before he'd left and after they'd fought. Her voice chipped at him, picking and nagging. He would have preferred the slur if she'd drawled because she'd been drunk. Would have served them both if she'd loosen up occasionally.

"Can't you even pretend to care?" He'd glared back, really and truly mad. The apartment was cold and humorless, just like her, with the same damned green velvet couch but other than that it was beige, and white, and all of that crap. Not even effeminate – just washed out like her.

"You enjoy your parties. Someone needs to worship you," he'd replied. "And it won't be me." Yes, he'd said it. The kids were away now, so he could speak the truth out loud.

"Have some more wine," she'd smiled. "Hope you come back," she continued over her shoulder as she walked out of the dining room. Did he really deserve that? Why, all of a sudden, did he hate her so much? Or perhaps he was just finally honest enough to admit it.

Oh, things had gotten better. Briefly. She listened sometimes, holding back her criticism. But the old resentments still hung there, filling the air, and he'd felt it. When was the last time she'd laughed with him?

His time with her had become scenes remembered.

Shortly after their wedding he had held her, watching a football game on their couch. "Who's winning," she'd asked, never one to figure out a score.

As he'd told her, the softness of her hair against his cheek had felt perfect. Now he was landing in a revolution and failed state. Could she figure out a score without him?

Perhaps he was too broken for her to hold together. Her world was pristine and controlled; his was full of bombs and the men who built them. Their respective choices over the years had driven them apart.

Let her file for divorce as he was running away. Her society parties would continue to support her and her ego. He wasn't there and, quite frankly, wouldn't be.

But still, her image hung on him and he couldn't let it fully disappear. Not yet.

"I love you," she'd whispered that morning, pulling herself close just as he left. She was in cashmere, a baby blue, fading color that matched her eyes while he'd been in cotton. That was the difference, wasn't it?

Why had she bothered? The kiss? The empty words? Was it pretense, that's what you did when your husband went off to a revolution? So he'd pretended too.

Perhaps she cared more now because he'd won an award and become a quasi celebrity. Perhaps she'd grasped the possibilities and decided to grab importance through him.

Or was he too jaded?

"Take care of yourself," he'd said, weak words, willing to add I love you. Just then the plane lurched, wheels hitting the runway, jolting him into his present reality and not the one he'd left behind.

Emine glanced over then went back to her notebooks.

George was too old for love. That was a young man's game and he'd left his marriage there long ago. Was it weariness or indifference? Studying the cracks in the mottled skin of his hands he wondered if Karen was having an affair. But he was in a new country now and had to leave that mess behind for a fresh one.

Packing *Alice* into his bag he looked out the window at the failed state and hopeful democracy. At least the Pyramids were still standing.

Sand

Khalil was walking around the Pyramids and the Sphinx, surveying them for security and a lack of security. In pictures they always seemed much larger and desolate than the actual reality provides. The desert was a backdrop on one side, with tall buildings and a crowded road forming the other. Nose-less and serene the Sphinx had never caught his fancy, rather it was the Pyramids that always made Khalil catch his breath. Stunning.

Sand crept into his shoes and he wished he'd worn socks. The usual men with camels and post cards wandered around looking for tourists, one of which Khalil clearly wasn't. He saw a sign for cold drinks and didn't even wonder. The marvels of surviving in a desert were ingrained in his memories of poverty-stricken youth and improvising to survive.

To bomb or not to bomb? So tempting to target a high-profile site, but he wasn't going to do it. As the Taliban learned after destroying the Buddhas of Bamyan, world opinion doesn't support the destruction of ancient historical monuments. Public relations are so important, especially with the Internet and its scalability. People vote for those they like and Egypt was facing an election in five weeks.

But Khalil needed to study his options and the Pyramids were so obviously one.

Khalil struggled to clear the clutter in his head. He had a job to do, but the details were excruciatingly difficult. And then there was Jennifer, so unpredictable and who kept spouting off ideas about leaving the jihad and settling on a beach somewhere. Jennifer's brain was healing but she had clearly lost her mind. Did she not understand his work and its global significance?

She was very pretty, however.

Focus. Work. Radwan had called. He'd been mugged.

"I didn't kill them. Punks," he'd spoken into the phone, taking away one worry but adding another. Radwan, so trained and angry, would be able to kill easily. The last thing Khalil needed was to find a new assassin because his old one landed in jail for murdering a gangbanger.

"Wise, wise," Khalil had reassured his charge. "I need you closer, again in Algeria." Khalil expected resistance and got it.

"I was just there! I need to be in New York, to finalize things," Radwan protested. Getting used to the easy lifestyle and comfortable bed?

Calm.

I'm not confident yet...no, too negative, he reminded himself. This boy was young.

"Radwan, do you realize how essential your role is?"

"Ahhh," was the response. Perfect. Or not?

Khalil had to wonder and question, the part of his job in which everything had to be perfect as his assassin couldn't miss with the plot resting on his young shoulders. They had the resources to support Radwan, but each man ultimately goes alone to his fate. Life was moving too fast and Khalil felt out of control, guessing at the future and knowing that sometimes he wouldn't be right. The revolution in Egypt was complex and added variables which shifted daily. You had to control what you could.

Things should be falling into place perfectly so why weren't they? Why couldn't he be confident with his carefully laid plans? This insecurity was going to get him killed.

Drawing the warm sand into his hands he watched it pouring through his fingers as it did when he was a child. The grains were powdery and sifted with an even weight. The sand here was like fine dust that by dawn would coat every exposed surface like a soft mist. Comforting? Yes. Predictability, patterns and certainties led to structure. The problem wasn't with his actions. No, they continued to be flawless, but the ancillaries weren't crystalizing as they should. Khalil faced cascading problems, possibly falling into an abyss of his leadership limitations.

The Pyramids loomed above. Man's will breaking the environment, with bricks leading up to the heavens and under a brutal sun. The Egyptians then had many Gods, leading them to build here on earth and not trusting Allah's divine will.

Khalil heard his cell ring, saw the caller id and answered it. His boss.

"I need an update," a harsh voice barked in Arabic.

"Radwan was mugged," Khalil said in response. "He's ok. I'm calling him home for more training."

"And in Cairo?"

"I still can't tell who controls the streets here," Khalil whispered, sifting more golden sand between his fingers.

"Why do I keep hearing that?" was the harsh response. "They are hiding too much with the 'Internet'." Silence. Khalil waited, knowing that he wasn't expected to speak. "Hire an expert. Find one."

"Will do," Khalil replied and then watched a man in a turban drag his camel toward two white tourists. Not too many of those visiting foreigners lately.

"Fast," the voice shrilled, then disappeared.

How would he find an Internet expert? Khalil texted Radwan. Right generation. Within seconds he got a number and began to dial. Didn't being part of a global organization mean that he shouldn't have to deal with this low-level personal shit?

The number was disconnected and he heard the static come loud and clear through his line. If you wanted something done right, you did it yourself.

Night Visitations

mine couldn't sleep. She never slept, dammit! Why couldn't she ever get past confusion? Certainly, most people didn't brood over things they didn't control to the extent she did. No one had time for the related guilt, frustration and helplessness. She wanted to escape too, but the Gods had decided to make her the one who repented, mostly in the middle of the night. Gods?

Ed was coming to visit. He missed her. She missed him. So what was the problem?

First, she hadn't left Paris that long ago. Personal space? Hot body, great sex, but he was starting to get clingy. Men often did that when she went to a work site. To Emine, the chaos was pretty standard, so each trip was yet another drop into a new world to be commented on and then forgotten. It was similar to shooting a movie except the bullets were real. Her vantage points seemed neither forbidding nor exciting, familiar, but to others they seemed thrilling and even exotic.

"It's so dangerous here right now," she'd told him earlier that night, on the phone. The rhythmic Arabic chanting from the streets, and with clanging music, was still defying the darkness. Smoke wasn't reaching into her air-conditioned hotel room but the raging fires were visible through her panorama windows. The mobs were getting angrier as they continued to starve even after the people's revolution.

Social change was never easy.

"I want to see Cairo; I want to see you," he'd insisted and she'd caved. He wanted her. Did he truly understand the danger; not just from the city but to his heart? Emine knew that she should be doing more to protect him. Ed was too perfect for her broken and lonely world and didn't have the tools to evaluate the realities involved. Meanwhile, she kept rushing into the world's hot spots, running to find a distraction and escape. How could Ed know the mayhem he was walking into since she'd shared so little of the realities? Mr. always did everything right and enjoyed going home for holidays. Perhaps he loved her because she was exciting and his life was anything but.

She did miss him, though. The solidness of his strong body and the way he gazed into her eyes. His gentle strong arms and how he held her just so.

Cairo was burning. Her job.

Emine had been drinking vodka tonight and was really enjoying it. The warm buzz dulled her apprehension and helped her justify the risk. Ed's risk. What if they actually got serious, this man who claimed to love her? She'd just have to drink more vodka until she figured life out.

Emine pulled her bare leg to her chest and grabbed a cigarette. Tomorrow they'd drive through the city, do some interviews and send the footage back to New York. Then, late in the day, they were going to the country's military headquarters for some interviews, with who was still unclear.

"When can I meet your parents, Emine?" Ed had asked. How about never?

"Well, um, I'm in Egypt covering an ongoing revolution. There are tanks in the streets and we…" she'd started. Her room was vast and overlooked the Nile. George had vetoed a pyramid-based location and put them in Ramses Hilton, near the now resurrected protests.

"Excuses!" Ed had replied; so naively confident she wouldn't yell. She'd damn well rather face his wrath than that of her parents. No one was ready for that meeting yet.

"Emine, Cairo is such a short flight to Istanbul. I'll fly from Paris. We'll make it a weekend," he said, persistent. Why she was still with him?

"I've never been to Istanbul before," he said.

"It's crowded," she replied. "And no."

Emine lit her cigarette, and puffed, watching smoke float to the ceiling. Her bed was standard; her clothes limited to a bra and matching aqua lace panties. The Hilton room service tray had more than enough food left. Her legs were thinner than normal and she pondered when she'd last eaten a real meal. The adrenaline rush that came from political turmoil was always so much more compelling than food.

Her nails were mostly broken now, she realized as she studied them. Anyone who lived as much in the mind as she did could pay only so much attention to her body.

"Ed," she'd begun tentatively, "my parents are a bit larger than life."

"Mine too. My mom will put you in a wool sheath when she sees your tattered jeans."

"No," she said, seeing Ed in her mind, so blonde and beautiful. Those blue eyes that stared into hers with such seriousness. Piers' eyes had been so green.

She'd stretched across the bed, settling in for a brave stab at honesty with Ed, easier on the phone than in person. "Do you have a few minutes to talk?" she'd asked.

"For you, of course," he'd replied.

So she'd begun the story, aiming for openness but not sure she could deliver. Her father was famous, and not always for good things. Mehmet was a big man, broad and dense with a commanding presence. Some of who he was definitely came from bluster but that was how politics were played in Ankara. Corrupt? Who knew? A behind-the-scenes-power-broker, absolutely. Liz was his biggest cheerleader, regardless of the rumors she must have heard over the years, and never fading. She shrouded her thoughts behind Chanel Number 5 and shopping bags from Paris, a good and respectful wife of a politician. They led separate lives privately. Life in the public eye was never easy, hence Emine choosing a different escape from her brother.

"He's tough," she'd stated and Ed hadn't argued. He must have done a Google search; lawyers do background checks. So she kept talking. The smoky rooms and hushed conversations. Her parents' lovers and the enormous boat. Her dad getting shot...some crazy Islamist ...and her mother only bothering to visit the hospital when the reporters were outside.

"I'm not some fairy princess who'll cook you dinner every night," she'd warned. "I write and travel."

"Ok," he'd replied. "I actually stay pretty busy myself, in case you hadn't noticed."

"Great," was all she could respond, aware that he couldn't comprehend a background as rootless as her own.

Ed listened for a while and then told her to get some sleep so she could face the poverty stricken mobs in the morning. A lovely man...but...no. That uneven smile with big white American teeth, so straight and gleaming. That patience when she rambled off on a tangent. His broad shoulders and narrow waist, tapering to muscular legs and buttocks. The curve of his hip and that firm, hard stomach. His hands as he touched her and most of all his deep lingering kisses. Shit, was she falling in love with him?

His apartment in Paris was all light and air, cool and angular with metal meeting white and a smattering of the right books. What was bothering her? Too pristine? Too safe?

Her phone rang again, "Hello," she said into the receiver, surprised that her voice didn't slur.

"Our driver, the one from the airport, was just found shot dead. Guess someone didn't like our first newscast," George said, his voice monotone and dry, as he did so well when challenged on television.

"Who told you?" she asked, instinctively, drunkenly falling into role. How she stayed alive.

"Bright. Our bodyguards are part of a security company monitoring everything. They told him before us."

"Would they have told us had he not wanted us to know?" Emine asked, and wondered at the speed of the murders. Who else was watching them? "So fast," she whispered.

George either ignored her or didn't hear her words. "Ben went to the morgue to get pictures."

"Morgue? The police are allowing pictures?"

"For our newscast, tomorrow," George replied, then laughed. "Makes no sense, right? We just arrived and already, this? Odd."

Emine took another a cigarette from her pack of Camels, lit it with a match and inhaled. Watching the smoke curl as she blew it into the air conditioner's blast, she wondered how to answer.

"Bright give you a raise?" she asked.

"Yes. You too," George replied.

"Bastard!" she said. He'd probably set the damn driver up, realizing the danger would start on day one: drama trumps reality. As if a city on fire weren't dangerous enough. Bright always had the biggest story, the best scandals and the highest ratings. Seeing her dead, so she couldn't say anything to his bitch of a wife about all his girlfriends wouldn't be inconvenient either. This was why she kept quitting. Only Bright always paid the most and would print anything. The no-limits rule … so she kept going back because no one else was as accommodating to ideologue journalists like herself.

What was in her best interest? How much did she trust George, still quiet on the phone? With all the vodka in her system she was best staying quiet tonight and deciding in the morning. Nothing was likely to happen before then anyhow. But Ben!

"George, don't go out. Not tonight," she muttered. Ben would be okay. He was as seasoned and shrewd as they got. And Bright needed those pictures while they were still for sale.

"Let's meet early for coffee and talk," she said and was glad George agreed. How savvy was George really? He'd been to Iraq and Afghanistan but always with a military escort and behind barbed wire. He would soon find out how different the streets here were.

Dispatches

eorge was restless as he stared out into the glittering darkness of Cairo and across the blackness of the Nile. Earlier, they'd landed and emerged into the burning heat of the late Egyptian

afternoon. Sweat had broken out on George's forehead and Ben, his new cameraman, had taken snippets of footage leaving the airport and driving through the city streets.

"We've just arrived here in Cairo and the airport is empty now. No one leaving or coming," George had said like a monkey for the camera. Emine gave him a thumbs up from behind Ben but didn't bother to smile. She didn't smile much.

"Fabulous," said Ben, ever the professional and used to coaxing his subjects. The great thing about being the one on film was that all you heard was praise…to elicit a better performance and presumably to protect the fragile egos of those who narcissistically sought an on-camera role. What a load of bullshit.

The air was hazy with so many toxins George didn't care guessing at its actual composition. His mood was shot, he was tired, and suddenly the reality of his decision hit him. They shot at journalists here. War zone. Failed state. Revolution. No safety codes.

They were herded into an armed van and Ben shot video as they left the airport for the city. The initial on-camera dispatches had been fairly simple; how much could anyone say about an airport?

The streets changed as they entered the city, dust giving way to grime. Most of Egypt is a desert with only that band bordering the Nile showing much green. Cairo itself is a modern city with the density of buildings and population, the filth, exhaust and other smoke, traffic and desperation of all such metropolises. But it also housed towering minarets and ancient mosques, ornate and holy. Mostly the city was grey but many old bricks had faded into a burnished gold. As each ancient land has its charms, depending on the street, he could feel a sense of the exotic and past mysteries that fed so many tourist illusions. Ben seemed to know the city well and agilely turned his camera back and forth between his commentator and the better shots in the streets. George was asked to comment here and there, but Ben did the real work.

And as they drove through the crowded streets, still bright but with the sun beginning to fade, curious faces peered into their van. The buildings got more densely packed as did their residents. As was always the case, people looked like people. The eyes were all dark and mostly George saw only the curiosity of men, but once in a while a startled woman would meet his eyes through bulletproof glass.

The hotel, the Rameses Hilton, was like any in the States and they'd been pre-checked in. Pristine and cool, it towered above the Nile. George was whisked to his room, where he took a shower then called Karen.

"Come home," she'd begged, surprising him by crying. Now she cared? Women made no sense and he was a damned psychologist. Men are from Mars and all that craziness? No, people just made no sense, period. And the older you got, the more you knew, the more confusing they were.

"Please," she'd begged. "I'm so alone here in New York."

That was it; apart from him she didn't have a lot of friends in New York.

"Get a life," he'd almost said but didn't have the heart. He loved her, right? Stretching out on the sterile bedspread, with the television in front of him and view of the Nile to his right, he realized how spoiled he'd become. Life had worked until today: at the press of a button he got whatever he wanted.

So every time he got comfortable he propelled himself into the midst of chaos – interrogating terrorists or documenting revolution. Karen was married to a seriously unbalanced man with an odd death wish, and she got left holding the bag of their life. He dimmed his lights and felt a wave of compassion. All she wanted was stability and a normal reality devoid of psychopaths and bullets.

"You keep talking about writing a novel. Leave academia and just write it now, Karen. The kids are grown and…" he tried to finish but only heard her sobs.

"I'm sorry I can't be better, Karen," he tried.

"You're good enough," she replied and he felt a tug at his heart. Why did they always fight? His cell phone started to ring and he saw that it was Bright.

"I need to go, Karen. I'm sorry," he said and took the other call, knowing that he was a bastard for doing so but doing it anyway.

"Brilliant footage, George," Bright said. "We're building a story."

"A story…" George replied.

"Let's frame the narrative. The world is changing and most people don't get it," Bright said. "The people have moved online and joined forces against the old social orders. Let's help them take over the world. It's a new revolution, George."

"You're crazy," George said, and wondered who wasn't. Karen?

"No, George. I'm like you and have a vision for the world and what it can be. We haven't made it there yet, George, but we will. Let's help these people." Bright sounded excited but George could hear a lack of sincerity in his tone. He only wanted the best story, didn't he?

"Amen," George replied, hired gun and influential commentator both. His jet lag was dizzying as he stared down at the Nile from his hotel bed, half in it already with a leg dangling. He hadn't eaten recently but all he wanted to do was sleep.

"I'm tired, Bright," he mustered.

"Pleasant dreams," was the response. George turned out the lights and slept surprisingly well.

Algeria

To most people Algeria is a mere blip on a map most famous for launching the Barbary Pirates. One of the original countries to earn the title of a failed state it passed through long periods during which a terrorized and starving population couldn't expect the basic rights of life. The fighting officially started in 1954 during the war of independence from their French colonial masters, but that brutal conflict only faded into instability then civil war. The current state of affairs was arguably only marginally better.

But Khalil called it home, and now that Al Qaeda had established a presence here he was safer within its borders than he'd ever been in his life. But failed states and deserts are never inviolable.

His team was well south of Algiers, the capital that glowed in white purity nestled up against a deep blue Mediterranean. The southern desert was a different place entirely, littered with Bedouin tribes and desolate villages. Paul Bowles's world of A *Sheltering Sky* seemed more surreal than visual, filtering through fingertips like the ever-present sand. And the heat was all defining.

"Ping, ping, ping," the rifle shots rang out across the parched desert as his boys practiced. He watched them and stared out over the expanse of sand at the colony of tents nestling on the edge of a shooting range.

French mixed with Arabic as the boys joked amidst target practice. A lone laugh echoed among the rolling dunes that seemingly stretched out forever.

His mother had died eight months before, just before the last of his operations reshaping his face. When he'd heard that she was in dire straights he'd luckily been just recovered enough from his latest surgery to fly home and hold her as her breath faded. Didn't the Buddhist say that death was life's only certainty? The stars had been out that night in full majesty and he hoped that Allah had taken her into his care, not renouncing her as she'd renounced him.

"Allah is with you. I love you ummi," he'd whispered as he held her, her breath increasingly loud and raspy.

"Allah does not protect women and poor children. He didn't protect you," she'd croaked, her chest rising and falling but her eyes still flashing fire. Perhaps he'd learned courage from her, but he'd never been brave enough to cry the way she had. Later, her bulk had diminished and she became a mere shell of her former body. He'd felt bones under her multitude of cloth.

They were in her small hut, a poor shelter from the sand that seeped in now that she no longer had the energy to keep it out. A small lamp lit her face, and the rest was blackness as she lay huddled on her cot. Poor but ever proud, her struggle to speak brought tears to his own eyes as he tried to meet hers for the last time.

"You've made your own future, Khalil, but you were blinded by promises of an Allah that does not exist."

Her labored breath hadn't lasted much longer than those statements. For the last time he kissed her cheek and prayed over her body before walking out into the night. The other women would see to the death rituals ordained in the Koran. He had too much else to do.

Now he was back and the sun blazed with the intensity of hell on earth in the summer. Had she found peace? If anyone deserved it, with her life of broken expectations, a dead son and deadbeat husband, she did. He hadn't cried again after that night. We must move on to our tomorrows if we can't face the pain in our past.

"Radwan, now," Khalil barked, keeping his voice sharp, as befit his rank. The boy had been arguing with another, the two yelling with sweat pouring into their eyes. They were dressed in loose cotton uniforms the color of the sand and used the sleeves to wipe their eyes.

"Patience is a virtue which most people don't possess," he told his recruits. "We've been fighting for centuries. Let the enemy tire for they don't have the stomach for a real showdown." Khalil studied the boy with his wandering eyes and tense shoulders. Radwan was a mere youth still and true to their nature had testosterone and impatience bursting through his veins. But discipline? *"Eternal is the Face of thy Lord in Its Majesty and Bounty,"* Khalil continued, quoting the Koran and touching the boy's shoulder to draw him closer. "Patience," he whispered.

Khalil needed to channel these men's aggression until he was ready for it. Like fighting dogs, these boys needed to rip into something; he should find some animals for target practice. A taste of power is all it takes to start a devouring, insatiable hunger and what better a motivation than real control over life and death? He'd been bitten by that scorpion himself. One must control his charges, absolutely.

He flicked Radwan's ear. "I'm headed to the market. Start practicing precision and not multiples."

The hot sun continued to beat down and Radwan blinked as the glare hit his eyes. "Should I come with you?" he asked.

"Why?" Khalil said as harshly as he could muster. "Did I tell you to come?"

Radwan gazed back and Khalil saw defiance so he slapped the boy, as his own father had once slapped him, a broad hand across the fleshy part of the cheek. His father had done it out of sport while Khalil needed to crush this boy for a different reason. As you brutalized fighting dogs, you needed to do the same with your young fighters. He grabbed Radwan and punched him in the stomach leaving him gasping in burning sand.

Khalil walked to his jeep without a glance back. These boys were still too soft; they weren't coeds, they were soldiers. He'd have them sleep outside and wonder at what lurked in the shadows. He could afford to lose a few of them as they were like cockroaches in the bazaars of Algiers. Turning on the jeep, Khalil wondered where his compassion had gone. They were his men, not just cannon fodder. Hadn't he nurtured his charges more in the past? Frighteningly, he couldn't remember.

But his real fear was ever lurking: would he ultimately have to be the one who pulled the trigger on KK's fatal day?

Perhaps he needed a mullah's calming voice to refocus his vision. Well, in this country the mullahs he knew had all been bought. They were like whores remarketed as virgins in a land where harem, all that was forbidden by Allah, was subject to the whim of whomever held the biggest gun.

But he believed, absolutely. "Allah, my merciful. Protect my path as I seek to do your will. Guide me." The last statement was a cry for help. The responsibility was grating on him and he wondered how worthy he was to lead a global jihad. "As Allah ordains, so I will follow." He drove on to the marketplace.

At least the French had left excellent roads, cutting through the bleak land with a determination Khalil knew he hadn't found yet in Radwan. What was he to do?

In his rear view mirror he saw that his boys had started an impromptu game of football. Yes, they'd spend the night outside in the desert. Did they think he cared whether one of them died? Better if one did, because then they would understand how seriously he took their jihad. He was training them to die anyway.

A snake slithered across the road but he didn't slow down. The wheels of history, or just the inertia that comes with our own fear? He would succeed.

His cell phone remained quiet and Jennifer hadn't called. He'd been told she was improving, but why hadn't she phoned to tell him? Time passed so slowly sometimes.

Turning on the radio, he heard Michael Jackson proclaim his love to Billie Jean, which only reminded him of San Diego yet again.

"Allah, be merciful," he prayed.

Father's Words

Emine heard the call to prayer as she tried to wake, the jet lag hitting her like a bullet between her eyebrows. Or was it the last slug of vodka that had put her to sleep the night before? Echoes of the ancient word filled the brightening sky, replacing gunshots and explosions for now, and she watched the play of a cloud through her expansive window. What color was the light? Pink, blending into rose then giving way to an odd orange? No, make that peach.

She got out of bed, naked, and made her way to the window. Further opening heavy curtains, she looked out at the Nile and city beyond. The oddly shaped pool was right below her room, glistening turquoise and angular but uneven. Cleaner than the deeper colored river it was early enough to be empty and looked like a jewel. Her room was high so she could see the vast expanse of Cairo, dense, hazy and filled with tall boxes and towering minarets. She loved these mega-cities: majestic, chaotic and teeming with life. Visiting the exotic was the best part of her job, and each city had its own personality and history. Now she was back in the cradle of civilization where people knew their country mattered

Inspiring.

Even though the unemployment rate was currently around 30 percent. And anyone wondered at a revolution? Seventy-five percent of those graduating college couldn't get jobs, and now that they could read about the whole mess on the Internet, they realized that other governments did better for their people. Never mix education and mis-management.

Emine was one of the lucky ones who could leave. She ordered coffee, toast and a list of other menu items while studying the streets below, noting the passageway to and from the hotel. The temperature would easily cross 100 degrees and it was dangerous. Bullets knew no ideology.

Still the ancient call to prayer rang out, familiar.

It reminded her of Istanbul and the soft hazy light as the sun slowly illuminated her ancient world living in modern reality. Istanbul, with its view of the Bosporus through large wood framed windows, with just enough breeze from the sea to cut summer's blistering heat. How she missed home, and yes, even her parents. But we all made our own choices and hers had been to run away.

Sometimes she felt almost lovely, a soft morning light falling on her pale and slim body, dressed in nothing but the remnant of her dreams and a few moments of quiet. But, shit, then reality struck and she headed to the shower to wash off her never-ending sins. Showering first, she slipped on a robe and waited for food.

Alone, and feeling it, she wondered what they'd walked into. Hung over and uncaring, she'd be fine. The only outcome was a focus on survival. Period. But…

The coffee came and she over-tipped the waiter; fuck Bright.

Gulping the dark liquid and choking down cold toast glistening with berry jam, water dripping from her hair, Emine called Ed just to say, "I love you, doll." She did have a sweet side and felt alone this morning and he was her "boyfriend". Still accepting thus far, but how much more did he need to discover before he dumped her?

"Enjoy the burning hot streets and ravenous crowd," Ed had replied in his light, professional tone. "Love you, Em." And she let herself believe him, suddenly acknowledging the void he left when not around. Why couldn't she be normal and sane with respect to relationships?

Emine swallowed hard. She wanted to tell Ed that she missed him and yearned for the expanse of his chest to shelter her before she faced the chanting, faceless masses. She understood the manic nature of a mob and, while happy to document it for news shows, couldn't help but feel a creeping trepidation. No one controls a beast. For just a second she wanted Ed's smile, along with the way his eyes grazed her face when she got quiet, and not just a cold phone. But he was too far away and she'd left him there.

"Cat got your tongue?" she heard, that hokey cliché he threw her way so often. Then, he'd just power through her insanity, pretending it didn't exist. Her moods, her paranoia and her ridiculous job. Which was a good thing... all of it. Emine wasn't going off to her office, though he acted as if she were, ignoring tanks, bullets and armed men.

She expected too much of him, didn't she?

"Miss you," she ventured. "But I'm still going into the heart of darkness today."

Then, in the midst of his laughter she heard his other phones ringing.

"Ignoring a big deal?" she asked, marveling that he could juggle her and a billion-dollar merger at the same time. Dressing as they talked, by now she was in old Levis, a long-sleeved t-shirt, despite the inevitable heat, and a skull head belt. Listening to him talk, she pulled on black lace-up ankle boots, flat in case she had to run. Her hair was drying but would end up in a ponytail regardless of what shape it assumed. Her coffee was now as cold as her toast but still she lingered on the line.

She'd meet George for hotter coffee in a few minutes.

"The papers here are full of stories discussing how the army and Muslim extremists are trying to manipulate the election," he said, and she stopped sipping.

"The election isn't for five weeks," she said. "Of course everyone is trying to propagate their extremist views, but can they pre-control it?"

"In a corrupt and chaotic nation?" Ed laughed. "Yes."

Emine felt even more unsure. The world was a mess, but the army here was pretty much holding the streets thus far, at least to her knowledge. She should call Mehmet, dad and political genius, and get his take on the situation before she stepped into the cesspool. She reached into her bag and pulled out a dark scarf to cover her head. If a true surge of support for radical Islam was building there was no point in provoking anyone.

"Ohh," she cooed into the phone, suddenly trying to figure out how to get Ed off the phone so she could quickly call Dad before meeting George. She gnawed her toast, thinking.

"Love you; gotta go," he said, saving her from the trouble.

She pondered what angle to take with Mehmet. She'd likely get only a few minutes and needed to have a focused game plan before calling as he usually gave her two questions before turning his attention elsewhere. She pulled her hair up into a high ponytail and surveyed her golden eyes in the mirror. She looked tired, with telltale red in what should have been the whites of her eyes. Could she continue this lifestyle much longer? Shit. Should she just marry Ed and put the Chanel back on? Looking at herself Emine acknowledged that there was no going back. Liz held the trophy wife prize, anyway, so Emine had to develop a different identity.

She picked up the phone and dialed Mehmet's cell.

"Allo," he barked, just as she heard the first ring.

"Dad," she said and heard silence. "I have a question."

"Yes," he responded. She twirled the end of her ponytail around her fingertip, annoyed at how childlike she continued to be with him.

Set the scene and ask question one. "I'm in Cairo and about to hit the streets. Does the army or Muslim Brotherhood control them and the election already?"

She waited through the silence on the other end. Mehmet didn't speak before he was ready and even Emine felt afraid when addressing him. The power he held, and who ever knew what he'd do or had done with it. That unpredictability and force might frighten her, his daughter, but it petrified his enemies. His eyes were almost green like Piers's and perhaps the common color had been a draw. Mehmet was more voluble, with a ready smile but a gaze that could stop you dead. Power was all he cared about. Well, maybe he cared about her as well.

"The army controls the streets; the Muslim Brotherhood has the hearts of many people. You understand the distinction?" he asked, careful and stern.

"Yes, Dad."

"Then explain it."

"It's an uneasy and delicate balance. No one is fully out yet; no one has won. Thus everything remains in chaos. The earlier people's revolutionaries are vulnerable because they didn't capitalize on their initial momentum."

He sighed. Things must be worse than she thought.

"Em, be careful," he added. Then, after a pause. "The people don't have a credible representative anymore, doll. And Tehran is an increasing problem for us all. Look there for insight; they see an opportunity and know how to strategically seize it."

She studied the phone. Shit. Today was going to be ugly; she could sense it and he couldn't - wouldn't – be clearer. No one was truly in control here, that much seemed clear.

"Dad, our driver from the airport last night was shot dead."

"Just meant to scare you, or they would have killed you all in the car. Who'd want to scare you and why?" Mehmet asked. Emine could imagine him, drinking his own coffee and reading through the pile of papers he devoured in the mornings.

"Em, you shouldn't be there, but remember to keep your eye on what doesn't make sense. Those odd patterns betray the truth behind the illusions. And, doll, we're not all that stable here, so I've only tangentially been watching Cairo. Our whole region is a powder keg,"

"You aren't scared?" she asked with a smile, knowing he'd reassure her because that was what he did.

"Em, I've set everything up in Swiss trusts, doll. Be careful, but I need to go." And with that his phone clicked off. Emine felt a sudden fear. Swiss trusts? So much for finding optimism and a can-do spirit in her father. Well, like him, she was a pro and wouldn't let her emotions show. Fear meant death in some environments.

With a swirl of lip-gloss she headed for the elevator, George and the mob, her camera poised and ready. Life really was too crazy for words so she'd have to revert to pictures. The secrets she'd keep to herself.

Dismay

George woke with a sense of unease.

Give people, and countries, the space to find you, he reminded himself. Restraint was the hardest quality to master, especially for someone such as himself who liked to control events. Patience unlocked secrets, while pressure drove them from you forever.

He wasn't comfortable here in Cairo. The mood was unfortunately familiar: poverty and a loss of hope. Why didn't democracy adapt more easily to desire? Not a prostitute but rather an ideology it asked for more than a gratuitous compliment before it opened up. Promises made to desperate people generally didn't end well.

Really, George felt like *Alice*, thrown into a new and unexpected world. His wife hadn't gotten tenure at Stanford for nothing, and her choice of books was as impeccable as her person. Great themes ran through history we just sometimes failed to recognize the narrative our own life was following.

The driver dead. Ben had called, late, but clear. "We'll need to watch each other's backs tomorrow," was all he said.

"How was he shot?" George asked.

"Execution style, back of the head."

A warning. They were being watched and forewarned.

Checking his email, George saw he had fifty-two messages, almost half of them from Bright or related assistant. Bright was as effusive as ever...the first video coming from the airport had been a viewer hit. The Democrats and Republicans in the US were still fighting over the budget. Karen had sent photos of wallpaper – all beige – and signed with an xo.

George gulped down some strong black coffee and ate half of his egg white omelet. The latter counted as food? Next time he'd order something he actually wanted to eat. Instead of facing himself he hurried down to the lobby to meet Emine, Ben and his two goons.

Emine was sitting deep in a couch and playing with her cameras. Dressed in unacceptable jeans, boots and a navy-striped and luckily long-sleeved t-shirt, she looked about twelve, but at least she'd pulled her hair into a high ponytail. Curiously, she'd also draped a dark scarf around her head and shoulders. The lobby was crowded and he sank into the pillows next to her. A waiter appeared immediately and he ordered coffee, American, no milk.

"Oh, George," Emine said, and he braced himself. Yes. He smiled, hoping to cut the tension. They'd agreed to meet early, but, really, not much had changed with the death of their driver. A revolution was a revolution, so they had to either enter the crowds or leave cowed.

"We aren't going home," he told her.

"No," she said and smiled back. She winked, bravado or not. "Let's roll." So much for his hope for a private conversation and more coffee.

He gestured to the group. Ben and their bodyguards had joined them, and they all headed through the hotel's revolving doors to their van. Introductions to the new driver, Ali, were made and George noted that the van had been supplied with bottled water and newspapers. The guns were hidden.

Grabbing the *International Herald Tribune*, George let Emine handle directions to the group. Wow, was she bossy but her Arabic seemed stellar. He abandoned his paper to watch her, glowing with purpose as she directed these resolute men double her size. Some people thrive in the chaos of a war zone and she was clearly one of them. Perhaps each member of their group had such a similar personality type: they were all seasoned and had signed up for the unknown, except for their driver, who lived here and was likely just trying to feed his family. George acknowledged that he was going beyond the barbed wire now, a bigger risk than his past not-at-all-safe roles, but he felt ready. We only grew by pushing ourselves.

The air-conditioned van was cool as it pulled out of the hotel, valets scattering.

"Follow George. He's the star. Watch his face as he confronts this fucking disaster," Emine ordered and her charges nodded. George burrowed into his paper until he remembered *Alice*, which he'd brought with him. Holding the book he ditched news for fiction.

Thinking again?" the Duchess asked, with another dig of her sharp little chin.

"I've a right to think," said Alice sharply, for she was beginning to feel a little worried.

"Just about as much right," said the Duchess, "as pigs have to fly."

George pondered the passage. Should man think?

"Shit, they're burning an American flag," Emine exclaimed and George's eyes darted from print to reality. God, he was an idiot. They were barely outside the hotel and the smoke was already noticeable. The van had slowed, blocked by the masses swarming the street. He noted more caps and beards than he'd seen in earlier news stories, signaling an increase in the Islamist element. The mood was tense.

Emine was clicking away with her camera, intent, documenting, her body rigid and no longer seated. Ben, cooler and calmer, was also focusing through a lens and capturing the sacrifice as it flared higher, orange so vivid against the sky, red – white – and blue. George was grasping for words, as Ben's transmission light was on and he was signaling for George to get ready. The in-studio interviews could only be so scripted, but at least he started out with a list of questions and a genteel expectation of civility. In these streets all bets were off and the rawness was palpable. This video was going direct to Bright in New York and George watched Ben counting down the seconds. Then the camera panned from the street and into his face. Words?

"Symbolic, burning the American flag. We've been here in Cairo for less than twelve hours and already our first driver has been shot, and now this flag is being burned before us. I don't need to say that we've entered a chaotic political system. Whoever is aiming at the hearts and minds of the city residents has missed their mark. These people are lashing out – not looking inspired but simply angry," George said, improvising and relieved when the words came.

He finished his monologue and Ben panned back to the crowd. He noticed that Frick and Frack, otherwise known as Carl and Bruce, had drawn their guns and that the driver looked resolute but unhappy. Emine and Ben, ever the professionals, were leaning out their windows to get better shots.

"What are they saying?" George asked, not remembering in the turmoil who in the car spoke Arabic but sure that at least Emine and the driver did.

"They want jobs," Emine said, pulling back from the window to stare directly into his eyes with her sparkling brown sugar ones. She looked determined but not scared. He was frightened but probably didn't show it either. Training, time and focus. The ability to act under pressure could be learned and was if you were to survive the type of hostile interrogations he'd done in war zones, even behind a fence.

"The flag...?" he asked.

She responded with a wry smile. "Your country hasn't branded itself so well. People identify with symbols. Burning American flags makes a clear statement."

"Iran," he started to reply.

"Did a good job at branding this sacrifice," she finished. "Over thirty years later you remember them burning the flag." She returned to her window. He'd think about how to address her points later. Jobs and basic human decency.

"They also want food, Emine," Ben said, breaking from his intense filming. George was surprised, as Ben seemed above emotion; nothing ever visibly impacted him, and no danger fazed him. "George, later, we'll cover it more fully. These people finally spoke up for change, dying, some of them. And they still don't have enough food. The fucking army is letting this country fall into chaos so they long for the old days under Mubarak."

"Bread and circuses," Emine responded, not pulling back from her window and camera this time. "Manipulating the masses."

"Oh, fuck off, Emine," Ben said harshly. "Don't listen to this jaded girl. These people had hope and they're losing, it so why wouldn't they be mad?"

"And dangerous," George said, watching as a face loomed up at the window, all wide dark eyes and a chanting mouth missing a few teeth. The man reached for Emine's camera and George could smell him, sweat and – oddly - smoke. Bruce leaned out another window and whacked him with the pistol. The driver tried to speed up and seemed to hit someone but drove on. What should they do? Continue? George was nominally in charge, so he'd have to decide.

The noise storming into the van was increasing and, unbelievably, the crowd was getting denser.

They noted his interest in their conversation.

"God, or rather Allah," Carl explained. "Chanting to him."

"No death to America now that they've moved on from jobs?" George asked, cursing himself again for focusing on writing academic papers rather than learning Arabic

"Bread and circuses," Emine repeated, without looking from her window.

"That too," Carl replied, gesturing to Ben, who was signaling that he wanted George to shoot more footage. George took the cue.

"Death to America and praise be to Allah," he said, Ben's camera light shining in his eyes and the van rocking slightly from the press of the crowds. Emine was now paying attention to him and kept mouthing something. He couldn't hear her, so just continued his broadcast. It was over quickly. Meanwhile the driver had managed to park. Ben put his camera down and George relaxed a little.

"While the army controls the streets, the Muslim Brotherhood is a close ally of too many people," Emine said, obviously repeating what she'd been trying to say earlier. He just looked back at her and watched as she adjusted her scarf. This moment was his last chance to stop them all from entering the volatile and burning hot streets, and he let it pass.

"That might have been true a week ago, Em," Ben replied. "But look around you and you'll see that the army has decided to step back and exert less control." George still said nothing. This anarchy was the risk they'd all chosen.

So they followed Ben, fearless, into the streets. George smelled fresh bread and exhaust. He'd lived through Iraq and Afghanistan; how bad could this be?

They were at the edge of the square and tall buildings sheltered the massive expanse. Tahrir Square had an interesting history, having been commissioned by a nineteenth century ruler who wanted to create Paris on the Nile. After the Egyptian Revolution of 1919 it became known as Liberation, or Tahrir, Square, though the name didn't become official until the Egyptian Revolution of 1952. Once again the center of a revolution, the vast space housed a plaza with a statue of nationalist hero Omar Makram, known for resisting Napoleon I's invasion of Egypt. The Egyptian Museum, Omar Makram Mosque and various government, or party, related buildings touched the square's borders.

A few silent men were resting in front of a teashop, sitting on the ground, proud and straight, with their legs pulled up tight to their chests. Red rugs lined the floor of the shop itself, a small room with a row of tea glasses lined up at its entrance.

George sensed his bodyguard and saw Emine's, burly and huddled close. Ben, alone, wandered into the crowd, video camera in hand. People parted to let him pass, as if sensing the Pulitzer prizes in the intensity he carried like a beacon.

"Stay close to me," Bruce said, and George huddled closer. Much as George joked internally, always the skeptic, he'd faced an open battlefield and survived many times in the past in part because he took direction from the security experts. This protest was nominally peaceful, but he could sense the hostile undertones and knew it could get violent fast. Crossing into chaos was a fine line and hit like a wild fire.

"The mosque over there..." Emine said, her voice barely a whisper.

George saw a few pillars sheltering an expanse of pavement under a domed roof and tiled courtyard. Then a bullet broke the silence and George had a flashback to the year before. He heard the loud crack of an explosion and saw the familiar plume of orange and red that danced with the sky before falling back to earth. He ran for shelter.

The air was thick with the smoke and screams disorder brings. He noted a door behind him but was more concerned with the chaos unfolding before him. Ben, of course, was filming it all and George tried to make his way to the video camera.

"Take cover," he heard someone shout in English, then another round of gunshots filled the square.

The creak behind him was barely noticeable, cloaked by the loud gunfight. His eyes were watering from the combination of smoke and dust. But the hand on his shoulder and cloth held to his nose and mouth were very real. George felt his legs give way as his mind lost its ability to control them. He heard a thud as something fell and wondered if it was his body. But all was dark by then.

Photo

When the gunshots broke out Emine felt utter terror. No matter how often she heard gunfire, the sharp click of a rifle always hit the pit of her stomach and she'd likely never grow immune. Today, in the midst of photographing the chanting crowd, bodyguard at her side, she'd been oddly surprised. Aware only of what she saw through her lens, she'd ignored her environment. She should have been watching the crowd more closely, being aware of its heightened tension, but instead she'd relied too much on a sense of safety from having a bodyguard.

Gunshots always felt like betrayal, emotionally they cut whether the feeling was rational or not. And feelings so often aren't rational but they still exist, and oftentimes take control. Men shouldn't wantonly aim to kill other men but they do.

"Cairo isn't at all safe." She was stating the obvious, ducking as a bullet whizzed by, speaking to Carl. "What happened?"

"I don't know," he replied. "But the shots are coming from that direction." Emine looked where he was pointing and noted that another round was coming their way from snipers perched on tanks.

Emine followed him diving behind a red Audi as they took cover. En route, another bullet whizzed by, real ammo, and she wondered why the army was shooting and whether the police were involved as well. There was a great story in this attack and her fingers itched to get back to taking pictures, so she shot a few of the cowering demonstrators. The real action was on the other side of the Audi but she wasn't ready to risk her life to document it. An alarm went off and she heard a scream. The smoky air made her eyes sting.

The smoke got denser and Emine felt her eyes watering. She began to sneeze and heard Carl coughing. Tear gas! The air had taken on a ghostly haze, spotty in its density and similar to clouds in the sky. The stone building sheltering them and the Audi looked fragile but had probably survived much worse many times over. Emine tried to take a few photo shots of the gas but mostly saw rocks and gravel through her lens. In one sense they were lucky that the substance, actually a fine acid powder, wasn't denser in their area. While she couldn't photograph it the stuff could cause blindness. The gunfire was also hard to catch on film though there was certainly plenty of it. Emine didn't see anyone hit so she couldn't capture that drama but she noticed a family cowering in a corner between two buildings, the parents sheltering their children. Pointless suffering. As if life didn't beat you down enough, violent men had to really fuck things up for the rest.

Emine willed her heart shut so she could focus on her work. Document, document, document. Her photos might eventually help identify the wrong – or right – person. Mentally, she pictured the process, locking up her emotions, keeping everything that was herself behind her thin rib bones. The camera should be all that existed now.

Looking through the lens she tried to identify pictures in the midst of chaos. Why were there tanks? The military was increasing pressure? She ignored her questions, head spinning, and just shot pictures. They'd just arrived and clearly hadn't been well briefed. Bright.

She tried to focus on framing the instant of a story before it passed – her job for three years now – and she'd gotten better at navigating the moral contradictions.

But Emine's mind drifted back to Sam, a soldier in Syria a few months before who had yelled," "Get out of the way. You'll get us all killed." She'd ignored him and photographed the two tiny toddler boys, brothers probably, holding hands in death. One of them had only half a head. A woman, their mother most likely, stood by wailing and shooting looks of hatred at Emine as her camera clicked away. None of that mattered, only the story did. People needed to see reality, and they only responded to violence against an identifiable individual. These gunfights rarely even made the news while the right pictures got widespread coverage – front-page stuff.

Sam had taken a bullet and she'd photographed him, screaming and bloody.

"Emine, you're crazy. Stop with the pictures," he'd shouted before passing out. He lived but never spoke to her again. Well, too bad. The soldiers had their mission and she had hers. Someday Sam might thank her, when he showed those photos to his grandchildren and explained what war was really like. Emine left Syria shortly thereafter. She didn't like it there anyway. Too many people were angry.

Now Cairo. Another bullet ricocheted by. What the fuck! This was supposed to be a peaceful demonstration.

Carl grabbed her elbow and pushed her toward their van, knocking over whoever blocked their route. Reaching it unharmed, they quickly climbed inside. The battle was over for them. She'd look at her results, the pictures on her memory card, in a minute. Leaning back into her seat she sensed that something wasn't right.

"Where's George?"

The men looked at her, but no one spoke. Ben didn't even pull back from the window reels he was shooting.

Emine grappled with her camera. The world of people flickered through her viewer, colors and limbs. On one picture she saw a man being dragged by two others. His hair was silver and his body was limp.

Shock

Khalil's narrative continued. "It is not that we have a short time to live, but that we waste a lot of it. Or so said the great senator Seneca." The crowd of men huddled around him stared with glazed eyes. They were sitting on the floor and various bright carpets with tea glasses clustered on small iron tables around them. Khalil was back in Egypt and just outside Cairo. Right when he thought he couldn't take on another problem, a new one kept cropping up. No one was seemingly in charge, his cover was blown (so he could be killed at any moment) and the men in front of him were not sold on his mandate. It had to become theirs.

Revolutions were such utter caldrons of indecision and shifting responsibility. A power vacuum was simple to spot, filling it much harder.

"The nice thing about the corruption in a failed country is that you can buy just about anyone. The downside is, so can your enemy," Khalil said. The men continued to stare in his direction. They didn't move and neither did anything else in the oppressive heat. The stench was becoming increasingly noticeable – too many people, unwashed and carrying too many odors.

"Is there a fan here?" he asked. A cooler room? No one lived like this, so there must be some way to get them to volunteer it.

"American," a man said. As if that meant anything.

"The fan?" Khalil asked.

Whalid, a particularly troublesome member of their group, stared back, not finishing what must have been his thought. A short man who looked to be in his early thirties and his mental development was stunted by an undiagnosed disease. His brother was a senior Muslim Brotherhood leader, so Whalid trailed through this revolution like a protected angel.

"An American journalist was captured," said Moha, a leader in the Muslim Brotherhood. More reasonable than some, Moha understood the delicate nuances of power and was willing to trade to build alliances. He understood the deal; most leaders in this revolution wanted to dominate, not recognizing how vulnerable that would make them. The one at the top gets blamed, and killed, first.

The Muslim Brotherhood was resisting Khalil's attempt to insert Al Qaeda into the local revolution. Years of stealth and intrigue had left them convinced that the country should be theirs. Having built a tenuous alliance with the army only to see it explode, they failed to notice that organizationally they were fracturing fast and had few truly big guns. Years of hiding their extremism didn't exempt them from needing real money now that an Islamic battle was being fought while the army, much richer, was winning. Meanwhile, the people's revolutionaries, upstarts still, lacked solid leadership so they were an even more tenuous ally. The army seemingly held the real power though Khalil was still guessing about underlying alliances and relationships.

Moha, thus far, seemed well respected across many allegiances within his group.

So Khalil couldn't just ignore Moha, though he really didn't care about an American journalist.

Moha gestured to a boy by his side. About sixteen and slight, the youth was Moha's oldest son and in training, as an assistant to his father, for jihad. The boy had a name, but Khalil neither knew nor cared what it was. He, quite honestly, couldn't leave Egypt fast enough as the country had always been bad luck for him; and now for Jennifer. Time remembering names or forming attachments was wasted.

But the youth was engaging, with big blinking brown eyes and a faded Rolling Stones t-shirt. He ambled over to Khalil and thrust a photo in his face.

Khalil's eyes returned to memories from long ago and cascaded through unreality. Had what he chose not to remember actually happened? Mental scar tissue, covering what was left of his psyche, began to throb and he couldn't grasp how to reason through what he was seeing. Clasping the picture, he noted the boy backing away and felt the room's eyes upon him. He strove to keep his face expressionless despite his inner turmoil. Everyone judged and everyone lied; don't trust that any picture is real.

Allah be blessed if the captured man really was George, his interrogator and jailor from the not-so-distant past. Had fate fallen so easily into his hands? Revenge was sweet, and if all he had to do was buy George, it would soon be his.

"What's this," Khalil asked, waving the picture freely. His tone was level though sweat beaded on his forehead. Words were worthless, but his body was being studied, for discussion later. Any visible desire on his part would only drive George's price higher, so he sat straighter, focusing on the stained walls with their few small windows.

"Can I see?" Whalid lunged and Khalil feigned indifference, letting him take the picture. "Ah, the American..." Whaled exhaled. Moha's boy watched, wide-eyed but quiet. Moha was also silent: scorpion to his spider. Not the best odds from his end.

"Moha, is that the American?" Khalil asked, pondering how to determine if this man was or might be his ally. Moha sipped at his sweet tea, wiping his mouth with the back of his hand. Clean-shaven and dressed in simple trousers and a long-sleeved tunic, he bordered east and west nicely.

"The Iranians have him," Moha said finally, still studying Khalil for some reaction. "You know him?"

Khalil could bluff and play the fool, but Moha seemingly knew his facts, so why risk it? The crowd around them was still, an ancient people used to letting time pass. This high-stakes drama was playing out in front of them and they wanted to see how it ended. Khalil would want the American, but how much would he be willing to pay? And, were the Iranians offering the trade to make money or buy loyalty?

The word that most stuck in Khalil's mind was "Iranian." The Iranians were too deeply entrenched in this struggle. Shiites, they shouldn't be in

Cairo. Radicals and of the wrong revolutionary bent, they only made his situation more complicated.

Including with respect to George since he wanted the man badly. Revenge was a wonderful pleasure but it rarely came so easily. The Iranians, unfortunately, had money and might not sell. Cash he had; influence he could ill afford to barter.

"Shiites; they are always looking for an opportunity to betray their fellow Muslims and take advantage," Moha said and paused. His message was clear: he'd align with Khalil for now and George was the payoff. Moha had bet wisely and Khalil would take this bargain. Everyone's palms would be greased in the process, but Khalil would win an ally and an enemy both.

Khalil felt black eyes burning into him as sweat trickled into his eyelashes. These men, sons of an old storied land, were still driven by ancient blood, even those with advanced university degrees. The Muslim Brotherhood had been founded in 1928 by Hassan al-Banna, an Islamic scholar and teacher. Banned and driven underground by the Egyptian government, it still managed to influence most of the 20th century Islamic movements. With the fall of Mubarak it had become a legal political party and reflected the more educated society that its former foe had built. *Islam is the solution* was their most famous slogan.

But the desert was a cruel master, rarely letting its sons go completely, and this bunch had chosen to congregate amongst the vibrant backdrops and brutality of the cruel sands outside the city and its prying eyes. The burning sun that nestled into hot dunes each night would outlast them all. No one could beat the desert.

"They'll kill the American," Moha stated, with authority.

"No," Khalil exclaimed, "I will kill the American." He saw his path to power light up. Simple. These men knew how to scheme and maintain the status quo, but they weren't risk takers, and now uncertainty had been thrown their way. None would be able to respond effectively but he, being Algerian, could teach them about revolution.

"Moha, I'd like to train your boy," Khalil said, gesturing to the child. "How old?"

Moha paused and the youth was staring at him now. Pride, love and determination showed in the father's face while the boy's expression was more complex.

"What do you want, boy?" Khalil asked.

"He wants to be a man and lead our country on the righteous path," Moha interjected but the boy stayed quiet. Smart kid. A true leader doesn't need to assert his importance. True leaders aren't about "me" but rather about their cause, and age is no barrier. Moha's boy was properly trained to wait and had demonstrated that discipline, of the desert but also beyond it.

Most of the world was crazy so you needed to grasp at those who weren't.

"The boy is yours," Moha said, and Khalil saw acceptance in the child's face. "And the man?" Moha asked.

"My jailor," Khalil replied quietly. "He's mine to address."

The men around him nodded and Khalil was aware that fatigue and heat were settling in. Life did get wearing and who cared about another man's blood feud? Perhaps centuries of being governed by pharaohs this country – in all of its history and majesty – had learned to give in.

"Bring the American to me," Khalil commanded and heard no dissent. George a journalist, he wondered? What else had changed and what would he do with George once he got him?

Little matter. George was cargo now; a bargaining chips in a fight between the Gods as Khalil too had once been cargo. And someone, perhaps Allah himself, had let him live. George might not be so lucky.

This group was a powerful one but their attention was shifting now, the conversation turning to more local matters. Khalil's mission had been accomplished and it was time for everyone to move on. Besides, this was what power looked like in the third world; local, sweat, sex, corruption and ready for dinner.

Khalil's phone rang and he noted Jennifer's name on caller id.

"One minute," he said to her through the phone line, looking strong but feeling concern.

"I want the American by this time tomorrow," he demanded now, assuming control. "Pay what you must."

The phone was released from its entrapment against his pant leg, muzzling sound, as he escaped into the dusk. The sun had turned a muted rose with lavender streaks as it nestled into the dunes, the deep crescents extending on forever, golden brown in the fading light. Feeling sand seeping into his sandals, he walked quickly to a bench across the street.

"How are you feeling?" he asked and pictured her full breasts in that flimsy gown she'd been wearing the last time they were together. Her nipples dark and visible through white fabric.

"Better," she whispered. "I miss you. Come home."

Khalil studied his toes in the sand. Jihad wasn't about home on earth, much as he wanted to see her. They needed to talk. He noted Moha's boy running toward him, sending sand flying in all directions. A plate of lentils, rice and noodles was thrust into his hand, then the feet scurried away. Khalil took a bite of the hot, fragrant food. He loved lentils.

"Jennifer..." he began and heard her tense as she braced herself. Why did some women seemingly know everything before it happened?

Fear

George didn't expect to wake up happy; perhaps lost somewhere deep in his dreams, he hadn't expected to wake up at all. He'd fallen down the rabbit hole and wasn't sure what Alice would have done in his stead. When he finally did wake up he was surprised to be surprised.

First, he heard Farsi. With Arabic there was a fifty/fifty shot of execution and a live video feed. With the Iranians who knew – it was a crapshoot. And what were the Iranians doing in Cairo? Didn't they have enough of their own revolutionaries to worry about? Then again, the Iranians were quickly building influence now that the United States had curtailed two of their big enemies, Saddam Hussein and the Taliban. All these years he'd cursed himself for not taking time to study Arabic when it had been Farsi he'd needed all along!

George felt his heart beating, faster than it should but thankfully unrelenting. His head felt groggy and he was ravenously hungry. Trying to move, George felt the stiffness of his muscles and a cramp or two, as if he'd been dumped into a random position upon arrival at this hellhole. He felt for his cell phone in his pocket but, not surprisingly, it was gone.

Now what? The argument in Farsi continued, loud enough for him to guess that it involved at least four men. Who knew how many listened silently, in deference.

But who had him mattered a lot less than that they did.

Glancing around his prison, George noted that it contained little beyond the cot. The room was dark and stifling, with one tiny window up high on the opposite wall, not enough for ventilation. The first glimmers of dawn's light were filtering into the room through the narrow opening. He could already see how the light in Egypt shifted over time. Anyone thought of a toilet?

Standing gingerly and carefully making his way to his open door, George peered down the hallway. He saw a group of men sitting on the floor, pillows scattered haphazardly around and under them. A large round table commanded the middle of the room and they were drinking tea and arguing. George smelled the vague flirtation of food.

"*Babdscao*," he heard, gibberish, passionate... nonsense. Clearly an argument, complete with waving arms and, oh no, a waving gun. Great. He slunk back to his cot to ponder possible options.

What was it the Iranians wanted again? Oh yes, death to the west and regional dominance. Nukes. Annihilation of Israel and all non-Muslims. Historically, they'd typically released their hostages but certain Americans from the late 1970s could testify firsthand about how long the process could take. Recently they seemed to be getting more acquisitive as the dissent (against their policies and repression) got louder. Luckily, he hadn't done too many stories about Iran lately. So much else going on....and likely he'd been only moderately insulting to their government.

But geopolitics was confusing these days and seemed to shift on a daily basis, depending on the news. What happened yesterday was no predictor of the future in the new reality; the whole thing seemed more illusion than reality anyway. They might decide to slap him up on YouTube and use his broadcasting skills to set an example.

He wasn't thinking clearly. To be expected given the circumstances? Now he understood how his detainees felt, both petrified and angry. George also questioned if he'd been drugged since his brain was working slowly and his head throbbed with pain. Was jet lag still a factor?

"Well, this is unexpected," he whispered to himself, still fighting the feeling that this situation wasn't real, indeed couldn't be real. This catastrophic change had happened so quickly and in a flash of gunfire, almost as if in a movie or an online game. Focusing, the crowds and his abduction came back to him.

On the bright side, he was still alive. Countering that optimism was the reality that no one knew where he was and that he was at the mercy of declared enemies.

George shivered, despite the desert heat. Or perhaps that coldness came directly from his heart. He looked at his watch, finally, and amazingly. It was just before 6:00 a.m. Great, his day was just beginning. An obsessive terror kept pounding in his head, a feeling entirely rational. Much as he willed it away, George knew he wouldn't succeed. "I'm going to die, I'm going to die," he whispered to the darkness.

George commanded himself to do better. He was an experienced professional who knew all about captivity and fear, albeit from the other side. He focused on his mind, entering it to control it, blocking off the sights and sensations of his surroundings. He'd studied this occurrence and knew the mentality that attached itself to a captive. The only way to survive was to control your brain, focusing on one thing at a time. He needed to distract himself, talk to God, to his children, to his parents (long dead but the memory was still a source of strength).

Prayer, hope and delusion.

Stay present, alert and try to escape. But try not to get shot.

Calm. Your own mind was almost more dangerous than the enemy. Well, okay, that last was a bit of exaggeration. But he was worth more alive than dead, right?

The voices continued, filtering down the hallway and modulating based on the speaker. One man seemed particularly upset: his voice louder than the rest and shrill. Wow, he had a lot to say. The passions that ideologies, self-righteousness or fanaticism can ignite. Are any words really that important? This man clearly believed so.

"*Resgnaop*," the argument continued. George still didn't understand a word.

All those articles and op-eds in the media at home missed the practical points of an undeclared war; he'd been guilty too. Compassion, my ass. Kindness? Trust building? What about how to deal with torture when you were on the receiving end? Was Iran observing the Geneva Convention these days? Journalists were suddenly getting kidnapped en masse with the consolation being that most were released into a book deal and minor celebrity. George already had a book deal and minor celebrity status.

George watched some bugs on his floor, crawling through dirt. So this was what captivity felt like.

Glancing around again, looking for a weapon or avenue of escape he noticed his copy of *Alice in Wonderland* and grabbed it, clutching it to his chest. How had that happened? Had he been carrying it as he left the van? Obviously he had. Fiction was a means of escape, though not the one he'd been looking for. This book, for now, was the closest thing to home he had.

George wished he could read, but the room was still too dark. Well, fuck this shit. He wanted some light, coffee and breakfast. Most of all, he wanted a toilet. He stood up but then had to steady himself against the wall when a destabilizing dizziness hit. Definitely drugged; how long had he slept?

George stepped out into the hallway, moving slowly so that no one would feel compelled to shoot. He was their guest and they were going to have to start treating him better. As he took another step the conversation stopped and all heads turned toward him. No one's eyes glowed red but they didn't look friendly either.

They all stared when George approached the group. The mass of dark men dressed in a hodgepodge of styles, blues melding into browns and then into oranges. He inhaled and willed his feet to keep moving. Predictably, conversation stopped. Each and every eye was dark and hostile. Well, so be it. If they were going to kill him the decision had probably already been made and what he did in the interim had little bearing on his ultimate fate.

"In'sa Allah," George mumbled. Was that how the greeting went, even with the Iranian Shiites? He had no experience whatsoever with Iranians, and, of course, no training in how to deal with them. Back to his original question – what were the Iranians doing in Cairo anyway? The Shiites and Sunnis rarely saw eye to eye, and Egypt was Sunni land. "I'm hungry, need a toilet and would like some coffee or tea." And how did you say please in Farsi?

George watched them watching him and felt his courage falter. He hadn't signed on for any of this because he was brave; he'd signed on because he was an idiot who couldn't say no. He'd never thought his own life would be one of those on the line. This was round two on that issue and he was starting to get fed up.

"I want…" the words fumbled on his lips but certainly he wanted. A lot.

A man stood up, disengaging from his group. They all had tea – in small clear glasses – sitting on the round table that formed their nexus. The man wasn't tall or impressive but had movie star good looks. His brown eyes were wide like those of a golden retriever except they were hard and mean; more pitbull. At least – if nothing else – he made an effort to smile, but it just looked strained.

"You are our guest," was all he said, yet George felt his anger building. No guest about it – he was a prisoner. Still, in this part of the world things were never addressed directly, right?

"Much obliged," George said and watched the man's eyes go blank. Probably a limited English vocabulary, so he'd need to choose his words carefully. The cluster, huddled around a dark wood table, was watching but hadn't moved as the light outside was gradually brightening. George felt ill.

"What I want is a toilet, some food and coffee or tea," he repeated. The floor began to dance in front of him and he hoped he wouldn't fall. What drug had they given him? All he wanted was to run, yet the reality kept hitting him in the face. And it hurt. How had this happened? Just days before he'd been on American television.

"As you are our guest, we'll do our best to make you happy," the man said, looking less than sincere. Truly, why even pretend? He started speaking in Farsi and people began to move. "The toilet is here. After that, please go back to your room."

George shut the door behind him and started to piss. He heard someone standing guard outside and was glad the door closed even if it didn't lock. There were no windows in the room let alone one large enough for him to climb through. He needed to find a way to escape. Better to risk death than wait for it, right? Well, there was something to be said for a little solitude. He'd never really wanted to face himself or his choices in life; he'd always been too busy. Perhaps it was time for him to try.

He pulled his pants up and felt that increasingly familiar dizziness. Exiting, George almost bumped into his host and wished the man to hell – but silently. Well, no one was deciding his fate, he vowed. These men were pawns, as was George, but he was smarter. They might have him now, but they'd have to hold him. His determination might be childlike; but without hope nothing was left. And the internal pep talks would continue, if only to keep his own morale up. Rule one of captivity was to keep your mental state strong. We are all our own worst enemy.

George walked back to his cot silently. No one spoke, even in Farsi, they just watched him. Next to his bed was a tray with some tea, flat bread and fruit. It was a start. He sat and drank a long gulp of the hot fluid. His guardian stood over him and didn't move. Let him. George ignored the invasive presence and tore off a bit of his bread. Things were truly bad.

Resolve

mine huddled on her bed and drank. She liked to drink, especially when alone and upset like she was right now. Ben was taking his turn on the phone with Bright, after she'd listened to their boss yell for a while. Hell of a lot of good Bright's abuse did George. Bright should be calling his senator, whichever one owed him the most, not yelling at her and Ben long distance. Once a bastard always a bastard.

Carl and Bruce were out cruising the streets, souqs and alleys, most likely offering large bribes. She was wearing only black lace bikinis and was quite drunk.

Bright had screamed rude obscenities. Shit, she was the photographer not the protection HE hired.

"You're my seasoned pro and were supposed to protect him. George is my star, baby, but naïve," he'd rasped, and she could hear the scotch even though it was early afternoon at his headquarters in New York. One thing they had in common: alcohol was their first solution to any problem. Emine pictured his dark blue eyes turning darker as they always did when he lost his temper. She sighed. The room was shadowy inside, but lit from the city lights burning below.

The Nile was lapping up against its bank, starting to rise in late May. Every year it rose and fell based on the rain patterns in central Africa. By September it would reach its heights here in Cairo, earlier upriver. The God, Hapy, was the river's life-giving force. Pot-bellied with hanging breasts and a papyrus headdress, in contrast to usually slim Egyptian Gods of antiquity, he'd been celebrated yearly before Islam breached these banks. The Nile still bound the people together and most Egyptians lived close to its shores. Like her, George might be listening to its gentle rhythms as he pondered his fate. They were all worried.

"Go to hell, Bright," she'd finally said, tired. "George has served in wars; he's not a baby and knew the risks. This city is a mess and worse than we imagined. Your research and briefing information are shit." and with that she'd switched from wine to vodka, courtesy of a large bottle the excellent concierge had found.

"Be careful, Eme. I'll fire you," he snarled and she'd pulled her naked legs, cold from the air conditioning, under her covers. Fuck him. He wouldn't dare. The scandal of the mission in shambles: one reporter kidnapped and the other fired.

"I don't see you getting your ass on that private plane of yours and flying over here," she'd yelled back. They'd always fought, which was why he could neither be with her nor fully let go. A domineering control freak, he needed a woman who obeyed; but he couldn't resist the challenge of one who didn't.

"Bitch," he said and hung up on her.

Emine started to cry. She pushed her bottle away and decided she wanted to be more than a drunk in a crisis. Ben wouldn't be drinking to excess now. No, he'd have a drink or two, then he'd pick up his cell and call every source he had in Africa and the Middle East to get information on George. Daughter of a politician, who attended Swiss boarding schools with lots of politically connected classmates, she had some good resources as well. Then there was that time in the field. Drunk though she was, she called Dad first.

"Allo," he barked into the phone. None of these men could ever risk sounding weak. She poured out the facts of George's disappearance.

"Not good," he replied; the briefest of answers. She felt the furrows on her forehead deepening as she waited. Mehmet had personally dealt with the crazy Islamists responsible for the kidnappings and bombs in Turkey. While a government could threaten force, often the real solutions were negotiated in private, since money speaks louder than guns.

"Emine, stop drinking," he said. "The disappearance is being kept quiet, right? Don't give those bastards any publicity. It'll risk George's life. No contact or request for anything?"

"No contact yet. We don't know who has him or what they want. Our first driver was killed the night we arrived, remember. After dropping us off."

Mehmet was quiet. Too quiet.

"Your group was targeted, but why did they take him and not you?" he finally asked. Emine ignored his request and downed another slug of vodka. Why not her indeed? She lit a cigarette with her Eiffel Tower lighter and noted that her hands were shaking.

"He's the one on TV," she said and wasn't surprised Mehmet didn't respond; he didn't tolerate dumb answers. George's profile only mattered to someone who wanted money or media coverage and not to someone seeking a political target, such as herself.

"I'll make a few discreet calls," he said. "You do the same, but keep it quiet until someone hears what they want, and you will hear. Then start writing. At some point you'll need to go public with print and that text should come from you."

"Got it," she replied, trying to sound brave.

"And, Eme, if they'd wanted you you'd be where George is right now. Still, be careful.

"Yes dad," she said and felt the tears blinding her. The moon was a full circle outside her window.

"Pull yourself together. Start writing and be strong for when the opportunity comes. And it always comes," he said. She didn't answer but did take another slug of vodka. "You'll likely get a call at some point, so be ready. Until then, write the stories and don't let someone scoop you.

Mehmet hung up and she continued holding the phone in her hand. Then she noticed a new text. "The Iranians; a few photos floating around" from Ben. She forwarded it to her dad, security be damned.

He wouldn't text her back…being more paranoid.

Her dad was outwardly so strong and, realistically, tough as steel. She'd never seen him show weakness or fear or pain. How did he hide everything and always present himself so impeccably? Had politics turned him into an enigma or had he gone into politics because he already was one? Mostly action with little talk, so even she, his daughter, had a hard time reading him. And he said so little regarding his true thoughts.

She hadn't been born yet when he launched his political career, and by the time of her birth he was flying between Istanbul, Ankara and the world.

Powerful and respected, rich and unstoppable. A populist, he gave time to everyone but his family.

Dad had been born to an impoverished family deep in the bowels of Istanbul, with its crumbling buildings and masses of barefoot children. His own father had been both enterprising and corrupt. An emerging economy offered many roads to riches, especially to those willing to grease the right palms, so by Mehmet's tenth birthday they were living in a large house near the Bosporus. He had loved that tangy smell ever since and wouldn't move away from its banks, though his houses got increasingly larger. His mother was pious, but also sickly. Her death freed his father to marry an ugly girl from a rich and better-connected family. Turkey then was in a period of instability and increasing violence as power shifted throughout the 1960s. But her grandfather had learned how to grease both sides of any palm and the family was safe.

Mehmet breezed through a quick college degree and from then on was always known as a powerful leader's right-hand man. He'd learned how not to argue from his own father. Whether his designations and relationships were defensible in a corrupt country like Turkey, Emine never knew nor tried to find out. Dad was her father and, like all children of little seen parents, she idolized him until she learned to hate him, then half forgive. Her grandfather had grown richer and richer.

At twenty-eight, Mehmet met Liz, the daughter of an old aristocratic family, on his father's yacht near Kas, in the southern-most part of the country. Against the back drop of lush sapphire waters and sandy cliffs he fell hard for her, in the midst of his busy life.

"She was like a vision from the heavens above," he'd proclaim. And a virgin, until he'd impregnated her, either against her will or with it, depending upon whose story you chose to believe. Then came a wedding, Selim, and, shortly thereafter Emine.

With his bird now caged, Mehmet had slipped back into his bachelor ways, and Liz had found her own nocturnal companions. The kids were shipped to Swiss boarding schools at eight, and Emine followed her father's activities in the *International Herald Tribune*.

"Did that really happen?" she'd ask him, breathless and having done her research, when he had time to call. Kind of sad, actually. But he'd laid out a political map for her long distance, when she should have long since been asleep. His world was all magic in her eyes, and she'd followed his activism into journalism, though not directly. While her mom opened up and softened over the years, Mehmet remained a fortress: approachable, but his defenses could never be breached. Sometimes she wondered about his secret thoughts but knew better than to ask. He probably couldn't give her an honest answer even if he tried, and he wasn't going to try.

Any bit of humanity Mehmet had shown disappeared when his only son, her brother, Selim had overdosed on heroin.

Thinking of politicians and bad fathers, she called her friend Bud, from her high school up in snow capped Swiss mountains, and was glad he answered. He sounded high. Nothing new in that. Bud's dad had always owned and run South African mining companies and operations throughout much of Africa, navigating a panoply of crazy governments. Bud likewise was a "businessman" and mining baron on the continent but based in Capetown.

"I want to rip off whatever you're wearing and fuck you," he breathed into the phone. Oh, he was also her occasional lover when their paths crossed. But, really, he was more like a brother; they'd been close for so long, concurrently traversing life's troubled path through good times and bad. And he'd been Selim's best friend in high school.

"A black G-string," she replied.

"So much the better," he said. "Take me less than a second. What do you need, Eme?" Emine inhaled and blew the smoke into the air. Bud had sensed from her tone why she'd called. Some people were so much a part of us they didn't require deep explanations to understand. She pictured his tousled sandy brown hair, always heading in a multitude of directions. Emine detailed what was going on and Ben's information as Bud listened, only interrupting occasionally with a question. Bud's network was the best in Africa and he'd get her an answer.

"Call you back," he said and hung up.

She got up from her bed she dumped the rest of her vodka down the drain, picked up a notebook and started to write. Gnawing a cold roll from her dinner tray she tried to sober up.

An hour later Bud called her back and sounded sober as well.

"Iranians had him near the Al-Fayoum Oasis south of Cairo. But they already found a buyer and no one knows who. Not a good sign."

"Shit," she said. "I would have bought him!"

He laughed. "So would I, but what's he really worth? I'd have given him to you in trade for your G-string. If the intel is dead, I'd say – in this area – it's Al Qaeda. They're working more cooperatively with Iran now, but the truce is an uneasy one. Perhaps George was a good will gesture."

"You'll keep looking?" she whispered, knowing that he would, and not liking what she'd heard. Exhaling, she pondered the gender divide. While men could be both demanding and jealous, when loyal they never fucked around with the truly important things. Women had fewer limits.

"Get some sleep," he told her and she complied. Just like her mother, she thought as she dozed off. Whenever she had a problem she called the men in her life and asked them to solve it.

Awe

It was a simple transaction. Khalil was willing to pay full price, and in such a situation most buyers are. He hated the Iranians, but they were rapidly becoming more pliable. Shiites, they would rot in hell. But *the enemy of my enemy is my friend,* and this was a simple business deal, so within a few hours George would be his. His off-again, on-again allies wouldn't cheat him, at least not on this transaction. Betrayal was rarely that direct in his uneasy alliances. Once he had his prize, they might try to blow him up, but that threat was hours away.

The shai (tea) was burning hot. In a Garden City manor, the suburb of Cairo with its crumbling early 20th century mansions, Khalil could see the greatness of a past envisioned but lost to corruption and economic decay.

The area, close to the British Embassy, had been modeled on an English garden city but had long since fallen into disrepair; as had much of Egypt due to its massive unemployment and stalled industries. How did history turn so thoroughly against a single country? Chasing the wrong side in a war, or just bad government – and that was it. The pharaohs were an ancient promise but only ghosts in the modern world, much as the term had been applied to Hosni Mubarak and a host of other dictators. Well, now the people thought they should decide.

"When do I get him?" Khalil asked.

"We take you now. He isn't far," his guide said.

They all invoked Allah on the deal and it was done. Things were seemingly going better.

Jennifer was doing well. Osman, Moha's boy, was surprisingly an Internet phenomenon, setting up accounts on everyone's behalf right and left. Their communication infrastructure was increasingly more sophisticated as it wove through faceless accounts and social networks, most encrypted, but others based only on old-fashioned computer coding. By posting discreet messages on various public web sites – in plain view – they were able to reach many without alerting the authorities. The reader needed to know the code and website to effectively track most of their communications, but such details were ancillary. In plain view was the easiest place to hide because it was so hard to flag them in the torrents of online data; therefore no obvious cross communications, just a group of men who liked the same football site…and visited it daily.

But life was never simple.

One of Khalil's facial scars had been bothering him in the heat. Overall, his body was wearing pretty well, all things considered, but he was forty now. The years fighting in the mountains and sleeping in the open had taken their toll. Injuries and surgeries. The continual travel and stress of planning big missions. The risk of getting caught by an unfriendly regime and having to hide in the daytime and slink around at night. He couldn't even feel safe going home; then again, no one had been safe in Algeria for decades. In an age of increased global security everything had just gotten that much harder, and he needed more sleep.

He was frightened; his cover had been blown. Practically speaking, what did that mean? Was he being hunted or merely followed? Khalil hadn't noticed any tails lately; still, relaxing in the face of such an identified risk was difficult when good shadows were hard to spot, even by him.

He'd be adding a prisoner to his risks. An American who was already the focus of a dedicated international search. So be it. He'd made that decision. Vengeance would be his, and so would George.

Khalil scanned the space around him, his eyes searching for patterns and especially abnormalities, or the oddities that didn't belong. One must constantly be on guard, and he needed to evaluate the entrances to the rooms and possible escape routes. The faces of those present were also key; emotions are only so hide-able, and his life depended on staying alert and making the right judgments. He'd paid, so why hadn't they left yet?

The mansion was like a labyrinth, and his first thought upon entering had been that there would be a trick. The long staircase in the entryway was lined with chipped paint and belonged in a Hollywood movie about a faded star. Furniture was sparse, peeling with decorative silk upholstery that was wearing thin. The breadth and details of the wood paneling seemed too large for the rooms, visually creating an image of vastness without the appropriate balancing furniture proportions. The upper classes used to drink and have dances, right? Had the rooms been sized for revelry and not piety? His home, Algeria, had likewise hosted the French and their similarly gauche debauchery.

As he drove, trees-lined streets had testified to faded wealth. They were, after all, in a desert, albeit close to the Nile, and water could get expensive. They met here because it was close to George and safe.

Amidst the Farsi he'd learned the details in Arabic. He was standing with the other men and studying a sagging piano as they spoke.

"We tracked the flight and killed the driver," a bearded man said. Khalil wasn't good with names.

"We knew we wanted the man, since he's famous in America," another man said, sipping his tea, then breaking off a piece of half melted Cadbury

Whole Milk from a stack of duty free chocolates in the center of a carved mahogany table.

"His boss is even more famous," a third man said. Khalil hoped they weren't trying to renegotiate the price. He'd brought cash...in American hundred-dollar bills. And two guards.

Explanations came easily. Khalil was nervous with the snail's pace as they kept appeasing him and periodically talking into walkie-talkies. He reminded himself that the Iranians were masters at subterfuge, so he should study them and not get impatient. They repressed their dissent better than anyone excepting the Chinese. Moreover, their Islamic government had spread its influence throughout the region despite being Shiites, a disliked minority. Guns, money, diplomatic support and counsel. Irresistible.

"We go," his guide said, and Khalil followed, one of his own guards a few steps behind. They headed out of the dark house into bright sunlight, then into a black Mercedes. A girl, surprisingly, was driving, but she was hidden behind scarves and dark sunglasses. She didn't look at anyone but pulled out into the streets, her gaze focused on the world through glass.

Within minutes, even in the dense traffic, they'd reached a poorer neighborhood just south of Garden City, which Khalil recognized as old Cairo. Full of mosques and even churches, it was tightly packed, with narrow winding streets. They were almost in the Coptic section of the city where the Christians worshiped. Heathens. The car slowed, then stopped in front of a dingy apartment building next to a teashop and restaurant.

"We'll need to walk from here," Khalil heard and nodded. He'd been waiting a long time for this opportunity. He suddenly felt hungry as the smells of roasted meat and spices hit him.

Reunion

The door was mostly closed, and locked, after that first morning. George searched for a solution – a way out. The fear was so crippling, sometimes he just lay in bed and worked on calming himself. No one spoke to him, and the days passed in slow motion and silence.

Two bearded men beckoned him after his first breakfast and forced him to make a groggy video. The mood was very different from his slick television shows with their witty dialogue from entertaining guests. Here George was expected only to say his name and beg for release, and he told his wife that he loved her. Like cowards the world over, his captors faced the camera with their faces covered by masks. One take done, they'd marched him back to his closet and he slept for hours.

The rest of that afternoon had passed very slowly. He prayed. Tried to reread *Alice in Wonderland*. It was a wonderful book.

"Would you tell me, please, which way I ought to go from here?" [Alice]

"That depends a good deal on where you want to get to," said the Cat.

"I don't much care where —"said Alice

"Then it doesn't matter which way you go," said the Cat.

Out! He wasn't having a hard time figuring out his own desired path.

The book's clever passages were a wonderful mental exercise and a great way to kill time. But he had difficulty thinking clearly and dispelling the fear that had settled over him like a cloak. His dire circumstances just weren't an avoidable reality, being far too important to ignore.

Ironically, in the moments leading up to the fall of that fateful hand, George had finally recognized that he was exactly where he wanted to be, amidst the chaos and mess of life and not hidden behind a camera or in a classroom. Perhaps certain people really couldn't stop moving forward to be more reflective on a daily basis and needed to be doing all the time. As a psychologist he could well understand the allure of denial and achievement over introspection. It left a larger footprint. Facing the inevitable reality of the related fall, he wondered whether he'd stick to his earlier resolve if he survived or if he'd scurry back to safety now that he knew what real terror felt like.

Something internal had been holding him back before and he hadn't paused to define it. Guilt at leaving Karen? The desire to be liked and have the approval of others by maintaining his stable and successful life? Fear of the responsibility? Of failure or of success? Well, now he had time to figure that out. And he was – after all – an expert at this sort of analysis. And a kidnap victim read pariah/celebrity. Realities of the media age meant that if he survived this unwilling detention he'd be even more of a celebrity. Ironies abounded.

George shifted his position on the cot. The room was filthy, grimy and with wafting smells of other people and too much sweat. At least – so far – he'd pretty much been left alone. He was clearly in a crowded part of the city and continually heard life outside his room, chattering and laughter. Smells of food that filtered in and the scents were warming. George could only imagine the world outside his walls but couldn't walk outside the door to put a reality to his imagination. The walls inside his own mind were only seemingly more controllable.

Fingering the book, George considered his options, which were few. How to pass his time until he could manifest one of them...but then the door started to move.

Khalil walked in. George sensed his stomach tightening and wondered if the throb extending up his chest was a heart attack or if he'd merely lost his breath. His vision was momentarily distracted by a flashback of Khalil's face as the gun went off, sending George to a hospital and months of rehab. What was the old cliché about how a cut on your finger only hurt until you broke your leg?

"Hello, George," Khalil said, and George stood up to shake his hand. Khalil slapped him across the face then whipped across the other cheek. George felt himself recoil but willed himself to stand firm.

"Are you going to kill me?" he asked.

Khalil had changed a lot, but George still recognized him. Having been under a plastic surgeon's knife, his nose was less prominent and his face was different. George couldn't quite place the variances and suspected they must be many and subtle. His adversary was thinner and had dark shadows under his eyes. The weight loss made the caverns in his face starker. Still, by his expressions, the way he moved and the frame of his face George would always recognize Khalil. George waited to hear his response – live or die?

"Not in the foreseeable future, old man," Khalil's tone was soft delivering the pardon – like a snake. Slithering until it lunged. "I already passed up that chance, remember?"

George laughed and shook his head. Even in his dire predicament he could see the irony of the situation. Circumstances change. He sat back down on his cot and wondered if things were getting better or worse.

"You came pretty close. How did you find me?" George asked.

"Rumors of a middle aged American hostage," Khalil started. "I saw a picture..." He paused then continued more softly, "I hear about most of what happens in this country." It was an excellent performance and George could see that Khalil hadn't lost ability to dramatize. How he waved those arms.

"Where am I?" George asked. Who knew where the Iranians had taken him while he was drugged, with planes..., so he might as well ask. Khalil's presence signaled nothing geographically, but later on whatever he said might matter.

"You haven't strayed far," Khalil said. A spider ran across Khalil's shoe, a pair of Nike's greyer than the blue of their origin. George watched it head to the corner and a pile of dust. Bugs were everywhere in this excuse for a room.

"Get up," Khalil continued, his eyes black as an oil slick in the middle of a vast ocean.

George studied him, gauging, only to hear, "Stand up." Khalil's voice was again rough and his face grim.

So George stood, fear almost paralyzing his limbs. Never show too much weakness; never openly challenge; never buckle under pressure.

"Hold out your arms," Khalil said, expressionless and giving no hint as to the direction this interaction would take. George watched as Khalil bound his hands in front of him, palms facing the sky and vulnerable, before being clasped together. The rope was itchy and the knot too tight. Khalil opened the door and pushed him through, then picked up *Alice*.

George saw the rest of the tawdry house, his eyes scanning for information, as they walked to the front door and a waiting car. It was all so ordinary. Khalil helped him into the back seat and a teenage boy was in the driver's seat. He didn't even look back. Momentarily, they were moving, and quickly through an older part of the city, dense with narrow streets and stone walls. George could sense his warden's unease and understood the sentiment. The city itself was striking, absolutely majestic, and they passed lovely mosques, minarets pointing the way up to heaven. Should he pray?

"Now what?" George asked Khalil.

"I don't know," Khalil said and shrugged his shoulders. He pulled out a cell phone and began a conversation in Arabic. George saw his one possession – a book – on the seat between them. At least he wasn't totally alone. The blindfold would come later.

Words

mine wrote. She'd spent the rest of the day in the streets with Ben, taking pictures of debris and the crush of the masses. When thrown, you need to get right back on the horse. Bright, a bastard who didn't want to be embarrassed by losing a celebrity reporter on day one in the field (bad research; bad security; bad network) bought a big team of mercenaries to officially take over the search. God bless, but she had a job to do and Ben felt the same. Thus they spent their time in the streets and on the cell with their network of contacts. Chastised, Carl and Bruce were only too happy to join them.

The people, for the most part, were lovely but desperate. How could a nation survive in the midst of rapidly diminishing hope? Their group wandered the streets avoiding – or at least trying to avoid – the worst protests, during which the crowd got out of control and violence ensued. The local women were sometimes a good indicator, and they tended to steer clear of the confrontations and chanting of slogans later in the day, when the men's testosterone would build and a lone leader would cry out for justice and Allah. The dense masses around him rarely declined to follow his chants and joined in, rhythmically mimicking his words. By that hour the heat of May, starting to build but not at the desert's worst, would be dying down and the charcoal of kitchen fires scented the air, along with rubbish and the human odors that settled over tent cities.

Tahrir Square had become a permanent rebel town in the midst of the larger Cairo. Young and old alike camped out and Emine tried to capture their humanity through her lenses. Everything looked different through the lens of a camera, framing reality in and out of context. Stillness allowed the capture of more emotion than most people could perceive crossing a face. The people here were mostly dark and thus she had to be careful with shadows, especially as the day wore on.

Life was in free fall and she was capturing the days before it hit the ground.

Ben was a master at video, while she knew still pictures, so they were the perfect team. He began to teach her when and how to zoom in and explained how to create narratives. His work was more creative than she'd realized and very much story based. A picture might be worth a thousand words but a video crafted a thousand stories.

Rumors were that George had been moved and was perhaps now held by Al Qaeda. Whoever had him wasn't sharing related information broadly. Well connected regionally or not the leads weren't panning out on her end or Ben's (or her dad's). Information was being closely held, which often meant, unfortunately, that someone important had him and was holding tight.

Now What?

George heard someone coming and felt the sounds like a physical blow: those creaks in the wood floor as a foot pressed down, then lifted itself back into air. Now what? He certainly hadn't been given the script for this reality – "Fifty-four year old esteemed professor and television talk show host held prisoner by his former Al Qaeda ward and killer". And, he wasn't even close to finishing out a week in the country. Bright better be using his resources to find him because this wasn't the land he'd been promised! Indeed, Bright's assurances of security and safety had been bullshit.

Khalil, not so surprisingly, opened the door and walked in. Who else would? "Hello George," he said, and quickly sat in the one rickety splintered chair. George conceded the dominant spot immediately and sat a few feet away amidst the grime and lord knows what else on the floor. He leaned up against the wall, which actually made endurance easier. That chair wasn't comfortable, and he was.

"Khalil, I guess I could say nice to see you," George said, half expecting a blow in response. Sitting on the opposite side of the table – metaphorically – was a tricky position for many reasons. Not only could his jailer kill him at any time and broadcast the assassination on Al Jazeera, but the power dynamics were so complex and layered with minefields, mine upon mine, step upon step. Like this damn country.

"Don't bother," Khalil said with that familiar dramatic wave of his hands, spreading out like wings only to return. George had always loved this mood in his adversary; it was expansive and almost giddy. How familiar the man was; even as circumstances changed, people rarely did. Khalil's weaknesses likely hadn't evolved much: that ego and complete denial when facing truth.

George's new room was a virtual palace compared to his previous abode. This one was fairly large, though all it held was a cot, one chair, George's books and the bucket that served as his nighttime toilet. The walls were chipped and had likely once been white. The house was sandy brick, like many here, and thus stayed cool during hot days. His window was tiny, its rough wooden edges framing the view of a courtyard with a lovely green tile fountain that ran 24/7. The room smelled of many things – none of them good and some slightly disturbing.

Having Khalil only a few feet away felt like a bad flashback. George waited for him to speak, but the man seemed in no hurry. Khalil liked to build tension in order to make his point. But the bastard also looked pensive, which George hadn't expected.

While waiting, George searched his memory for those fragments of information he had about Khalil's background. Torture? Interrogation? He remembered munitions expertise, but the briefing file had been light, purposefully so. The United States still hadn't gotten its various agencies, or even the people within each agency, working together. But emotionally George knew the man like he knew his own wife, well not quite but a solid start. Proximity builds a shadowy intuitive sense of another person if you pay close enough attention.

"What do you want to talk about, George?" Khalil asked, not moving as he spoke. His legs were stretched out as he sprawled across the rickety chair, wearing baggy pants and worn navy t-shirt. A baseball cap, sans affiliation, completed the look. George marveled again at how much the plastic surgeon had softened his features, making him look not western exactly but effeminate and handsomer. Meanwhile, the cheekbones were still harsh and set the clear boundaries of his face, leaving him with an edge.

Someone was playing a Frank Sinatra song and it filtered through the thin walls. He was flying to the moon while George was stuck on the ground.

Fly me to the moon

Let me swing among the stars

The deep voice, the memories of another time and then the here and now.

"Let me go – how about we start there?" George asked, smiling to lighten his delivery. It was never good to challenge your warden too directly because he might feel a need to retaliate and show who was boss. But being too meek and frightened gave him all the power. Better to flatter him but with a slight edge to your banter as it struck a balance between deference and confidence.

"I haven't decided what I'm doing ," Khalil said. "Letting you go isn't likely at this point." Khalil crossed his left leg with his right and he looked troubled. "What would you do?"

Outside their room George heard a merchant hawking something in Arabic, beyond the prison walls and somewhere in the streets teeming with life and freedom. Life went on as usual in this neighborhood, his plight ignored. The sense of unreality in the midst of normalcy only heightened George's unrest.

"What would I do?" George replied and his mind ranged across so many thoughts but where to begin...and what to suggest? Search for the logic in the insanity?

"What do you want to accomplish, let's ask that question first?" George said, deciding to adopt the mentor role. You never knew going into a situation which approach would succeed, so he'd learned to follow his gut. They already had an established relationship and in Khalil's line of work he had good reason to feel alone and uncertain. So much was at risk, including his own life, so George should exploit that fear.

Khalil stared back at him but George found his expression unreadable.

"I want a lot right now." Khalil knocked off a fleck of wall plaster with his shoulder. "But I guess I need to decide what I want the most."

"I'm not the enemy, just a symbol of something you hate. I gave you a chance. Give me one."

I could have killed you outright, but shot to the shoulder so you'd likely be okay and..." George watched Khalil blink, his typical way of showing emotion. Khalil shouldn't have made that confession and normally George would have felt a surge of adrenaline at having played the trump card. But now his life was on the line and he knew that the repercussions could surprise him. At what point did he beg? Every man had his breaking point if you pushed hard enough.

Not today.

"Aim for democracy," George tried and watched his words fall flat.

Revenge?

halil was in charge, which was nothing new.

George was his prisoner, but that was of secondary importance. He had information to plant, a bomb to detonate and an assassination to facilitate. He needed better support and a path to success since his tasks were too complex and disparate to accomplish alone. Osman was a step in the right direction. Adding the boy meant his communication network had taken a leap past the present and far into the future thus his plot was proceeding faster. His cell phone usage was pretty much dead now except for a few calls with Jennifer.

Now, they were doing everything through dissolving emails and web sites...many of which lasted for mere minutes while others kept going indefinitely and appeared faultless. Hiding information in the cyber frontier was a cinch once you had a guide. And the technology had so surpassed the laws, creating a confusing morass of opportunity, so at least one area of operations was off his plate. Osman was only sixteen, but had grown up in a country with a sophisticated online community and was a wizard. Increasingly, where ever Khalil went he brought Osman along.

He'd talked to George but was still unsure what to do about his prisoner. It was like lovers being re-united; at first they had little to say but then all fell into place. Physically, they were awkward but had willed their way through the barriers built by time. Khalil hadn't killed George outright because? Well George had showed him some humanity, and there was so little of that in life. So they'd talked, haggled and ultimately reached an impasse. Again.

"Let me go," George had said.

"Tell me what you know," he'd demanded.

"I'm a journalist now," George said, and there was truth in that perhaps. Khalil observed the fine veins that filtered under the thin white skin. George had aged and the lines on his face were noticeably deeper, like creases in a dry riverbed. He reached out and caressed the one that ran from George's right eye into his hairline. George winced but Khalil didn't respond. Some of life was merit and other parts were luck and the greater world was indifferent to both when it judged us. He smiled, feeling the thrill of being master now.

"So, George, tell me about Alice," he asked and the tables were turned. Khalil got to ask the questions and guide the conversation. He let George talk for a while. The walls crumbled around them and the lighting was dim, while the air was heavy with exhaust, human stench and meat. Khalil was free to call the shots now; all prisons are bad but less so when you ran them.

"Let's talk about democracy, George," he interrupted. "How do I win this upcoming election?" he asked and watched George wince. Good. The man's clothes were dirty and he had sweat beading around the perimeter of his face. His weary smile in response was perhaps the only reason he was still alive. George was the enemy, but he was still strong and noble, even in defeat. Those little things make the difference between life and death, success and failure, up and down. Khalil wanted to tap that laser insight into the forthcoming election upon which so much in the region depended. He felt an itch at his ankle but didn't want to move and distract his prey. A child screamed for his mother and then began to cry. Khalil felt his own anxiety rising but he waited, looking for an answer but knowing not to push too hard.

George sighed then spoke.

"Do you want to win? Should you?" George asked, then waited but Khalil said nothing. The greatest hardship was to wait, in silence, when answers didn't come.

"First, ask whether it will be a fair election or not," George spoke, pushing on as requested but with little insight as yet into Khalil's relative position or candidate. Khalil would get better information by sharing the detailed facts but wanted George's raw analysis before disclosing anything. Would George aim to enlighten or to dodge? "You need to know the playing field." George's grey eyes twinkled as he spoke, but otherwise his face was neutral; he had to be scared. "Many people don't vote, at least in my country; you need to mobilize them. Are they literate? Not necessarily. Focus on the message you want to spread – which should inspire them in moral terms, not practical ones. People here are hungry and want jobs." George was now studying Khalil.

Khalil returned a half smile.

"Touch their hearts?" Khalil asked and was rewarded with a nod from George. They were comfortable together, despite the circumstances, having spent so much time in a small room previously learning the parameters of each other's personality. "A chicken in every pot?"

"It's been used successfully before!" George responded. "Go American – we do campaign slogans well. 'The people's economy and a fair chance for all'."

"I like it," Khalil replied. He appreciated the sounding board, especially knowing that he controlled the freedom of the person providing it. For now. We could never ultimately control another man, even if we had the illusion of doing so at a particular time and place. "This time I have books for you, George," he said and handed George a stack of books. *The Cairo Trilogy* by Naguib Mahfouz and a boxed set of four novels by Lawrence Durrell about Alexandria in the mid-20th Century. "Learn about the locale," Khalil said and left, closing the door softly. He'd send the man extra lentils and return with more questions. Democracy indeed?

Machiavelli had said, "Entrepreneurs are simply those who understand that there is little difference between obstacle and opportunity and are able to turn both to their advantage." Khalil was running a business and now he had a democracy expert in his hands. What luck when trying to sway an important Egyptian democratic election? Ever the opportunist, he'd get what he needed out of George before setting him loose on the world like a bomb.

Squiggles and Beds

mine stared down at her notebook and wondered at all the lines and squiggles. Her penmanship was almost illegible but her points were dead on. How did a country survive the reactionaries in a revolution? It usually didn't, with the result that violence was almost inevitable, even as the world pretended not to notice.

Braving the air conditioning in yet again another lace outfit, this one a negligee with soft apricot flowers sprinkled sparingly across the sheer white, she was curled up on the bed, her chosen desk. To write she needed to build a mood. Perhaps due to Liz's perfectly coiffed hair, inevitable makeup and wafting perfume, Emine needed to look pretty to feel creative. Liz liked to be polished and predictable; Emine preferred a more Victoria's Secret look.

Well, she had a different focus in life, didn't she? Liz, the political wife, hid the truth while Emine, a reporter, exposed it. She should ask George about that dichotomy when they got him back. She'd never give up, which meant they had to get him alive.

The doorbell rang, but Emine had already been forewarned by the front desk and Ed's many calls en route. Wondering where she'd left her train of thought in her draft, she opened the door quickly, and then felt suddenly crazy dizzy. Looking into Ed's blue eyes, her body tingled with a desire she'd forgotten. How could he just walk into a room and make her feel both numb and desperate to touch him at the same time? As he kissed her deeply she melted into his warmth.

"Wow," was all she could say, taking a deep breath when he pulled away. Ed looked exactly as she remembered yet she stood transfixed. So tall, his shoulders broad, narrowing to a trim waist, Ed, her not-a-boy-friend. Very blonde and pale from too much time inside working, he nonetheless kept his body firm and cheeks healthy (he didn't drink the way she did). But she poured him a glass of deep, dark Burgundy, which she'd started on while writing. Then she hugged him again, greedy, before retreating to the couch to recover. How could another body feel so heavenly as it crushed into hers?

She'd almost forgotten the strong attraction between them. Sex the first night they met had been divine, so she'd kept him around despite how different they were. He played games willingly but retreated into respectability when their clothes were on. No man was perfect.

Ed sat next to her on the brick red couch, adjusting the exotic orange striped pillows away from them both. He pulled her close again, and she smelled the sweet rankness of his sweat and felt his unshaven cheek against her smooth one.

"Long flight?" she whispered. He responded by kissing her deeply. She ran her fingers across his back and massaged the muscle beneath his neck and shoulder. How soon could she get his shirt off? Suddenly he jumped up.

"Can I take a quick shower?" he asked, probably wanting to wash off that distinctive smell she loved so much. She nodded and he flashed a broad grin before heading to the bathroom, leaving her speechless. He'd just arrived and was already leaving her alone! He stripped off his navy polo shirt and loose khaki pants with brown belt en route to her tiled bathroom and she heard the clothes hit the floor before the shower began to run.

How had he happened? A thoughtless pickup in a bar…turning into an almost boyfriend. Had she forgotten Piers so quickly and perhaps started falling in love again? Love was such a troubling word, heavy with responsibility and guilt; so she'd rather park her life in lust. Thus, Ed's appearance thrust her into emotional turmoil; well she'd forget that baggage for now and just fuck him. Soon he'd be back on a plane to Paris and she'd be aiming her camera at the sweaty desperate mobs of Cairo's revolution.

Ed's shower lasted too long but eventually Emine was under him on the bed. Her flimsy lingerie hadn't been much of a barrier and she felt his hardness brushing against her thigh. But what did logistics matter as he entered her, so swollen and firm, thrusting deeply between her legs? They moved in conjunction and she felt herself letting go, slower and then faster, with his little butterfly kisses, until they came together. The rest of the afternoon was a blur of sweat and more kisses, broken by the calm of limbs entwined and voices speaking softly, until the evening call to prayers and shadows of the descending sun marked the day's passing.

Emine stared up at the white ceiling and felt the breeze from the air conditioner brushing her skin. Her body was numb, but happily so. Could she ever fully remember the endless variations of movement that had formed their afternoon?

"Oh, God," was all she could whisper. Had she found her God?

Ed's eyes scanned her body, then he drew her tightly to him as he kissed her again. So quickly he was hard inside her. Was there truly a world beyond the crush of his body? Nothing felt as good.

"I love you, Emine," he whispered in her ear and she didn't want to respond. What was wrong with her?

"I love you too," she whispered back, anyway, then hid her face in his chest. He felt so good, but her heart was cold, no confused. Warm and safe, he smelled familiar yet still didn't settle her. A tear pooled in the corner of her right eye and she started to laugh, demonstrating her lack of sanity, or at the very least, clarity. She adored him, yet wasn't sure about love or even what it meant.

The phone rang, but Emine didn't answer. The machine picked it up and she waited, knowing she'd lunge if a voice carried news of George. Bud's voice came clear and loud, and she felt momentarily guilty but not too guilty.

"I found where they're keeping your man," Bud said, his voice deep with the familiar lilt.

"George," she told Ed and lunged for the phone. He nodded.

Bud read her an address on the phone and hung up. How these Africans worked she'd never understand. Reasonably, Bud had probably bribed someone for the information. Part of the cost of doing business locally, and he could afford it. Likewise, she'd die for him and he knew it. Her second brother and....

Bud hadn't even stayed on the phone long enough for her to say thank you. Perhaps he'd known or sensed that she wasn't alone. Emine wouldn't put it past him to have her followed. And he'd justify the act by saying he was only concerned that she'd stalk George into his abyss. She had calls to make. Bright? Could she count on her boss?

"You're the best thing in this broken country," Emine breathed, almost choking, as she turned back to Ed. Why was she such a fucked up mess? She gulped the dregs of her wine and knew she'd order more even though Ed would be shocked. So be it. "Don't leave," she whispered and let him pull her close.

Finally, she'd found a good and decent man. Ever more fascinated by danger, she'd still kept Bright, Bud and her dad on speed dial. Ed was an emotional risk; they were physical risks. Not hard to figure out which one frightened her more.

Touché

Now George was evaluating, and the man in a grubby pullover, more grey than brown, stared back defiant and likely angry again. Khalil had rage issues....go figure, right? Then again, George tended to fall back on intellect even when confronted by difficult, irrational or plain mad men (we all have our issues). No point in responding with emotion, since it would just ratchet up the tension and, here, likely get him shot. When they'd sparred before, with Khalil as prisoner and George jailor, the balance of power had been exactly opposite. But, old habits died hard, and Khalil was used to confiding in him. George would coolly bluff.

Having a clear strategy and objective bestowed power. Not enough; but he wasn't desperate just yet. Khalil had stopped hitting him and the sun had risen in the east that morning.

"I like to give people a chance," Khalil pontificated. He'd reverted to the role of philosopher, hearkening back to his years as an undergrad majoring in philosophy. Why so scared if he was free now?

"Only they can find the will to fight and stay alive," Khalil said. "I like to watch the process, though I never thought I'd see you again. You're mine," he added with satisfaction.

Wait, George reminded himself. An opportunity always presented itself but most people lost heart and didn't see that one shot when it came. Keep your mind clear and don't let Khalil rile you as he'll keep trying.

"Why so philosophical these days?" George made his words deliberately vague to see how Khalil would interpret them.

They were both stretched out on the floor, their backs propped up by the wall. The lighting was bad and the chair had been banished after it gave off too many splinters. A typical shitty third-world house but George should feel lucky to be so safe. Funny, though, he actually felt put upon being kept in this rat hole against his will.

"I was reading a lot more for a while," Khalil mumbled, shuffling his feet. Frightened as he was, George could sense this conversation getting interesting. Coping mechanisms help distract us from the elephant in the room, so he might as well grab at whatever distraction he could get.

"Reading what? Back to philosophy?'

"Yes, I was sick...my mom died...I started re-reading some of the books I'd read in school. Machiavelli. Spinoza. Plato."

"And?"

"And nothing. I just like to read."

"You've been given a big job, haven't you?" George probed. "You're now the boss of something and feeling the pressure?" George saw Khalil's eyes widen and kicked himself. Some people didn't like to be called into account and Khalil was one of them. Like a child he now seemed to be hiding out in stories, from books and from a false God who told him to kill. Stupid to call him on it. George shut up and watched.

"No, you're wrong. I like to read. You need a Quran, George. I'll get you one."

A million cute remarks flashed through his mind but George knew when not to push and simply lowered his chin respectfully. "Thank you, Khalil."

The man studied him for a moment then his face softened.

"I didn't feel safe when you had me in that cell," Khalil said, his voice distant. "The future was so fraught with risk. I wasn't petrified of death because Allah would have welcomed me, but you don't have that kind of faith. What will you do George, now that you're here and my prisoner? I own your fate. You need to find Allah."

"And if I do will you let me live?" he asked.

Khalil just stared back.

George opened his hands to expose his palms. "My faith is different from yours, but that doesn't make it any less real. I don't glorify death as you do. That lapse doesn't make me evil or weak."

"Allah will help him who moves in the way of Allah, said Abu Bakr. The choice is yours, George."

"We never did agree on religion. Or politics." George replied. "And I note that while your Allah makes promises, you don't." As they sat in silence and the street came alive through the flimsy walls with ongoing chatter and motors blaring.

"You aren't going to give up, are you?" Khalil asked.

"I never do. Then again, neither do you."

George smiled back, trying to reach the humanity in Khalil. It was there; they'd broached that path when Khalil had broken past pain and fear and addressed his brother's death and the years of trauma that followed. But that was a long time ago, and the background noise now was in Arabic, not English. How could George touch that soft spot again, in the former prisoner who now held the keys?

Directly? Never.

"What's happening in the streets? What am I missing? The political situation here is uglier than I expected," George asked, choosing a neutral subject that wasn't so neutral. Khalil's Al Qaeda presence here couldn't be good for Egypt. Extremism rarely trod lightly.

"There is no balance in revolution," Khalil replied, and George noted a sadness in his eyes. He waited. Never push; at least not until the right moment. "I grew up in one. Algeria is always at war. With our French colonist overlords, with our own government, against our own people. The most brutal always have an advantage."

"Your group was among the most brutal in Algeria. Muslim extremists killing Muslims," George reminded him, trying to keep his tone neutral but irritated at the utter denial in Khalil's comments. One didn't kill freely without emotional repercussions.

"The government stole our election," Khalil responded angrily. Justification. "We needed to be stronger than they were but didn't have their professional army with big guns and the international community's support. Everyone loves an ally, even if he's a dictator."

George thought for a minute. Algeria's battles during the second half of the twentieth century made the Arab Spring look like May Day. Starting in 1954, with the launch of the War of Independence known for brutality and massacres, the Algerian people had known mostly terror. In 1991 an Islamic party, the Islamic Salvation Front, had won the first round of elections.

The military had intervened and declared a state of emergency, suspending most of the people's rights. The election was cancelled and the old ruler, Mohamed Boudiaf, reinstalled until his assassination in 1992. During the ensuing Algerian War everyone was targeted and brutalized. It was into this reality that Khalil had been born and raised so he would have defenses related to it, but also sensitivities. Then there were all of those years fighting as a jihadist. This man's psyche was a mess. Cairo must feel more than a little familiar.

"How many people died during Algeria's civil war?" George asked, and watched as Khalil lit a cigarette. Settling in for a bit?

"They say over 160,000 people were killed between 1992 and June 2002, but the true figure had to be much higher. I knew so many...". Khalil inhaled, then exhaled. "People here have no idea what path they've started on. Revolution doesn't come with peace, just chaos."

George couldn't deny the truth of Khalil's words. The expectation that life would get better immediately contrasted with the reality that nothing worked initially when social structures broke down. Coming from a democracy, his countrymen knew they had a voice in shaping policies and the resulting realities. yet often shirked them.

"What are they doing here, now?" he asked Khalil. This man had been walking the streets, speaking to the people in Arabic. The best he himself had, for now, had been a cameraman and an air-conditioned van.

"Imploding."

Small surprise.

"Your group is exploiting that?" George asked, then watched anger flash across Khalil's eyes as he crushed the butt of his cigarette into the grungy floor. George needed to remember that their positions were reversed. However, percieved power was as good as real power.

"George," Khalil began, and George braced himself. "Most people only want food and a decent life for their families. We try to provide that, along with Allah's divine law. These people need help desperately. You and I differ over ideology, but we both have the people's best interest at heart."

George smiled, seeing that he'd succeeded in touching Khalil's vulnerability, if only for an instant. This was a boy who'd never had a safe home in his life and struggled to find a place of power in an ever hostile reality. The people lining the streets really were his compatriotes who shared his desperate pain and longing. Khalil was the perfect example of the birth lottery's ugly side.

"Khalil, our ways of caring for the people are vastly different. You kill so many, negating their choices." George tried to find comfort in his four peeling barren walls. Nope.

"Not everyone fights the same war and your methods don't belong here," Khalil responded, his rage on the rise once again.

"Democracy can work for everyone, eventually, if the right systems are put in place first," George replied, trying to bring the conversation back where he wanted it. He was increasingly less sure that his words were true as he aged, but currently his concerns revolved more around staying alive than being ideologically consistant. Realistically, how could the poor fight the corrupt at the ballot box, and how could Western values be exported to countries that didn't necessarily want them? But how could you not try to give everyone equal rights and a voice?

Outside, the nightly chants and pledges were starting, following that rhythmic undulation so characteristic of the nation's music, a chant followed by the crowd repeating it, then the masses clapping and shouting summation. Khalil nodded toward the room's excuse for the window. "The night begins," he said with a smile.

"You'll go out into the streets, tonight?" George asked, feeling a stab of fear. Was his safety dependent on Khalil's? No one knew better than he how quickly a crowd's mood could change. He'd been in the middle of the local quagmire and had ended up here.

"Worried?" Khalil responded. "Like the father I never had," he said, referring to the man he hated. They'd discussed that reality long ago.

George shrugged. "Ever been followed?" he asked only to sense Khalil's sharp attention before hearing an urgent, "Why?"

"No reason, I promise. I'm just not liking the mood in Cairo and can't figure out why it feels so menacing and burdened. And I was followed, as you know."

"What are you?" Khalil asked. "You can't fight, but you also don't break – even now. Many men would have begged me for their life already. You're like the sphinx, and no less impassive."

George just smiled. The word for what he was happened to be "stuck" but somehow he didn't think that answer would satisfy Khalil.

Grime

George was grimy but still looked clean. His fatigue pants were ripped in a few places and his t-shirt looked browner than whatever its original color must have been. That was his way; even rumpled he was composed and dignified. He really was a professor through and through, never abandoning that paternal leadership role to become more humane. Or, perhaps dignity was the ultimate quality a person could acquire and once established became impossible to dislodge.

Khalil recognized that, while the dirt sat lightly on George, he himself was filthy. The heat, dust and smoke of the city made staying clean difficult, as if he even had time to worry about doing so. Jennifer, still white in her hospital bed, hadn't complained.

He studied George and wondered, how much did this man really know, and how could he discern the extent of Khalil's internal database? He owned George, could probe for information or even resort to torture. He could kill him, quickly or slowly. The tables had turned, but somehow the situation didn't feel as rewarding as it should.

"Stupid – I suppose," George finally replied. "I didn't have to come to this country and end up here, a lamb waiting for slaughter."

Khalil stifled a smirk, not wanting to look weak or soft. And George did inspire respect with his useful intellect and fighting spirit. A rare man could sit with him in the dirt, a prisoner, and crack a joke. Khalil needed men like this to fight for him, but they were few and far between. Perhaps, with the right inducement, George might barter for his life. Not likely; but one could never really guess at what a desperate man might compromise. A plan was beginning to formulate in Khalil's mind, its tangled skeins taking on a semblance of order and an outcome. Keep your friends close and your enemies closer? Yes, until you decided to set them loose on the wrong path.

He had to ease George onto that path carefully.

"I'll go with crazy," Khalil said with a half smile, then led the conversation in another direction. "How do you get someone to love you?" he asked.

George's eyelids didn't even twitch. Deceptive bastard; he could hide pretty much any feeling, couldn't he?

"Khalil, what an excellent question!" George responded, as if he were at a podium facing his Godless class, or worse, mass media audience. "I wish more of your leaders asked it. But love in what context – personal or professional?" George looked intrigued, even excited by the question. Khalil noted that his beard was growing in, the hairs fine and silvery, as he studied George's face for a response. He kicked at his Nike while pondering how to answer George's question.

"Personal." he replied, not meeting George's eyes. Was he wise in raising this topic? It didn't much matter. He so rarely had an expert in men and women before him, and he could limit the information he shared with his prisoner. Besides, there was no one else to ask.

"I heard something once that I'll pass on to you." George paused and studied Khalil's face. They were like two primates. Khalil hated this particular look; it reminded him of when George had been the interrogator and had treated him like a surrogate son. Or what he imagined would be the way a father treated a son, since his own had abandoned him long ago. He'd shot the man himself after his mother's death; she'd always forbidden him before. Khalil couldn't stop shuffling his legs from discomfort, but cursed himself for doing so, hoping that George wouldn't sense weakness in his incessant movement.

"If you make someone happy, why would they leave you?" George began, his voice deep and firm. "If you make someone unhappy, why would they stay? But somehow we can't seem to take that advice." George looked away from Khalil and his eyes had gotten misty.

"And sometimes different things make people happy, right, old man?" Khalil responded. What messes they both were. Aging men teary eyed at the mention of love. Time to end the conversation for now. Khalil hopped up en route to the door.

"Shalaba will bring you what you need." Khalil tone was all business now. "She speaks very little English but is smart and can understand more than you'd guess. She won't help you, so don't bother trying. A widow, I employed her so her children don't starve, and she won't survive if you try to use her for your own ends." Khalil said and left, locking the door behind him, waiting for that click.

The air was sweltering, and for a second he wondered if he could possibly find someplace to escape the heat. Summer was coming too rapidly. Khalil had a lot to do, and George just added one more dimension.

"Get the man a Quran," he told the guard and liked seeing him jump.

Hot Streets

Then there were the interviews. No one listened to the common people, or so Emine believed as she dragged Ed with her, and Ben. This time, with no George, she took center stage on camera. They did four interviews, then Ben quit and Ed supported him. She yelled at them both in the middle of the street.

"Emine, you're filming them in Arabic, mostly. Who's going to bother translating that? And the streets aren't safe," Ed began, his blue eyes wide and the people around them staring at someone so obviously American and out of place. Tall and hot, he belonged in a polo club or her bed, not a winding alley smelling of urine and blood.

"This is what I do for a living," she said. The Egyptians were a sophisticated and cultured people and she wanted to document their perspective on film.

Ben cut her off. "'This is bullshit, Emine. Trash and not worth my time. No one cares what the street people say. The revolution is the story." And with that Ben left her, camera in hand, and got into the van. Their driver started the vehicle and both Carl and Bruce shuffled their feet. Damn Muslim country, no one was ever on the woman's side. She joined them; sitting down with a thud, then had drinks at the hotel with the lot of them. Turncoats, but what could she do if they refused to listen?

As with many other Anglicized hot countries, afternoon tea had evolved into an excuse for getting drunk (among non-Muslims). The hotel's Sherlock Holmes pub had genteel seating and a long gleaming wood bar. The lighting was soft and someone had ordered a Shepherd's Pie for the table, so she kept picking at the mashed potatoes.

"I want a human rights story," she said and kicked Ben under the table when he openly laughed. "You're so jaded," she added.

"Yes, but we want viewers, and viewers want action," he replied, sipping at his water instead of his gin and tonic.

"Burning flags and tanks," Ed piped up: Ben's new ally.

"Do the math," Ben added. "We get what? Thirty to sixty seconds of video time on air? Not a lot of words, but quality time for action. The video needs to make an impact. Word are passé since no one reads anymore."

"Nobody cares," she said, knowing she was being petty and that people actually did read, especially her present company. They were just busy.

She took another slug of her Singapore Sling, a holdover from her time in Asia, and wondered if she should order another. Too many years of radical totalitarian governments for the people to expect better than abject poverty? No, not really, but transitions could be hard. Dictators often looted; the Middle Eastern ones had largely arisen from the socialist path laid down during the 1950s and 1960s. Poor men originally, they aimed to level society and succeeded in bringing down everyone but their cronies. In any country with a supreme ruler, those around him had to be prepared to sacrifice any pretense of ethics or morality to ensure that the boss stayed supreme. But this country's boss had been fired.

She smiled at Ed and gestured him upstairs, leaving the chatter behind. Too much politics eventually bored her; Dad's business. She documented but wasn't deeply interested in making policy (just influencing it with pictures).

Ed kissed her in the otherwise empty elevator, and she stared up at the scalloped ceiling, detached but willing. Too many clothes but not for long; once they were in their room, he stripped her bare and laid her down on the bed. They spent the early afternoon exploring each other. Since no one would take her back into the hot streets, she had to find action elsewhere.

Later, they were watching CNN when she decided enough was enough.

"You've got to go," she started and watched his face fall. That was his second mistake of the day. First, she didn't like men who told her what to do and treated her like a girl. Second, she didn't like men who cared too much about her. Piers had been the exception; but he was always emotionally in a cloud; thus his love never felt like pressure.

"I need to work," she continued, caressing his shoulder, moving on to his bulging bicep. He did have a nice body and worked long hours, leaving time for her own mission. Usually men were clearer: yes or no.

"Fuck you, Eme," he said, surprising her, and she saw the flash of anger in his eyes as he grabbed his shirt and started getting dressed. "I fly out here, hit the squalid streets of a country in turmoil and actually care about you, but you just like to push people away. And now I need to decide whether I'm going to let you do that to me."

She turned from him and grabbed her cigarettes. Not facing him, she could collect herself for a moment. She lit one and saw her hands shake. Ed was something she wasn't ready to let go just yet. So she turned to face him. He was still there but pulling his pants on.

She inhaled, choking down the acrid smoke, and tried to analyze her emotions. Every time she began getting close to a man she panicked but couldn't figure out why. It was as if, once she became vulnerable, her brain shut off and she was left unsure of what questions to ask. The more time she spent with a lover the less she seemed to know him and a resulting gap of trust grew. Did intimacy drive her expectations higher, or was she just an emotional mess? Piers had been different because he'd trusted her

131

immediately and thoroughly. Then he asked for so little emotionally in return, seemingly able to survive on air, red wine and plain bread.

Ed was watching her now and she sensed him waiting. But for what? The room had darkened, lit mostly by Cairo outside. Neither of them was the type who turned the lights on first, so they gazed at each other in the near darkness. She inhaled on her cigarette and he coughed. He hated her smoking. She hated his job.

The phone rang and she didn't speak up when Ed reached for it. Depending on who was on the other end of the line, she might have created one more problem.

"Hello," Ed said, "Emine's room," he added, sounding polite and American. But she knew that he had different facets and his greeting was only the public side of his persona. Courteous now, he'd be fighting her again in minutes depending on to whom he'd just said hello.

She pulled a shirt over her head, cigarette in ashtray. People were mostly concerned with their own problems, and Emine knew she was no different as she sat, plucking at her thin white t-shirt. Waiting.

"Got it. You want to talk to Emine? No. Okay," he said then replaced the phone and turned back to face her. Even under his loose shirt she could see his muscles move and felt strangely vulnerable.

"That was your boss. They verified where George is being held. Bright is flying here so he's local when the rescue mission starts." Emine tried to evaluate the new data, which hit with minimal warning. Her anger at Ed was deflected, careening from self-blame for not appreciating her almost-but-not-quite-perfect boyfriend, to fury at the attention-seeking ex-boyfriend who was her boss. Bright would, of course, want to be there for the photo ops attached to any rescue mission.

But her questions abounded. Government run or privately hired mercenaries? Legal or illegal? No wonder he hadn't wanted to speak to her. He knew she'd ask the tough questions and try to stop him from risking George's life for extra publicity. Ed had been the perfect vehicle for Bright dropping his bomb.

Meanwhile, back to Ed, her immediate reality and problem. One of his good qualities was that he let her daydream when the mood hit. She could sense his patience wearing thin today as her mind was jumping.

So Bud's information had been verified? Would they be able to rescue George safely?

"I'm sorry," she said to Ed, surprising herself but knowing that she had to regain control of all her situations.

"Seriously?" Ed asked, with a smile, sitting down next to her on the bed. "That they've found George?" She blushed and he reached across the pillows, to caress her thigh. The room was so dark now and she couldn't make out his expression.

"No, of course not. Our fight," she added, resting her palm on his hand.

"Well, I'm leaving anyway. Don't want to meet your ex-boyfriend, now boss, if that's okay with you." Even in the darkness she could see his eyes were sparkling.

"You knew?" she asked. Surprised, but only mildly so. Bright, being married, had expected some discretion during their affair but not an excess of it. He liked being known for his nocturnal successes.

One moment your life is a stone in you, and the next, a star, she whispered quoting *Sunset* by Rainer Maria Rilke.

Emine picked at a loose thread – the shirt was her favorite though it probably looked like a threadbare rag to most people. The holes were getting bigger…as her life's purpose was coming together.

Our most important relationship is with ourselves. But what if you have no self? What if it never developed? So she let it go and focused on the man in front of her. Hopefully, George would be the next live male she had to confront (and Bright would stick to his suite and rolling cameras).

Curling into Ed, she smiled and let her back arch as he drew her closer, questioning. For now, she couldn't calm the chatter in her head and wasn't sure if stowing another person in her room was such a great idea. She needed to think. No one else was looking out for George quite the way she was, and he was the only one who really needed her right now.

Clocks

George had reached an impasse with time. It had stopped moving forward and he couldn't seem to make it move backwards. All of those "could have," "should have" and "would have" arguments played in his head.

Outside his tiny window the small crescent moon ignored him, preferring the darkness.

A snowball was already in motion, and as George mentally watched it roll downhill, growing bigger and bigger, picking up speed, he could only marvel at how inevitable this moment had been. Everyone who took big risks eventually came out on the wrong side of one.

He'd known that flying into Egypt and taking to the streets for filming was a risk. Hell, the shit had already been hitting the fan when he allowed his team to exit their van and head into the crowds. Maybe he'd liked the idea of being a real journalist, not one who just sat in a studio. Perhaps it had been the diamonds given to Karen, along with an insurance policy. Ok, that later precaution had been a sure indication of possible danger.

But he'd felt compelled to come back and jump into the danger that existed. Like a child who kept putting his finger in a light socket, he kept searching out trouble. Cairo, better known for its Pyramids and antiquities, was now among the most interesting places on earth. No longer just part of civilization's cradle, it was charting a new paradigm for those Internet-enabled to learn the truth and be heard. No one remained dispossessed anymore.

Who would have predicted that George would chuck tenure for more exciting pastures? Some of this path – the interrogations – had been a fluke based on a mere article, a related award and a call from the CIA. A leave of absence to "consult" had led to interrogations and Khalil. He'd been shot and almost died. Yet he'd left his safe life to re-enter a country known to be more than simply dangerous – crazily so. He'd never planned any of it. Events had happened, and they fit, strangely, as had events for poor Alice in her Wonderland. Until now – when the stakes had gotten too high – and they didn't anymore.

Granted, he was still alive. With life came hope, which was what faith was about. So, now the question came, did his faith match Khalil's? No, his exceeded Khalil's because his God had no desire to speed up an exit from the life he'd bestowed. Best to pick our deities carefully.

Still, George's pain and fear were debilitating, and he had to keep fighting the urge to drop into insanity. How had his detainees survived this hell? He was well trained, but the reality was so much worse. First, you were fine until you tried to move any part of your body – at which point you risked your mental balance. Next, you couldn't eat, sleep or think. Then came the fear that washed over you and swept you into an abyss of uncertainty and imaginative loss.

He didn't want to die.

George had welcomed danger into his life, and now he had to live with the consequences. He took responsibility for his choices – painful though the outcome was proving. The only question was what to do now. Looking back got him nowhere but what could get him out of here?

He needed to get out alive before pondering geo-politics.

Stay quiet – rule number one. Look obedient. There was an advantage to surprise and he needed it. Weakness was closely tied to verbosity. Insecurity led to shooting off one's mouth, which led to death.

Rule two – pretend nothing was out of the ordinary. The only chance he had of surviving was to keep his wits about him. Panicking, overcompensation or desperation also led to death.

Rule three – always be calculating. Everyone got a chance so he needed to be ready when it came.

Shit.

Not technically in a war zone, now in contrast to the past, when he'd been hidden behind barbed wire and big guns, George had finally entered the war, and he wasn't in Kansas anymore. In the States, even in Iraq and Afghanistan, he'd been able to take his time. Even though lives were at stake the primal desperation of a country at war wasn't his daily reality. Now he was in a big time negotiation – for his own life – so he had to face it with a new intensity. He knew he had the raw materials to see this catastrophe through and survive. Arrogant, maybe, but so be it. He wasn't emotionally ready for the situation but had no more choice than George Washington's rag-tag troops who had taken on the most powerful empire on earth and won. That American spirit in action.

Anyone fighting an organization as ruthless and competent as Al Qaeda had to be prepared for the same in return. Thus far, the bad guys might be taking out a hotel or two but they weren't winning. The situation wasn't personal; it was about the survival of the world and anyone fighting had to accept the gravity of this new global order.

George picked up the book Khalil had given him: Graham Greene's *The Heart of the Matter,* and paged through it. He deliberately ignored the Quran. He'd get to it, but not now. He had few avenues of discretion left these days but he'd take each and every one. Later George would read the holy pages and attempt to understand the enemy. For now, he'd lose himself in fiction – suddenly not stranger than fact.

Wilson sat on the balcony of the Bedford Hotel with his bald pink knees ...

George would read for a moment to relax his own unquiet mind. He'd read the book years ago and remembered the message – does a "good" man sacrifice out of a will to benefit mankind or out of weakness and the inability to face himself?

George had tried to be a good man, and look where he ended up. No more. He was going to fight for his country and for the life of each citizen. Whoever – and whatever – came down in the process was tangential to his end goal. War was hell, and he was going to embrace it and not pretend it was anything else.

Now how did he get out of here?

Aswan...Dam....

Set, Aswan to blow up in fourteen days. The new dam and not the old.

Aswan, Egypt's gateway to Africa, with its wafting smells of sandalwood and spices, and its souq cluttered with Nubian talismans, sharp Sudanese swords and stuffed crocodiles. The people got darker here, and the town graced with palm trees and black granite boulders nestled against a wider section of the Nile, stunning in its beauty and flowing from Lake Nasser. Colorful Nubian villages touched the edges of the river against the backdrop of the desert sands. Much of Nubian antiquity, the pyramids and stone temples, had been moved or buried, along with the villages, when the new dam was finished in 1971. That pool of water was about to be unleashed again, and the valleys would settle into their natural patterns, uncovering what had long been hidden and burying a different expanse.

A governorate capital with an esteemed university and active tourist trade, Aswan would soon be wiped away by the exploding waters the bombs would release. All wild things ultimately want to free. Khalil could watch from a rented felucca, but he'd leave that torrential experience to the visiting Americans and European who'd never see it coming. Indeed, Khalil wasn't sure how the water would disperse itself once freed from the constraints of the massive structure.

Now mostly a tourist destination, a spot on a Nile tour close to the Temple of Isis, Aswan was famous for its relaxed lifestyle and gentle sunsets. The heavy-lidded Nubians intermixed with Egyptians and a motley assortment of tourists and residents from the deeper reaches of Africa. Man shouldn't be trying to redirect Allah's will in one of his lands. The bombs would be placed strategically in the days leading up to the target date. Hitting the structure at regularly placed spots would weaken it irreparably and the water itself would force those cracks open.

Soon.

Khalil pushed George's door open. Little did his prisoner realize that he had a role to play. Everyone had to work for room and board, even those who preferred not to stay. He smiled when he saw George sitting on his cot reading the Quran. George was coming along just fine. Nothing like fear to spur obedience. He tossed George a new book, on Cleopatra, which he himself had just finished. They might as well both learn more about this accursed place, the gift of the Nile and cradle of civilization.

He sat on the floor, back against the wall again, and gestured for George to move closer. Khalil had the power to bring in a more comfortable setup but they wouldn't be here long, so why waste the money? Out of the small window he could see the minarets of the medieval Al-Azhar Mosque, with its mix of sandy bricks and white. The view placed them in the Islamic – older and crumbling – part of the city. Whether George could find the area later was of little use and the streets were so tight and crowded he'd never find this specific set of rooms. And even if he did, Khalil would string it with so many explosives the investigators would be blown sky high before they crossed the threshold.

Then there was the election in six weeks.

His phone rang, and he answered, spewing forth in Arabic and ending with "Aswan." George's eyebrows shot up before he directed his eyes down, pretending that he hadn't heard the word. Oh George, little do you know.

"We need to move," he said and watched George's blank slate of a face. He wasn't in the mood for this crap. Khalil was now being actively followed in the streets; a reality that had become increasingly apparent over the past few days. Why were they being so open? Dark and seemingly from deeper Africa, this was a new bunch. He would need to disappear again, but first he would have to solve the George problem and fast.

"Thanks," was all George said. He paged through the book, spreading it open on his stretched out legs. The pages were an off-white color, barely, with rough edges. The book was a lovely contrast to the poverty and squalor of this neighborhood and the life they had decided to enter.

Khalil's phone rang again and he checked caller id in case it was Jennifer. No. He'd sent her back to the states and she was allowed to call him once: upon arrival. The closer a major strike loomed, the quieter communications got.

"So, when are we going? Where?" George mumbled, sounding indifferent, probably knowing Khalil wasn't going to provide much information but at least making an effort.

Good boy.

"Aswan," Khalil said, "Didn't you hear me on the phone." He laughed at George's response. Yes, it was too pat not to be a trick. Which is what made it such perfect information to share.

Cleopatra

George looked across the smoky air at Khalil. This part of the city stank. Sewage, spices, smoke, petrol, food and Khalil himself. It was hot and stuffy. Loud. He'd found hell. *Cleopatra* was a nice book; wouldn't *Dante's Inferno* be more appropriate? His nostrils spewed forth in black, and filth coated his eyes as he wiped them to grey on his sleeve, the only handkerchief he had.

Aswan. He'd never been, and it sounded exotic. If he survived. Was Khalil lying now or just planning to kill him in sharing that information? The mental games were never-ending and there was a new energy in Khalil. Why? Perhaps Khalil was planning to strew him with bombs and detonate him at the dam. Shit, was Khalil going to blow up the dam?

Information given? But why? You always had to question the information provided and the timing before you could access its quality or reliability. Khalil remained as enigmatic as ever.

"What are we both doing?" he asked and watched his adversary stare at the wall. A regular mutual past time. George waited. The din outside of yellers, horns and barking dogs was a welcome distraction. He heard a loud boom and let it go.

"The food is good here," he said, finally interrupting Khalil's reverie. "I had a wonderful spicy lentil and rice dish for lunch."

"Shut the fuck up," Khalil yelled and George just looked away. You got more confident if you didn't get shot first thing during captivity. Perhaps it came from a certainty that they were keeping you alive for some reason. Probably a misguided ideal and not worthy of pushing the limits yet being too subservient was always a bad idea because you lost your humanity. Meanwhile, coming on too tough got you a bullet. The balance was delicate to achieve. George just started paging through his book again. Ever mercurial, Khalil was getting increasingly jumpy.

"George, I'm going to need your help. I'm being followed. And it isn't only the Americans. I need a decoy."

"Not at Aswan," George replied, ever more confused. Khalil seemed different, all over the place and not thinking clearly. He wasn't normally this scattered but rather tended toward reptilian guile. The pressure of a bigger responsibility? Well, George knew weakness and how to strike. Khalil was slumped against the wall and sweating, but elegantly. It was his darting eyes that revealed the pressure. And those hands, long and tapered, with a sprinkling of evenly sparse black hair. They kept moving, which Khalil did whenever he lied. George needed more information, so he had to fake trust, which meant not being too outwardly trusting, a paradox but anything that came too easily was always suspect.

"Happy to help if you let me go afterwards," he said with a smile and watched those cold eyes focus on him.

Then the early evening call to prayer started, echoing through the tight alleys and hallways. That characteristic bump on Khalil's forehead was testament to the likelihood he'd leave for prayer. The raisin as it was sometimes jokingly called by the faithful who knocked their foreheads on the floor day in and day out all in the worship of their beneficent Allah.

He watched Khalil walk out on him.

Empty Nights

Khalil wasn't sleeping. The heat hadn't lifted from inside the small house and he shifted on his cot as he tried to sleep in the quiet of a deep night. He was still worried. The weeks were rushing by while his list of tasks seemingly only grew. Khalil wiped sweat off his forehead and heard himself sigh. Nothing in this plot was easy. A bomb only needed to blow up to take out the surrounding neighborhood while a bullet had to hit one man.

Then there were the false starts, the diversions and the surprises.

The realities were hitting him and thus the sleepless night. Radwan wasn't intelligent enough to ever truly become seasoned; he didn't have the ability to stay alive that long. He was basically a foot soldier acting out a more senior role. An assassin had to be so much more. A mistake? Khalil didn't even want to acknowledge that possibility. So much time and energy had been spent developing Radwan and he only needed to get one bullet right. Back in New York again, scouting his neighborhoods, Radwan was already happier. Africa, his home, was rough, and he'd already begun settling into delivered food and dry cleaners. Could Radwan toughen up enough in time to understand the gravity of the plot?

What set elite fighters apart from the rest? The qualities were easy to articulate but harder to predict, and not so different from what determined greatness in most areas of life. An ability to act under pressure and with judgment trumped pretty much everything else...but who could evaluate in advance how someone would behave in a crisis? It took character not to run when frightened or if events didn't go as planned. Intelligence helped, but it wasn't critical; instincts were better.

Each year eager young recruits joined his organization. They all assumed they'd survive training, even though their leaders knew otherwise. Should they be better vetted? In a volunteer army you took all comers.

Khalil had survived and, oh, what he'd survived. He thought back to when he'd first met his jihad, in a narrow Algerian alleyway, lit by rays of sunlight and coated with a fine sandy dust. The buildings were whitewashed clay, cool inside even on the hottest days. The air itself was heavy with the fear and violence of a long civil war that pitted brother against brother.

Getting recruited had been easy.

Khalil always loved school while his brother, Hassan, and cousin, Josef, not so much. Hassan had been a jihadist first, before Khalil stepped into his dusty footprints. They played soccer often before that, kicking a ball through the streets, shouting boys in tow. Later Khalil sheltered his brother in his arms on the same street, the blood draining until Hassan's breath ceased. His eyes stayed open but the light left in the instant it took to swallow hard and become a man. Hassan had died fighting, his thin arms hurling stones at the government soldiers until they extinguished the protest with a hail of bullets.

"Allah be with you..." Khalil had whispered as the parched earth accepted the blood sacrifice from the brother he'd worshiped since birth. The martyrs were starting to pile up even then. Everyone in Algeria fought. As a result, twenty percent of the population died within a few years. Protests in a poor country typically helped only the ultimate victors – who for some reason often seemed to be the targets of people's initial demonstrations – while the masses were left still begging for bread.

"Will you go?" The Imam asked, drawing his cloak around him. The hot sun burned into Khalil's flesh and his sweat dripped. But this was a holy man and he had made a request.

"In'sa Allah," Khalil whispered. He'd meant to be a philosopher and not a soldier. "Everything is moving so fast."

But the Imam walked away and Khalil picked up his burden. He was sixteen and his first mission was to aim sniper shots at government soldiers. If he did well he'd be on a plane to a training camp for the summer, then back in school.

"You may not return," the Imam said, refocusing his somber eyes on Khalil, ignoring the others. Dust was rising amidst the stone walls around them. A baby was crying.

"As Allah desires." Khalil tried to remember his dead brother's face, but he was just so tired and the guns were heavy. He started to walk, following the boy in front of him.

His mother would be angry. She'd cried when he'd brought home his brother's dead body. Most of the other mothers were proud to claim a martyr.

"Allah is a farce. No mother should face such grief." Miriam, in her hijab, face covered, had cursed at the women who tried to comfort her. The room was small with clean white walls and a few flowers in a vase, her rare but favored luxury. Hassan's body, still warm and soaked with blood, seemed to fill the space and he was settled on some pillows. Would Khalil be next?

"He died a martyr's death," the cobbler's wife said.

"A saint…" said the baker's wife.

Miriam spit at them and sent them away, cradling the body and alone, her husband long gone.

"For you, my brother, forever," Khalil whispered, shouldering his burden and heading off into the unknown. Even then he'd questioned the information given but it came from a holy man so he listened.

Not many years later he'd be in San Diego studying philosophy. And he'd learn about Machiavelli with his philosophy that the end justifies the mean. We all needed to reason through our choices, and always, Allah had to prevail. Even a boy could grasp that concept. But sometimes Allah spoke so quietly he was hard to hear, and then you needed a man's word to fill the void.

Khalil regularly called his mother, Miriam, both ever loyal and waiting by a phone at the baker's shop.

"When are you coming home?" she'd say, unafraid and defiant, alone without a husband or sons but never faltering in her bravery. Even a woman could be an inspiration.

"Soon, mama, soon," he'd lie. He would be sitting in his cheap apartment, without a stick of furniture, dirt poor but proud. Like her since he'd grown through her example and effort, a shoot that sprouted on different soil but with the same soul. They both knew if he went home he'd be killed by the Algerian government given its policy of no dissent. But someday…

"Allah be with you," she lied. But he knew she didn't really believe. The next call would be from his Imam.

"I have a mission for you," the holy man would whisper into the phone, and Khalil always listened.

Apples

eorge tried to sleep but thought instead of the apple tree, darkness not sheltering him from fear. Captivity. Not his strong point. Mostly, he created his own psychological turmoil but

143

now, when he finally thought he was freeing himself from those internal restrictions life had shown him how truly wrong he was.

So he turned his mind to the apple tree instead. For the short term, surviving his physical captivity was all that mattered. And having been on the other side so often, he knew, theoretically, what worked. Yet was theory ever important when reality looked us directly in the eye?

At least the apple tree was something concrete. George had grown up outside Boston, in Lynnfield, a small suburb. He didn't remember the town at all, having moved away at age eight, never to return, but he did remember his backyard. The vast lawn sloped down to a densely forested area in which he'd lost himself each afternoon, playing at being a knight, or Robin Hood, or a dragon.

The apple tree was on the front lawn next to the compact white house. Daffodils had bloomed on the lawn each spring, replaced with cascading snow each winter.

George had climbed the apple tree almost every day for years. From a few branches up he would jump and make pretend he was brave. Even then he had continually aspired to do better. If he died here and now how much did those ideals ultimately matter?

Coming home from work, his father would walk up to the tree and address George who was perched up on a branch.

"Nice day, George?" he'd ask, his grey eyes sparkling in the fading light.

"Yes, Dad," George would always answer. His days were so happy then: roaming around his backyard, making up fantasy worlds. "I killed a dragon in the jungle today. And how was your day?"

Then he'd jump down, always, to hug his dad.

"Tell me more," his father would ask, then listen for the answer. Years later, George would learn to listen as well but back then he'd just spoken.

"I took my sword and chased the dragon through the forest," George would say.

"Which brave knight were you?" his father would ask. "Did you think of ambushing him?"

"I didn't think that through, Dad," George would answer, in awe of his father's brilliance. "What else?"

"Don't quit," his father had instructed, his voice soft and his eyes, George's grey eyes, serious, perhaps beyond the gravity of the situation. "Always fight your enemy using any tactics that will work. If you don't, who'll protect the princess?"

And what had George learned from him, other than self respect, fairness and kindness?

He'd learned about cars. His father owned a Ford dealership, back when it was a thriving profession. So different from Emine's elite background but the lessons they'd learned seemed similar? Never give up and fight for what's right. Assume responsibility and face fear head on.

The cot was rough and the small house was hot. By day, guards watched his every move and their guns were real. Dialogue was non-existent; if they spoke English in this prison, no one had bothered to inform George. He had only Khalil, which was not enough, and the veiled woman who visited his room occasionally, bearing food.

But no half-assed, corrupt, stressed-out terrorist was going to beat him! George had found his rage and he was going to get out. He was going to survive. Khalil couldn't stand in his way forever because George would find a way around him.

"If not now, when? If not me, who?" George whispered. Rabbi Hillel's words, those of a Jewish scholar, were perhaps not the best way to fight an Islamic radical, but they were all he had.

"I'll make you so proud, Dad," George whispered. He wasn't afraid anymore. Finally, he'd really joined the war, and no one was going to fuck with him or his country. He wasn't some crazy kid on a suicide mission and he didn't want to die, but there was no part of war he didn't understand. Everything was, finally, making sense.

The war wasn't inside him anymore.

George shifted on the cot. His back hurt and he was deeply tired. How could he get out? The window was too small. Were the guards sleeping? In life there was always a way, if you just looked hard enough.

The tree's apples had been green, hard and tart; Granny Smith. George willed himself to remember, that time when he'd been strong and confident, though perhaps ridiculously naive.

Outside his room a shadow shifted and George knew someone else was awake.

Aswan. What did it mean? One thing for sure, he couldn't trust Khalil or his motives. If a 777 could disappear what other surprises could fate deliver?

Clarity

Khalil still wasn't thinking clearly. His world had gotten too risky and he didn't know how to fix it or even how many things needed fixing. Well, he didn't have the luxury of not moving forward because of the risks or a lack of information. If he ever stopped, the best he could hope for would be to get shot. The worst was so much worse.

He'd been followed in the market again today after being certain that he'd shaken the earlier tails. This crew was persistent and seemingly worked in teams. They also, oddly, didn't seem to mind that he'd spotted them. Seeing their black skin and robes, he couldn't place their exact ethnicity. Cairo was such a melting pot from around Africa that one needed to be an expert anthropologist to discern all subtle distinctions in the ever-transitory population. Would they reach out to him at some point with a message? Was that why they were circling ever closer? Had they wanted him dead, the opportunity had already presented itself many times.

In front of a café he said, "Aswan" loudly into his phone and left it at that. A tipoff for friend or foe? Khalil's life was full of risks and he wouldn't be as successful as he was without taking them. More forces wanted to stop a bomb than ensure it went off. Or a gun.

Still, his proximity to the unknown motivations of other men made him nervous. As the real danger of his own team was their willingness to die, these men's boldness showed a similar nihilistic attitude, ideology cloaked in service to the divine. How to respond? Especially when being wrong could mean death; he'd already been warned about his blown cover. Not that he wasn't happy to join Allah and the fellow martyrs but...

Mostly, this assassination was just a lot of work and so detailed in its precise planning. Targeted assassination was a relative unknown for him; he'd never attempted one in the United States before. So much could go wrong, and he trusted no one else in the chain of participants. His temple would start throbbing and he'd lose the ability to think. Luckily, this rarely lasted long before he'd get distracted with a detail and forget the fear.

He kept hearing Jennifer's last message: *In New York.*

Was she all right? She'd followed orders, and her message told him nothing.

But first, he had to get George on his way to Aswan without getting distracted by a woman. These next few steps were clear, and George was the perfect decoy. The media would love the story and it would get great coverage. A leak first.... Here and there another dropped comment or two.

Khalil stood up from his cot and headed toward George. Leaving his office, even smaller than George's room, he noted how little a man needed to survive. Osman had created a little shrine to his new technology with a laptop and stack of assorted disposable phones. A few t-shirts, some loose pants, a Yankees cap. Another pair of Nikes and an empty glass. His three books, for now, dog eared and friendly: *The Prince*; *The Quran*; *The Social Animal.*

The narrow hallway was empty, and paint peeled from the scuffed walls. George probably didn't realize how close their rooms were, and didn't need to know.

"Hello, old man. What have you been doing?" he said, entering the room and tossing another book George's way.

"Hello yourself, Khalil. Do they have toothpaste in this country?"

Khalil smiled. He should just shoot the pig. But he wouldn't.

"Hand me your Amex and it's all yours," he replied. George was reading that damn rabbit book and reclining like a lord on his rickety cot. The natural assurance of the man was unnerving.

"You're more western than you admit," George replied coolly, looking up from his book. "Is that an Under Armor shirt? Whose back did you rip that from?"

"George, let's talk about manners."

"I'm not happy."

"I know; but you'd be less happy if I killed you."

"Good point. What do you want?" George asked then got up from his bed to slump against their usual place against the wall. Khalil joined him. *I don't want to be here either, George,* he felt like saying. *I've never been safe myself. I envy you in that at least you have and yet you chose this bullshit.*

"Why are you here, George?" Khalil asked.

"Trying to right what's wrong. And you?"

"Same reason, I guess."

"We just don't agree on the ideology," George said.

"Is the ideology all that separates us?" Khalil asked. He valued the answer but didn't wait for it, having larger concerns. "Work for me, George, and I'll spare your life."

"Thanks for the offer, but I don't know how to take it."

Khalil watched George as he delivered the next part of his message. Still curious about the man's response or did he just want to see the resulting pain? "You may die."

"As my God and not yours decides."

"Tell me what you believe," Khalil requested and recognized suddenly that George was worth the money. With George he could talk, ask questions and learn. They had some time to kill. Why not enjoy insights from someone brilliant and knowledgeable? Not a lot like him in this corrupt and accursed country in part because those who had such intellectual gifts were hiding! Khalil felt the grubby floor beneath him as he sank deeper against the wall and waited for George.

"What I know or what I believe?"

Good question.

Dinner

Bright walked into the restaurant where Emine was waiting at the table with Ben, Carl and Bruce, sipping her dark Turkish coffee (the Turks, or at least the Ottomans, had ruled Egypt for hundreds of years not so long ago). Looking like Julius Caesar with his soft brown curls and broad shoulders, Bright carried himself like a conqueror. Emine noted that at 5'8 he'd never attain the full impact of that imperial air. Grudgingly, she acknowledged that he took over the room anyway.

He walked up to their table, waiters scattering, before him. He could have pulled a gun and shot them all in the softly lit room with its floor length views of the Nile and oyster white tablecloths. Still angry about his long distance rants she nonetheless held her tongue. A cold and calculating bastard, he did fly his own ass to Cairo to help his man out. Most billionaires wouldn't do that, even for a star hired hand like George.

"Our team just went to get our man," he announced, grabbing a chair with a smile and shocking them all. "Your man Buck, Eme, helped us out there."

"Bud," she corrected and pulled her cigarettes out of her bag. Having seen Ben's shock at the news, she knew enough to let him reply. Fearless and insanely talented, he had a much better relationship with Bright than she did.

"And who's filming it?" Ben asked a long pause, outwardly calm. Emine had to chuckle at his preternatural self-control. The tension in the air was thick.

"No one. I decided not to risk anyone's life this time," Bright replied with a smile. He snapped his fingers for a menu. "A few mercenaries but no trails back to us. Shit happens all the time in Cairo, and I've got lawyers to support our strategy of non-negotiation. I'm officially here to discuss whether or not I can pay a ransom." A waiter hovered.

Emine had to smile back. She watched Bright order a lamb kebab plate and a bottle of scotch with many glasses. Contemplating salads, he decided to forego one. Practically, he'd hide his tracks in rescuing George; then, if the shit hit the fan, his lawyers would support his bluff. Safety of plan for George was a crap shoot, but one had to at least question its possibility.

The soft lighting highlighted the dark circles under his eyes. Still attracted to him, Emine had a lot of questions for Bright and bad wishes for his wife, but she remained silent. Ben was fiddling with his cameras now, probably processing the data and wondering how to respond.

"Footage isn't worth jail or death, I suppose," Ben conceded and sucked down some coffee as Bright handed him a cut crystal glass of amber scotch.

"The US government has a policy against paying ransom," she finally told Bright, curious to hear his response. The Americans, of which Bright was one, felt that going to the media or paying ransom only encouraged more kidnapping and put the individual at greater risk. Rescue operations were okay, but often a long time in coming. Paperwork; policy; politics; excuses. Mostly, the official line encouraged waiting for communications from the captors before negotiating.

"Didn't pay any ransom," Bright responded as he attacked the breadbasket. "Came to negotiate only." He grabbed her glass of water, sloshing a little on the table. His grey suit, lavender shirt and silver tie were impeccable despite the flight and heat. Of course, he would have flown private and been met by a car.

"I like that Buck." He looked at her coldly.

"Bud," she replied and let Ben take over the conversation, describing the turmoil on the streets and rumors he'd heard from other journalists. She noted that Ben got a smile, which she hadn't.

And

"The end justifies the means?" George asked, curious at how much Khalil's mood had changed since he'd last seen him. Then, Khalil had been jumpy and distracted. Cranky. Mean. Now he seemed patient, as if he had nothing better to do than squat in the dust and chat. Neither was the real Khalil, but this one was a crudely veneered imposter. What was going on?

Khalil had gotten into the habit of quoting Machiavelli, so perhaps George could probe and find out the genesis of this new interest. Granted, Khalil had majored in philosophy about twenty years ago, but why this author now? Somehow George was skeptical that the choice tied into his mother.

When something made no sense check your assumptions and get more information. Doubtless you were missing an important fact.

Besides, George's best option, since he had no power, was to destabilize Khalil. Failing that, the more information he could extract from his adversary the more ammunition he had. George was still resolved to escape soon, tonight perhaps. But first he had to get through today.

This situation was grueling. George dug his fingernails into his palms and ignored the decrepit surroundings. Ancient worlds in the digital one weren't so backward anymore, despite their appearance, as technology and information had infiltrated minds globally.

"You quote a man who advised a prince on retaining his throne because you seek to prop up a likewise vulnerable deity?" George asked, alluding to Khalil's God but not wanting to be killed outright for disrespecting him.

"Western thought and not Islam," Khalil responded with a look of curiosity in his eyes.

George felt like Shahrazad, the queen of 1,001 Nights, who kept herself alive by intriguing the sultan through stories that carried over for said number of nights until her life was spared.

"So you've adopted it? Interesting," George flashed a grin of bravado. Even the weak sometimes had their pride or perhaps folly. He wasn't ready to show weakness; animals attacked when they sensed an opening, and Khalil could be primitive with that temper and willingness to kill. Fucking vampire, feeding on the weak and blowing them up. Quickly, George tried to force a more genuine smile, hoping that his thoughts hadn't just flashed through his eyes. Animals like Khalil survived on instinct and subtle unconscious signals.

Likewise, he sensed that Khalil, staring at the tobacco white wall, wasn't really paying attention. Also not his norm. Was he becoming bipolar out in the real world? So George pushed a line, again.

"Killing innocent people just to make a point...".

"No one is innocent," Khalil said, his eyes flashing. "And infidels are to die."

"Because it's in the Quran?"

"I can kill you for that, George."

"You seem to have murder on your mind today, Khalil. Why?" George saw Khalil back down. Which was a surprise. "I'm asking a question," he prodded, "You kill for a lot less than that, so should I start my prayers?

"Stop," Khalil said, and finally looked at George. "Tell me about why people love someone."

George couldn't believe his ears; talk about a switch in conversation. If Khalil wanted to talk about love he'd do it; even killers fell in love. Conversational topics didn't really matter much when your life was on the line.

"Well, we don't know exactly, but we do know a lot." George leaned into the wall, glad of its presence and taking the question seriously. He heard the familiar sounds of the street: the merchants, kids laughing and playing, the horns in the distance. The role of professor came easily to him. "Love has both a biological and a psychological component. There are neurological changes when someone is falling in love that we can track via a brain scan. Emotional need. And there is something in the eyes. People connect there, and studies can monitor the impact of certain interactions and how they affect eye contact. Have you felt it?"

"George, I don't fall in love. I travel." Khalil shuffled his black Nikes in the dust.

So why the questions?

"Of course, but you can fall in love. Everyone can." The dark eyes, with those amazing butterfly lashes blinked back at him, hooded and defiant.

"What am I going to do with you, George?" Khalil asked, not looking unsure but certainly deflecting the topic.

"You'll either kill me or you'll sell me for something you value more."

Khalil studied him quietly. His captor looked scrawny, yet he had all the power now. Before their situations reversed George hadn't realized that Khalil wasn't the type who needed to exercise power but rather wore it lightly. Especially interesting among terrorist leaders (boys playing with really big toys to prove that they mattered).

"What are you worth?" Khalil asked and George wondered how to answer.

"Depends on the currency." George closed his eyes. This situation was wearing on him. "What's her name?" he asked, merely eager to deflect the conversation off himself.

"Alice," Khalil said, and George opened his eyes in surprise to see Khalil holding his book. "I told you I need your help, George."

"You can borrow it if you like," he told Khalil, ignoring the reference to plans or plots. When the time came....

"She may have a name one day. What if she did?"

"We're not carrying on the same conversation," George said and studied his adversary.

"We never did," Khalil said. "That's why I was able to escape."

"Yes, but to what? This?" George gestured around the miserable hut. When Khalil had been in captivity he'd been in better accommodations by far.

"I'm free now," Khalil said, and stood up.

So that's why you're running away, George felt like saying, but watched Khalil slink out of the room instead, Alice in hand.

Just then he heard a loud explosion and the room shook. Not again.

Shadows

halil noticed the shadows moving outside the house when he left George's room. The late afternoon dusk was starting to fall and the buildings around them had taken on a golden

glow. Evening activity was picking up and the usual stench was replaced by smells of roasting meat and fragrant rice sprinkled with cardamom. He was dressed in simple jeans and a fitted shirt. Slipping out a side door leading not into the street but a neighbor's house he listened for sounds to follow the initial burst of explosions. No one was home as he walked into the cluttered room, with its mattresses and lone fan. Anyone there would have ignored him anyway, being his allies.

In Cairo the commotion that accompanied a bomb was decidedly less than in a western country. He could hear heavy boots and shouts next door. Exiting from the front he tumbled into the massed crowd, most gathered from a safe distance to observe the disruptive events. Based on the Land Cruisers, foreign here and thus owned only by those with too much money, someone fancy had come to spring George. "In'sa Allah" he whispered and headed to the Nile, quite a walk, but he wasn't needed anywhere else and could hear about the day's events there from those leaving Tahrir Square.

His implant George was good and ready to go with the whisper of a plot and his freedom. Khalil studied his new acquisition, Alice. They no longer had to figure out how to plant George; someone had done it for them. Smelling the food in the air, he felt hungry and decided to get some dinner first.

Smoke and Screams

The loud bangs, shouts, smoke, screams....familiar. At least here there were no alarms going off and further shattering his nerves. A lot of yelling in the streets but no sirens. Khalil didn't seem on his way back. Thankfully. George looked down at himself and all parts seemed okay. No blood. Now what? Had the danger just increased or decreased? The answer depended on who just blew the door open. If it was the good guys, then the next question was who would reach him first. George slumped on his bed and prayed to his own God, who seemingly did exist. When in doubt, what else can you do?

No. He stood up again, still in hell, of course, but when in doubt get out. The door was, surprisingly, unlocked when he gingerly tested it so he exited into a smoky hallway. Fire, tear gas, something else? No one in sight, so from memory he tried to retrace the original steps that had taken him from the front door to his jail cell. Right by the broken doorway, left past the wood frame chair, and then to the left of the water pipe. The rooms were small but pretty empty. Evidence of people was everywhere, from shoes to shia (tea) to a radio, still on and speaking forth on something in Arabic. No person was visible, nor did George hear gunfire. Had his guards abandoned their posts, or had something more sinister happened?

He continued his course, trying to reach freedom. This escape wasn't exactly what he'd been planning, but who said he got to decide when opportunity came.

A man grabbed him from behind, and he jumped.

"Quiet, I'm your friend," he heard in a harsh whisper against his ear. Khalil had been his friend, too? The accent was hard to place, especially with the soft tone. Well, clearly the gun in the man's hand had some bearing as to how friendly George would be. He felt another arm on his elbow guiding him somewhere he wasn't sure he wanted to go.

The man was wearing a mask (which seemed to be the thing in Cairo these days) and was dressed in a baggy black t-shirt and dark camouflage pants. George could see the bulk of muscles under the slight shirt and knew he wasn't some flunky. A pro? Not middle eastern. They rarely got that gym strong and bulky. He prayed for a rescuer. American. They weren't far from the front door, and George was gratified to see that his new friend used his own body to shield him as they made their way. Certainly a good sign. Nearing the door he saw a few similar-looking men providing cover, and one nodded.

Just as they were about to exit the front door gunfire erupted in their direction coming from the street. He heard the soft ping of a bullet hitting flesh and heard a soft cry. The gunfire on both sides continued, and then he saw a flash backing them up from a black Range Rover. Some scraggly looking men ran for cover, and one slumped as a bullet must have found a new home somewhere in his back. A dog began to howl and the evening call to prayer broke out, its long peals shattering the first fall of darkness. Luckily, the crowd began to disperse. Gunshots had that effect.

This part of the city, the old Islamic quarter in a city of mostly Muslims, was more devout than some other areas. The stone walls intermingled with cheap, bright storefronts and teashops decorated with those big smoking pipes. All of the signs, including the street signs, were in Arabic so it was only the golden mosque spires that gave him any sort of geographic orientation. Not that knowing where he was much mattered since his body had just changed hands from one group to a new one, which seemed friendlier. George felt his world like Alice's had turned unreal yet again. The choices we made could lead us into the strangest alleyways.

"Bright hired us," someone whispered in his ear, then hustled him to one of the two SUVs, providing cover until he was safely nestled in the back seat. Once inside, he was given bottled water, not so cold, and an *International Herald Tribune.* Since he didn't know the date, he wasn't sure if the issue was the current one. The President of the United States was making threats about the budget, and Israel was almost at war. China was building up their military presence. Burma was holding a free and fair election. Surprise. Meanwhile, his driver was on a walkie-talkie and his escort seated beside him, big gun and muscles tucked neatly in place.

The car started and within minutes was pushing its way through the throngs of onlookers, prayer goers, kids playing football and a peddler with lentils and rice. George had emerged from his hellhole with less than he'd entered having lost Alice. He hoped the book burned with Khalil in hell, along with the copy of the Quran he'd been given. What a way not to win a convert. He'd been somewhat positive about Islam before, but now just wanted to avoid it and all organized religion.

A few manic police cars flashed past, caught in the dinner and prayer-time crowds but making good time regardless with horns, sirens and lights going strong, George watched one hit the brakes as a donkey wandered in its path. Heading to the scene of his commando rescue and those gunshots or another crisis? George scanned the crowd, curious. The little round caps and long, drapey robes of the more religious were almost as common as Western dress in this neighborhood.

"What's the date?" George asked his rescuer, glad to be with people who spoke English. Briefly, the thought of Khalil and his current status crossed his mind, but he let it pass. He'd have time for all those issues after he'd showered and slept in a safe bed.

"On the paper," was the response, and the man gestured out the window at the massed faces pressed up against their windows in slow the traffic. Gawking. "Natives," he said, gesturing.

"I figured that out," George responded. "What happened to the people holding me captive?"

"Well, you saw that one guy got shot. Not sure who he was. The rest ran. We weren't there on government business and couldn't hang around asking questions or taking prisoners. Our goal was to get you out alive."

The man studied him coolly, brown eyes steady, and George recognized the glimmer of a South African accent. Mercenaries, but who was he to complain? Must have cost Bright big money, for George knew without asking who'd funded the mission. Karen would still be in their penthouse talking to his former government employers and doing as instructed. She'd complain that this mission was illegal, but – being the one just rescued – he was past caring about legality. He hoped Bright had concocted a cover story better than the truth. Alive and illegal was better than legal and still prisoner.

They were stopped at a light now, and a policeman with a rifle was waving it at the passersby as he blew into a whistle. The crowds didn't glance his way as they pushed through at their own pace. Soon the SUV was moving again. The sunset on the Nile was crimson mixed with burnt orange as they pulled up to the Ramses Hilton. Bright, in a crisp suit, was at the front doors to meet him with a hug.

"Let's get dinner," Bright said, tightening his arm around George's shoulders as he waved his two black Land Rovers away. He'd already paid them? What if they'd brought George back in a body bag? George marveled again at how easy and seamless the rescue had been, as if his captors hadn't even been trying hard to defend him or their abode. He couldn't help but wonder at their fate and that of Khalil, who seemed to have slipped into the dusk.

"Your captors ran like pussies," Bright declared, his eyes red but not slurring at all and his breath perfumed with expensive scotch. George could use one or two of those himself.

"Strange?" George asked and headed with Bright toward the fancier kebab restaurant inside the hotel, aware of the turned heads as he walked through the lobby but beyond caring.

Bright just shrugged his shoulders and like everyone else pushed George's elbow. George didn't resist, though what he really wanted was privacy, a shower and a good night's sleep. Getting information and updates from Bright was probably a better choice and he'd be able to get a drink faster that way too.

"Thanks for rescuing me," he said, feeling tears beginning to flow. Good God, he appeared to be free and safe, so why cry now? He'd have to call Karen, he reminded himself.

"I need an interview. Did you take any pictures?" Bright asked. George just shook his head. Now he really did need a drink, badly.

Bright handed him a new cell phone, a glistening touch screen model. "Lost yours, right?"

With regret, George nodded. All those numbers and pictures gone. The new phone already had two new calls and messages for him. He couldn't even shower and shave before being back at work?

Noting the stares as they entered the restaurant, George knew his clothes were as dirty as his body and a scraggly trace of a beard completed his look.

Bright ignored it all and kept talking about the plans and broadcasts. He was considering staying in Cairo to watch over George personally.

"No need," George mumbled before Bright was off and talking again.

New Direction

"What a mess," Khalil mumbled as he got behind the wheel of his Fiat, whose back seat was still stained with his lover's blood despite the efforts to clean it up.

His minions had fled during the raid and George was gone, clearly back to the Americans. The seeds of his role had been planted within, but Khalil had wanted to add a lot more disinformation. Now, who knew how George would use the limited information he thought he had about Aswan? Of course, Khalil had already been planning to release George, although that would have been difficult without raising suspicion. At least that issue was resolved even though the timing was terrible.

Thus Khalil had shot the head of security at their ramshackle little prison in the heart of Cairo, aiming the bullet right into the soft spot where the skull met the spine as he blubbered and begged. The rest of the guard's on duty had trembled when the gun went off, so he sent them to a camp deep in the Libyan desert, with its high white sand dunes and snakes, near the border of Gaddafi's former country. Only one of his men had shot back during the commando raid, and that one got to remain in Cairo. The rest needed more training to learn what real terror awaited them, should they run like cowards again at the sound of gunfire.

At least Khalil hadn't seen his dark African tails in the streets that day. They must have been the ones who betrayed his prison and George's captivity, stalking him until they accomplished their goal. How they'd found him he'd never know. But no secret was ever safe when more than one person knew it.

Would the tails of darkness re-appear and start shadowing him again? Their disappearance indicated that their only interest had likely been George. They were probably mercenaries who didn't want to mess with geopolitical games or squabbling with other armed organizations. A fight over a man was honorable and to be expected. Fights over ideology led to wars.

He himself was in the desert now, heading for Aswan. He could have sailed on a chartered felucca or crowded steamer, but too many people would have seen him, a risk he didn't want to take. Khalil was also avoiding the narrow strip of fertile and hydrated land that tracked the Nile upriver and deeper into Africa. Ninety percent of the country's people lived in this band, not the vast rolling carpets of barren gold sand dunes. Driving through the lightly traveled desert made him invisible, and he chose the roads to the west, meaning the Sahara, or Libyan, desert. Horned vipers and cobras kept him safely inside his car. Besides, he'd already spent plenty of time in these locales and was in a hurry.

Five oases nested like green islands amidst the khaki ocean that spread from the green perimeter of the Nile across much of northern Africa with no boundaries to mark borders or tribes. Fresh water springs, palm trees and men carrying coolers of iced cokes littered the greener stops, but in the distance were mountains, in varying shades of black or white. The valleys were strewn with the wrecks of Roman mud brick forts, long ago built to defend trade routes that had since been buried in sand. The Romans, when they had long ago controlled Egypt, irrigated the land and planted grapes and wheat, exporting it to Rome. They also built temples for worshipping their own gods but eventually abandoned their settlements to the tougher nomads of the desert.

Seth, the ancient Egyptians' god of Chaos who'd murdered his own brother, Osiris, ruled here and the harsh territory seemed his due. His ethos seemed to be rapidly spreading beyond the sandy expanse of this realm.

Of course, in ancient times, before the water dried up, the desert had been a savannah supporting both plant and animal life. Lions, giraffes and elephants had roamed the vast plains, and left fossils as a testament to their presence. Ancient man hunted in the same areas through which Khalil now drove, though he was winding along one of the many roads built when Nasser re-connected the country to its deserts. As with many reforms, the effort had limited long-term impact since it never led the Egyptians to leave the densely populated Nile Valley and re-settle this land.

But Nasser had led the last Egyptian revolution in the 1950s. A lot had changed in Egypt since then, but not the desert.

So Khalil kept driving, listening to his new right-hand boy, Osman. What a coup. Osman had an encyclopedic knowledge of technology and knew which types of torrents, or packets, or lockers, or bits and bytes could be sent and how, then tracked or not tracked. The words whizzed by Khalil's ears, and he understood little of Osman's insights, but what he did comprehend was that some computers and sites couldn't be traced and, while encryption was better, it wasn't always necessary since the digital world was too large to police or patrol. The laws and law-enforcement capabilities hadn't kept up with the technology, which was to his advantage. Moha wasn't the only smart one in this family. Khalil's digital education was proceeding as they drove together.

"Nothing lasts and nothing is traceable," the boy said solemnly, staring out the window and whispering more to the wind than to Khalil. "We change logins, identities, postings, messages and even web sites at will. Disposable, pre-paid phones and codes with as few lines as possible leading people nowhere online. No one needs to ever connect with a real human being."

Osman gave Khalil a quick glance, then studied the smartphone in his hands. Android?

"To what purpose?" Khalil asked, not taking his eyes from the road long enough to evaluate the device. He still wasn't sure he could trust the boy's driving. Sixteen at best? But he always had some electronic device in his hands and spare batteries in his pocket. Most of it was clean, so no-risk. Games and homework? A definitional distinction.

"Keep your network invisible," Osman continued, confident in his technology. "The authorities can't even estimate how much piracy there is online, let alone stop it. The same with fraud, gambling, drugs and prostitution. Done right, you've found a new frontier."

Osman shifted in his seat as a big overloaded truck passed them on the other side of the road and the tiny car shook. Khalil sped up and passed a mostly empty bus, blaring loud techno-Arab-rock into the vast air. In an

Aerosmith t-shirt, battered jeans and black rubber sandals, Osman looked like any teenage punk, but his mind was already automating the jihad and taking over Khalil's online organization. Support sites, YouTube sermons and sites both selling materials and accepting donations.

"As long as no one can trace it back to you, anything can be posted online. The worst thing that happens is it gets taken down."

"Well," Khalil interrupted, "We don't want our messages found and understood." The risks could be devastating.

He slowed behind another one of the puttering buses circa Moscow thirty years before with men hanging off the top and out the windows, robes and shirts blowing. Their Audi's air conditioning was dead, so everything inside their car was blowing as well, warmed more than cooled by the hot air. Closing the windows would have cooked them both.

"I can guarantee that they won't," Osman said with a smile. "You studied the code? We can hide messages in pictures, then fade out some pixels, or colors, to make them readable. Put them on a blog or sharing site in the comments based on a code. Create web sites that are re-built every half an hour. The possibilities are almost endless."

"And unless the authorities capture you, I'm fine?" Khalil glanced over at the boy. So young, smart and brave, he needed more soldiers like this one. Moha should be proud; he'd raised a valuable warrior who wasn't destined for the front lines, now or ever. This one might eventually run the whole organization. Khalil was protecting him from the camps and battlefields where he rarely ventured himself anymore. The closest they'd get was KK's assassination since it was too important for Osman not to be directly there. He'd probably monitor police dispatch information from a hotel room. He could text a warning, then make it evaporate in an instant. The miracles of technology. File-sharing sites, pixels and password-protected sites. Facebook, Twitter and Google +. Never Foursquare! He was learning a whole new language of code words and digital concepts with so many places to stash and hides bits of information and, eventually, money.

Before going to Aswan they had to stop at one of his blistering hot training camps in the desert to check on his less golden boy, Radwan. The

burning sun had moderated, and Khalil saw that the shadows were length-
ening as evening started its descent. They should arrive at the end of dinner
and could grab food at the camp. Would he be happy with what he found
there?

Scotch

mine watched George across the table, saw his head drooping
almost into his grilled kebab nesting on rice, another expensive
scotch in his hand as Bright toasted his courage. George had
a grey shadow across his cheeks and chin that in this part of the world
wouldn't even be called a beard. He looked dirty, his clothes were a mess,
and those smells…! Bright had already gotten Ben to shoot thirty minutes
of them both talking on camera, loving the look of his star reporter just back
from captivity, dazed and half drunk. No one else got a word in, except,
barely, the star reporter himself.

"Just glad to be back," George slurred, exhaustion and stress evident.
Emine downed a slug of the scotch as she studied him, feeling the rough
enveloping warmth.

The restaurant, Falafel, one of the more touristy in the Hilton, featured
traditional food and over-the-top gilt décor. Deep blue walls were accented
with gold trim and red panels. A short stage commandeered the center of
the room, where belly-dancing shows were mostly staged for foreigners,
though increasingly frowned upon in modest Cairo. Indeed, since the 1950s
the dancers were no longer allowed to show their stomachs, which had to be
covered up by baggy harem pants and coin or bead-heavy bra bodices. But
her group wasn't here for the food or the show. They were here to work, and
Bright was domineering Ben's camera work. Streaming live? She hoped not,
but wouldn't put it past her ambitious and competitive boss.

Emine picked at her fish, ignoring the rice and guzzling down the imported deep red wine. She preferred darker crimson wines – with and in
preference to – just about any food; the heat here had killed whatever hunger

she might have felt. If she stayed in Cairo much longer she wouldn't be able to eat on the streets during the day. Ramadan was coming and the alleyways were getting crowded with pilgrims ranging from the deeper Muslims of Africa to revolutionaries and Islamists.

And Bright had managed to slip that reality into his interview with George. He loved to attack Islam, hoping to incite some Fatwa, or pronouncement of death by fanatics, so long as it didn't fall on his own shoulders. Up the ratings.

The press. Her world, but too often just about the next hot story, never mind the glazed look in George's eyes and the hell he'd narrowly escaped.

"Leave him alone, Bright," she said, wrecking that part of his interview with his zombie boy on film. But Bright just gestured Ben and his camera in her direction.

"Tell us your version of the kidnapping," her boss requested. She thought about telling him to fuck off but knew if she did he'd just harass George instead, so she complied, reminding herself to stay away from the wine as she did so. No pictures with alcohol. Besides, didn't the people of Egypt deserve to have their chaos reported? She could fill that role to give the poor a fair hearing, with the rampant corruption and lack of jobs, while she had the spotlight.

"These people are starving, but more slowly than in a normal famine zone. They have no hope or jobs and the revolution is creating utter chaos."

Bright cut her off and Ben avoided her eyes as he turned his camera away. The truth about the masses never sold as well as personal drama, like George's story of being a captive American.

Ben began checking his footage and taking an occasional bite of some sandwich he'd ordered. She knew that Bright loved Ben's quietness. "Ben is all art," he'd bark at her when she argued over how he wanted to slant a story. "You're just a pain in the ass." Got to love him.

Bright's cell rang and he sprang up. "My lawyer. Gotta figure out how to keep us all out of trouble. The Egyptians are more worried about their damn revolution than stirring up a scandal. Just need to know if we can ever return to the States."

Ben's eyebrows shot up and he stared at his boss; then he must have realized he'd been holed up in his hotel room when the commando mission went down, so he'd be fine. In a second his eyes were back on the footage, and Bright was out the restaurant, leaving his own food untouched. Emine noted that he'd taken his drink.

"Aswan, they're planning to strike at Aswan," George said as soon as Bright was out of earshot. He must not trust their boss, either. With Bright everything was a story; George was ex-secret service and public service; she was just a fanatic.

"How do you know?" she asked, curious but also suspicious. They hadn't expected him to escape when he did, but – nonetheless – why would his captors trust George with key information? Unless they'd been planning to kill him?

"Khalil mentioned it. Wanted me to help him. He had a task for me, but the raid happened before he could set me in motion." George guzzled his water, then started to cough. "I need to call my old boss in Washington. It's still afternoon there."

"Go," she replied. "I'll tell Bright you were exhausted. We need to get down to Aswan. Was Khalil headed there himself?"

"I don't know, but that seemed to be the implication," George stood up from the table and wobbled a bit. Emine felt herself soften. Ben's eyes were on her and returned her glance. The expression in his eyes was complex, but she knew him well enough to guess at his emotions. George was a pawn in fate's hands now and was of little consequence in search of the bigger story. They all did it; George as well. Once the scoop started to roll, they'd all follow.

She turned back to George, who had noticed the look that passed between her and Ben.

"We can leave first thing in the morning for Aswan," he said, foregoing any comment on the personal. "I need to reach Washington first, even if that just complicates things."

"Shower and sleep also!" Ben said with a smile, but his eyes were floating down the Nile already heading into the depths of Lake Nasser, the manmade lake that had resulted from the newer dam and the rushing waters of Aswan itself.

How to deal with Bright? Had she been a coward, she'd have left it to Ben and his gentle touch. But Ben caved too easily if it meant getting a better story. Bright needed to bring additional security if they were to chase the story, and she'd be the only one with enough nerve to suggest they do the right thing.

As Emine guzzled more wine she heard Arab music start, throbbing with emotion, melodic and modular. The belly dancing was beginning, and three women with flowing costumes and long dark hair came out onto a small stage. Slight, but curvaceous, they began to sway with the music, their bodies mimicking the repetitions of the traditional musical phrases. Tension built, then climaxed, repeating the pattern again and again, with bright colored scarves waving like hummingbirds. Emine found the crowd's response more interesting than the somewhat predictable dance, more hip than belly.

Glancing at her phone, she noted a text from George: "They're sending a team our way...." Bright had already charged the dinner to his room, so she gestured to Ben and they headed for the hallway. He nodded, and she understood that George had texted him as well. She'd need to find Bright and fill him in: he was no longer master of this production.

Rabbits

eorge reached his room feeling as though he hadn't yet emerged from his rabbit hole. Nothing around him seemed any more real than it had been when he was a prisoner. His ability to think clearly had seemingly vanished.

He should have called Washington first, but Bright had grabbed him, grungy from the filth and squalor of his captivity and gotten him on camera ASAP. All in the name of authenticity or some such bullshit. Stripping his gross clothes he dropped them into the trash. Now he was taking a shower to wash the grunge and desperation off his skin. At some point he'd call Karen though she'd already been notified he was okay.

His fear was starting to lift, but his replacement emotions of concern for what Khalil intended to blow up next were building fast. Why couldn't the bastard just stop killing people? As if the world itself wasn't bad enough!

Lathering quickly he skipped the shave; the dam was being targeted, so he had to move. He slipped into light cotton sweat pants and a white oversized t-shirt and turned down the air conditioning on his way to the phone. Why did the room temperature in Western hotels seem to be inversely pegged to how hot its location was? He also hit the minibar and grabbed another scotch. He hadn't yet had enough to drown his nightmare.

Dialing the number he still remembered so well from eighteen months earlier he got a secretary.

"May I help you," she said, not identifying whose office he'd reached. But he recognized her voice.

"Beth, it's George Harris. I need to speak with Tom. It's urgent; national security." George heard the silence on Beth's end and the inhale and exhale that accompanied it. He used that second to bolt down his scotch and immediately felt warmed. No, he shouldn't drink too much before the call, but it was too late now for that concern.

"One second," and that was that; he was on hold. God bless her for being able to prioritize and get him quickly to the right party. Bullshit questions only wasted time. Staring at the wall, he couldn't believe he was still conscious. The room was fine; in a slightly aging chain hotel, it had been kept in pristine condition. Things were too beige for him, but such seemed to be his fate whenever he wasn't fearing for his life. Nothing like the Indiana Jones movies he'd watched, envious. Still, the lights on the Nile outside his window were pretty great.

"George, heard you got nabbed," Campbell said, a careful tone in his voice. Waiting. Never lead anyone when you aren't sure whether they're safe.

"I'm out. At the Hilton and..."

167

"Shit, George. You need to be with a government team to give them a briefing on what happened! What are you doing at the Hilton? What if someone else comes after you? Again."

George understood Campbell's frustration and momentarily wondered at the coincidence of his former government work and how quickly he'd been nabbed. But why hadn't his captors pushed for more intelligence information? Now a minor celebrity, googling him was barely an effort and his whole past filtered through Wikipedia and myriad other sites. Khalil already had much of the history, so why hadn't anyone pushed him harder for data or at least insight, even though he'd been rescued surprisingly quickly? Something didn't make sense so his assumptions must be wrong.

"You're right," was all George responded, feeling his fatigue and unwilling to speculate on the unknowable. He wondered what would come next in his crazy mixed up reality. He'd clearly been a pawn, but whose pawn? Did his role fit into a larger scheme or was it just a random piece in a freeform game? He couldn't help suspecting that Bright had set him up somehow. At one level, it didn't make sense, but at another, only someone with a reckless mindset would send a former government operative into a war zone. Or was George now getting paranoid, as prisoners were known to do?

"You were reported missing, and we were working the streets, government and military. Waiting to hear anything. Tough, you know," Campbell said, understating.

"It was tougher on me," George replied. "Iranians nabbed me and sold me to Khalil…"

"Khalil!" Campbell exclaimed. Would he stop interrupting?

"Listen to me….Khalil mentioned Aswan. He was going to use me in some plot there somehow, but I got…um…out." George realized he hadn't heard back from Bright about how he needed to legally phrase his "escape" so as to protect the mercenaries who'd risked their lives to save his. Damn, this maze was complicated.

"The dam or the town?" Campbell asked, his voice calmer now.

George could hear the question hanging unspoken in the air: when? But on his end the nagging unease about how few questions he'd been asked kept building and distracting him. How had events unfolded again? They'd caught him his first morning, out in the crowded streets after the military had fired on protestors (the last not unusual here). Who had known he was coming? Everyone. Bright had covered his assignment on air, internationally. Set up, he'd fallen into a neat trap? Then, he was handled with kid gloves? Well, he didn't know what to think any longer.

"The plot thickens," he whispered.

"George, what did you say?" Campbell asked and George heard sirens outside. Sometimes Cairo made Manhattan seem like a ghost town.

"Nothing, really," he replied. He needed to control himself. Once you realized your vulnerability, playing it cool was best so no one would notice how weak you really were. He was caught between strong forces: Bright and his obsessive search for the perfect story, Campbell and his cold focus on national security, Khalil and his complex and twisted aim of destroying the western world, and Emine and Ben, who wanted to win Pulitzers. George was a mere vessel for their desires. Then there was Karen and her ambition to ascend Manhattan society. He just wanted to hit the pillows and get some sleep. He also wanted to stop Khalil from blowing up the Aswan Dam. That he could do.

Such a potentially destabilizing blow made a twisted sort of sense. Seemingly, in any crisis these days in a Muslim nation, it was the Islamists who filled the vast gulf of immediate needs. They were the only ones who had the organization and resources to provide food, medicine and shelter. Egypt would fall apart if the newer dam blew and flooded the crops and countryside. Khalil's group could organize the ever more chaotic country.

Not on George's watch. He'd do whatever it took to ensure that didn't happen.

"Khalil going soft on you?" Campbell asked.

"Amen," George responded. "It doesn't make sense, does it?"

"Hell no. Too bad you got out." George heard Campbell chuckle but couldn't join in. Something about him being the pawn wasn't so funny.

"Now what?" he asked.

"We'll need to de-brief in the field. You'll have a plane to get to Aswan in the morning. Eleven-thirty a.m. with my team on board; they'll pick you up. I'm going to have a busy evening, but at least that much is confirmed."

"You can meet that timetable?" George asked. Skeptical? No. He was a believer but not trusting much right now since the basic facts seemed improbable. He really was like Alice in her Wonderland as everything kept turning upside down. Campbell was a pain, but he knew how to work the powers in Washington.

"Things are more bureaucratic than before, but I'm willing to push hard on this one. We need to stop Khalil, and I'm willing to fight to for that goal."

"Let's get dinner when I'm in Washington," George replied, reaching across the miles of fiber optics trying to reestablish their once close bond.

"You won't make it to Washington…or I won't be here…or something. But I like your show."

George felt the familiar discomfort whenever someone said so as he hadn't adjusted to being famous yet.

"Too true," was all he replied. Campbell was always the pragmatist, which meant George would get his flight and team but not the dinner.

"Now I'll ring off," Campbell stated and George heard his stress. He rubbed his forehead, feeling the same. "But I might call with a few questions later. First, what exactly did Khalil ask and what were your answers?"

George heard the question, but his exhausted brain started to spin. He was so tired.

"There's been chatter," Campbell said when George didn't answer. "Aswan has been a recurring theme. I'm trying to get clearance to disclose more. What else do I need?"

George yawned. Need? So much. How about a time machine to go back into history and reduce the economic equality, hatred, lack of opportunity and desperation in these countries falling into revolutionary turmoil.

"You need to share information with me," George asserted. How else could he stop Khalil? "The turmoil here is terrible, and if he succeeds I can't begin to imagine the repercussions."

"A revolution is an idea which has found its bayonets, as Napoleon Bonaparte once said," Campbell responded. The closet intellectual? "I don't envy the Egyptian people."

"We need to help. Hellish hatred and a violent mood that just hits the crowd out of…".

"Gotta go," Campbell snapped and hung up.

A flight to Aswan tomorrow? Would Khalil be there?

Night Sounds

Khalil woke to noises that didn't fit the desert night. The air was cold and the vast emptiness a deep darkness befitting Allah himself. Infiltration? No, he didn't sense that danger. So what were the sounds and why did he feel so uncomfortable?

The moon shone brightly this evening and he spent a second, once he'd left his bed, pondering it. Distant and mysterious, which also made it harmless, it was a constant and shined nightly. Did one always want to explore the unexplained?

Well, he did. With war came danger, and his war trumped personal safety. Khalil grabbed his flashlight and headed into the night.

In the desert at night the risks are few. Snakes and other reptiles fear the cold and dark, and they hide when the evening chill settles. The winds might blow, making flying sand a problem, but the real risk was always other men. Here armed guards and booby traps protected Khalil's camp. He headed to the sounds, unsure but somewhat confidant.

They came from a tent not far from his own. The grunts unsettled him but knowledge is power and he had a gun in hand. "Allah, guide me," he whispered to the night, what he might see beginning to dawn on him.

Squishing through soft sand, Khalil ignored his surroundings. The moon lit the flat desert but he wasn't interested. He drew apart the flaps of the nearest tent and let his eyes, used to the dark by now, take in the reality. He'd use his flashlight only if necessary.

Khalil saw a man's back and buttocks, jutting and moving in a motion he almost recognized. Under him was another man, similarly grunting and undulating. The man on top was Radwan, and Khalil recognized the receiving partner as Aaban, a Somali. The sounds were louder now that Khalil was in the tent and he knew he'd never look the bottom boy in the face again. Pussy.

Martyrdom erased all sins and this one was large. But it was also a reality dating back to antiquity. Deny men access to a woman's open legs for his cock to run wild and he'd turn to other men or even boys. Then there were those who preferred a man's hard body to a woman's soft one. Were the virgins in Allah's paradise male or female? Perhaps it depended on the martyr and his definition of paradise.

Men liked to fuck. What they fucked mattered little if they cleansed their souls in jihad. Radwan would be blown to shreds and Allah would accept what was left of his soul. Now the boy couldn't argue his earthly fate; the boy was impure and had to be freed of his sins and he could face his choice of virgins later, after their mission and his martyrdom. Sin was Allah's blessed responsibility, while Khalil had to focus on the actual shot that took a man to paradise.

The panting from the tent intensified and Khalil heard the men as they cried out louder. He stifled his disgust. The cries signified a loud end and the motions stopped. Khalil turned away and let the tent's flaps close behind him, making his way back to his own tent.

He owned them now. Looking down at his cell phone he grinned as he scanned through the photos of firm buttocks and faces in bliss. We are our own assassins, he thought and dived back into bed.

Khalil's cock was firm now as he slid under harsh blankets, the cold biting against his skin. He rubbed himself and thought of Jennifer, how she let him ram hard into her with little warning. Front or back, she was always open. How those western women begged, always the whores.

The promise given was a necessity of the past; the word broken is a necessity of the present, as Machiavelli said. Khalil had hoped he could keep Radwan, so highly trained and valuable, alive in the KK assassination. Now he realized that his wish had been a violation of Allah's will. The original Assassins had always known they would die; that certitude made their success guaranteed as their focus was on success not their own base fears and desires. Khalil was guilty of a sin as well...protecting his asset, who was but a base sinner. Now he decided that Radwan should take more risk to succeed. His accomplishment would be his salvation, and he needed to make a grand gesture. Khalil tossed and turned, not sleeping, as he tried to envision what that would mean. A grand gesture in Manhattan? He had a tough act to follow in that regard.

We're our own worst demons.

A new plan began to ferment in his mind. It would take some effort to get it appropriately ripened but, if he could make it work, the results would be divine and a credit to his cause. The world was increasingly eaten up by protests, spreading from Africa through the whitest parts of Europe. What he needed was a sacrificial black, yet Radwan was much too light. But his lover, Aaban, with those high cheekbones and lovely mahogany eyes, was very black indeed. Pledged to do as the jihad required, he'd be thrilled to go to New York with Radwan.

Khalil, comforted that he had a new branch of his tree to seed, finally fell into a peaceful sleep.

GET LOST

Airplanes

Emine was packing again as usual, headed someplace new. But for a change she was going to do more than take pictures. Entering George's world had upgraded her into participating in important events. Some people are meant to create history; others document; more just wait for events to unfold. George seemed to have a nose for the former. What other journalist kept finding himself in the middle of key plots of destruction? One of the documentarians herself, she envied the intrigue of his life.

His manner remained so cool, as if he hadn't spent a grueling hour on the phone with national security after Bright's interviews not to mention being held by his ex-Al Qaeda prisoner for almost a week. He'd called her at 12:01 a.m., though his voice wavered, to tell her to pack for Aswan in the morning.

"How are we getting there?" she asked.

"Don't know," he responded. "Got to get off the line and call Bright."

She hung up, wondering why Bright was always just Bright, with never a first name. Then she requested a wake up call and tried to sleep without success. She'd lost the two people she'd loved most in life and sometimes, mostly at night, they haunted her.

Piers, of course, her fiancé and more but what exactly she was uncertain. Was he, perhaps, the first person who believing in her had taught her faith in herself? When you're used to disappearing into the background such lessons can be hard to grasp. But he'd also set her free from many fears to begin chasing dreams. Before, in her world, only men, like her father, had been allowed to change the world. Piers had led her to Bright, his boss. And that affair, when she'd been so broken, had given her professional opportunities that she'd never believed possible.

Selim, her brother and only one year older, was a more brutal loss. They'd been sent away young to boarding school, like many of their friends. She'd never been alone at school until the year he graduated, leaving her behind. He'd headed to London and hard-core drugs, teetering further and further toward the edge until he fell off.

In high school she'd started dating and having sex with Omar, that beautiful Saudi boy with the butterfly eyelashes and six-pack abs. Her first boyfriend. New to the school and having no friends there, he'd spent hours at the gym. Omar had gotten a teacher fired because she seduced him. Rotten old witch. Emine. still a virgin at sixteen, had been eager to try sex. With Omar it had been divine. Neither of them feeling alone anymore.

"You'll never leave me?" she'd asked Omar once – and lived to regret it. Everyone had always left her before, and she'd wanted something of her own. Which was Selim? Perhaps he'd gotten jealous, but he challenged her and her lover. She had sex with Selim in front of Omar, then her brother bought them all an extravagant trip.

Omar faded away after that and she never missed him. Selim faded into drugs, she'd faded into shopping and parties. Too many men.

The question always remained: how could she have saved Selim? She'd seen the increasing drug use and risky behavior as he sped his Porsche along the hairpin curves on the roads near their boarding school his senior year. Drunk or stoned most of the time by then, his friends seemed to pull back from the worst of Selim's excesses.

Bud had tried to shelter her from the worst. "You don't want to see, so go to sleep and let me handle him," he'd urged, and she'd escaped for a while.

Then, late one night, Emine had walked out on him, snorting cocaine as if his nose was starving. A drop of his blood hit the mirror he was using, a red spot in the white snow. His new girlfriend and worst influence ever started to laugh hysterically.

"Idiot," Emine said as she left with a banging door and hard feelings. The next morning was their last final and Selim joined his girlfriend on a flight to England. Emine had rarely seen him after their fight but they still spoke often. Her last year at school had been lonely but she graduated and moved to a little apartment on Paris' Left Bank.

The night she heard Selim had ODed she thought she'd have to kill herself. Even in their worst times he'd only been a phone call away, and their late night conversations had never ceased, even as their lifestyles diverged.

"Eme, I'm always here for you. Always. You know that," he'd say to her when she got scared and felt alone. Then one day she really was alone.

So she drank. And took pictures. Now she was going to Aswan, following someone who probably knew more about real life than she ever would. Perhaps if she paid close attention she'd learn why everyone clustered around George, her new magic man.

And so she finally slept, wrapped in pillows, a comforter and not much else. Waking to that cottonmouth of a serious hangover again, she ordered coffee and started throwing her stuff into duffel bags. This was her life.

Outside the sun promised another blistering day. Aswan. She'd never been. No reason before for a war photographer to join the tourist crowd. Would George get her a Pulitzer? One thing she knew for sure was that her chances with him were better than without.

They were quite a team, with the ambitious Bright and Ben tagging along as well. If nothing else, she was preparing for a real adventure. Khalil preparing to blow Aswan and flood Egypt? George had better have intelligence to share.

Darkness

The knock on George's door was startling and the room, heavy curtains drawn, was still dark. He glanced around, relieved that at least he was in the Nile Hilton not his back-alley jail.

But he'd gotten little sleep the night before.

"I have another question," Campbell would ask long distance, his voice mostly patient but developing an edge as his own night deepened. The time difference between Cairo and Washington DC was six hours. George, well into his own nighttime, had reached Campbell late in his afternoon. Both were testy. But Campbell kept calling back with more questions, even though he'd acknowledged that a personal de-brief would be necessary.

"I wish I were still a field guy and could join you in Egypt," Campbell said finally. "But I can't leave here, so I need to ask one more question."

"It's very hot in Cairo," George replied, feeling his head as it threatened to crack open and so tired he could barely hold himself upright. Finally, at 1:30 a.m. Cairo time, he called it quits.

"I just escaped my captivity. The questions, you know, will go on and on. It's late."

"Fine," Campbell responded curtly. George could picture him, the sort who disappeared into the background and quietly listened. Until he started to yell. There was always more to these spooks than there seemed.

"We're sending you two agents, for both protection and support. They'll brief you," George watched what appeared to be a dung beetle, the ancient sacred scarab, scatter about his room and pause at a crumb.

"Goodnight?" he asked, deciding to rest his head on his pillow.

"I need a few more minutes from you," Campbell insisted.

"Not another question," George whispered, hoping not to fall asleep mid-sentence.

"Tomorrow then," Campbell barked and hung up.

George wondered what the spooks would disclose, or if they'd just ask questions. In the past, he'd complained bitterly about the "classified" information kept from him. And he'd officially been CIA back then, though not at the highest clearance level. Now he was a reporter.

He knew his old boss would be on the phone all night, begging, conniving and negotiating. Government could be brutal. But he also recognized that he couldn't be in better hands. People had died in the previous go-round with Khalil, also a last minute exercise, but many fewer than would have been sacrificed in Khalil's larger plan targeting numerous McDonalds.

He settled his head deeper into the soft down pillows but couldn't quiet his mind. Would Campbell get him better security clearance and solid information? He needed it to stop Khalil! His head swam and the scotch finally took hold as George drifted into sleep. Only when he woke to the morning realities did he remember that he hadn't called Karen.

Now he couldn't because he had guests.

Jumping up, George, clad only in pajama bottoms, threw on a faded t-shirt and headed to the door.

"Can I help you?" he asked, careful to check before opening.

"Tom sent us," was the reply from a voice echoing no accent. George opened the door to see two men standing there. Spooks. Their eyes gave them away with that distinctive wariness and the unnerving ability to scan the surroundings while looking at you simultaneously. One of them held out a Styrofoam cup of what smelled like coffee. Momentarily, George wondered if he should have the man test it with a first sip. But this wasn't a movie; this was his real. He gestured them in.

"I'm Jim and this is Bruno," the taller one said. About 6'0 feet, but thin, Jim had the rugged looks of a Mediterranean family tree. He wore jeans and a black t-shirt. Bruno was a few inches shorter, but wider. His blue eyes were light, almost icy. His wide smile was warm. George was momentarily reminded of his wife. Bruno wore khaki pants and a navy t-shirt with a bandanna tied around his left wrist.

"Shall we sit?" George asked.

"Are you packed?" Jim asked.

"Yes," George replied. He'd thrown everything into bags while on (and off) the phone the night before.

"Lots of chatter," Bruno said, his voice gravelly.

George prayed that Bruno would give him better or at least more detailed information than Campbell had thus far shared.

Jim sat next to him and fingered the edges of a small fatigue green backpack he was carrying. Folding himself deeply into a plush chair, George waited to see what Jim had to deliver. It was a photo of Khalil, the new version, post plastic surgery, and in a vast desert, golden dunes cascading behind him. In his right hand was a Kalashnikov, the infamous AK-47 rifle, long and dark against the lighter sand. He looked like a movie anti-hero with a navy scarf flowing behind him and his other fist in the air.

"We've been tracking him for days now," Jim stated. "We found him after we started inquiring about the Algerian holding an American. We got his cell number and tracked it for twenty-six hours before it went dead."

George felt the old anger stir within.

"You were about to rescue me?" he asked, only to watch his goons blandly meet his eyes.

"Confidential. Can't comment on possible military or other governmental missions." George glared at them both. Then Bruno started laughing.

"What do you think? Time for us to plan anything, with our checks and balances, given that the cell phone number is days-old information and we lost the signal?"

George smiled back, aware that if his new team saw humor in bureaucracy something constructive might actually happen in their hands. It was the ones who obsessed about procedure that slowed opportunity to a grinding halt of lost chances.

"He was in the Libyan desert near Aswan," Jim said, without a trace of humor. However, his eyes said, "bastard" and George realized that Campbell had sent him good men.

"This guy is both ruthless and brilliant," George said. "He's one of the best operators I've ever encountered and we must stop him this time. He's emotionally haunted and that weakness is enough to take him down."

Knowing that the three had only a short time to speak privately before joining the larger group, who weren't privy to this confidential information, George tried to focus his tired mind. The world will trample you if you let it so you must always maintain mental focus and strength. George was now effectively back in government employment and, like it or not, going on another field assignment after Khalil. Desert or dam, he'd be under the protection of these two men, and they'd be judging him constantly.

Would his entourage of Emine and Bright's film crew and bodyguards be coming on the flight to Aswan? How to be more conspicuous he couldn't imagine. So he raised the issue.

"Is my film crew with media hound boss and his private army invited?' George tried to ask nonchalantly but the words sounded so ridiculous rolling off his tongue he had to laugh. His mirth only increased as he saw the look that passed between Jim and Bruno.

"No," Bruno said.

"Maybe a small crew of Emine and Ben," Jim replied. "It will be great cover and you are a known journalist. But not the bodyguards as we need control over those functions."

"I like it," Bruno responded.

Set to leave in ten minutes, the two men quickly filled George in on the chatter they'd gotten from Khalil's phones. He was using a technology that made his text messages disappear sixty seconds after receipt, but they'd caught a lot in those instants. Encrypted, encoded and deciphered, the name "Aswan" was prominent, as was a birth date of next Tuesday, five days away. Related? They thought so.

George quickly threw on some khakis and a hunter green polo shirt. Heading toward the elevator, he didn't bother glancing back. Once inside the lift he realized that he still hadn't called Karen. Bright didn't take it well when told that only the skeleton crew of Ben and Emine would make the trip to Aswan. Not that they could stop him from flying down separately.

"Damn press censorship," he muttered and stalked away, unwilling to make a scene in the hotel lobby. Even he knew better than to draw attention to government entities unless he had a mass pulpit.

Desert

halil watched his charges as they shuffled before him, standing in his tent and staring at the ground. They were blessedly quiet, as he spoke.

It is better to sit alone than in company with the bad; and it is, better still to sit with the good than alone. It is better to speak to a seeker of knowledge than to remain silent; but silence is better than idle words.

"So said our greatest prophet, Mohammed," he told the boys, Radwan and his boyfriend, Aaban. Aaban was the name of the angel and this boy needed some soul cleansing if he was to live up to his promise. Boys with boys was not an earthly pursuit but one suited for the afterlife and rich rewards of paradise. What they didn't yet realize was this conversation would address that reality and its consequences.

He let them squirm a bit, biding his time. The young must develop patience. Radwan was peering intently at his toe and using it to shift sand back and forth. The boy was leaner then when he'd returned from the States and his propensity for enjoying food was entirely unsuited to harsh desert camps. Khalil had beaten him enough to know that the boy, wily in some ways and relentless in pursuit of environmental control when setting up a mission, was essentially happier with his comforts than with challenges. Those fringed eyes were never quite wary enough, given that he'd been a trained killer since age twelve. Now in his early twenties, the boy did have a focus critical for assassination, where attention must take in a controlled visual frame so different from the battlefield's chaos. Specialized, Radwan was mission sensitive and expendable.

Sweating in his cotton pants and loose Coca Cola t-shirt, cleanly shaven, Radwan looked of questionable nationality. Like many traditional men that had been westernized he seemed more lost boy than holy warrior.

Well, lost boys were the easiest to control. These blank slates followed any message if the mission was articulated well enough and promised glory. Radwan was also anxious to return to the States. He liked it there, too much, and Khalil worried about this propensity. Would the boy carry through his mission or go to authorities instead and buy himself a visa with information?

Aaban, Khalil's new insurance policy, was of a different sort altogether. Radwan had grown up on the streets of a chaotic and insane Algeria, where even your brother was a suspected source of betrayal and all walls had ears.

The boys from Algeria learned to survive. In contrast, Aaban was a Somali, which made him even more dangerous. Algeria was just short of a failed state, but at least some parts of society functioned. Somalia was utter and absolute anarchy.

The latter boy was tall and very dark, with the delicate bone structure of his race. Flawless skin and large, rounded eyes added to his youthfulness and hid the piracy in his heart. In Khalil's opinion the Somalis couldn't be trusted: growing up with no order, they knew only tribal honor and he wasn't of their tribe. Khalil had been suspicious of Aaban from the beginning, sensing the boy's self-serving soul. He wouldn't regret sending this one to a holy death and eternal rewards.

Radwan's eyes softened as he gazed at Aaban and Khalil understood why. The boy was beautiful. Smart, he spoke rarely, so couldn't help but live up to people's expectations.

And Aaban, the angel, didn't make patterns in the sand with his toe like Radwan. No, he gazed up at the sky. They were a strange pair, but jihad attracts a motley assortment of the bright and ambitious as well as those desperate to make a mark, irrespective of their skills. Khalil could and would work with them all: he needed men and recruitment was lagging.

If only his newer and bolder plan would work. They'd have to move out of Egypt faster than he'd expected but that reality had become inevitable anyway. Time waited for no man. So Khalil prepared himself, knowing he was more than skilled enough for the upcoming negotiation.

Softening his expression, he forced himself to smile at the boys.

"Allah has spoken," he started and watched Aaban's eyes dart to the left. Shifty kid, not the least bit trustworthy, eyes always flying off to avoid direct contact. For this mission that quality might be a good thing. Liked to get fucked, did he? Well, he had the ultimate fuck coming.

"Aaban, I need you to go the States with Radwan," Khalil said and watched the boy's eyes dart to meet the others, incredulous and suspicious. He tossed a passport at Aaban, and watched him drop it. Then he waited until the boy retrieved the booklet from the sand, letting the small grains fall from where they'd taken a respite in the mostly blank pages.

The camp around them was preparing for evening prayers and then dinner. Shortly, the call to prayer would ring out among the dunes and jolt the camp back to a focus on eternal life and not the heat of their worldly one. Stomachs would be sated later and already the smells of grilled lamb and fragrant rice filled the still hot air. Khalil could see the first lights coming on outside his tent flap.

"You've sinned against Allah. He forgives those who cleanse their souls in jihad, so I'm going to let you join Radwan and meet your eternal paradise."

"But,..." the boy started, causing Khalil to stop his lips with a finger and then a caress to ensure that his message was not only delivered but also heard. "Go to the address clipped on the back here, in Harlem. They'll take things from there. Leave in the morning and I'll be there in two days."

Aaban looked reluctant, but not chastised. Little did he know that this new twist in his role required only a body present at the right place and time, and an empty mind. The boy was perfect. Khalil knew he couldn't trust Aaban, so would keep him uninformed beyond minor details. On American soil he'd be hidden away until unleashed to be in the wrong place at the wrong time. Once dead, he'd have no recourse. But his role would be tricky. Getting the American police to shoot an innocent man was a formidable challenge, though it was possible. Riots over a dead black man in Harlem murdered by police? Stranger things had happened, and the States were overdue for such violence. The downside risk was so low Khalil might as well try: a fake passport, plane ticket and Aaban's short-term living expenses. If necessary, he'd fire the fatal shot himself.

"The virgins in heaven await you boys," he murmured as the call to prayer started and he gestured for them to go. Those bumps on their foreheads testified to their devotion.

"For the US trip, stop letting your head touch the ground during prayer," he barked and watched the boys jump. Well, at least most Americans didn't know that the bump signified piety and was common among those in his organization. Beards, another such sign of an Islamist, could be eliminated with a simple shave. Luckily, the boys wouldn't be long in the States before ascending to their maker.

Khalil kneeled and began his Salah, one of the five pillars of Islam. Washing first with water, the drops hitting the hot sand before being absorbed, he knelt and visualized his home. Salah means connection and is more than simple prayer; instead it is a connection with Allah performed five times a day starting with an absolution, basically a cleansing with water or dirt when water isn't possible (a practical reality in desert countries). As the Quran stated:

O you who believe! when you rise up to prayer, wash your faces and your hands as far as the elbows, and wipe your heads and your feet to the ankles; and if you are under an obligation to perform a total ablution, then wash (yourselves) and if you are sick or on a journey, or one of you come from the privy, or you have touched the women, and you cannot find water, betake yourselves to pure earth and wipe your faces and your hands therewith, Allah does not desire to put on you any difficulty, but He wishes to purify you and that He may complete His favor on you, so that you may be grateful

Murmuring, Khalil started the prayer, his hands raised to shoulder height and fingers slightly apart. The ritual was comforting, amidst the darkness that had already settled and solitude was its own reward, though sometimes it felt more like a punishment. Jennifer was in New York now and he was alone, again. Of course Allah was always in his heart and watching over him like a blessed shining star from above. Khalil had no allegiance save that one, for our earthly reality changes but our God never does.

This country, Egypt, wasn't far off the map from his own, but he felt an eternity away from the life he'd lived as a boy. This was the breadbox of civilization while Algeria, much conquered during ancient times, had an even more tumultuous past.

Going through the rituals of his prayer, Khalil couldn't help but revisit the memories of his mother, much as he knew that he shouldn't. His past had haunted him ever since her death. She wouldn't have minded his distracted prayer as she'd believed in Allah's betrayal.

His father, Ali, a brutal and violent man, had deserted them for another, younger wife only showing up occasionally to demand money. His behavior was permissible under their religion, and they'd starved as was the custom, Miriam begging for any available work.

But now that she was dead Khalil he missed her soft touch and accepting love. Oh, he had sisters, shrouded and burdened with husbands thanks to Ali's heartless will and absolute right to make such marriages. His brother was dead. He heard a beep and saw that Jennifer had sent him a text from her new disposable phone, using the name Clare. Perhaps she'd save him from loneliness. He opened it quickly, knowing it would disappear within 60 seconds.

"I miss you; I love you. Clare"

And he watched it dissolve into the digital divide lasting nonetheless forever in his heart. His next steps would be difficult and complex but he'd make the plan work as he generally did. First, a man had to die so that Egypt wouldn't become a model for a new progressive Muslim society. Then it would be time to bring Allah back and ignore the dictates of a corrupt west and the call for equality.

The desert chill was settling in and Khalil felt an ache in an old scar, the one slashing across his ribs where a bullet had almost ended his life at twenty in the mountains of Afghanistan. Soviet Kalashnikovs and frigid air had led him to war after war. Now he wondered if the opportunity for his group of Islamists hadn't perhaps passed by, a mere whisper left unspoken. Really, democracy and open social networks had been the catalysts for driving local dictators out of power, and not the promise of Allah's golden state.

For decades the mosques had been the only refuge from repression until the Internet created another one. His group wasn't ready to surrender the power they'd built during that time span but then again Mubarak hadn't been either and look at him now. Were ideologies being replaced with tweets and calls to worldly action, forgetting that eternal life and Allah's judgment lasted much longer?

How to regain the emotional hold over the young and old in Egypt? This country must form the foundation of a new Islamic Caliphate as where it fell would lead others, it was too important to lose. Among other things, Khalil had been given this mandate too. Osman had been a needed blessing who took over the Internet dialogues as one born to an online world, already building him a mass pulpit. It was one part of his movement that he could delegate for at least a few weeks. But he was learning and appreciated the relative safety given the lack of guns, germs and steel.

Seeing the soldiers clustering for dinner, Khalil hurried to join them. A leader had to be seen often to inspire confidence, and he was hungry.

Aswan

Rising up, white and expansive against golden sand, the New Aswan Dam controls the flow of the life-giving Nile River. The Dam was constructed between 1960 and the early 1970s after the Aswan Low Dam, completed in 1902, failed to sufficiently moderate the Nile's annual flooding. Massive and commanding above deep blue waters, the structure towers above the landscape. Rushing waters create hydroelectric power for all of Egypt.

Since antiquity the Nile has been flooding its banks every year during late summer as water from its East African drainage basis flowed down the valley. These floods distributed nutrients and minerals, creating the fertile soil that supported the country and its civilization. But in high water years the Nile over-flooded crops and in low years left them parched, leading to droughts, famine and a destroyed cotton crop. The new Dam was built to complement the older low Dam and better regulate the water's flow, thereby protecting the farmland and has had a significant impact on Egypt's economy. The reservoir storage also preserves water for when needed.

Through the lens of Emine's camera the water cast dramatic lights and shadows, and she loved the effect, especially against the vibrant blue sky and camel colored vast desert. She snapped as fast as she could, fully aware that she and Ben were a side dish not the main course. Essentially, they were just a cover for the government mission centered around George. Feeling a hand on her shoulder, she looked up to see George's worried expression. She followed him to a bench and they both took a seat.

"What do you think?" he asked, a broad question and probably deliberately so. They'd arrived a mere hour before and had headed straight to the dam without first checking into the hotel. Then came the dam tour and now a break. Staring at the deep circles under his red eyes and the stubble that would never be a true beard, she smiled.

"Even when you're a mess you look cool and calm. But your eyes are troubled."

He flashed a half smile, then looked out over the vast expanse of water. She waited, but like her, he never felt obligated to speak until ready. The sun was in both their eyes and the air heavy. Like a lightening rod George attracted followers of which she was but one. He had his government shadows, Bright had wanted to come (and he followed no one), Ben was busy editing footage of George framed by water and she was just watching. Later she'd write.

His mood was difficult to read and he let silence hang. What did she think? She hadn't much time yet to think and, really, she'd been more focused on herself and her own problems. His reappearance came quickly.

"Nasser built the New Dam in the 1950s and 60s," she said, deflecting. "It's so important to the people and the economy, essentially feeding a hungry desert so food can grow," Emine continued, her words almost disappearing into the noise of the water. But George was watching her and seemed to be paying attention. While she was now in baggy army-style khakis and another dark t-shirt, he wore crisper, neater khakis and a more formal polo shirt.

In sneakers and ponytail, with dark glasses to shelter her eyes, she was comfortable physically but feeling the pressure from George's stillness. Sunglasses likewise shielded his eyes, but she still sensed his glare.

"Tell me something I don't know," he said, and she stared into his dark lenses, hiding behind her own.

Emine studied the rock and clay walls cradling Lake Nasser but her focus was on George's voice, and it cracked.

"Khalil is going to bomb this dam and plunge people into a torrent of water, sweeping everything out of its way, destroying homes, crops and families. It had mixed origins but must stay standing."

"Soviet money?" she said, gesturing to the Lotus Tower Soviet monument in the distance, its white stakes pointing up at the piercing hot sun. "This," she said gesturing, "is a Soviet symbol. They helped design it and loaned Egypt the funds."

"The world is complex and Khalil fought the Soviets years ago," he responded. "But his group of extremists wouldn't want the blame for the ensuing chaos and massive destruction."

"Blaming it on us?" she let him lead the conversation, skipping around as he was.

"Or forcing us to do something?" he asked.

"Or deflecting," she asked softly and it was only then that he seemed to see, or hear, her.

"Yes," George exclaimed, suddenly animated. "Why blow up the Aswan Dam? It's irrational as the Islamists don't benefit from harming their fellow Muslim countrymen, not that much of what they do makes sense."

"The chatter backs it up?" Emine asked, wondering if George would tell her anything about the related government data.

"Dream, try, believe," George mumbled. Had he heard her? Sometimes George seemed to be living entirely inside his own head. She'd known other people like that over time but few who could then suddenly hone in on the answer to a question that came from nowhere yet was somehow relevant to what they'd been discussing.

"Khalil said it once, a long time ago. About Don Quixote," George said, pausing again. Sometimes Emine forgot how much time he'd spent with Khalil and how well they knew each other.

"Why did Khalil buy you? What did he get out of it?" she asked.

George's small smile told her all she needed to know. He not only didn't hate Khalil for his murders, he also truly knew the man behind the acts and cared, in that odd way that men have when respect enters an adversarial relationship.

188

"We don't know and can't figure it out. He didn't even ask me much." George shrugged his shoulders. "Khalil is both different and somehow the same now but he's not so self destructive that he'd blow the dam."

Emine sensed George's escorts closing in. Additionally, a small cluster of men who had been watching their group was slowly hovering closer. Dressed in Western clothes, the group didn't look exactly threatening – perhaps merely inquisitive. The white people with cameras stood out but curiosity exists in all parts of the world, Aswan being no exception. The group looked like native Egyptians, though this part of the country was such a diverse mix with the darker, taller Nubians being a big presence along with that wide spanning hodgepodge of Africans following the wealth of the Nile. The men were mostly silent, but occasionally someone made a comment in guttural Arabic. An African Albino stood out with his mottled light skin and colorless eyes. Saying nothing, and a seemingly unnatural addition, he was lucky to be alive since in much of Africa witch doctors used Albinos in their cures. Emine was used to crowds with guns or machetes, so to her they looked tame, so far. But Jim and Bruno would want to protect their charge and not surprisingly were hovering close. Any crowd could morph quickly.

"So, what does your gut tell you?" she asked George, knowing that their intimate conversation was about to end and still not sure why he'd pulled her aside. What she really wanted to ask him was why the world was so unstable now.

"Chaos," he replied as if answering her unarticulated question in addition to her voiced one. "Al Qaeda's calling card. But I'm missing something. You're perceptive. Watch for me."

"Chaos to blame on Israel?" Emine asked him, as their minders closed in.

"No. Lenin once said that a natural disaster creates an ideal condition to bring about a revolution. Those damn Algerians learned from the communists before they became Islamists."

Interesting.

"George," she ventured, almost daring to ask him a bigger question.

189

"Web chatter's still picking up," Jim stated, cutting her off. "It's steady but hard to decipher." The tall man stared her down, even though she had sunglasses on and he didn't. Had he sensed something challenging in her or just wanted the stage?

Jim continued, "They found a football site that's harboring encrypted messages, to be picked up from random computers and cell phones at will. Difficult to trace, but implying a hit in the next few days to blow up the dam."

"Too pat," George replied, rising from the bench and physically submitting to his group, as Bruno gestured to their new mini van. Emine lagged behind and tried to hear what their clustered groupies might say as she passed. Learning Arabic had been time well spent and only seemed to grow in value.

"That's him." She heard the Albino speak for the first time. Funny, the damn African could have been sent by her friend Bud, by Khalil, by a mistrustful Bright or by none of the above. This story had too many characters, each harboring innumerable secrets, to make rational sense any more.

More men started to gather. These new additions were darker and looked like menial workers, in loose tunics and trousers, dirty and with rubber sandals on their feet. Gathering and staring, they reminded Emine of hungry dogs circling a wounded one. She hurried her step and wondered whom to trust, not liking the mood in the streets here much more than in Cairo.

Time Travel

Walking into the hotel, George had to admit that its sheer beauty was stunning. He felt like he was stepping back into a grander time when travel was a magical adventure allowed only to those rich enough to afford lodgings like this one. The Old Catarack hotel sat on a pink granite shelf, amidst a garden, and overlooking the vast and luxurious Nile. The river here was wider, stunning in its vast expanses of clean blue, the white sails of the boats billowing. Also visible were Elephantine Island and the ruins of Abu in the vast golden desert. The scenery was among the most beautiful George had encountered, a mix of striking colors and palm trees blowing against a pristine sky. The Nile and the ancient stone architecture of the city met its complement in the Victorian building, invoking the romance of countless novels.

An old fashioned veranda above the water was where they'd meet for drinks before heading to a strategy dinner in a private room. Until then, they each needed to wash up and make whatever calls their respective authorities required.

He was stone cold tired but burning from the desert heat. George's body was that confused and his mind unsettled. Something wasn't making sense. One of his assumptions had to be wrong and he couldn't even begin to guess which one.

In his expansive suite, he wandered to the balcony and surveyed the majestic Nile. Everything moved at a soothing pace, completely unlike Cairo's utter chaos and din. He could stay here forever and part of him longed for such an escape. Would this hotel wash away if the dam blew? Who really knew the impact of that vast amount of water unleashed; it hadn't happened before.

He fingered his new phone, supposedly more secure than his old one but none of them were really. His old phone, battered, familiar and comfortable, was also gone. Did Khalil have it? The Iranians? Who knew? Luckily he'd never input a full address book, only occasional numbers, so his captors didn't have his home address. Then again, global jihadists could probably find a way to get it if they really wanted. Was he listed in the phone book?

What next?

Oh, damn. He still hadn't called his wife. Studying his phone, George realized it was late morning in Manhattan. She'd probably be mad but since that was seemingly her normal state, did it really matter? The new phone was blank absent a few key work/government numbers, but he could dial his home from memory.

He heard the ring and marveled at how small the world had become.

"Hello," she answered, and he wasn't sure how he felt at the sound of her voice. This woman who'd borne his children and lived next to him for nearly thirty years now. She was far away yet was that distance so simple to breach as a small phone and a wireless connection.

"Karen," he said, then felt his emotions hit. What could he say? That he was exhausted but alive? That he had no idea what to do next but everyone kept looking at him like he had all the answers? Or that he probably wasn't going to be home anytime soon.

Surprised at the how scattered he suddenly felt, George acknowledged his severe emotional trauma and this new disorientation, was his reality for at least a while longer. But he needed to pull himself together.

"George?" he heard Karen's voice through the phone line, and had to sit down. He could picture her, probably still carting around a large mug of now cold coffee, heavily dosed with sugar and lots of milk. She'd carry it around all morning as she made her calls and read whatever sites hosted the academic papers and news that she deemed important. She'd be in pants, her fine blonde hair pulled loosely back into a ponytail and in those soft loafers she loved. Their apartment would be quiet, since she only had help occasionally now, preferring the tranquility of floating above Central Park and doing whatever it was she did when no one was around.

"George?" she asked again.

"Yes." He choked and couldn't believe the tears in his eyes. Wasn't he considering divorcing this woman? Yet how did one leave a woman who had been at his side for almost thirty years? She might be difficult and demanding, but he could at least anticipate her moods.

"I'm so glad you're all right! I got a call late last night and couldn't wait to hear your voice."

"Yes, yes," was all he could say, filled with emotion and the crash from the adrenaline that he'd been running on for so long. He was carrying too large a burden and just wanted some warmth for a change.

"I'm being interviewed tomorrow on your escape, and now I can say you called and we spoke. Can you give me some details so I can sound involved?"

Her voice had that whispery softness that had initially attracted him years ago. "I love you," she whispered, and he had to wonder.

"National security," he responded, pulling himself back into his role. Even with her? "*New York Times?*" he asked. Since his escape was news and Bright was tight with the paper's owner; it was a natural fit. Or his own show?

"*Vogue,*" she replied, sounding happy. "And they're taking pictures of the apartment. It's getting cleaned and primped now, so I can't talk long. Oh, and, where are you now? Darling."

He stared out at the white crested boats on the Nile and thought back into his own antiquity. She'd been a good mother but less so a wife. Hot and cold, she'd alternately flattered and then pulled this sort of shit. Life wasn't always about her. But the problem for their relationship was that it was increasingly about him and she felt she had to compete.

"Cancel *Vogue,*" he said, wondering how she'd reply.

"I can't, my love," she responded. Some would say that Karen was the perfect wife, stumping for him and presenting the dream to a large audience while he pretended to live it. Others, that she was a self-centered bitch who needed to be the center of attention.

Yet he loved her. The softness of her belly when she lay next to him in bed. How she massaged his shoulders, her fingers surprisingly strong as they dug through the knots built from his daily tensions. And how she always proclaimed that she loved him no matter how ugly a tone their fights took.

Then there was the guilt. They'd had a true partnership once, advancing both careers to tenure and raising two great kids in the process. But George had left self-promotion behind and Karen was holding down the fort for them both in that arena.

She prattled on about something else, and he hit the new mini-bar. Before long he was off the phone and dozing.

Then the phone rang again and Bright was pitching some shots of the Dam with Ben in charge. George listened to the monologue and realized that all was not without its reasoning. People pursued their own angle irrespective of his values.

And, by the way, the Aswan Dam was at risk.

"Rumors on Aswan?" he asked Bright. "Are you having me followed?'

"Yes, well, about that," Bright began, but George already knew not to listen. He'd guessed right and his boss would offer some half-right excuse, but George didn't owe any of them a front seat ticket to a major terrorist plot and had no intention of risking anything to deliver it. The people of Egypt would hopefully never know that they had him to thank for saving the dam even at the expense of ratings.

"And?" he asked Bright.

"No one can figure anything out. But Khalil's ex-girlfriend, the blonde...".

"Jennifer?" George asked, surprised. This 'girlfriend' was a new addition to his information.

"...turned up in Manhattan two days ago. She'd taken a trip to Egypt before. Imagine."

Imagine? What in the world did that mean? And all George wanted was sleep. Suddenly, he couldn't. Life ultimately often came down to pattern recognition and a woman visiting the current abode of an old boyfriend could only signify one thing.

Entrapment

Khalil left Egypt far behind, Osman at his side. He'd originally intended to make a stop in Aswan but then decided against it, since he had bigger battles to fight for today.

The concept of freedom had been nagging, a relentless ache that meant he was running away from something important. He'd escaped a cage through craftiness and sheer will, blowing up Americans in the process, but he wasn't really as free as he'd hoped to find himself. Instead his past and present conspired to lock him in a cage of his own making and he'd seemingly lost the key.

Could he ever be free, or, once entrapped in a cause or otherwise, was such flight an utter impossibility? Osman was a wanted distraction but not enough, not now.

The boy was taking over, and Khalil struggled to keep up with his technological advances. Osman had pitched Khalil's trusty phone into the desert and given him an iPhone for data only and a disposable phone for calls. Since it was programmed with nothing, Khalil was forever pulling scraps out of his pockets to dial numbers. The new security procedures drove him crazy much as he understood their value and knew getting caught again would be bad indeed. Still, part of him yearned for the day when everything wasn't encoded and he got to keep a device for at least a month. Next, they'd be using video sites to hide messages – or so Osman had promised. Forty-eight hours of video are added to YouTube each minute, totaling eight years of content a day, an ever growing number and, while much of it was monitored, the practical reality was that it was a moving-picture wilderness and an easy place to lose a video clip. Never trust an American company.

But free? Finally. From being followed? Mistrust? Incompetent minions? Snakes, spiders, dirt and rebellion? Hardly. He was just headed to the States, JFK, where he was on a most-wanted list. Understandably nervous, Khalil knew that his new passport was fine but didn't know if his new face been entered in any security databases yet. Whenever he boarded one of these flights he took a risk.

Khalil looked at his charge, asleep in the dark cabin and breathing heavily. A mere child taken from his father and told to be a man. As they all were.

Events in New York would move fast, so he'd have to forget about Egypt. The country had always been bad luck anyway. Captured shortly after leaving a mere two years ago then sent back, he'd been a victim of the Egyptian military, then shipped to the Americans. Memories of torture died hard, yet now he'd been negotiating with those same captors and asserting that, truly, in this Islamic revolution, they were all on the same side. Thus Khalil was thrilled to leave this ancient land for a newer one, with bigger opportunities.

Keep your friends close but your enemies closer? The lines blurred. Islam was a unifying force but other loyalties could prove stronger.

America, a president weakened and a country divided. Like Egypt, they had few jobs and little left of that long-promised opportunity. Khalil regretted his plot choice now; the Egyptian President instead of the American one. Could he change it? Would the US President be at the same UN meeting, staying likewise at the Four Seasons?

But could he really up the ante and switch KK out for the American President? Certainly Osman, his wonder boy, could find out if the President was attending the conference at any point. The boy seemingly could find any information electronically, a magician of amazing powers. Then the only relevant factors would be luck and logistics, and the name Khalil would be famous forever as he'd willingly take that shot.

Timing in life is important. The world was falling into a vortex of desperation and nothing seemingly was working any longer. Whores and money were the true masters of the West and the filth of its corruption was spreading, a ticking bomb of moral corruption. What man didn't want a willing Western whore with her legs spread open and a panoply of cars, boats and money? After all, he'd returned to Jennifer.

Time for the Americans to taste war and chaos on their own shore. They'd so willingly disseminated it across the last century.

Balance

mine was getting phone calls.

Men often liked her, and the more unresponsive she was the more they pursued her. Eventually they tried to take care of her, which, because of her experience with her dad, she knew was about control. For whatever reason, the men who chased her were all about control, while more balanced men left her alone.

She'd pondered those realities once when, in a rare burst of introspection, she wondered why none of her boyfriends accepted that she'd make her own decisions and do as she liked. Her girlfriends didn't get the same hassles.

She was a free spirit, which drove her control freak father, used to Liz and her passive acceptance of everything, crazy. But she was used to men like Mehmet, so seemingly she continued to attract new iterations of that model. And, trained in evading their control by being elusive and non-committal, she drove them as crazy as they did her.

Moreover, her warlord and politician interviewees tended to be control freaks, a source of their success, so she could pull her hot-and-cold routine with them and get great interviews as they dodged and weaved, trying to impress. She rarely got stellar interviews when her subject was a woman. Perhaps they saw through her act, practiced and precise, or maybe they just didn't like her type. Since women were the minority heading renegade armies or countries, her career wasn't negatively impacted.

What if she married someone like Mehmet? Now, she was already feeling hounded by Ed's clinginess, a much lesser version. Then again, no one could marry her without that "I do" she had no intention of uttering in the near future if ever.

And that's the other reason so many men liked her: she was all sex with no commitment.

Ed, her boyfriend, and Bud, her not-boyfriend but still boy toy, wanted her out of Egypt. Revolution heating up. The papers. The rumors. The bullshit and deluge of lies. Islamists taking over? The army? With all of the rumors who cared! The country was chaos, and the people hungry with anger.

She chided them. Never, ever argue directly with a man. They don't forgive it.

"I'm a war reporter," she cooed. "This is a revolution. My job needs me here." What she wanted to tell them was that they weren't her fiancé or husband and thus had no say. Her father was different. He at least was blood. But on this one front, ever the progressive Turk, he encouraged her to deliver the news. Willing to risk the safety of his last living child, Emine could only admire his courage. Perhaps they were just a reckless family.

So she talked sense into her boys.

"No bombs in the streets of Cairo," she stated firmly. Not yet, she whispered under her breath, sensing the undercurrents than ran through the streets once the insane protests began. And nothing had changed thanks to the Arab Spring: the poor still starved.

"You want what from me?" she asked and emailed them pictures of the desert, set so stunningly against the sapphire foreground of the Nile. Maybe she'd move to Aswan and take up with a Nubian.

Or not.

"Aswan isn't happening," Bud said. Trust me.

"Aswan! No! They can't," said Ed.

And Emine thought back to her lost angel, Piers. He would have shrugged his shoulders at the debate and gone to fix things. Perhaps the ones we truly love become more present after we lose them when our evergreen mind refuses to drop them from those internal dialogues. Still, we're left with the survivors and the world as it is. Her reality was that Bud, a well-connected warlord school buddy and sometimes bed partner, was skeptical that Aswan would blow.

"It's stupid. Al Qaeda makes mistakes, but they aren't dumb."

"Take the world back to the time of Mohammed?" she asked. Or Lenin?

"They're already heading in that direction fast. Before you know it, they'll all be riding camels and lobbing cannon balls."

"So says he in the fine safe state of South Africa," she replied.

"I'm in Paris, doll," he said. "Where you should be. You live here, remember?"

Emine glanced around her hotel room and wondered which girl he'd taken to dinner before, reminding herself that she had to meet her group for drinks and didn't care anyway. She didn't want a committed relationship. Right? Especially not with someone as flighty as Bud.

They hung up, and she looked for her lace-up black stilettos, with those long thin straps that wound up her calves. Bud's information was generally solid and seemed to confirm George's suspicions. Something was amiss in this plot but the chatter kept saying otherwise, confirming the impossible. Damn intelligence. Sometimes it defied common sense.

Grabbing a drink before the drinks from the wine she'd ordered Emine pondered Bud's words. Such a smart bastard, but he liked to fuck with her by embedding hidden meanings into his sentences. Was no man ever straight when speaking to a woman?

"And you're hearing that where?" she asked, but he never answered.

Emine swirled the wine in its glass and noted its buttery yellow color and smell. The future was always such a strange balance between desire and fate. For tonight she'd see her group and they'd strategize, coming up with steps for the next few days. She'd find her way, one day at a time.

Perhaps it was time for her to re-adjust her goals. She'd come to Egypt looking to do a tome with George on terrorism and ideology in the age of rage, including some pictures of the turmoil, and perhaps an additional long story. She'd found a revolution and a bigger book. Now she'd added this Aswan plot and her government escorts, so maybe she'd even find a movie in it.

So why did her mind keep wandering back to broad shoulders and two bulging bicep muscles? But whose? She wanted to feel strong arms around her and defer to another's judgment. Could a man fill that job description, or was she just looking to escape and not face the problems she wasn't solving?

Perhaps Liz should have been the one to call for advice, but Emine avoided the phone, preferring to talk into her glass of cool Chardonnay.

But then her cell lighted with a call from Bright and she picked it up, too eagerly. He made her laugh. Always the bastard, they argued, he cheated and went back to his wife but he always supported her, professionally and otherwise. Working almost exclusively with men, she'd learned to tolerate their eccentricities.

"Emine, I told George that we found Khalil's girlfriend in New York. You need to push him. That bastard knows his terrorist, so what isn't he telling me? "

What isn't he telling us all, was her first thought, realizing how little George had been sharing about his time with Khalil. Perhaps he'd told the Americans more? And what wasn't Bright himself sharing?

Curling up in a ball, staring out at the dusky Nile, knowing that she was late for drinks, Emine questioned how to proceed. Part of her hesitation was the realization that neither words nor actions can be rescinded and their impact reverberates across time.

What she really needed to do was to stop drinking alone and head out the door to do something constructive. Being right was never a meaningful victory.

Imagination

How do you imagine a world that doesn't yet exist? Drawing on history is a start but it ignores the complexity of what happens every day as time ticks on. We want to fall back into the comfort of the familiar but the world ignores that option and decides its course irrespective of our desires.

And George was in the midst of many desired outcomes, depending on his conversation.

Currently, Egypt was a mess. Mubarak's ghost hovered over the whole environment, his spirit haunting each disparate group differently, Islamists and independents alike. The balance of power was a crapshoot, George's new favorite word. And his conclusion was based on the intelligence shared with him by his spook partners, never the most straightforward or forthcoming group. Revolution equals chaos, as Khalil had said. Which way the world order fell was more luck than science, and history seemed to dictate that the most ruthless group would be the ultimate victor.

"The Muslim Brotherhood benefits whether the dam blows or not? Al Qaeda?" he'd ask anyone who listened. And the answers would come.

"No one in Egypt would benefit. It makes no sense so the question becomes who benefits from utter chaos."

George continued puzzling over the implications of the dam's destruction. Massive loss of life, confusion, blame, a military crackdown? Egypt's crops and homes flooded? Whoever took such a step, if identified, would be hated in these regions, and the tribes of Egypt had a long memory.

But Israel and Iran were the ones who benefited because each could blame the other and hope to shift the regional power dynamics in their favor. Would either be so brazen and why would Khalil get involved? Then again, it had been the Iranians originally who nabbed George, only to turn him over to Khalil. Damn. And the Iranians had released most of their Al Qaeda prisoners, sending them out into the wider world to wreck their havoc. Why hadn't he probed Khalil more when he had a chance? Yet he knew that their time together had revolved more around his personal quest for survival than any desire to figure out the next plot.

Khalil was never direct, anyway, creating the first of many contradictions; he should never have mentioned Aswan to George in the first place. True, their positions had been reversed and the escape mission wasn't expected, but doing so was sloppy, unlike the usually meticulous Khalil.

Which meant?

Something was amiss.

George admitted to himself that his problems included distraction, along with Machiavellian politics and a ruthless terrorist. Did anyone care that he was sitting in a hotel room puzzling over a million implications, most of which he seemed to be missing but the outcome of which meant the difference between life and death?

Relieved when the phone rang, he answered quickly to escape himself.

"Okay, so what else did we miss?" he asked Emine, his new nightly call. Karen would be at yoga now.

"Khalil said Aswan, right?" Emine asked. "He must have wanted you to hear it because someone like Khalil wouldn't slip twice. He didn't kill you after a few days, thus he wanted you alive; the man was controlling your life, after all.

Emine, perhaps better than anyone, understood the complexities of a broken ethical system and the difficulties of achieving desired outcomes within geopolitical realities. He was better than Emine in understanding people; but she grasped the politics with an instinctive precision that he'd never achieve. Emine was of that class who grew up in the halls of power and internalized its realities, having a politician parent to teach her the subtler rules.

"I escaped?" George replied, catching her meaning. Khalil made so very few mistakes. The man was a machine with spies throughout Egypt, thus could have known when George landed in the country. So how had a raid surprised him? And where was Khalil now? George knew he wasn't overreacting; these dangers were real.

"Khalil isn't in Egypt anymore. His phone was ditched at Heathrow," was what his spook friends said. Could Khalil be headed to New York and Jennifer? London had connecting airports.

"I've heard this isn't happening..." Emine said. "A friend."

George looked at the clock and saw the time was close to 11:00 p.m. He liked to speak to Emine after dinner like this, when they could talk alone. She had a remarkable source of information, one he was better off not asking about.

"We're going to New York too," he decided. He wasn't needed here. What, to recognize the surgically altered Khalil, who seemed to have jumped off the continent? Yet. Instinct mandated otherwise. And Campbell, on DC and not Cairo time was only in his afternoon, so how quickly could George persuade him to okay Manhattan? And why was he bringing Emine with him? Well, he'd bring Ben too. They might not be able to shoot footage of what ensued – this damned national security bullshit, but they were his team. In Aswan George was just chasing windmills again.

He dialed his next number.

"Campbell, it's George." Hearing breathing on the other end of the line, George decided not to allow any response before he finished. "I need to get to New York."

"Okay," was the response. "I'll call you back."

Weakness

Khalil knocked on the door, hoping that Jennifer was there and alone, that she hadn't set him up. Could a woman be trusted, or were their minds too weak? How could she truly love him after not seeing him for so long?

The cheap hotel was the type of place to fade into amidst peeling paint and the din from Grand Central Station, perhaps his least favorite place in the city; but being anonymous was easiest next to a transport hub where people slipped in and out at will. Khalil didn't want the attention of a hotel where the staff cared.

Outside he heard the sirens and horns of a big city and felt the adrenaline rush of finally being closer to achieving his mission.

The door opened and a blonde tumbled into his arms. *Malak*, his angel as decried by Allah. She smelled and felt like Jennifer but his senses couldn't process more. Rose, violets and a muskiness that made him dizzy with desire. Jennifer's head was almost level with his. They were about the same height but she was much slighter and he loved how her body gave. His was always tense. A wet saltiness of tears brushed across his cheek. He didn't cry anymore, so they had to be hers, and he was touched.

Pulling away, she looked at him and he studied her back. Her limbs were long, yet their lankiness yielded to soft curves in all the right places. Her blue eyes blinked and the mascara was smudged like kohl around her eyes. But she was smiling.

"You're here," was all he could whisper. The pressure of her struck more then the emotion. Jennifer was a presence where most people just felt like clutter. He had a man to kill, was still being followed and he'd mixed her into the jumble. At what point did it all tip over? Wasn't there a point to running so fast no one could keep up?

"You're learning that you love me?" she asked, seemingly expecting an answer. Right? No?

He caressed her bare back, glad that her jeans were topped with a loose t-shirt, allowing for free exploration of her skin. And he let his hands run free across her front, noting how her nipples hardened at his touch. She did understand that he was fighting this war on her behalf as well? Allah's will had to reign supreme if they were to reach his kingdom beyond this earthly one.

Was he learning that he loved her? How could she ask? As if risking his life wasn't proof enough.

"Can you raise boys without women and expect them to learn later how to be men?" Khalil said, finding his voice and wondering if he had just spoken his first true sentence since childhood. But, still, he deflected her question. Love?

"What?" Jennifer pulled away, shock and a harsh tone coming into her voice. After all they'd been through, was she really going to insist on hearing what he couldn't say?

"I'm not sure I know what to do," he said, trying to gently nudge her inside the room. Exposure was always dangerous and anyone could notice them in the hallway. Her blue eyes fluttered and thankfully she yielded. He hated the chatter of women when they felt wronged or misunderstood. Many things in life might make sense over time or through greater learning but women weren't one of them. Soft fingertips brushed his shoulders, and he was glad that, while Jennifer had a bad temper, she rarely showed it.

"You asked me to come all the way across the world and then back to New York, leaving my life and safety behind," she started, and Khalil, exhausted from his flight, stifled a groan. "And you didn't think through what you'd do when I asked you to admit you love me?" she finished, her large blue eyes flashing sapphire and sparkling with something he couldn't identify.

He waited for an explosion, but she only led him to the bed, its brick-colored comforter too close to crimson for his taste. What a grim room. Small, it was neat and dark, with only a few pieces of furniture. Her suitcase was on the floor, open and messy. Through the windows he saw another building across an alley. The air was stuffy from the summer heat even as dusk was falling. But he liked the comfort of the street noises, which took him back to the clamor and heat of Algeria. Honking horns and people talking, which are the sounds of large cities across the globe.

And she kissed him.

"Yes," he found the word to answer when she drew back, and then watched her laugh. She curled into him on the bed, her fingertips fluttering across his chest. He liked her this way, exposed and at risk, with only him as her savior. That was why people needed to be removed from their area of comfort. The resulting disruption created a void easily filled and made them dependent on you. She couldn't go back to her old life easily now, not after traveling with a wanted terrorist.

He brushed away a section of her hair, falling into her eye, to uncover her face and returned her kiss, but much harder than before.

"Men, you're all the same," she murmured when he finished, then bathed his neck with light kisses. "You just want to get your way and don't think through the consequences."

"How many men have you known?" he asked. The shamelessness of her dragging him into a broader pool of men. His eyes bored into her, and he knew he should back down but was unable.

"More than I'll ever tell you about," she said, laughing again but not lightly now. Her gemstone eyes were flashing and he wondered whether she'd protest. He leaned back against the wooden headboard. She couldn't learn bad habits because he wouldn't tolerate them. Complicating his life with a woman was about as big a risk as he'd take, so she had better be an obedient adjunct. Men in this country pretended to treat women with respect but usually just used them like the whores they were. He'd train her as he did his troops, letting them come after him. He watched the storm rage in her eyes but noted she didn't fight. Enough decisions like that and she'd be tamed.

He caressed her gently.

"You're perfect," he said, her reward for backing down. He watched her face light up as she curled more tightly into him. Denial was such a powerful tool, and most people wanted to believe in the fiction of a life you narrated to them.

He'd been reading and becoming more conscious of the tools he'd used with his men and in his missions. The psychology mattered more than the reality. George, his nemesis and decoy, a mentor really, in a sense, had instilled in him the spark to question and learn. The one that had been extinguished at sixteen when his brother died and Khalil left his beloved school for a jihad that just didn't end.

Women may fall when there's no strength in men, as Shakespeare had said. Jennifer couldn't navigate his world. Like any new recruit, she needed to be trained to survive. Most wanted lists were the real deal, especially in the digital age, where hiding your identity became increasingly complex. Jennifer was his and would rise and fall on that reality. She was also a beautiful woman in his arms.

"I'm glad to see you," he told her and looked deeply into her eyes, reassuring, wanting, but not having time. Some things were more important than sex and he needed to get two men shot during the next week.

"I have some calls to make," he said, caressing her and feeling the hard curve of a hipbone. Her fingers wandered down and started to unzip his jeans. He loved these western whores sometimes. So brazen. Then again, sometimes, they were just a pain. He pushed her away, knowing he was being rough. He could give her a fake American smile, like the men here did. But no.

"You just got here," she said, her voice disappointed. She'd get over it. Or maybe not. Why not.

"I want you first," he said, changing his mind. How long would fucking her really take? Peeling off her clothes, he saw the confusion her eyes but went on anyway. Time to ravish her, a Moor returning to long abandoned but never forgotten lands and he wanted it rough. So he took her quickly, ramming himself into her before she'd even gotten warm. He felt himself explode almost immediately and kissed her hard on the mouth, nipping her lower lip.

He heard the ceiling fan whirl above as Jennifer shuddered under him and he felt her come. She was perfect for him sexually; she only got off when he dominated her completely. Perhaps that was why he'd never forgotten her after all these years; their bodies were in tune even if their minds sometimes floated apart. Most women either just lay there or actually expected something in return. Jennifer thought she loved him, so she tried to please. And she always had. More women should learn that trick – making a man happy, without the prattle of stupid conversation.

Feeling himself harden again, he kissed her gently, she'd earned it, then rolled away and grabbed his cell phone – the newest in an ever revolving succession that he used now for business.

He dialed and heard a man answer.

"The explosives are lined up, under the water. Any explosion will be muted when compared to one above the water. The pressure of the water weight will push the force tighter into the dam and send a strong wave upward and out." The voice seemed close but was oceans away. That harsh guttural Arabic of the coast.

"But will it work?" Khalil asked, and was glad that Jennifer didn't speak Arabic as she was watching and listening, intently. Women. He caressed her soft white cheek.

Clouds

Ben was staying in Aswan and Emine wasn't happy.

"I'm a cameraman and photographer, and no one seems to have a clue what's going on," he stated, sounding patient but determined.

"That means?" she asked and watched his lips twist in irritation. Ben, preternaturally calm and someone she knew well, was wrong on this issue. Like all good cameramen, he let the picture guide his actions and even in the midst of gunfire seemed to emerge like a divine angel with his perfect shots.

"If the dam blows, I want the video. What am I going to do in New York?" Perhaps witness the next 9/11?

They were sitting on a large rock outside their hotel in the soft light that dawn cast over the Nile. None of them had slept much as they struggled to decide whether to go or stay and George handled government logistics out of Washington DC.

There are those moments in life, dead center in the midst of chaos, when everything feels perfect. These interludes are counted in seconds, and remind us why everything outside of this perfection actually makes a kind of sense. Listening to the momentous stillness of the Nile's water as it brushed ever so gently against the sandy shores, Emine could only stare at the sky's fading stars and wonder why men seemed so intent on wrecking the world's tranquility. And Ben was going to stay in case he missed that momentous shot which would risk his own life.

"What if you get washed away?" she asked and ignored his look of deliberately ignoring her. Of course, they all risked everything when they walked into a war zone or revolution, but they did it anyway. Someone needed to report the news.

"Please come," she said, unsure why his decision mattered so much, yet wanting his ongoing presence. She studied him in the warming light. Ben was like her in that he faded into the background, with those soft brown eyes and a floppy patch of light brown hair. A studied exercise of quiet he had strong political convictions, he rarely spoke but acted instead. Ben favored loose light t-shirts and those pants with many pockets, for his lenses. He favored video over stills but could capture the camera's passing reality on any device. And he had height, which wasn't always common in many of the battle-scarred countries they inhabited and helped her spot him in a crowd. She kicked his shoe and gave him a half smile. He met her gaze but seemed lost in thought.

As the sun's first ray crossed his face he was looking again out at the river. A call to prayer rang out, echoing and other-worldly. Ben still didn't answer but he did almost smile back.

"And?" she asked him, aware that he'd chosen not to speak. What exactly did she hope to hear since he obviously wasn't changing his mind?

His eyes were still focused on the water. The first boats were spreading their white sails and the sun was increasing its span. How to explain an ancient river facing yet another day, with the myriad of voices and faces that lined its banks and the history which never repeated but must eventually begin to look familiar? The desert beyond was quiet and vast, a companion to the slow moving waters that licked its sand.

"And?" she repeated.

"Emine, I want these pictures," Ben said suddenly, his voice alive. "Chatter never means nothing, and if it's centering around Aswan chances are some story will rear its head. If you're in New York, then you can handle whatever crisis hits the city. Besides, one of us has to stay. We need to get the comprehensive story and not both chase after one possible part."

"So be it," she responded, disappointed but deferring to his logic and desire. Bright had yelled when she informed him of her departure, so he'd be thrilled with Ben's decision. Their boss wanted Aswan pictures, and was perfectly happy to assign someone else in New York (a city with plenty of reporters). Ben could have ignored Bright's pressure as a rare soul who got away with following his own antenna so intently that bending him was virtually impossible. Emine smiled at the conversation she imagined between them: Ben didn't cower and Bright rarely reasoned, preferring the faster tools of abuse, rewards and threats. At least he was never cheap.

But Ben had decided to stay on his own.

"I'm going with George to New York. Khalil seems to be there," she stated the obvious to close the conversation.

"Give him my best." Ben gave her another half smile before glancing back out at the water. Who had the better nose for a story, she wondered? The one who guessed right at the action shots would have a hell of a scoop.

Was it instinct or judgment based on experience that led you down the street chosen by government tanks for their massacre? Which chatter resulted in a successful strike and which was just chatter? And when did the instinct for finding a story lead to death, as it had with Piers? Would his ghost watch over her and use its otherworldly knowledge to send her to glory or back into his arms? The uncertainty and stress were heavy as the world's chess pieces shifted each night while they slept, hoping for peace. Well they'd stumbled into a story, all right, and something big seemed about to happen. Khalil was the real deal, and he didn't touch terror unless many lives were on the line.

George hadn't shown his cards, but Emine knew his position: he was going to find Khalil, the Aswan be damned. Obsessive? Absolutely, as the best at anything had to be, throwing themselves into their objective, never pausing to question the wisdom of utter conviction in pursuit of a goal. George had the passion.

Stretching stiffly, she studied Ben. God bless him if he got the photos of the year and won a prize. She'd pledged herself to George, so it was the best possible division of powers possible.

"I want coffee. I'm tired," she said.

Cards

Ge.orge was going to New York to get the bastard. The US government had a solid team on the ground in Aswan, and his presence really couldn't add value. Khalil and numerous indications pointed toward New York, so it was best to hightail it in that direction. The asshole was likely already in George's new hometown and not planning anything good. Any welcome home parties would, he hoped, be absent body bags, dangerous gases or a bomb.

Well fuck Khalil. Manhattan wasn't that big and George didn't plan on letting him escape this time! He would do whatever was necessary to ensure that his nemesis failed and was recaptured.

Of course, George still hadn't called his wife to tell her that he was on his way home. Quickly he typed out an email, and it was done. At least she'd pretend to be glad when he walked through their arched doorway and they resumed their perfect life.

He took a deep breath, looked around his room to triple check that he'd packed everything and suddenly felt his age. Why wasn't he content to enjoy the fruits of his labors and instead doing battle with men who had no scruples and nothing to lose? Once someone had relinquished a common sense of humanity he enjoyed an advantage in that his behavior had no limits, while someone like George was constrained by his commitment to the sanctity of human life.

Aswan wasn't his problem, and leaving it behind was a perfect example of picking your battles. People died under tragic circumstances every day, and no one could save them all. Egypt was a lovely place, but for countless centuries it had managed to find its own way and survive. The United States was on less stable ground in the forthcoming weeks, with Khalil on the loose. And its inhabitants' expectations were so much higher – which in this world of flattening realities had to eventually mean trouble.

Being the one in charge meant being alone. Everyone he spoke to had their own agenda, and he had to deal with the related bullshit. Did no one tell the truth anymore? George was seasoned enough to recognize the feel of crunch time. Again, with Khalil, he was placing his professional reputation and judgment on the line. Either he won and crushed his opponent or he failed, and lost the respect and goodwill he'd spent a lifetime accumulating. Then there'd be the bodies. Khalil wasn't risking Manhattan for its excellent shopping.

His phone rang, and he saw it was Campbell, perhaps the only other person risking more political capital chasing down Khalil. The games it took to affect a positive outcome in the quagmire of government bureaucracy these days.

"You're coming?" Campbell asked. They'd been through a lot together, and George trusted his old boss almost completely.

"I am."

"He's here, in the States, and was spotted. You aren't coming back for nothing."

"How do you know? Do you know where he is?"

"I'm not cleared to know his exact location yet. Perhaps by the time you get here...".

Shit. Same old, same old.

Manhattan

Khalil wandered the streets of Manhattan, walking back and forth between the Four Seasons Hotel and the UN Building, with a soundtrack of traffic and the hum of people mixed with water. He knew that Radwan had repeated this walk many times.

Aaban was adjusting to the city and spending his time in a cavernous Harlem mosque getting to know its community of people. His role, unlike Khalil's and Radwan's, was to be as visible as possible.

And this part of the plot was taking Khalil to a new level! Shooting KK was explosive enough; but Khalil was framing Aaban, weaponless, to create controversy. Then the Americans, with their fragile balancing of both ethnic tensions and economic disparities, would hopefully see a riot. These big cities, with their scattered pockets of desperation and poverty, were powder kegs where revolution just kept spreading, unchecked and uncontrollable.

How?

Aaban would become known at the local mosque as a pious, if radical, immigrant with limited understanding of English or the city. A few ill placed comments would only cast doubt later, when the police questioned people. Radwan would die after shooting KK, whether shot by the police, security or Khalil. Aaban would run from the building on cue, thinking he was just a lookout and not realizing that his prints were on the gun.

Complicated? Absolutely, and that was Khalil's expertise. An easy strike couldn't have the same debilitating impact or create the right network of fear. Khalil reminded himself not to let ambition override his major objective: the only element which really mattered was ensuring that KK lay dead in a pool of blood with the rest being a lucky perk. KK's progressive politics couldn't be allowed to take hold in Egypt.

Khalil gazed at the tall steel towers around him, majestic and massive, while the cheaper ones were starting to tarnish with soot, even the best sheltered kabob shops and the ubiquitous McDonalds.

He enjoyed watching the people. Worried always, of course, that he'd be picked up again as had happened two years before in London. The hand firm on his arm, brown hair on white pasty skin that led to a horrible span of nine months. Solitary confinement is hell, every minute of it. Time passing like water drops on a hot rock in the desert…disappearing into nothingness such that it never seemed to pass.

Next time they'd have to shoot him before he'd surrender. Now Khalil knew how bad captivity was with its torture, prisons and prying Georges. Walking in the humid heat of a New York summer, he felt gloriously free and soaked in gratitude. Allah had provided, and he therefore had a debt to pay in killing KK. These people walking the open streets in a mostly free country didn't realize the price to be paid for their arrogance and attitude of entitlement. He wasn't their property, so why should he accept their classifications and prisons?

He dialed his phone keypad and called Jennifer on her disposable. Three calls was Osman's limit, then the trash bin. The boy was holed up in a safe house right outside the city and Aaban, his dispensable one, played phone courier in and out of the city. He'd toss this phone right after the call.

"I love you," she whispered into the phone and he wondered at her judgment. He really was the best she could do? These Americans had such complicated relationships, as the songs he kept hearing on the radio attested. So be it, since he still wanted her around. Those other men from her past had been fools who left her vulnerable to a dangerous tramp like him. And she was lovely too.

But he wasn't ready to tell her he loved her – or perhaps he had nothing to lose in letting go of that fear. Her silence over the phone line make such a stark contrast to the bustling city. Those years alone had been so like the chaos of the streets around him, thoughts heading in all directions. Now he had a place he wanted to go at the end of each day but didn't offer much in return.

"I love you too," he replied, surprised at his words yet suddenly knowing they were all right. "I'll bring dinner back," he told her.

"Oh, can't we just go out tonight?" she asked. He watched a taxi almost knock over a man in a trim grey suit, his briefcase swaying as he jumped out of its path. The yellow cab just sped off. None of the pedestrians slowed down either, preferring to head off into their own realities unaffected. It was that sheep-like acceptance of oddities in the streets that made his job easy. Now if only the authorities would stop trying to find him.

"Fine," he responded to Jennifer. "I'll be back in forty minutes."

Tossing the phone into a garbage can, he was glad to be in a light polo shirt and khaki pants, not a grey suit. The people on the street were a full spectrum of colors and nationalities, and he actually fit in quite well.

Before seeing Jennifer he had a bribe to pay. Doormen didn't make high salaries in this city. Not even at the Four Seasons.

Home

George stepped into his apartment, relieved that his key still fit the lock. Truth be told, he was just glad to be home and was even looking forward to the reunion with Karen. She might be a bitch sometimes, but she was his bitch and he wasn't always easy to be around.

They'd left Cairo that morning, ending up on an Egypt air flight to JFK arriving just before 6:00 p.m. Government escorts got them through customs and immigration in a flash. Emine had been deposited at the LeParker Meridian, not far from his apartment, and it was now close to 8:00 after bags, traffic and the rest – thus the middle of the night in Cairo – and George was exhausted. He'd slept little on the flight, mulling over possible clues to Khalil's erratic behavior.

Khalil was a dangerous and tricky killer. He was unable to abandon his tortured fight against the west, whatever desperation or faith bound him. Emboldened by crazy revolutionary rhetoric from the Castros and Lenins of the world, he chose to destroy so that a new reality could arise from the resulting ruins, like a phoenix from its ashes.

His group, the Salaafists, an affiliate of Al Qaeda, wasn't doing well geopolitically, being increasingly marginalized as other Muslims grew weary of the body bags and bombs in their streets.

Dropping Aswan into their conversation on more than one occasion wasn't like Khalil, who was careful and quiet to a fault. That characteristic had made him damn near impossible nut to crack, each word drawn through complex manipulation and psychological maneuvering. Khalil was as chatty as a rock.

Then Khalil had swept through Aswan and bolted to Manhattan to meet Jennifer, the girlfriend George himself had thrown back into his path. Why now? A quick trip? Had he already left the country again? What kind of game was he playing?

The certainties were rapidly running dry.

George had left his two suitcases and carry-on bag by the front door, planning to deal with them in the morning after he got his much needed sleep. Now that he was home, everything he needed was here, organized and within his grasp. In his living room he headed for the bottle of scotch and glasses they kept on a side table, right next to his favorite bookshelf. *The New York Times* had once printed a photo with ereaders on the shelves of a similar case. While George had and used a Kindle, while traveling, for example, he still liked his paper bound books. Some were old friends and had stayed with him through the passing years. Karen, understanding his passions, had let him commandeer the location by the scotch and piles of books.

Pausing by the bookshelf, he saw that all was as he'd left it, familiar and grounding. George considered grabbing a favorite but took that extra step to the scotch first. Pouring himself a solid slug he suddenly noticed how quiet the apartment seemed, especially after the chaos and noise of Egypt. Karen hadn't come to welcome him yet and he felt that lapse deeply, a familiar ache of not connecting. Yet we can't force people to do our bidding just because we wish it. Karen was especially independent with George's increasing absences, as he seemed incapable of turning down each new challenge. And she wasn't the dusty-clothes-in-a-war-zone kind of girl. He'd joked about it being "her loss" but knew that their relationship was the real victim.

George got up from the couch to select a book. Fiction or non-fiction? Light or not? An old favorite or something he hadn't yet read? He grabbed *Anti-Americanism* by Jean Francois Revel, the French intellectual. He'd read the book before and wanted to revisit the reasons that Revel believed so many in the world today hated Americans.

Why do so many people bother hating those they don't know anyway? Hardly the most productive use of energy. But somehow it was a very popular activity and political tool used to divide and conquer. Did the addiction come from a sense of helplessness, narcissism or insecurity? Well, any sort of rigidity was a toxin that exposed a perceived threat, either from the inside or out. Perhaps people needed to use the contrasts with others to reassure themselves of their own superiority. But as Buddha said, all suffer – they just suffer in different ways. Compassion seemed a better mindset. Alas.

George looked at the words, black letters on white paper expanding page upon page upon page. He slugged down the last of his scotch and went to bed. The world's problems would have to wait until he got some much needed sleep.

Trust?

"Don't trust me. If you truly love me, you'll accept that I will do things you won't like," Khalil said, staring into Jennifer's deep blue eyes and letting himself fall into them, if only for an instant. Why did she continue to trust him? Trust: that word had little meaning anymore and only put her in danger. Jennifer. Smart girl. So what was she thinking? Khalil would be more comfortable if he believed that she understood the risks she was taking and would act accordingly, since he wouldn't be there to protect her. Still, her naïve faith in whatever she thought he was did have its appeal.

"Khalil, I do trust you," she said, all wide eyes and innocence. She was too old for such blind faith, wasn't she? Perhaps we're all just looking for an ideology onto which we can channel our utter submission. Or was she lying?

"Don't. You should have learned that much already," he replied, letting the topic rest there. She'd been warned; no point in fighting, since his responsibility was now over. "Let's go get dinner."

Were they being reckless by eating dinner out and not in? Khalil was unsure. He'd suspected a tail or two, yet couldn't be sure. But the best hiding place is always a large city with its transitory and unconnected population. Few would recognize him, especially after his surgeries, unless they were looking for him – in which case it was only a matter of time before he was arrested or shot.

The smells of early evening Manhattan filtered into their budget hotel room. Near a pizza shop, with its expansive skinny pies, the smells of yeast and tomato sauce filtered into the air at mealtime. The room's air conditioner didn't work well, so the temperature served as a reminder that the humid city was warming up with summer's coming. At least the bed was good, wide and soft, which was a rarity in less expensive hotels. He could have sprung for something nicer, but at a Four Seasons he'd be noticed and followed as the staff strove to offer impeccable service, including remembering his face and name.

And Khalil was starting to feel trapped. Sure, he'd invited her. But years of living without having to answer to a "partner" had made that his established practice now. In his world he was either in charge or took orders. Sure, a war allowed for some "partners," but not really. He'd never answered to a woman before or been with one who actually expected him to. His past women had mostly been paid to keep his house and provide other services. They didn't talk back or even express much of an opinion, and he would have hit them, had they done so.

The one little girl, the rail-thin Dinka from his time in the Sudan, had gone so far as to decorate his home. But she'd stopped at that meager liberty and thus had been allowed to stay a while. Jennifer was a whole other story and, while he'd forgotten the Dinka girl's name, Jennifer was the one back in his bed.

"Why are you looking at me like that?" she asked, and he saw her temper flare. With the world crashing and burning around them, she was complaining about his look? Mostly physically healed after her bullet scare, her behavior had improved. Perhaps reality was dawning and she was seeing that everyone's skin was equally helpless while bullets were impervious. But they didn't discuss these things, nor did he want to discuss them. So his guesses were merely that, another shot into the darkness of her mind.

He finally had Jennifer, yet was too nervous about his work to appreciate her. Was that why she'd been touchier, yet also more tentative, than before her injury? Realizing that she was making sacrifices but not understanding that his were so much greater?

"Let's get dinner," he repeated, softening his voice. How could he protect her? The truth was that he couldn't. Tomorrow more money would get transferred and in less than two weeks the hopeful Presidential candidate would die. Egypt would be left without the great reformer currently being glorified globally as a humanitarian and job creator, and it would continue in chaos. Then his group could swoop in, seize the reins and bring a different sort of order.

"Where do you want to go…oh, what's close…?" he asked, staring into Jennifer's blue eyes again but paying attention this time. People's eyes changed less than the rest of them over the years and hers still fluttered the way he remembered them doing in San Diego.

"I don't care," she replied, grabbed him and planted a deep kiss on his mouth. Still, he felt the tension in her affectionate gesture. She must be petrified, poor girl, yet she still didn't realize that this was the easier part. Every day their risks only grew. She was in jeans, a touch too tight and framing her ass. Lovely, with a softly yellow t-shirt setting off her hair, she really was a sweet companion. Glancing around at their lone bed, couch, table and luggage, he knew that he could and would give her better. He'd actually saved a lot of money and skimmed more. Maybe sometime soon he could retire, if his organization let him.

"Forgive me," he said then watched the mist gather in her eyes. How could she still know so little? Grudgingly, he admitted that if she knew more she'd leave him and probably abandon their love for good this time. He fingered the thin material of her t-shirt as she kissed him again and he held her tightly. Her touch was his only respite from the world around him.

"No pizza." Jennifer laughed as she pulled away, then headed out the door. Following her, his cell rang.

"Tomorrow. One. In front of the hotel. Red shirt." A man's voice spoke then broke off.

Yes, the Assassins – those political suicide killers from the Middle Ages – were back. Meanwhile, Khalil trailed after his girlfriend in search of hot food. Catching her, he enfolded her in his arms.

Abruptly, she stopped and turned to face him.

"I'm so flawed, Khalil," she said, her voice husky with tears. How could such a smart person otherwise have so little control? Whoever said love was blind missed something. Love amplified our beloved faults, and we assumed shame for them. Thus came those moments when love and hate mingled, as we struggled with taking on someone else's weaknesses, committing but also pulling away.

Yet he couldn't bear to be apart from her, not even for an instant, not with the way she melted against him and whispered into his chin.

Exiting the small elevator, they headed out into the crowded streets near Times Square. A rushing heavy-set man almost knocked them over without pausing or offering an apology.

"I saw a Thai place down that street. It was pretty crowded, so it must be good," Jennifer suggested, pointing. Khalil nodded and followed her, dodging the crowds swarming from work, to dinner or to Broadway shows close by. Thai food wasn't his favorite but he'd never been a picky eater.

"There," he said and pointed, touching her shoulder gently. They headed to the small brick-red store front, the restaurant name displayed on a deep Kelly green sign with white block letters.

A man scurried behind them and Khalil worried, wondering if he'd was being followed, always paranoid and careful. His lifestyle required such vigilance though didn't most of us carry our own burdensome fear? He just knew what his was. Scanning the street Khalil looked for sheltered areas and escape routes. He'd had brought a gun but didn't want to use it so hopefully they'd make it through dinner unbothered.

Entering the dimly lit restaurant they were greeted by a young Asian woman in an asymmetrical dress. The room was a wide rectangle and most tables were full while a dull hum of voices mingled with shouts from the kitchen. Khalil gestured to an empty table in the back and she walked them there before handing out menus.

As they sat the waitress asked, "Anything to drink?"

"A beer, please," Jennifer said, as she opened the menu. Khalil's muscles tightened. Women shouldn't drink alcohol. Oh, he knew that she done it before, when they were younger at college, but he'd been borrowing her then – with no intention of keeping. The standards were different now.

"You shouldn't drink," he said, trying to keep his voice level but hearing otherwise.

She looked up. Her eyes were wide open and her lips parted as if in surprise. "I'm going to pretend I didn't hear that," she said and then directed her attention back to her menu, letting the order stand. Khalil tried to read his own rolling list of specials and curries but instead felt forced to fight his rage, which he resented. Whore.

The beer arrived, along with his bottled water. She took a long, deep gulp, watching him defiantly. Then she put it down and smiled blandly. "What do you feel like eating?"

Khalil thought, trying to weigh each possible option though he really had too many variables to analyze in a few fragments of a second. The reality was that if this relationship was going to work not only would she have to change but so would he.

"Steak, rice and some eggplant," he responded, choking and gulping his water as she studied him. He tried to smile but failed so took another swig of water. Never make a decision in the midst of emotion.

"Perfect!" was all she said. Now what would they discuss?

"Do you like New York?" he asked, hoping she'd pull out of this odd mood. What was wrong with her? Seemingly he'd done something egregious and Jennifer didn't want to enlighten him with the details. Lucky at her age to have a man even if he wasn't the greatest catch. And Khalil was both rich and famous. Wasn't that all American women cared about? Perhaps he should tell her so and thus improve her behavior. Cheap, old, drunk whores lined the streets of this city.

"It's okay," Jennifer responded slowly. He felt the pause since she made it obvious. "You love me, but do you respect me? Do you respect women at all?"

This fight he wasn't having. He was with her and risking his life (and hers) to do so. She could get drunk and fight with another man. He wasn't tolerating such ridiculousness.

"What will you do tomorrow? I need to work," he said, ignoring her question. Her eyes flashed anger and she took another gulp of beer. "Come on, let's not fight," he said. She nodded and again he saw those tears bunching up in clusters on her eyes. What was it with her! Khalil knew he must be missing something important but couldn't imagine what. Then he realized how few common interests they had to discuss. Their lives were so different and he couldn't talk much about his while hers was boring. Helping rich and poor people deal with the American court system? What did he care about civil lawsuits? If she'd done more criminal work perhaps he could have learned something useful.

"I don't know," she murmured, finally giving him a genuine smile. "I guess this city is lovely....but I haven't been here for a while." A dish of some dumpling appetizer she'd ordered landed on their table, wafting a garlicky aroma. He realized how hungry he was but held off from the food, letting her begin. Gingerly, she used both a spoon and a fork to deposit a few dumplings on to his plate before taking some herself. She gave him a shy smile.

"Is this what our life will be? Running from one country to the next?" she asked and must know that he had to lie. The truth was that only when assembling a big plot did he run like this. Other times he waited and did very little, living where ever he pleased.

"I can afford it," he responded only to see her shake her head.

"That isn't the point," she replied and he bit down on the fragrant dumpling, the tender juice spilling out. It was delicious. He'd avoided marriage this long to run head into this mess? Apparently.

"What do you want from me?" he asked her, finally worn out from her mood. "Have another dumpling."

"You aren't planning something are you?" she asked, ignoring her food. "We're in New York so you can kill people." His first instinct was to walk out on her but he didn't want to give her that information, implying that he cared she had such concerns.

"You aren't watching me for signs of anything, are you?" he asked, trying to make it sound like a joke.

"I lied to you in college," she started, tears now taking over her eyes in puddles. "I got pregnant and had an abortion without telling you. I still wonder how our lives would have been different if I'd given you that chance to be a father."

Khalil just stared, seeing through and behind her but not focusing. He felt like he'd been hit hard in the head and couldn't recover his wits enough to respond. She'd just said that she aborted their child while they were dating twenty years before? She'd kept that secret for so long?

And now she was staring at him in a cheap Thai restaurant in mid-town Manhattan dropping her own bomb? What did she expect?

"I'm using the bathroom," Jennifer mumbled and left the table, her food and him. Khalil struggled to figure out the implications of her words. Was she a plant or just crazy? Was she working with the government? Perhaps that's why she'd agreed to see him at George's bidding two years ago when he a prisoner and again after he'd called.

And was she telling the truth about the abortion? He didn't have a clue.

New York

mine was in Manhattan and she just loved New York. How George planned on finding and capturing Khalil made no sense whatsoever but seemed to have the makings of a novel, with its elements of intrigue and tendrils of danger. Find a dark guy in a city of over eight million very diverse people?

Spending time on Wikipedia, since George was at home and she was alone, she'd already learned that Manhattan was the oldest and most densely populated of New York's five boroughs. The area was also among the most densely populated in the world and had a per capita income of over $100,000. Manhattan was also the third largest of the five boroughs in population but the smallest in size. Home to Wall Street, the NY Stock Exchange and much of the city's government and country's media titans it seemed delicately poised to continue being a major terrorist target.

Emine loved the winding Hudson River, lush Central Park and even, yes, she loved the stores, and not just Fifth Avenue. No, she'd gotten past high end and now wanted the curiosities. The bookstore with old first editions. Artisan jewels...not the cheap or predictable branded stuff. Knick knacks and the exotic.

They were on the cusp of summer and the temperature was rising.

Being housed at the Le Parker Meridian meant that everything worked. And when so little else in the world did it was nice to find a place where order and efficiency weren't a problem. The hotel had that vast white feel she so craved, and her room was likewise neutral with a killer view of the city streets.

Emine stared out her window, pondering the vastness below and the limitations of her knowledge. What she understood was that Aswan was seemingly still a target. Underwater or from above? Which was more likely to work when accounting for the heavy weight of the water itself? Not a munitions expert, she'd listened to George explain the repercussions of each possible course. A strong explosion under the surface would create tremendous pressure from the water itself. A kick back action would send up a huge wave and push into the dam with additional force, crumbling the structure. If not enough munitions were used the water would crush the impact's spread and devastation. Water is so very heavy. From above, well, boom.

Khalil was in New York or wanted them to believe so? One random phone found did not a pattern make. But George was obsessed. And, if Khalil was in New York, home of 9/11 and George's apartment, with some luck they could find him before he did any harm. As if terrorists came to Manhattan for a little deli and a photo of the Statue of Liberty.

Shit.

Watching George Emine had witnessed firsthand how smart he was.

Then there were Mehmet's words. "Some people have a special antenna and see the world before it happens. I don't have that skill but try to follow those who do. George has that distinctive insight and, Emine, so do you. Follow no star but your own."

Thus she was ready to start sorting eight million people until she found the one on her agenda. Why not? Nothing much on television anyway, as if she cared since the real world was so much more interesting. Bright had assigned a team of people to help her sort and process data in the hopes of a non-government driven lead. He also wanted to give her a cameraman to replace Ben. Hell no!

Emine sipped, deeply, crimson, and she thought: her angle was ...?

People would see things of interest but wouldn't have the resources or contact base to reach out with their information. You sound crazy when you see terrorists in Manhattan because, oh gosh, for a million reasons. Emine could set up a web site and call in number. A Facebook page. Or Bright could put an article in one of his papers, asking for tips, but she'd have to pen it first.

Her not exactly boyfriends were trying to keep her good and distracted on the personal end just as she had a major scoop falling into her lap. Sensing her independence?

Ed…"come to Paris and I'll take care of you…".

Bud…"I'm finally ready to love you. My sources say both Aswan and Manhattan are dangerous so let me know how I can help."

Now! Really?

And a girl had to choose the way she always did…by following her heart. But first she had to find it and that's what where her big bottle of French Burgundy came in handy. Maybe some women didn't run at threats of a commitment but she did. That crushing sensation of expectation that took her very breathe away. Wasn't there some balance of power in romance, as complicated as geopolitics and just as dangerous?

So Emine intended to to drink herself to sleep tonight and see what clarifying dreams the moon and her muddled mind concocted. Tracking a killer, wiling to risk his life to enter the States again, wasn't a challenge to be treated lightly by falling into romance and fairy tales. Tomorrow her wits would matter, tonight, intoxicated, her subconscious would be free to range possibilities and fantasize answers. Realistically, she only had room for one man in her brain now and his name was Khalil. Ben, the Feds and the Egyptian government could handle Aswan…hopefully…but if not she wasn't even there any more thus couldn't help.

"Disorder leads to power shifts, like a comet hitting the earth and no less violent," Mehmet had said, ever a calculating politician. "Happy people want the status quo thus anyone aiming for change must prey on the unhappy." The miserable were everywhere, even Manhattan.

Emine took a slug of crimson and tasted the chocolate intermingled with woody musk. This room was comfortable, and she looked down from her perch at what felt like the top of the world. Below people were rushing too and fro, living their lives just as she was. Time for reflection comes too rarely so she savored it.

She'd ordered hummus, with a spread of salads, adding cheesecake, since she was in New York, then found she couldn't eat it. The dense dessert was too rich, after her normally spare diet, so she picked at the strawberries with whipped cream. Standing up and tottering only a bit she looked down at the streets. He was there, Khalil, wasn't he? Walking, talking, eating, sleeping and breathing. Intelligence days old wasn't worth much but Emine sensed that he'd come here for a reason and hadn't yet achieved his purpose. The whole world had been waiting for another Manhattan disaster and Khalil seemingly would be the desperado to take aim at that crown

Chasing a man she'd never met and who was an enigma left her grasping at the unknowable, and adrift. It would be George's heart they'd all have to follow. She prayed that he'd caught the right emotional subtleties during their more recent interactions and knew that regardless, they would persevere, painfully if need be.

Emine never believed in chasing after men. Letting them come after you worked so much better. So how to dangle a prize before a criminal such that he had to come running? What was it that Khalil really wanted?

To succeed at his worldly aims or to be loved despite the miserable person he'd become? How do you become whole again after making too many bad choices?

Night...time...

eorge couldn't sleep. His repentant wife had returned home tipsy. If nothing else, she always had the ability to surprise, most likely why he'd married her and stayed. He understood and analyzed people professionally, at the absolute highest levels and she was sometimes an enigma! What other new surprises about her would he discover in the days to come?

"You're going to be elected President, George," she'd mumbled before crashing onto his shoulder where he'd fallen asleep on the couch after only a few slugs of scotch and paragraphs that made him feel hated as an American. Thirty years of marriage made that a normal experience.

The sounds of the door opening had woken him and he'd jumped in fear before realizing that he was finally home. And he hadn't even been gone very long, despite all that had happened. Then George recognized the soft tread of her step and braced himself, not knowing what to expect.

"Everyone hates politicians," she started and he smelled the wine she'd been drinking. At least her aroma was from a good vintage. "And if you catch Khalil they'll love you. You'll be the Ike of your day."

He almost followed her logic. "Or Ulysses Grant? Another general who won the presidency after winning the war?" he asked, thinking that comparing him to a great general was quite a stretch, even drunk. She stared back, blinking like she always did when tipsy, as if her eyes didn't see right. Wearing a simple bone-colored sheath, her shoulder length hair pulled back into an elegant and wispy ponytail, she looked clean and safe and familiar even in her present state. She was as much his home as his scotch, bookshelf and ugly green velvet couch.

226

"Exactly," she said with a smile. Well, never argue with a drunken woman. He hugged her and was relieved that she hugged back. Tightly. "I missed you," she murmured, all sweetness now. And they kissed softly. Quit frankly he was just too tired for anything else...or not. He might be old but he wasn't dead.

The sirens and horns outside near Columbus Circle had almost stopped for the night. Later, George slept deeply, his delicate wife breathing gently next to him and nuzzled among soft sheets and cushy pillows. But then he'd woken, stirred by the shadows that a city's omnipresent lights filter throughout its inhabitants' lives. There was no dark here.

His unconscious worked such mystery and haunted him on evenings when a tough (or impossible) problem nagged away at his rest. Neither the scotch nor the wife had robbed him of the tension that he could feel paralyzing his limbs and worse, his brain. George got out of bed and headed back to his cut crystal bottle and its amber resident.

The pressure was intense and the repercussions from his choices kept rapt pursuit. As he'd, unwisely, decided to stay in the streets of Cairo to get kidnapped he'd now decamped Aswan to its fate and landed back in Manhattan but for what exactly? Fate was the unknown that played its hand unexpectedly.

George surveyed the facts he'd misinterpreted in the past. Khalil had likely known about his entry in Cairo before he arrived or if not him than someone affiliated with his organization. Their driver's death and how quickly and easily George was nabbed were the work of pros. He could speculate and wonder at the exact details but they didn't matter for invisible eyes shockingly did watch. Khalil must be tracking George; not difficult for someone in his line of work to accomplish.

And now the bastard had lured him back home.

George sipped again, dressed in baggy cotton sweat pants and a faded black t-shirt. The fluid was a warm balm, soothing and needed. Seemingly George was starting to appreciate the green velvet couch, his main companion this evening, and a welcoming one after splintered chairs and dark alleys. Soft, comfortable and familiar! The city below was quiet but Central Park hadn't changed and was as lovely as ever.

Why did Khalil want him here? Did Khalil want him here or in Aswan? That Khalil would track him made sense on so many disturbing psychological levels. First, there was the Stockholm syndrome of identifying with your captors. He'd been virtually the only one nice to Khalil in over a year of captivity and his only pseudo-companion. That was how George broke men: torture didn't work as well as promised. Men would say anything to end pain and did, true or not. Offer them understanding and support and you won them.

Next, Khalil was a psychopath.

George was supposed to know Khalil but how well did he? Ultimately we never know someone rather just what we've seen of them in any given set of circumstances. At this stage of the investigation, despite their recent interactions, George could only guess at why Khalil was in New York of all places and what was his ultimate destructive endgame.

George felt no strong advantage.

But having worked with sophisticated killers over the years he knew the drill. Instinctively, after spending a certain amount of time with someone you knew them better than your insecurities let you believe, and you knew them well enough. George would have to trust himself, despite all signs to the contrary, and follow his gut despite any conflicting evidence that pointed elsewhere. People rarely act out of character. Even Karen had her patterns in her unpredictability. Khalil liked to surprise, but George would subconsciously, though not consciously, adjust for that factor.

Why did he have this overwhelming sense that he was being stalked?

No wonder George couldn't sleep.

Somewhere off in the distance he heard a siren and hoped things turned out all right. President, huh? Exactly how much did Karen drink earlier that evening. And with whom had she been conversing?

Coffee

Khalil guzzled from a paper cup of coffee, a Greek looking thing found throughout this city with symbols and pictures all around. Blue. He also gnawed at something called a "scone" but not at all like what he'd eaten in London. The US and UK really did speak a different version of the same language, with slang and assumptions thrown in.

George must be getting up by now, with the soft filters of a summer sun, while Khalil was sitting on a bench in Central Park and staring up at his window and drinking coffee, extra cream. He'd left Jennifer in bed and had come here to join the joggers and homeless. Hot coffee was nice but the city's humidity was already noticeable and he was glad to be in short sleeves.

He was dressed lightly, in loose cargo pants and a white t-shirt. Thin but muscular, his body type was an oddity here this morning despite the multitude of runners. Americans were just bigger, both in bulk and height, as their diet was richer. The park was pristine and lovely and Khalil savored the moment of reflection that wouldn't last.

He'd had an early morning call about Aswan, which was what had originally driven him from his hotel room and warm Jennifer.

"Aswan is set. What do you want to do?"

Why of course he didn't know.

Originally, the Aswan plot had been meant as a diversion. They were going to have it "revealed" and "save" the dam. But the potential bombing proved so easy to put in place! Egypt was a country in sheer chaos with the authorities' attention on the mobs and the power struggles preceding the election. Planting grenade like bombs at strategic spots across the dam had proven simple.

Planning to debilitate a dam shouldn't be so.

His analysis now that a hypothesis had become reality?

As always, one needed to consider the desired effect before picking a course of action. The deeper the water in which the explosion took place, the greater the impact on the water. The recoil would hit both the dam's solid mass and the surrounding fluid with great force, sending them flying. But water had weight and needed to feel a big explosion if it was to share. A higher up explosive, closer to the top of the dam, would be more predictable and would blow off the dams top but the deeper waters would be untouched.

Khalil had decided on the deep blow and sent in his diver, a munitions expert careful in the most delicate missions. He thought they'd be caught planting the device, risking his specialized man but worth the fear a bombing would engender, but weren't. Was Egypt rapidly becoming such failed state that they couldn't protect their dam, the source of their fragmented shards of prosperity?

Now it was his decision whether or not to detonate the bombs. He held Egypt's fate in his palms so what would he do?

First, he sipped at his bitter coffee and stared up at George's windows. No one ever really forgets anything, he whispered in Arabic and knowing that likewise no one understands. He hadn't been followed; tossing his cell phone each day seemed to work well for keeping his location a secret. So many ways of tracking a man...

He'd held George once and could grab him again, should he so desire. For now he didn't.

But his problem was KK first, the dam second and the dam today. Time was running out and then if lucky he'd take his woman and escape back to Brazil and his plastic surgeon. If...only...if...

The sun was brightening and the streets getting more crowded with that flash of busy feet headed somewhere. This city was like any other, from the river that had propelled its original growth to the smelly traffic that now clogged its arteries. People would wander through their realities and never recognize how events tied together, rarely random. History was as Allah ordained and humanity just did his holy bidding.

Aswan would be decided today while Khalil had just over a week to kill KK.

Machiavelli had said: *God is not willing to do everything, and thus take away our free will and that share of glory which belongs to us.* Now the burden was his alone.

Khalil gazed back up at the white column of a building. So what to do with George? He sipped, and then nibbled at his crumbly scone, thinking, but not really letting his thoughts head anywhere important. He'd deflect this decision because too much was pressing on his mind and he could no longer think straight. His mind was a jumbled mess, tangents leading to order to utter disorder.

Jennifer.

Khalil needed to go back and deal with her. She was a risk now, he recognized and acknowledged. Jennifer of those soft kisses and lush breasts, her hair cascading against the pillows as he'd left her asleep before the full sun's emergence. Lovely, but perhaps an illusion camouflaged as an angel. How skillfully could she lie? Someone prone to tears might merely be a good actress.

Observing a fellow dark man with a coffee cart and pastries serving a crowd Khalil went over to him and watched as the vendor moved his fingers quickly, spouting frothy milk and wrapping all in napkins. The man was about his own age but of a darker hue. Egyptian? He wore a Yankees cap and *I Love New York* t-shirt with jeans. Going for the tourist crowd? His patrons seemed to like him, as they chatted about sports or the weather and kept calling him Reggie. Sensing a break Khalil went up to his cart and whispered an address.

"There," Khalil pointed at George's building. "Two coffees, black. And two bagels." The man nodded yes as Khalil handed him fifty dollars. More would have been too conspicuous. He smiled at the man and walked away, confident that George would now have a fresh breakfast with his own hot coffee.

Voyeurs

mine was on the phone with Ben. It was God awful early and she had more than the whispers of a hangover. She was also feeling the flight and time change and honestly couldn't remember what she did the night before. Thankfully she hadn't eaten the cheesecake brick and had woken up alone.

Between their frantic calls this morning she'd managed a quick shower but her hair was still dripping wet. She was wearing an American Apparel lace one piece, black, and had slipped a robe over it when room service rang. Bright was on the warpath and Ben had been ditched by his Feds, who were seemingly in a panic. Everyone wanted information but she had none.

Emine picked at her breakfast. For some reason pancakes had seemed like a good idea but then came the syrup and all those phones calls. She cherry picked the berries and used them to sop up her syrup. The coffee was perfect, deep and dark, without that watery taste so common in the States.

It seemed no one was sharing information, if they had any, everyone wanting it desperately instead and thinking that with her proximity to George she might have some. George was the one not calling or answering his phones, which went straight to voicemail.

Bud didn't know anything, deliberately. She could tell.

"Eme, I helped you rescue your business partner but mostly I stay away from terrorists. They kill people, you know," he'd said into the long distance call, in Mauritius now and probably with some girl, much as he kept saying he loved her. "Not even wealth makes you immune."

She was dressing, having abandoned her soggy towel to the floor. Today she'd...?

Walk the streets of the city, peering into faces. Eat an ice cream cone and walk to the park. Call her mother. Damn! She last called Liz when? And meanwhile she'd been phoning Mehmet so mom would be mad.

Picking up her cell she heard her room phone ring. Conflict? No! Answer the phone that's ringing because that was the person who wanted to speak with you now.

"Emine?" a formal voice said, which since it was Bright signaled trouble. She breathed in deeply and braced herself.

"My reporters are getting shut out," he said sternly, a fake control apparent in his voice. She waited. Let the bastard stew; she wasn't giving him what he wanted. He was a cold fucking snake and she knew his utter control in the thralls of anger. He'd deal calmly in the moment then kill you later when an opportunity presented itself. She felt a chill run through her at his tone and wondered what he wanted.

But he waited too. And since she worked for him she recognized her reality...she'd break first with the only variable being how long she'd wait before doing so.

"That's not unusual," she responded. "Especially when someone, the government, doesn't want leaks." She slipped on some ballet flats and reached for petal pink lip-gloss. This city started getting increasingly humid now, at the end of May, so she was atypically wearing a light sundress with bare shoulders and a flowing skirt. The shoes would be her insurance in case she needed to run. Bright was still waiting her out, even though she'd spoken first. Damned game player. So she continued.

"Where are you?" she asked.

"Downstairs," he replied. Hadn't he been in Aswan with Ben yesterday? Well, she wasn't bringing him along if, when, she reached George. It was already 10:00 a.m. and she hadn't heard from her local "partner". Ben was waiting for some direction but no one seemed to have him on speed dial any longer through he was perhaps within a mile or two of the greatest terrorist attack ever contemplated.

"Kidding," he said. Phew!

How to extricate herself and solve Ben's problems at the same time...

Emine checked herself in the mirror and was heartened by what she saw. Growing up in utter chaos left her particularly suited to it and she absolutely glowed. Somehow with all her drinking and gritty assignments her skin and eyes were clear and her face lean. Perhaps the passion she brought to her work got the credit?

You can't fight life because it wins. So you need to work with it, with the Buds and Brights. Khalils, Omars, Mehmets and Lizs. And if you're really smart, like George, you can dictate the cards that got dealt and perhaps even a rule or two.

Life was the dealer and we all got played.

How was she going to handle the asshole on the phone? Seemed like a good time to start bluffing which since she didn't hold any cards was her only option.

Chaos

Saving a nation first or your family, George asked himself. He really had a lot to do and it was all relentlessly crushing. Increasingly he believed that Khalil was challenging him on his home turf. The delivered coffee from an Arab guy in the morning was just but one more clue. Cute.

Khalil was a sick fuck...that's what mass murder did to your psyche. It had an impact even if you'd started down that road out of necessity and not desire. How someone dealt with the first kill made all the difference. People tended to shut down, reeling as the fight or flight syndrome kicked in but it was the defenses that you built in response that defined the person ultimately. Did you seek to justify or dehumanize your victim or did you turn on yourself?

The coffee had arrived with the sunshine and George had dumped the mess down the garbage disposal. Karen didn't understand and argued.

"Go pack or you'll be dead soon," was his response and he knew that his attitude wasn't constructive. A smart girl, for once she did as instructed and mostly held her tongue. But not without a question first.

"Nicolas and Natalie?" she asked. Their children.

"Protection program and I'm on it. Now pack quickly. Whatever you need."

Then he yelled at Campbell, also not constructive but he was beyond that. He'd been so obviously tracked before and kidnapped so why had they sent him home without better security detail? This was his tax dollars at work. Campbell got guards for George and protective custody for his family.

Only then did he start making coffee. Real coffee, home coffee and not blood coffee. Karen talked him into a shower, promising to patrol the door. The hot water as it hit his body felt like he was already in heaven.

He could taste his own fear and tried to wash it down the drain but it wouldn't obey. Thankfully, Karen for all of her faults tended to coldness not emotion which was useful in his own panic. He wanted her and their children safe.

Sick fuck! Was Khalil imploding and trying to take George with him? Thinking back and realizing their earliest interactions had been so very long ago George remembered the calculating prisoner that was Khalil. He'd been strong, and hadn't ever broken completely, instead always plotting and planning, using his weaknesses as an advantage and not a liability. Dribbling out bits of information, enough to help plan his own escape, though also enabling George to stop a string of domestic McDonalds from blowing up. But even then Khalil had been more in control than he was now. What had led to the change?

Khalil was scared. So he was coming back to what he knew...George... but what else? The spider, with a complex web of patterns in his plots...why contact George before and not after completion if the chatter was right and a major strike was planned?

It had to be personal. Revenge? Obsession? Or anger that George got away? What about Aswan? All George had was questions, much as he'd spent the morning on the phone with Campbell.

"We lost him in New York."

The girlfriend. Missing too but George wasn't the only old face with whom Khalil was reconnecting.

Then the updated file had arrived from DC...no one had thought to get him a copy while he was in Egypt and George started devouring, reading and pouring through what was a much deeper and denser packet than earlier data he'd seen.

Karen slipped into the room.

"George," she asked, a few times it must have been, before George heard. He was so intent on his file and all that was new and important. Khalil's mother had died earlier in the year as he'd said and here it was confirmed! Could she have been the rock that kept him stable? He didn't seem to have anyone else.

But Karen was standing there and talking so he had to engage with her before she left. Hopefully, they'd hide her somewhere nice with a beach and strong Internet connection for her research. She was dressed in simple trousers and a loose short sleeve blouse. Always appropriate, her hair was again pulled back loosely and she wore her favorite diamond earrings. Smaller stones encircled a larger one, creating a gem flower and the diamonds glistened as they caught the morning light. Her make-up was light and her mood seemed fine, all things considered. George and Karen had never been tracked in his home before. Indeed, they'd never been tracked until recently.

Trying to smile, he recognized that his mood wasn't holding up as well as hers. "Hi," he tried, really wanting to engage but not having more to say. He couldn't even be fully honest with her. National security.

"They're here for me," she stated, and gave him a real smile. Running hot now, and not cold, she was back to being a trouper of a wife. Thankfully.

"I appreciate your support," he mumbled. "I'm sorry. This wasn't supposed to happen." She laughed and her eyes reflected sympathy not scorn. Marriage was so complicated. His wife frequently yelled about his "attitude" but when he put his family in mortal peril she didn't.

"Oh, George, didn't anyone ever tell you that if you hang with the tough guys once and a while you're going to swing?" She went behind him and started to massage his shoulders. "I'm just glad the kids were easy to find and have already been whisked away. Imagine, being tracked...". Her voice trailed off and George could feel the tenseness in his muscles, too stiff for the release from her fingers.

Looking at her over his shoulder he decided that he'd rather stand and give her the hug she deserved. Fragile in his arms she was also familiar and smelled like home. He'd been through the peaks and valleys of life with this woman and she'd mostly done fine by him. Her clothes were soft and her perfume reminded him of a musky garden, exotic but still sweet.

"I took your advice and started writing a novel," she said softly, pulling away and meeting his gaze with her icy blue eyes, a rare version of azure that was all the more striking for its almost lack of color. He hoped the book wasn't about a man who kept leaving his wife to follow an impossible dream. Don Quixote had been sympathetic because he didn't have a wife; otherwise he'd just have been one more commitment phobic bastard singing to some pathetic wench and the moon. George waited for her to continue as Karen held the floor today.

And he wasn't disappointed as her pause barely earned the title.

"I decided not to compete with the great authors I teach in my classes. I'm writing a historical novel about missionaries in China. Something completely outside my daily world and yours."

George started to laugh, for the first time in what felt like forever. The chuckles rippled faster than he was ready and his side began to cramp. Instantly, his pressures and cares lifted from his body, as if each giggle expelled some ghost that needed an introduction to the divine. The more he laughed the less possible stopping seemed and Karen smiled at him, looking a bit worried but also seemingly sympathetic. As he gradually began to slow, wiping away the few tears that had gathered, she gave him a last soft kiss.

"I'm bringing books on China and missionaries into what I'm calling a spiritual retreat. And others on religious mysticism. You go on your mission and I'll go on mine. We both have some deep inner mystery we need to solve."

"Demons to exorcise," he whispered, recognizing that his wife touched on genius sometimes. She was frighteningly accurate for a literature professor and yet the concept had slipped through his never ending and seemingly very lacking analysis. They'd both been so intent on clawing through their daily lives, with its tasks and other flimsy diversions, until now. Yet he'd never questioned that a different man had made the choices he'd made years ago. People evolve, their priorities and tastes change and the world itself moves into different realities. He hadn't taken time to adapt to whom he'd become, or perhaps as important, whom Karen had become. Did he truly know either of them anymore? Well, he'd lost site of the inner voice of his psyche. And no one knew better than he how the unconscious doesn't forgive getting ignored. Ultimately, we punish ourselves more harshly than does the world.

What had he learned while in captivity? Anything at all as they could both use time devoted to spiritual reflection?

Karen had pulled back and looked resolute. A tear rolled down her cheek but her mascara was still dry and in place. Always together, even today heading into government protection.

"Good bye," she whispered.

"God bless," he said and gave her another quick kiss. If she was going to explore religion, that mass propaganda of the centuries, he could at least support her. How religion was used for purposes ranging from the divine to the devilish was a topic on which he was an expert. They'd have interesting conversations later, once this Khalil crisis was over.

He watched her leave with a wave and smile then bent back over his file. What else had he missed? The dead matriarch. Surgery. Jennifer. Obsession. And...

The phone rang and looking at his caller id saw that Emine was on the line again. He ignored the call and let it ring into voicemail as he wasn't ready for a reporter and her probing questions yet. His guards and voicemail could protect him from the outside world while he figured out what else he'd overlooked. The answers were always there but did he have enough information to find them?

Start at the beginning, George reminded himself, and don't get lost in the clutter. Every narrative is simple; the human mind just often looses sight at how obvious the clues to the truth are, adding complexity and confusion through over analysis. Most people stopped believing their eyes and their hearts, the only two things that could be relied on not to lie if you listened closely enough.

So what did Khalil want? He wanted George in some form. Jennifer too? He wanted to destroy the west and kill lots of people. He was willing to get plastic surgery to keep running his marathon jihad.

But did he really want to die or had he managed to survive his dangerous lifestyle precisely because he didn't? Seemed the most logical conclusion to an American psychologist but did terrorists act so rationally? Blowing themselves up for Allah and some promised "virgins" (how long were those "virgins" meant to stay pure and what were their value and the related sacrifice after they were despoiled) didn't seem fully rational to his Western post-reformation mind?

Dam

"We're set to blow the dam is eighteen hours," it was the voice again, and Khalil disengaged his limbs from Jennifer's softer ones, sliding out of bed into the night air. He hated hiding in the bathroom to speak but even though she didn't know Arabic he still favored it to discussing his work in her presence.

The dam was scheduled to "blow" not in eighteen hours but next week. Moron! Swine! He had women on his team not the capable men he needed.

"You're timing is wrong," Khalil barked into the phone, comfortable in the language of his childhood and watching the city of many youthful dreams out a dusty window. Traffic was finally moving at this late hour and a mist was settling on the asphalt.

"I report to others as well and you were overruled on this one," was the response. "In'sa Allah."

"What other circumstances have changed?" Khalil asked but the line was already dead. Had his bosses decided to punish him such that he'd need to call them, begging, to be re-instated as head of the mission? Or had he been played and they hadn't shared that the dam was really meant to blow until now, when preventing it would be difficult. Fools! The dam couldn't really be destroyed as they would lose Egypt permanently should the truth ever come out.

It must be a power game, plain and simple. Global jihad was big business and staying on top was never easy if for no other reason than that drones kept randomly taking out leaders which left those alive angling for more control. His job was best compared to being one of many snakes in a basket with the end goal of wriggling to the top.

But then you added in personalities and individual power struggles. From the wise to the brutally ruthless, being a senior leader in a terrorist organization was never easy. Power attracts those willing to fight and angle for it and these men were ruthless in winning.

How to respond?

No groveling; that would be showing weakness and they'd circle him like hyenas sniffing blood. Well Khalil always had a plan B and spy in place, which was better than falling into the whirlpool of desperation when plan A derailed. Shit has a way of happening.

Part one of Plan B was his boy. He'd sent Osman back to the dam to "help", instinctively suspicious a few days prior but not able to explain why and he was right! Perhaps he could learn something from the boy's insights now that he was back home in Egypt. Men too often ignore the invisible eyes of the young and this child was sharp. He'd hopefully have found his way to the important information in the local huddle.

The dam had been meant as a distraction for the authorities so KK could slide into the States without fears of danger shadowing him as they were focused elsewhere. For a second, Khalil had held the Nile Valley's fate in his palms, and since it was his plot the ultimate decision had been his. He'd stuck to his goal of removing the Islamists' biggest electoral threat, choosing politics over destruction.

That omnipotence was gone.

"Yes," Osman's voice whispered through the phone line, across a world and a history. Khalil was sitting on the toilet, seat down, and his feet were propped up on the sink. They room smelled of chemicals, not people, which was all too common in America. As if they could pretend that their people didn't live, breathe and sweat but rather wallowed in detergent and deodorant. White porcelain and a swaying ivory shower curtain to hide behind rounded out the decor.

"What's happening?" he asked, starting with an open question. Would his boy perform? One must always be testing people because sometimes they broke. No, they all broke at some point but predicting that point could be a crapshoot. Every man deceived, you just had to hope it wasn't on your dime.

"I don't know for sure since no one will say much. But I hacked into some cell calls and got an inkling."

Osman. He had no morality but rather lived on curiosity and an innate ability to find his way around boundaries. Luckily, the boy was doing as his father had ordered and staying loyal to Khalil. Or so Khalil hoped. When in the company of thieves...and the machinations kept getting harder as technology continued improving seemingly overnight.

Khalil crunched the tiny phone into his ear and adjusted himself on the cold seat. Ask Osman how he intercepted calls? Why? Did it matter? Khalil needed only to know that it could be done and hire those who did it with ease.

"4:00 a.m. But not tomorrow, the day after I think, but am not sure. Getting people in their beds," Osman said and Khalil felt a deep unease in his stomach. Their goal was to rule the country right? While flooding the dense population base around the Nile certainly seemed one way to bring back the time of Mohammed since most infrastructures would be wiped away - so would the people. He'd flirted with the power of the concept but backed away at the implications of such devastation. Terror wasn't a weapon to destroy but rather to provoke your enemy to over retaliate, thus shaping public opinion.

And the imagery was too Jewish for him, as if Moses (or in this case Nasser and the Soviets) had parted the sea only to dump it back on Pharaoh's people. No, he had to stop this biblical revenge move unless he could ensure Israel took the blame, which he couldn't.

Jennifer was knocking on the door. "I need to use the bathroom," she yelled.

He lunged for the knob, turned it and burst past, pausing only to spit on her. As if he wasn't carrying the world on his shoulders she had to pee. Storming out into the hallway he headed to the streets. In a global metropolis there was always somewhere to go, and someone else to curl up next to, even late at night. Bitch.

Khalil felt a tremendous pressure in his head and had to struggle to focus. It was a boulder digging into his brain that seemed to be coming more frequently as he dealt with the pressures of his role.

A puppet now, with a new face and a girlfriend to match, he was taking on a Herculean task trying to fill a global leadership void after so many others continued to get killed or caught. He had no choice now did he, wanted and chased, but to shelter himself under the protections of his own organization? In charge, he decided who lived or died and didn't leave those decisions to a potential enemy.

They want to do what? No, we want to do what?

"Osman, tell me, what will happen?" he asked the boy, knowing that these ears could guide him, like the blind man he was, an ocean and a world away. How many hours would pass, as he counted them down and wondered at all that could go wrong. His heart was still wrapped in being what he'd been told, at sixteen, would save his brother. But over twenty years later his brother was still dead and haunting the increasingly crowded martyrs' regions of heaven. Yet the echoes in his head kept driving him forward, seeking vengeance and running from pain.

These people lining the dam, mostly Muslim, shouldn't be the next round of martyrs and this faked plan had taken on a cancerous cast.

And his brain kept hounding at the question, what's really happening? Khalil should be in charge and making decisions. He had planned the carefully spaced bombs; about 50 meters below the surface, but clustered low enough to ensure a massive onslaught of released waters if detonated. A fireball would blow up and out, forcing ripples of water and a bubble, which would explode creating a shock wave into the air. A plume would send water spurting up, creating a dramatic but deadly effect. Water is very hard coming at you with great force and speed.

Only the bombs lining the dam's neat golden stones weren't supposed to blow. They were a plant, meant to be discovered and shift attention to KK's home and away from his person and forthcoming US visit.

Indeed, the bombs were meant to be discovered by Khalil's group not detonated by them, he kept repeating to himself. Too bad they couldn't frame the Israelis but they guarded their weapons more carefully which were thus virtually impossible to buy on black market. The Iranians handed them out like candy, bought originally from China and Russia.

Most importantly, each plan had to be orchestrated by one man. The complexity level was so great, and the players so varied, one person needed that ultimate final control to keep each element in its place and on schedule. Conflicting generals made conflicting decisions and confused their own troops. So if Khalil wasn't the conductor but merely an instrument then who was leading the band? What other decision changes, with little or no forewarning, had been made without him being informed even as he risked his own life on the premise that he controlled the related path?

"What's happening?" he asked Osman again, and wondered if the boy could be expected to understand when his boss was so uncertain.

"The blind sheik is here and he wants the sins of the world to be washed away," was all Osman replied.

Khalil glanced around, still in the building's hallway, a long line of doors leading to their own personal dramas. This country, with running water for most and food stores for all, what did it know about deprivation and the hard lives of those wallowing in a different reality? A people's history determines their character and Khalil was still struggling to understand what defined the American people.

For the blind sheik was an American, a traitor to his homeland after discovering jihad in Afghanistan against the Soviets. Khalil had fought with him then and knew the man to be a cold-hearted mercenary. Until he lost his eyesight in a brutal battle out in the Hindu Kush, that mountain range straddling central Afghanistan and northern Pakistan. Then a mullah handed him a brail Koran and he started to proclaim the divine. But when had he become powerful enough to overrule Khalil and blow up a dam? Short answer was that Khalil didn't believe he had.

Khalil trusted only one thing: his instincts. This was a blatant grab for power, sensing Khalil's weaknesses from across an ocean and having been recently out of circulation and in jail. Still, it was a misguided effort to fill his shoes and obviously one viewed through a westerner's lens. For when a people counts in centuries of what value is a year or so? Quietly, he hung up on Osman, having already alerted him too much. All fear must be contained, internally.

And the sheep on the ground would just take orders, never questioning that they were coming from another general. Trained to obey, they would.

Osman was a mere boy but Khalil had other men on speed dial that weren't and could solve this problem. He dialed a number etched in his mind.

"Yes," the man said, his voice gruff and raspy, fading into barely discernable. But this man wasn't the sort who needed to speak in words, choosing action instead and never missing a shot.

"Kill the sheik," Khalil told him.

"The blind one leading the world off the edge?" he asked but Khalil didn't need to answer. If this man knew of the problem why hadn't he called Khalil first? Normally Khalil knew that his order would be executed quickly and perfectly. Now he wasn't sure who to trust or what to believe when so much more typically was understood.

"If you knew why didn't you call?" Khalil asked, probing.

"I thought you sent him. You didn't tell me much about this plot, remember. I'm just here in case you need me but not to get involved otherwise."

"Yes," said Khalil, knowing there was some truth in the words but fearing nonetheless. Everything was veering slightly off, and then there were the tails. Did he have a traitor filtering information to an enemy? And if so, which enemy when he had so many?

"Today," Khalil clarified.

Malik, master or king in meaning, was one of his best and most loyal fighters. Khalil didn't trust anyone but if he had to, Malik was the one. First, he'd kill the sheik. Then he'd have to take over and ensure that the dam plot was revealed in time to prevent the explosion – as originally planned.

Would Malik succeed? Allah would decide.

Khalil's own name meant beautiful or good friend. And he was giving this friend a chance at eternal glory. Was anything better than that?

Phones

George still wasn't answering his phone but Ben was and Emine didn't like what the latter had to say. Quite frankly, she preferred reporting on events and not being part of them. With the former, she could hide behind anonymity and a lack of responsibility. Now, she was included in finding a solution in a reality where half the puzzle pieces were missing. How the fuck was she supposed to help when no one knew what the expected plot was?

"The military is here," was how Ben started the conversation. Great. But Ben at least had some amazing shots while she sat in a hotel room and kept hitting redial. Tanks lining up against blue water and cascades of golden dunes billowing behind them. If she turned on Bright's station she'd doubtless see his footage with its big guns and jazzy uniforms. Luckily the boss himself hadn't called (yet) to yell at her for doing so little. If he did, she'd just plead "national security" and not admit that George was ignoring her. Had it not still been morning she'd be drinking more than coffee. But, really, how much alcohol can one person drink in a day?

She cuddled her coffee in her king sized, white hotel bed and curled deeper in the covers. Had she been wearing clothes the air conditioning wouldn't have been so harsh but the covers were lush enough to solve any chill.

"Tanks," Ben said. "So many tanks."

"Didn't the US fund them?" she asked, grabbing her iPad to do a quick Google search. Where did the Egyptians get their weapons from again? It had to be to US. Egypt had been their geo-political baby for years, since they were the first Arab state to recognize Israel.

Yes, the Americans were giving them about $1.3 billion a year in military aid during the Mubarak era which buys a lot of guns. Thanks Wikipedia!

"This place is swarming but no one will talk," he continued. "They keep massing, and the general is in our hotel with his new stalker, Bright."

Emine pulled herself up.

"Bright's still there?" Confusing! "It isn't safe there so what's he doing?"

"Emine, if an important general is here he must think he can get some sort of coverage without taking too much risk. We're close to a great story somewhere, I can feel it." Ben sounded tired, a rare thing with a reporter of his caliber. Ben was a constant not a human being.

"Hot?" she asked. "You aren't sleeping?" she continued. "You have no story just a bunch of tanks?" she finished, sensing and knowing at the same time. Did George have better information? Sure she and Ben were press but they were also now intimately involved so why shut them out so completely? Or, maybe that was exactly why...national security...

"The mood is brutal, Emine," Ben said, but then paused and she sensed him weighing his words. We all need to talk and men liked to talk to women. Would he? "Everyone is desperate. The buzz is about the dam and they're swarming like nothing I've seen. But they clearly haven't found whatever it is they're looking for".

But I still haven't found what I'm looking for, she sang. Ben didn't respond.

Damn. He was going to win the Nobel Prize and she'd be stuck drinking vodka and coffee naked in a New York hotel room. With the tanks and generals she'd just bet no new journalists were getting into the area. Ben didn't even bother asking for her updates as he'd know that she'd share if she had anything. He'd clearly drawn the more interesting stick.

She let him go, knowing he was heading back into the street in pursuit of a story and envying his opportunities, dangerous though they were. She gulped more coffee, a milky cappuccino, strong this morning and starting to cool. She'd also ordered bagels from room service as she loved them, dense and chewy with crispy toasted edges. Spreading raspberry jam on top of her cream cheese she savored the mix of flavors and found herself downing a second one.

But she couldn't just sit here all day eating until it was a respectable time to start drinking. Really.

So she called her mom. It was afternoon in Istanbul.

"Baby," cooed her mother into the phone. "What's going on?"

Normally, a question like that was somewhat innocent but today Emine sensed an edge to her mother's normally languid tone. Everyone was tense today. Why Liz?

"You tell me," was one way to start an interview, so why the hell not? Crazy, really, putting her own mother on the spot. Ah, but would she learn something?

"Your dad is so tense. Always on the phone, with the door shut, if he's here," Liz said, her voice childlike but throaty, with the drama of a toddler. But she'd hit the nail and figured the mood. Everyone was waiting for a big strike but didn't yet know how to stop it, much as they sensed the imminent danger. Indeed, they must not be sure of what "it" was at all or they'd be doing more.

So Emine started discussing her problems with Ed, more to distract Liz than anything else. Her mother liked girl talk but got increasingly more uncomfortable when substance was thrown into the mix. What Emine didn't mention was Bud, the family friend and Selim's old buddy, who was calling her daily now.

Bud her mother knew well and that made his name unutterable since Selim had been brushed under the carpet of denial. Coping with the death of a child was never easy; drugs and years of neglect only made it harder.

Selim had been such a needy child, grasping for attention in a house where there was none. Younger, Emine still remembered how he'd cried on the nights their parents left for yet another party. She'd been the one to comfort him, standing next to his massive bed in her white night dress, with the Bosporus glowing glorious outside his window, the soft touch of the moon illuminating Selim's tears.

Until one day he matured into teenage rebellion and an overdose. Now, no one spoke of him as if that sensitive boy had never tugged at all of their hearts. Emine hated that denial in her parents and couldn't help but judge, not caring if she was coping maturely or not. Cowards. Still, she needed them....for now and perhaps would forever.

"Do I love him, mom? Do I? How would I know?"

The silence on the other end of the phone line was palpable and odd. Liz liked to chatter away, especially about romance, but apparently not tonight. Her silence could mean many things, but none was obvious with respect to Ed. She'd never even met him!

She'd also been deathly silent at Selim's funeral, with much of Istanbul in attendance, hiding behind a veiled hat and sunglasses. Mehmet had cried silent but visible tears as dirt hit coffin. Emine had been still numb and feeling alone. She'd wanted to jump into the coffin with her brother but that was a different culture and not acceptable in her reality.

So for now she just waited for her mother's response and found her mind wandering to Bud, not Ed, en route away from Selim's memory.

"You don't love him, Emine," Liz said, softly and stern. "Ed just looks good on paper but that's the extent of the appeal. He's shallow and you aren't." Emine heard a hard won honesty in her mother's voice and had to credit the effort. And her mother was right.

"What's going on?" she asked, voicing her real concern. Liz had to know something since she was married to a very important man.

"I don't know but it's big, whatever it is," was Liz's answer and Emine heard the exhale of cigarette smoke as she lit her own. Perhaps the nicotine would help them both think.

Hiding

eorge ignored the phone. He wasn't checking caller id though he tried to take Campbell's calls or at least ring back. But the information shared wasn't making him happy. Spotty, risky and not under control.

Mostly, he felt like the onus was on his shoulders to figure out the bastard Khalil, who spider like, had crawled back into a hole with seemingly poor phone reception. Or he'd learned how not to get tracked via cell signal, yet no one can vanish into thin air. So what was George missing? The answer, more often than not, really was right before you.

Karen was thankfully gone (he loved her but she was a distraction) and he'd banished his goons to the kitchen. His wife had put a television and computer with Internet in there when she ripped out the old to replace it with much pricier new so they should be happy.

His wife. She must hate him sometimes for how he prioritized his life and put his own goals before hers. While he wasn't always honest with her about it, paying lip service to the concepts of equality and togetherness, he was at least becoming more honest with himself. But really, who knew why he did it? To sacrifice your life to save the world wasn't fully emotionally healthy, which he could diagnose professionally, and the world could never be saved. Yet he was too old to change and hell bent on destroying that murderous bastard. Didn't the definition of addiction hinge on self-medication?

Well one thing George felt strongly sure was that Khalil wasn't coming back to this apartment building; even he wasn't that bold. Thus his goon duty was playing Angry Birds in his kitchen and George was pondering impossibles. Point taken; next contact would be an unexpected – not expected – one.

Aswan was swarming and everyone was waiting, petrified. A bold plot or a distraction? The risks of the structure possibly being fatally damaged were so massive no one could ignore the possibilities and just hope nothing went wrong, especially with a forewarning.

So what did Khalil want?

What George wanted first was more black coffee, but what he most wanted was an answer and no one had it so the burden of discerning one fell solidly on his shoulders. Was too much of the national security budget going for paper pushers or body scanning tourists in airports? Shouldn't Khalil have been caught crossing the border? How could one dark man just disappear into the streets of Manhattan?

So what did George know for sure, besides whom his focus was centered on? Khalil was close by, whether in abode or just in visits to the city. He'd confirmed his presence by delivering coffee to George. The bastard seemingly knew his phone was being monitored and wanted to be tracked but not found. Khalil only spoke in obvious strokes…like Aswan…when he wanted to be heard, which was often. Now Aswan was overrun with tanks and Manhattan was on alert. What had the man accomplished? He'd created a spectacle and seemingly on purpose, pre-event not post. Red herrings?

The phone rang and he let it ring. Fuck the calls.

But instinct or responsibility compelled George to look at the caller id and he saw "private caller". Normally, he wouldn't answer but he did anyway.

"Hello," he said, regretting the word as he spoke it. He shifted on his green velvet couch, HQ central with its view of the park and central living room location, impatient.

"George, grab a pen. I'm telling you where the bombs are on the dam. You may not have a lot of time," Khalil said and George jumped. This man was seriously sick, and even more unpredictable. Grappling for a pen, he wrote down the logistics and before he could ask a follow up question Khalil had hung up. So much for tracing the call.

Starting to laugh, nerves, George picked up the receiver and called Campbell. Who knew whether the information was good or not but it had to be passed on to those who could find out.

Briefly, he wondered at whether Khalil was loosing control within his organization but didn't yet have enough information to decide nor time to figure out. There were so many reasons why that turn of events made sense.

Crazy, out of control, destabilized or just manipulative, George had not a clue. But the exact placement of some bombs was a good piece of insight regardless of the larger picture.

Freedom?

halil curled up on his bed sleeping and Jennifer let him, watching some cooking show with little volume. He tossed around not because of her but from an unquiet mind. By now, the blind

sheik should be bobbing under water and tied to one of the bombs, his eyes gauged out. Divers would be defusing the explosives, then dismantling their components. George could be counted on to follow up quickly.

The sheik had once been Khalil's friend but sometimes life irrevocably changes the course of a relationship. Long before he'd tried to take over control of this mission and usurp Khalil's power the man had been a trusted ally as well. Khalil felt the bitter taste of an unexpected betrayal and wondered at why friends felt the need to challenge someone of greater authority. Envy? Ambition? Was no one immune from such bitterness?

Years before, they'd been camped in the snow, their thin tent scant protection against the bitter chill of an Afghan winter. They'd had a small dinner that evening, with hot tea and supplied by the local village, but mostly they weren't eating. The Soviets were getting closer and shelling the area, dimming the appeal of creature comforts. No one dared venture out during daylight but out of necessity did attempt dinner in the blackness of a late night. The moon was low so the cover was perfect.

The Sheik was called Rafi then, and dressed simply. American that he was, he liked to talk, even when there were rockets zooming above. A donkey was hit and screamed as life drained out of its body. The stars glistened, imperturbable and vast.

"I couldn't afford college and had to drop out," Rafi was explaining how he'd ended up with his less privileged friend, here. The world around them went on.

Being in the middle of a bomb storm is petrifying. No guarantee exists that you won't get blown to kingdom come as in a movie theater reenactment. Inevitably, a bomb drops too close for comfort and a companion takes the hit. One minute a compatriot is a few tents over and then a crater is. Rafi wasn't used to the violence and Khalil had talked him though their first night of the bombardment,

That night they'd been chewing tobacco, not wanting to risk the small red dot of a cigarette as target practice for the Soviets. Snow was falling and not much else moved under the clear half moon. Rafi told a joke and Khalil laughed. Suddenly, they heard a loud screech and Rafi threw Khalil back.

Hitting a boulder, Khalil felt his shoulder splinter. But worse was watching Rafi's silhouette highlighted against the bomb as it blew up not far from where Khalil had been moments before. Rafi recovered but his sight never did.

Now Rafi was dead. Fate was rough, but we all want to survive and Khalil was no exception. In the battle between life and death, all bets are off.

So for tonight Khalil slept, knowing that his plot was back on track. He was running this show until someone killed him and that was the deal. Finally he had some rest and his head was comfortable on his pillow as he dreamed. Jennifer let him and would have been comforted to know that Khalil dreamed of her.

Water

Emine was listening rapt as Ben detailed events as they were happening. He was shooting video and Bright wanted her to write it up ASAP. Ben only had so many hands. The cusp of dawn was breaking in Aswan, a pink milky glaze slowly illuminating the Nile's waters and the streets around the dam. She was watching the live video feed on her computer as Ben scanned the rows of clunky military vehicles, police cars with sirens blaring and motorboats scanning the area with spotlights. One side of Aswan was waking up normally while the other was a war zone. Ben knew how to frame war shots and not lose the imagery in too much bright light and commotion. Unless staged carefully, as in a movie, movement looked cluttered.

Spare was always the best aesthetic when you were limited to the geography of a rectangular screen shot.

She'd tried to reach George to tell him that a big raid on the dam was happening but she only spoke with his answering machine again. Men! They just wouldn't communicate when they didn't want to. Didn't they realize how unproductive that attitude was? Thus Bright optimistically sent a courier to track George down at his apartment as if the doorman might really yield access (George still technically worked for Bright). Had her media boss been in New York he likely would have gone himself but instead he was planning to be the on camera narration for Ben so the latter could focus only on visuals. He urgently needed her writing skills so she couldn't be spared to stalk George. Indeed, as it was, she was alternating between two laptops and emailing the station and paper editors as events materialized.

Bright loved having the exclusive story; no other journalist had been embedded with George in Egypt so hadn't been alerted to the crisis or allowed in the area. Well, hopefully, he didn't get both himself and Ben arrested now that the situation had dramatically escalated. Egypt wasn't known for its free press orientation and reporters were repeatedly carted off to jail. Any rumored terrorist related raid carried too many risks to detail.

"See, in the upper corner of the screen, the divers are going into the water. We haven't been told their mission and with the number of people it's hard to tell what's actually happening. A clear shot is impossible with so many people swarming everything."

And indeed, Ben's footage confirmed the confusion and seriousness with which the authorities were responding to whatever information they had received. His mumbled explanations were of little help but since they hadn't been briefed by anyone about the mission even being present was a coup. Clearly it involved a high alert centered on the dam itself; Emine felt both fear for and envy toward Ben. Unleashed water could hit at remarkable force but in the meantime he was shooting amazing video.

"They're letting you film this!" she exclaimed, as she watched the details unfold, including the arrival of another two helicopters. Most governments wouldn't want such a raid on film, especially due to the high probability that something could go wrong.

"We were commanded to add a 30 minute delay before showing footage and might make some careful edits," Ben mumbled. "I think there was a lot of cash involved paying for these press 'rights'." Transfixed, Emine watched her screen as she saw him zero in on a boat hemorrhaging divers who appeared to be taking cameras underwater, along with a hodgepodge of other complicated looking equipment.

"Fucking corrupt bastards all around. Can't trust anyone in this country," Ben mumbled and Emine laughed, trying not to let him hear. The unflappable Ben must be going nuts with all the high level machinations to shoot something that shouldn't be on film. Bright didn't know the meaning of no and had the money to be so arrogant.

Emine watched the arc of the sun as the lighting subtly changed on the screen and the images began to drop their haziness. Really, everything moved so slowly until it didn't. Thankfully, there was that delay requirement and the editors at the studio could craft a more riveting narrative. No one wanted raw footage in this time of immediate gratification and fast moving video games. Reality was a poor second to a well-written story.

She observed, alert but her mind also wandering, trying to stay engaged but doodling on hotel stationary with a hotel pen anyway. Wearing red sweat pants and a large white t-shirt she was ever glad at how much of her work could be done in private. Why she craved alone time so much was only somewhat of a mystery but then again most people just talked too much. They judged and demanded and she unapologetically felt little need to fulfill their expectations. It wasn't like she told other people to do things…well, except professionally but that was her job.

Ed kept texting her and she sent him a few halfhearted responses. What had her mother said about Ed again? Not the right man; she didn't love him; he looked good on paper but hadn't engaged her heart.

Hadn't she always told him that she didn't want to get serious? Well, she wasn't serious so why had he seemingly headed down that path? Shallow or not, Emine was caught up in the realities of her very exciting job. Seriously, a commitment? Now! She wanted to win a Pulitzer Prize and was worried that Ben would sweep this one out from under her.

She heard a roar through her speaker.

"Shit," Ben said and she could see what prompted the response. Military helicopters were swarming and Emine realized they were American. "The team that went under was probably Seals and not Egyptian, just cloaked in native boats. This was big. Bet the US authorities didn't know about Bright's side deal to film the unfolding events.

By now, the landscape was fully lit and Emine could sense the sun's harshness from how images were highlighted against stark backgrounds. Temperatures rose irrespective of how burdened men were with uniforms, guns and other equipment. She saw no women and indeed locals had seemingly been barred from the location.

"It must be bombs on the actual dam itself. I wonder how deep," Ben murmured, and Emine smiled at his tone. She knew him so well and loved him for a breadth of reasons but mostly because he aimed for doing what was right, taking whatever criticism resulted and moving imperviously on. Life disappoints but he never let it. She let it.

God, her head hurt. Late afternoon here, she snagged a scotch from the mini bar and downed it straight from the bottle as the action on her screen heated up.

"I'm getting pushed away," Ben exclaimed, and Emine watched a sweaty Bright in flat front khaki's and green t-shirt with company logo arguing with men pointing big guns and in full combat gear. The Arabic mingled with English and she hoped her boss backed down even if he didn't understand the language and believed himself above the law.

"They're going to shoot you," Ben translated and Bright immediately smiled at the men while raising his hands in an airborne surrender. Emine could hear Ben asking for specifics, using that flattering, flowery Arabic of a journalist in trouble.

One man replied. "The bombs are being defused. Another had a booby trap, which wasn't expected because the others didn't. They aren't sure when it might go off...but...,"

"Stop!" his companion ordered and the man ceased speaking, using the scope end of his rifle to push Ben, camera and Bright away from roaring waters and dam. Ben was still shooting but seemingly pretending not to thus the picture wasn't centered. Most of the boats were zooming away, presumably letting the helicopters take over area coverage and heading for a safer distance. If a bomb really blew on the side of the dam would there be a safe spot? That really depended on the explosion size.

Ben seemed to trip and the camera view shot up to the blue sky. Emine gulped another scotch and decided to call room service for a bottle. Dinnertime was rapidly looming but she wasn't in much of a mood to study a menu. Her cell rang.

"Emine, what the fuck?" the station manager shouted at her. "Why the fuck are they still there shooting footage? A death wish? I don't want a flood shot."

"You need a mini-bar," was all she replied.

"As if I'm not drinking too. What the fuck? What the fuck! And his wife is a lunatic," Emine silently concurred. As if she wanted to work for that bitch who couldn't like her should Bright return home in a body bag. "Is this story worth it? Can we even show it without facing some sort of governmental probe? I feel like WikiLeaks."

"You always wanted to be an esteemed journalist," she responded but also didn't like watching the area clear out, taking on a ghost town feel. Ben hadn't deserted his post and was just filming from a greater distance now. The vehicles were exiting and the helicopters becoming denser, which couldn't be a good sign. One boat bobbed solo, highlighted against the gold stone dam.

Suddenly, Emine could hear footsteps moving quickly and she saw Bright running closer to the water. Since most authorities had moved out there was no one to stop him and the camera shook, distorting the picture, as Ben tried to keep up. Something was bobbing on top of blue but the camera lens wasn't zooming in enough for her to identify it. Suddenly, Ben stopped and Bright began to talk.

"The divers are re-emerging and appear to have some large sandy colored discs. The bombs? We can't see well due to the distance but can count… one…two…four… eight…no eleven of them." Emine watched, transfixed, as the boats and vehicles started to return, as if by divine calling and the helicopters swung hooks or some similar apparatus down to the water level. The divers began attaching the discs to those hooks. And then she watched Bright get handcuffed before the camera went dark.

"Shit," she heard on the line before realizing she was still on the phone. "Guess I should stop talking to you and call legal. Idiot," he said. Shit was right. So was the whole mess over and a success? No other station was covering the raid and certainly not live so she had no way of knowing. But she did know someone who had a direct line to the government even if he still wasn't returning calls. She texted George then grabbed her menu. If she had to wait at least she'd have a nice meal. Still daytime in Aswan she could see outside her window that evening had fallen on Manhattan.

Daylight

Time to emerge? All George wanted to do was stay holed up and ponder imponderables. He liked his apartment, with its book lined walls and fully wired existence. Fat chance. His adversary had broken and he had to chase him down while the bastard was weak. Khalil must be finally feeling the stress of being an international exile, a pariah among civilized men, and all around murderous jerk. Time to reel him in, though that would, naturally, entail personal physical risk. So much for retiring onto an elite television interview show. After this, George would really need to make an effort to learn the word "no" and actually use it.

Campbell had phoned and he'd taken that call, though no others. Indeed, Campbell was the only one to whom he'd given their second private number and Karen was forbidden to use it for now. Only a few close friends had gotten through over the past few days and George was enjoying the silence. After all they'd been through together Campbell counted as a close friend and he added confidential information into the value proposition.

"Eleven bombs. Watertight plastic casing. Set to go off within twenty-four hours. The sixth one had a booby trap, smack in the middle. Luckily, our guys are the best."

"So all is ok?" George asked. "Damn, Al Qaeda likes the number eleven."

"Apparently. Ultimately it's never done but just one more step in the right direction."

Wasn't that the truth? Problems were like a Wack a Mole game, and terrorism was no exception. No matter how hard you wacked one terrorist or plot on the head another one just popped up anew. And they kept getting more sophisticated. Khalil was one who just wouldn't stay down. Why he'd stopped this plot, bombs on the Aswan Dam, George had no idea but guessed that his motives weren't pure and something bigger must be brewing. Khalil being a nice guy? Yeah, right, and there was that bridge for sale.

"So now what?" George asked, wondering if Campbell would tell him anything even if he had information, more worried that there wasn't anything to tell. What was chatter anyway? Usually, the most valuable information came from recent captives, trading information for privilege. The bad guys all realized now how easily anything digital could be hacked and tracked.

"We're still looking for your buddy Khalil. Any more calls?" George loved the lack of a real question in Campbell's voice and didn't respond. They were just two old and jaded warhorses waiting for the next fire drill, weren't they?

But how paranoid could you be when men never deviated too far from themselves? Thus, timing and location were variable while whether Khalil would kill again wasn't. Why he'd prevented this plot was a mystery but didn't reflect a change of character. And someone, somewhere would be mad that the bombs had been discovered thus would retaliate against Khalil if they guessed at his role. Mysteries unresolved lead down strange paths.

"A dead guy was strapped to the bombs: the blind sheik," Campbell muttered. "American but we didn't kill him for a change so the press can't go crazy."

I am the press now, George thought.

"Wow, they bothered to strap him to the bombs," he said instead. "How long dead?"

"A very short time. We also have men scanning the dam's video monitors. Nothing so far but I'll keep you posted. Security was surprisingly lax given the risks," Campbell added thoughtfully.

"Well, the country is in turmoil," was all George could think to respond.

George watched the people on the streets below him, hurrying from work, to dinner or home, the joggers heading into the park and the hot dog vender with his ever-present line of patrons. They all thought they were safe but with Khalil wandering these same streets who knew. Life didn't promise us any warnings or sense of infallibility. Indeed, Khalil could be staring up at him now, his dark eyes glistening in the bustle of a sunny city day. Life was like that; the obvious could stare us in the face but if we didn't want to see it we wouldn't. What was he himself not wanting to see?

He loved this country, his country. He loved how he could say what he liked, complain and pontificate, right or wrong. He loved the will and drive and optimism of a people that had never seriously lost at anything. The economy would rise and fall, some people would drop through the ever-larger cracks in society, but at least here existed hope and the American dream.

His job. Speaking of which…

"I'm back on government payroll, aren't I?" he asked Campbell, knowing there couldn't be any other outcome. We need to accept fate not fight it. After all, he couldn't be a journalist and still privy to high security information. Eminent domain could attach to a person, not just a piece of property and if the government wanted to own you they did.

"Yes, and you know the drill. It's all confidential from here. We'll get you a new cell phone,"

George interrupted, "It's never safe."

"Right. We keep sweeping your home lines so hopefully they're ok. This job isn't getting easier just because we have more equipment."

"No," George said, "they have it too," and he hung up. He'd also noticed seemingly sparse updated information on Khalil. In Manhattan and doing what other than having coffee delivered?

George saw that Emine had sent yet another text. He'd ignored them all and her messages as well, not ready to confront her. Smart girl, and a journalist, she'd ask him questions he didn't want to face let alone answer. But our heads can only stay stuck in a hole for so long and everyone eventually comes up for air. Plus George owed Emine his freedom as a friend of hers had been the one to track down his Cairo location (read paid a lot for information) leading to him escaping alive.

"I have to tell you what happened! Now! Aswan." her text said. As if he didn't already know more than she did and would be gratuitously filling her in, as appropriate. They'd play some game of dodging substance and information then he'd sneak in the facts he wanted her to know.

Meanwhile, their book had become a minor distraction in a storm of overwhelming proportion and she was halfheartedly - seemingly - typing a word or two on it daily. Perhaps chronicling an ever-changing world had been a mistake what with the new realities they kept confronting in a kaleidoscope's shifting lens. He'd tried to escape into her media world but was really a driver and not a commenter, a fact he was slowly facing.

But before George returned her call he needed a better grasp of his objectives. Never follow up until you're clear about the desired destination; as with Alice if you don't know where you're going any road will take you there. So....?

First, he wanted out of the book. Period. What he did took time, focus and confidentiality and the book clouded the whole lot.

With Emine? She had noble ambitions and her father was among the most influential men in the world. She should be writing a book about him, before he got assassinated, or writing the one George had been helping her on alone.

Assassination. Why did that word make George so uncomfortable? Something...something...something... he was missing something. Did Khalil say something? Yes, Khalil had mumbled allusions to the Assassins and past greatness of their mission so long before but the details had gone over George's head at the time. He'd been petrified and worried for his own life, not caring about those of others (funny thing about being held captive by a murderer). Hopefully, he'd remember at some point and in time. But this thread was one he'd need to pick up and start unraveling now regardless due to the severity of the threat. Instinct told him that he'd just hit inspiration.

If I were Khalil whom would I kill? The question was haunting him.

And Emine? He'd have to extricate himself from their book while maintaining her help stopping Khalil. Suddenly, George had an idea.

He dialed her cell, and when she answered he heard the slight slur in her voice. Good.

"Emine, I apologize," he started, then waited for her response.

"George, there was a raid on Aswan today...," she started and he felt bad cutting her off. He was so much older and experienced.

"I know, I'm working for the government again," he said and let his words sit, seeping into her reality. He glanced at his scotch but that would be for later and this conversation was too important. He counted silently, giving her time.

"Oh."

"I can't do the book. National security," he said, pausing, counting again. "You should write about your father. He's much more important than I am. Or do our book alone since you don't need my input anymore." He paused again. Counting. She needed the pauses; he couldn't look eager even though he was. Now, time to pounce.

"I need a favor, please," he said and waited again. He could almost hear her gulp on the other end of the line, her thin frame hunched up likely with a glass of wine in hand and unsure where his word were leading. She had to answer before he proceeded.

"Ok," she responded and he heard the exhale of a cigarette's smoke.

"Ask your father whom Khalil plans to kill," he said, more on a hunch than a fact. Khalil usually bombed, being a munitions expert, but those hints at assassination added a new whiff to the scent of his schemes. George's memories from his own captivity were a haze, coming and going, but hadn't Khalil brought up Martin Luther King, assassinated, and how sometimes there are those who propel social progress that must be stopped?

And when Emine exhaled George knew he'd won and she'd use her access to help. Mehmet was a geopolitical master strategist (better by far than George) and a Muslim whose nation was hanging on that omnipresent thread of barely stable. Turkey walked one of the most difficult diplomatic tightropes by bordering Iran, Iraq, Syria and that failed economic reality (or unreality) of Greece thus had to be ever careful. Unstable neighbors spread their problems across borders.

George needed all the help he could get.

And so now he wanted to change the subject.

"Sorry for disappearing. I had to," he lied. "What did I miss?" And he let her talk, knowing that she'd filter her information to suit her purpose, he knew more about almost everything than she did and he'd learn a lot from how she said what she said.

Women

It was starting. All the other boxes were checked and Khalil now had to ensure that KK ended up dead. If he could also create a revolution or at least a riot in one of New York's boroughs so much the better, but that was mere icing on the cake.

He'd heard nothing officially, internally, about the disaster at Aswan or the blind sheik's death. Front page on most newspapers, the watered down version had made the mass media rounds. Someone somewhere would be angry but wouldn't retaliate until after KK's assassination, his death being the real goal and ultimate objective. Khalil was one of the few elite fighters left who could make it happen.

Like all leaders Khalil sometimes got tired of running his own show due to the pressure, bad or middling employees, impossible variables and the many small details, all of which could go wrong. But he loved the power that came with responsibility and directing meaningful change. And the biggest problem of leadership was that so many followers were frightened by the risks inherent in charting a new route. They faltered and failed, leaving him to carry the heavy burdens.

Aaban had been complaining.

Sometimes, putting yourself in another's shoes could be the hardest exercise and Khalil was a harsh master of his boys. He'd been trained to be demanding of himself and others but that discipline was why he'd excelled at his profession. Not everyone was cut out to succeed at a global level. They were the ones he blew up and he had plenty of them.

Jennifer had complained that her normally skintight jeans were too tight today.

"Am I getting fat?" she'd asked him, her puffy and new little stomach creeping outside her too low cut pants. Really? He had issues of global importance on his shoulders and they were discussing her eating too much and adding a muffin top? But he wasn't going to fight with her over a topic so pointless.

"You're beautiful," he replied, neither lying nor answering.

His hands found their way to the lush softness of her breasts and he reached to the firm nipple under cotton and lace. It was the deprivation of years that made her skin like the sticky tape children used to bind their fragile art projects, memories made such that years later they'd be remembered with less fragility than their foundations.

She was faith, and hope, and the only love he'd ever felt. Whether any true affection had come in his direction otherwise he couldn't begin to judge, mostly the skin had been cool and hadn't warmed his heart. He'd pushed the others away, never trusting their affection or that he'd deserved to be loved. Jennifer was burning hot, and every time his hands ran along her soft skin he felt a confusing and disorienting burn.

Why her? Of the women he'd fucked she seemed the most improbable. Dangerous in every sense, their timing couldn't be worse, not the first time they'd dated and not now, yet she'd haunted him for years. Jennifer was elusive, alternating calm with that occasional tantrum such that she moderated his moods until she excited him. He resolved the latter sexually, when she let him get rough and he rammed into her almost violently, releasing whatever pent up emotions he was too frightened to face. Yet she asked little emotionally, perhaps having learned long ago to live without expecting support, masculine in her fierce independence.

Alone for most of his life and thrown early into the street, he'd resisted cheap feminine tricks of closeness and bonding. Such insanity was for pussies and Jennifer never pulled that crap, letting him get close to her physically and never expecting him to "open" up or "express his feelings". Practically, he couldn't begin to even guess at how he felt or the darkness hidden deep inside and she'd have been asking him for something that didn't exist had she asked for more. And the less she asked the more he started finding in himself.

Khalil had chosen to always do, moving forward shark-like and knowing that if he stopped he'd die. Introspection was for those not skating life and death, trying to change the world. He hadn't reached that ideal which was why it stayed the perfect goal and ever elusive so he'd never need to face himself.

Touching her, the white skin milky clear and electric underneath his fingers, he felt the only life he'd known. The rest had been just a build for this moment and his deprivation had built a hunger such that her body could never fully sate it. Instead, he'd become addicted to the rush of caring about something, and of finally feeling that he had a body. Before, his limbs had been functional, and he'd deprived and disciplined them, forcing performance at ever tougher and higher peaks. Climbing mountains in Afghanistan, trekking across the border into Pakistan and then flying to the deserts of murderous Algeria and battle wracked Iraq. He'd pushed harder and driven the distance between himself and his body ever wider until she brought him life and didn't seem to understand the importance of her presence.

Fat? Really? How could she ask him such an insignificant question?

Khalil continued caressing a lush breast as he pulled Jennifer onto the bed. He tried to focus on her full lips and those blue eyes, glistening and seemingly penetrating into his heart's secrets. Had he truly never understood the world before? The more time he spent in her presence the more she enchanted him and the harder it became to refocus on the real world, of KK and his plots. Once you've found paradise, that ultimate escape, how do you go back to our world's harsh realities? He tried to break apart her elements after they made love but could never remember the act clearly only the ecstasy that was like a drug in its high and no more recallable.

He just knew that like an addict he wasn't there for the memories but for an escape.

She nuzzled closer as he entered her, and gently exhaled against his neck. Like a dove, she cooed softly and moved as if a part of him. The first woman who'd ever given herself to him completely, when she was in his arms he sensed her ultimate surrender and felt a surge of control. Most people in life resisted and fought, always aiming for the upper hand and fucking you over. There was so much more power in surrender.

And he did, into her. The electricity didn't pass just because the act did and he pulled her closer, hiding his eyes. How could he let her see the emotion, harder to keep in check now that he'd reunited with it? He had a bad feeling that his newfound heart wasn't going to help him win the war but we all take risks. And now he knew, without a doubt, that all of Allah's promises were true as having tasted paradise the clarity of its certitude and the toll of related sacrifices begged no further question.

So he kissed her again. KK had eight more days alive on earth and then they would leave this dangerous country forever, heading into their own sunset if lucky. For now, Khalil could spare a few hours enjoying his own life in a cheap hotel room with the woman he loved. Jennifer smelled of acrid sweat and whatever perfume she wore with jasmine and her distinctive sweet bitterness but little else. Roses, lilac, who cared? He studied her body and saw some truth to her earlier concern for while her waist was small her belly really was rounding out. We all age.

Jennifer's lips began with those butterfly kisses for which she had such a talent. Starting at his shoulders, he could feel the soft crush of her lips as she wound her way down his body, inch by inch. Flesh feels different when its owner truly loves you and the resulting touches nourish. Khalil sensed the first real love he'd ever known and vowed to enjoy it since nothing is guaranteed to last.

Hugging her tightly he wondered at how sometimes only his body could communicate while his lips existed without words. Should he have told Jennifer how he felt twenty years earlier, when they'd been dating and before he left? Well, the answer scarcely mattered anymore. There is no turning back in life and momentum keeps propelling us forward sometimes, no matter how hard we struggle to change its course, if we even know which course we want to take.

Task oriented, Khalil knew what his next week would hopefully bring. Beyond those ambitions he wasn't prepared to start asking bigger philosophical questions let alone come up with truisms. And there wouldn't always be a tomorrow to figure out any answers so perhaps ultimately they didn't matter.

Silence

Well this situation was tricky, wasn't it? No contact for over a day. No return calls or texts. No book. Little information and a direct question for her dad. What was in this situation for Emine? Please? Really. Nothing...

Got it.

She'd call Mehmet and ask the question anyway. Sometimes decisions in life aren't just based on what we obviously get from them. Of course, George was playing her but did he have much choice and was he hiding it? He was doing so to stop a murderous killer and foil another likely plot after risking his own life to stop an earlier one. She'd already watched him place team and mission above self-aggrandizement. Bright had given him a global television platform and he'd fallen back into anonymous government instead. Used to idealistic men, she'd support yet another one.

Who would Khalil try to shoot and would he succeed? Was Khalil rationally going to switch from bombs to guns, though he was a fighter so realistically guns weren't anything new in his fingers? And what's right in a terrorist plot when a terrorist is merely a warrior without a supporting recognized government? Definitions of terrorist, revolutionary or soldier often came down to the definer's ideology and relative position.

If Khalil wanted to harm Manhattan he had almost too many options though she wasn't an expert at which choices were practical ones given the many security measures in place. Strike where: shopping malls, restaurants, planes, embassies, government buildings or private buildings? Or a person, hence George's question.

She let George end the call, deciding not to question his demons as they were all feeling the pressure of a shoe (or bomb) about to drop. He hadn't even mentioned Aswan but her text had. His information was probably better and she wished she could probe and write richer related stories but as always Emine also let those questions slide so she'd protect his trust, which a probing, inquisitive journalist wouldn't.

Back to work.

George seemed to think that Khalil was going to kill someone and was concerned enough to ask her father for insight, an interesting turn of events and her dad would be intrigued! But one key related question was Khalil's current location as it had huge potential implications, even in the day and age of air travel and the likely outcome. Well, if George had any inkling he certainly hadn't said.

Emine lit a cigarette and watched the smoke blow in curls, pondering her words. She wasn't calling Mehmet until she knew exactly what to ask and how to phrase it. Men like him, even your father, never give you much time to speak.

Was dealing with Mehmet's type only so much manipulation? Yes, pretty much. Some people never saw past their own agendas and you needed to address them within the confines of those interests. The problem with individuals pushing political end games was that your goals could never compete. No appropriate counter existed to a person attempting to save the world or right global wrongs and arguing was ultimately futile. A further complication was that only the most ambitious wanted to save the world and were often perfectly willing to use anyone to achieve their goals. Or sacrifice anyone.

She and Selim had been sacrificed to Mehmet's ambition. So had Liz. But her dad had arguably made the world a better place though in a net balance he'd probably come out even as his means could get rough. How much different was George really?

And Emine could call George on it and point out what a bastard he was being: reneging on the book, ignoring her, refusing to share information and then using her father for insight, and perhaps, answers. Weren't they and Ben a team? But she was a trained enabler and willing to get thrown under a bus for the right cause. The world needed help and her feelings had never much mattered before so why should they now?

Besides, Emine had no obligation not to use any and all information for her own maximum benefit. If George owed her nothing she owed him about the same. That was the law of the jungle at work and power was the domain of the ruthless.

Emine thought back to a walk with her father when she was eleven. He'd decided that they'd hike up the winding Istanbul streets below the Hagia Sophia and Blue Mosque. Using the tiny narrow back alleys rather than the wider main road, they'd explored the older district, with tiny tea-shops, narrow apartments and crumbling shops. The closer to the monuments they'd gotten the more touristy the stores had become, littered with postcards, jewelry and decorative dishes. The aggressive and ever present "Turkish" carpet sellers ignored them, seeing that they were locals and not game for a hustle. And being from Istanbul Emine had wondered at her father's decision to take her to the most touristic part of the city. She'd seen the monuments before, many times of course, but usually when her father was giving a tour and wanted to imbibe it with a family flavor.

They turned the corner on a cobblestone street and she could see the famous holy buildings only partially. Set up on the hill, they overlooked the city and flowing Bosporus River, with its tour boats and commercial ships. Two massive domed structures, gardens and a majestic fountain separated them. Emine could remember running for the sprinkling water as her father called her back. Impulsive, she'd usually ignore him and suffer the punishment. Dashing through scattering pigeons she had no intention of letting him keep her from the magical plumes of glittering water. It had been summer and very hot. Puffing, her large and unfit father would catch her slowly.

Surprised when he didn't she'd turned to look for him. Silhouetted against the expansive dome and four minuets of the older Hagia Sophia she saw him in rapt conversation with a darker man, dressed in Arab robes, with two boys of about her age. She recognized the man from a dinner party her parents had hosted the night before. Peeking from atop their grand staircase she liked to watch the well-dressed and important people that her parents would gather for their parties. This walk must be "politics" and she had been brought as a distraction.

Her initial response had been annoyance but then self preservation kicked in. If she helped her dad and distracted the boys so he could persuade their parent (unofficially) to do what he wanted not only would she likely not get in trouble for her dash he might be pleased enough to get her ice cream. If he didn't get what he wanted, she'd be punished for sure. So she ran to the group and grabbed one of the boys.

"Hello," she said, "I'm Emine. Do you know the mosques?" The boys had deep, dark eyes and she watched as they met each others' and seemed to pass a secret message. Kids learn how to communicate without speaking and she could sense they were deciding whether to engage. Well, if their dad knew her dad they must be used to these unofficial, off the record machinations and probably just as skilled at working them to advantage.

"Hello," the taller boy responded gravely and the younger boy took a step backward as his father's head turned to the children. Seeing Emine, he relaxed.

"She'll tell them about the mosques, it's all right," her father said, putting his hand on the man's elbow and moving him away.

"The Hagia Sophia was dedicated in the year 360," she started. Her parents had forced her to memorize the facts so she could mimic a tour guide as necessary. The boys looked polite and perhaps even interested as she droned on, but were clearly frightened of their father. They were dressed in Arab robes as well.

"Originally a Christian church, it was repeatedly destroyed by earthquakes, age, invaders and other factors. Considered one of the finest examples of Byzantine architecture it was finally made a mosque in 1453 when the Ottoman Turks conquered Constantinople, Istanbul's original name."

Emine glanced at the old building, with its four minuets, three of red brick and one of white limestone and sand stone, and too wide a dome, the latter of which had put crushing weight on the walls for centuries. The builders had managed to line the bottom of the dome with 40 windows, further weakening the structure but gracing it with its mystic light. It had held the title of largest church for a thousand years until 1520 when the Seville Cathedral had been erected in Spain.

Perhaps heavier and less well preserved than the newer Blue Mosque which only dated from 1616 Emine had always loved Hagia Sophia more. Inside were both Islamic tile work and the elegant Christian mosaics of saints and Christ himself, in tiles or gold. The church had been built from materials spanning the earlier empire, including green marble, black and yellow stones and eight Corinthian columns from Lebanon. The largest columns weighed over 70 tons and were made of granite.

Tinted red and yellow from a 19th century restoration, the sun directly above it was blinding and Emine watched as the boys squinted, looking like they were trying to live up to their social obligations as the two fathers chatted quietly off to the side. The younger one made a comment to his brother in Arabic but Emine wasn't fluent in that language then so didn't understand nor did she care enough to ask, just pointing at the domed building. Their accent was one she didn't recognize and the words were hard to discern as well.

Suddenly, Mehmet swooped between the boys and put his hand on their respective shoulders, ignoring Emine.

"The structure is very complex," he began instructing them, and Emine could see that their father was watching Mehmet, approving of the attention he was showing the boys. People are suckers for those who flatter their children. Mehmet continued his speech, "The dome is carried on four concave triangular pendentives that serve to transition from the circular base of the dome to its rectangular base, and juggles the massive weight. The walls needed to be reinforced. Emine, explain the Blue Mosque," her father ordered and she knew his show was over. For him it was all negotiations and she'd have to entertain their guests. But first.

"Pappa, can I buy them ice cream?" she asked sweetly and gave him a smile. Watching as he peeled off some bills, as she'd known he would so he could quickly get back to business, she pondered what flavor she'd choose. She'd always favored the simple vanilla. But, first, her job.

"And the Blue Mosque there is a mix of Byzantine and more traditional Islamic architecture and is considered the last great mosque of the classical period. Note a large courtyard, as with the Hagia Sophia, but two additional minuets, and that light elegance so much its own." Emine watched the boys make those mocking faces which only children could pull off. Was she pouring on the tour guide talk too much? She sounded like a trained guidebook but too often that was the role her parents expected.

She knew the story of the dome and how the mosque was also a mausoleum for its founder. The Sultan had been the only one to enter the delicate archways on horseback and had a chain hung just low enough that he would have to lower his head to enter, signifying his humility before the divine. With over 20,000 tiles handmade and in over fifty tulip designs, along with fruit, other flowers and even cypress, the mastery of artwork itself was awe inspiring but Emine could tell that the boys were bored now so kept that information to herself. One started splashing around in the fountain, throwing water at the pigeons and his brother, who joined in laughing. Their fathers ignored them, as did Emine who redirected her attention back to the mosques. The boys would be fine without her.

The Blue Mosque was perhaps classically more lovely, lighter and more delicate, with over 200 stained glass windows and a spattering of chandeliers. She loved to sit inside and let their heavenly lighting filter across her, knowing that so many others had experienced exactly the same. Her home town was littered with history, and the Hagia Sophia especially had been built across cultures and religions yet always steadily watched over the city from its perch above sapphire waters, speaking to her personal concept of eternity. People are transitory but in historic cities such as Istanbul the holy places survive even if they adapt to modernity.

"Ice cream" she yelled, regaining the boys' attention, and the children ran off together to the vendor with his tourist oriented cart, littered with English and post cards for sale.

George was acting like Mehmet now and using her as a decoy so he could get information. Normally, she'd work her angle to get an ice cream; people use each other all the time. But now she wanted to help George stop a killer. Would Mehmet give her the information she wanted assuming he even had it?

So how would she get Mehmet to provide the answers George needed? First, she had to try and figure out her own father's goals in helping. He'd guess why she was asking her questions and his answers would be driven more by his agenda than the truth. Evaluate people objectively when you want something from them or you may end up being the one used.

She lit a cigarette and starting charting the world as she knew on a piece of paper. Geopolitics. Who wanted what these days, and as important, what did they not want to happen?

Patience

Waiting is the hardest thing to do when you know that a plot is unfolding before your eyes and people might die. If you miss clues the blood of innocents will stain your hands, haunting your dreams and the shifting realities of your daytime. As Lady Macbeth found red is a color which isn't easily cleansed.

George had enough blood on his hands already. In his line of work you always missed something, a tone of voice or a name. That one coincidence which only seemed so obvious a month later when you couldn't sleep and kept turning over the words of a past interrogation, the detainee long gone.

No one escaped their past: George's had found him and he pondered why.

Khalil shouldn't be in New York. He shouldn't be getting close to George. A sane man didn't stalk his ex-jailor in a country that had him on a "most wanted" list. Then again, a sane man also didn't spend his life plotting to kill innocents and blow up buildings: that was the job of Hollywood or a novelist. Khalil wanted something and George was grasping at what it was. He'd stopped Aswan....

Practical realities standing in the way of his answer.

No one was telling George anything; but someone had to know more. The modern ironies of the information age meant that the only facts you could get were those you didn't want. George wasn't even told his security clearance but assumed his venture into international journalism hadn't improved his standing. Morning now, he waited for what the day would bring and expected a surprise. Again. The sun gleamed metallic as it ricocheted across the building tops, blindingly harsh. Summer with its unforgiving heat was coming; life can be similarly unforgiving.

And Khalil was ultimately his responsibility, George being the only one who understood the sick fuck in the process of unraveling, his words and actions becoming more disjointed and even random. Which meant? George knew the realities behind the behavior changes and understood the signs of a man breaking under too much pressure. Good.

George scanned outside his window. Central Park was before him and headed north to the upper east and west sides, with their affluent housing, one old world and the other new, then to the Bronx. New York was such a hodgepodge of people, mixing colors, religions and beliefs into that American melting pot of vibrant substance, hearty like a stew. He was more acclimated to northern California with its rolling green hills and geek talk in every Starbucks or trendy barely good but expensive café. Engineers didn't focus on food...or ambience...though universities did and Palo Alto was a campus town. Manhattan was a different beast entirely. The old mixed with the new to create a striving energy re-created by a rare country let alone city.

Palo Alto was the vibrant future; New York just mixed in that added kicker of history. There was so much to see, do, taste and smell. The smoke coming up from the manholes reminded us, no just him, of all that deceptively lay beneath a surface.

He grabbed a bag of pumpkin seeds and poured some into his palm. He loved pumpkin seeds that were well roasted, balancing smooth richness with salt, or just overly salted ones. These were his favorite and he downed them quickly. George had to acknowledge his burning hunger. Physical or mental was of little matter, the seeds quenched it so he kept eating, popping one after the other into his mouth and crunching.

The city was stunning, vast and teaming with vibrancy, and he reflected on why he'd appreciated it so little. Why was his heart always searching and missing what was before his eyes.

Times Square, Greenwich, Soho, Tribecca, Lower Manhattan with Little Italy and Chinatown thrown in. Then heading to Wall Street and what was left of the World Trade Center site. So many of the names were familiar yet only the city residents lived the brownstones, traffic and corner shops. And the neighborhood looked so different in a movie but the threats here were real and the people lived and died them. Not Tel Aviv, Beirut or Homs quite yet but braced for the worst.

Even terrorists had rights here.

So what were his clues? Or at least the ones he'd managed to grasp thus far from his muddled and overflowing mind. Shit. Why couldn't he be smarter?

Martin Luther King Junior, out of nowhere and for some reason. Aswan, which Khalil had thrown, lobbing a mysterious soft ball in his direction The bastard hadn't killed George. The Iranians and Cairo. Coffee in disposable cups. Practically, none of that information seemingly mattered.

Only one clue did and that was the assassination of a high level target in Manhattan. All else faded to background noise when George did the analysis.

So what one person in Manhattan could change Khalil's world for the better by dying? George knew his time doing Internet searches wouldn't yield nearly as much as his government researchers, with their endless minions and databases, could provide (if they'd tell him), thus he continued pondering his adversary's character. Cold, tough and mean, Khalil would need a massive amount of pressure to crack. But one thing George recognized was that Khalil was thus splintering.

And the world itself was also unraveling for some inexplicable reason as if God had just decided to stir things up, knowing how unstable social orders inherently were. We always need to regress to the mean...a basic Darwinian reality. Balance, patterns, order and synchronicity would ultimately bring a new normal.

Here in the United States the protests had continued, rising only to fall, and the people demanding better. As the upper classes quickly lost numbers but gained in income the population around them noticed. Being rich was becomming tougher as that minority plummeted and everyone else asked why, you? The conflict of democracy was that the majority could hold a minority hostage and George now inexplicably found himself in that top tier of minority million plus earners. Luck or skill? But George wasn't in it for the money...he was risking his life to do his job. Except.

No one had told him not to go to Cairo and indeed, his wife had been paid off in diamonds.

The world still needed Khalil in jail thus the less important value judgements would need to wait.

So why in the hell was Khalil in Mahattan? If he was after an American why New York? Wall Street, Fleet Street or politics? A strictly political target – domestic – would come from Washington DC. But, what if it was a foreigner? Now you opened up a number of big cities and only then did Manhattan make the most sense. Who lived here or was coming to the United States?

Now George studied his scotch but decided he needed to keep his head clear. Massaging his sore knee he wondered at risking a run in the park; life is not lived by treadmills alone. The somewhat humid air was less than ideal but the outside exercise would do him good and clear his head. We think better after a tough workout. Morning was the perfect time to run through the park and he'd have that runner's high to confront whatever else hit him today. Yes, he'd do it!

George stood and headed for his side closet, housing his running shoes and favorite shorts. As he was about to leave the room, the phone rang and George swerved over. He saw the 201 area code of Washington DC so he answered it.

"We have a break," said Campbell.

So much for that run.

Surprises

Jennifer was watching him and Khalil had become convinced of that unpleasant reality though he was unsure of her motivation. Changing phones, that one risk at least was contained. And the men following him on the street seemed to be back full time. What other dangers was he missing?

Women were all whores so why did men need them so much? He studied his and still loved her, much as his trust was dissipating.

Radwan was actually doing surprisingly well suddenly. At least something, someone, was succeeding because too often Khalil felt like he was merely spinning wheels and heading out of control. And Radwan was truly the only thing that mattered because KK had to die and Khalil was increasingly worried. Sure, a well planned assassination by someone willing to die in the process was hard to thwart but like all strikes it was still tough and the tools to prevent it had sharpened.

Now you really only had two choices if you were serious about your desired end result being a high profile dead body. The first was a brave and showy self martyrdom....but by a very skilled warrior. Or, you just blew up everything in the vicinity of your target. Both were less likely to succeed than you'd expect as life, once in motion, tends to continue going in that same direction and only a big effort can change that momentum. Skilled killers, now that the cold war was over, were rare and blowing up a whole block is hard. Electronic monitoring, scans, cameras, night vision, even nosy civilians just made strikes tougher.

Then there was the biggest enemy of all: yourself.

Khalil was now doubting his girlfriend which strangely made him value her all the more, between his tense calls in Arabic and late nights pondering every detail. Her skin was a creamy white but her words seemed increasingly black with deception.

As if he had time to deal with Jennifer. KK was now arriving earlier in Manhattan than originally planned and with a large entourage, including a general. He'd come straight from a tour through the Middle East, skipping Iran, and thus would land in New York three days before his UN conference.

To chaos? One could only hope.

Violence generally came without warning. There was rarely a foreshadowing and it happened ever so quickly. A ball thrown your way could just as easily be a fireball and once it hit the only thing you saw before death would be a flame and a blur. We give too much breadth to the things that move slowly, expecting that they'll create change, but it's what we don't see next to us that wacks us in the face.

Khalil now knew it was Jennifer and he loved her still. She had to be a plant.

Those eyes, blinking but rarely, would gaze into his, holding him enraptured and plotting his demise. He'd run his hand across smooth skin, with roughness at those bended joints, and know that she was plotting a way to trap, or worse, kill him.

And after he'd told George about Aswan, Osman among others had gone quiet and Khalil was increasingly finding himself alone. His phone suddenly rang, unexpected, and he threw it to the floor, crushing it beneath his heel and knowing he was making the right decision. No one should be calling him now.

The cell groupings in his organization worked based on the number three. Unless you fell into the very rare leader class, as he did, you only ever knew of three other people (outside of the training camps) and thus could only expose the organization to the extent of that limited circle. Each person in a cell only knew of the two people in their own grouping and one other. Thus deception was harder since the repercussions were minimal, touching an additional man or so at a time.

With KK in New York early should Khalil's plans change? He now had a few additional days of opportunity and a multitude of new options. Security would only tighten as more world leaders arrived and so perhaps moving sooner made sense. The counter argument was that being disciplined enough to stick with a plan set apart one man from the next, deciding who ultimately won.

Khalil heard Jennifer on the phone talking to her mother. But was she really? Perhaps the words were a code and only meant to deceive and betray. He'd need to watch her closer now as the stakes continued to rise higher. Khalil wasn't being grandiose when he pondered about how the fate of the world was increasingly resting on his shoulders.

And the Aswan fiasco had led to so many arrests within his organizations and endless internal strife. Was chaos good for someone ready to seize advantage and exploit opportunity? In a global organization with no real leader he who pulled off the boldest stunt would rule. Look at Fidel Castro.

One moment everything was fine and then in the next a lens changed and a different picture replaced it, whether through a flash of fire or another eraser, which wiped your panorama slate clean.

Zuccotti

mine wandered through the pristine confines of Zuccotti Park with its neat rows of tables and grey benches, all angular, like the tall office buildings towering above. Light reflected from the glass and she felt watched by the corporate occupants, still alert over ten years after the World Trade Center was destroyed a mere block away.

It was mostly deserted; Occupy Wall Street was over for now.

Liberty Park or Zucchotti, the former being its earlier name and the latter being the chairman of its owner, Brookfield Properties, had returned to its normal calm Protesters had spent months camping here to decry what was wrong in America, from its protected elite to the lack of an ongoing American dream. As with much in America, they'd been moved from this private park due to sanitation and safety issues, a loophole in the zoning that required a 24-hour open to all policy. In some countries repression restricted protests; here it was rules and regulations with the net result being the same, but with fewer body bags in lower Manhattan.

She tried to imagine how the square had looked when clustered with tents and alive with music and camaraderie. Delicate flowers filled the neatly tended planting beds, a clear demonstration of well-managed corporate order. United States Steel had originally created it, filling a space of about 33,000 square feet it. Many public works and museums in the United States were likewise built by rich corporations or individuals, which felt both self aggrandizing and also admirable. Damaged during the World Trade attacks it had been renovated at a cost of many millions.

Two sculptures added aesthetic appeal and quirckiness. The first was a very American visual of a seated business man while the other was a 70 foot tall red abstract. Lightly populated with affluent looking business people, Emine tried to tie it with the earlier pictures and videos she'd seen from the Occupy Wall Street protests, messy and dirty. So odd to hold a protest in a corporate owned park near the site of the WTC disaster and then get evicted for too much trash and not enough toilets. America.

Emine was waiting for her dad's return call after reaching only his secretary. "Emergency meeting," was all she was told and didn't like the sound of those words. Such were the mysteries of government. She was also on hold with George who was clearly and openly not sharing information or actions citing "national security". When Mehmet and George were ready to talk they'd find her.

It was a muted Bright that had sent her here, to this now again sedate park with the tumultuous history. He'd also been getting a similar brush off and suggested she start a series on revolution and protest. Good idea or bad? She had little else to do other than drink so she might as well write.

Grabbing her camera Emine started clicking away at the square's confines. Small and tidy, the boundaries didn't amount to much and dimutitive shops littered the neighborhood, offering newspapers and oversized sandwiches. What could people in this ordered society have to complain about, especially compared to the brutal realities of sustenance survival and war in other less fortunate locales? Yet no man, rich or poor alike, is free from worries or problems.

Here the people knew they had a voice, expected and demanded it, along with accountability and equality. Such an odd foundation upon which a country might build itself.

Still, the Tea Party, Occupy and the ever vocal press with their related demands for fairness were so optimistically American. Things didn't always get better because you pushed for change; sometimes they got worse. Was this country increasingly putting fairness and equality above democracy as they strove for the right ideology in practice? Equality when there wasn't enough to share could push living standards down for all and such were the common results of Communism. But perhaps justice, even when most people were poorer, led to greater happiness.

Who was she to judge? Mostly she wrote about repression, war and abject poverty because she'd stumbled onto that path pursuing an escape from herself. A richer country wasn't her domain to understand but Emine enjoyed pondering the questions.

Khalil must be similarly lost. They both came from Muslim countries with gross divides between the rich and poor and little accountability at a time when media was Westernizing their expectations. But while his homeland had lived in constant war hers, the gateway to Europe, was arguably more stable. The Ottoman Empire had once ruled half the known world, a thundering and fearsome presence. Now, still within the domain of generals until very recently, Turkey had mellowed, perhaps in deference to its more volatile immediate neighbors. Crossing cultures could be confusing.

America was so very different in certain respects yet lived in by people the same as those the world over. We all want more don't we? With not enough resources globally and inequities now splashed across the Internet the world was increasingly in turmoil. So many souls striving but for what and could most even articulate their amorphous desires? And Khalil? Did he ask himself these confusing questions as he navigated his way through the same chaotic and confusing streets? What was his desire?

Emine took a photo shot at a pigeon, using black and white film, and her pocket started to vibrate. Shit, she'd forgotten to put the ring tone on and she grappled to pull the iPhone from the front flap of her jeans, which were slimly fitted thus resisted her advance.

"Eme, I'll be in New York in a few days," said her father's voice, far away but sounding near. "There's yet another conference at the UN Headquarters and I'm attending. We'll be hearing insight into the global protest movement and what's working from the government end," finished Mehmet, in his gruff but formal voice. Emine sat down on a bench and felt its cold cement through her jeans. The sun hadn't yet built to heat.

Was Khalil interested in these dignitaries discussing global changes? Sounded like a great opportunity for a man trolling a target.

"Dad," was all she said instead, noticing the glances of two businessmen passing by. Her shirt was more gauze than fabric but this was the big city so a flash of skin was nothing new; she smiled anyway. Bright pink wasn't a local color but she wasn't local, was she? Mehmet was explaining a number of upcoming global elections and her head began to spin at the possibilities. It wasn't like she could just figure out which country was the most potentially unstable and thus made the best target. So who's absence would spur a change most beneficial to Khalil and his group?

"I wanted to know, who would Al Qaeda shoot in New York, and perhaps at that conference?" she asked, deciding to keep her question and facts spare. Don't guide the answer with your question's phrasing. Like a predator he'd jump on any glittering detail that caught his attention and build from there.

"Al Qaeda is planning to shoot someone in New York?" he muttered. "The conference would be perfect." His voice tapered off and she stayed quiet. Occasionally, he thought out loud and she'd hear the complex number of variables that weighed an eventual conclusion in his sophisticated mind.

As she waited for Mehmet's answer another question began to nag: why was Khalil here now? It was a timing issue. He shouldn't risk arriving too far in advance of whatever plot he was planning since that time span would only increase his risk of being caught. Thus?

She wished she were at the UN Headquarters now so she could study the complex but it was forty or so streets north. Mehmet kept muttering... the names of countries and people...alliances and deceptions.

Emine kicked at a napkin lazily wafting by. A hint of a breeze propelled it forward, then to the side and forward again. Overhead, a cloud followed a similarly leisured path, as befit the moderate temperature and mood of the day. This park, much as it was in the midst of a tall city, was a respite from the sidewalks' frantic pace and truly pristine. She liked hearing her father, an ocean away, talking and reassuring. They might not know what was happening, but with him as an ally stopping Khall was a step closer.

"Saudi Arabia," he finally said. "Then the suspicion will fall on Iran as they'd tried a plot against the Saudi Ambassador on American soil before. The crisis blew over but someone seemingly wants a United States-Iran war. They don't even need to succeed in killing anyone as the threat will be enough to create a real risk with tensions already running high."

"Brilliant!" she responded and his words did make perfect sense. Getting the Americans into a war with Iran would be among the most dangerous ways of neutralizing the world power. And if it happened, with whom would China and Russia side? The First World War was triggered by an assassination; would the third be likewise started?

"The Islamists want chaos and wars," she said, hearing a similar mumble in her tone. Like father, like daughter.

"Yes."

But Emine wasn't done with him yet and needed more ideas, in case he was was wrong. Nothing was ever as transparent as it might initially seem. She'd interviewed many "terrorists" and they all considered many plots before deciding on one.

"Who else?" she asked, and held her breathe again. For that was the problem with Mehmet: he'd always give you the answer that suited his purpose, not the best answer. Iran was a constant thorn in Turkey's side and had sheltered many of its dissidents over the years. A better option might be one he didn't want to publicly acknowledge, not even to his own daughter, as it might put their country at risk.

"Egypt, KK, the moderate candidate and favored to win. Egypt is key in Middle Eastern politics and vastly impacts policy throughout the region. The Islamists need to win Egypt or they'll be marginalized to crushed."

"Syria?" she asked.

"Why?" he barked, impatient. "Currently, Syria is only valuable as Iran's partner but in chaos would become an unimportant failed state."

"They're educated?" she responded as a pigeon boldly landed next to her, staring gingerly.

"And they should kill an American instead," Mehmet continued. "What a glorious win that would be, if he was important enough. Perfection."

Emine heard in her dad's tone that his mind was now wandering. He had given her a minute, for which she should be grateful, and some insight. Pragmatic but biased, his viewpoint was still one of those she'd trust the most.

Yes, Saudi Arabia. Egypt. She needed to find George to tell him though none was a surprise. But first.

"When will you arrive?" she asked.

"Four days. The conference starts the next morning."

"Tuesday." That didn't give her and George much time to find and stop Khalil, if Mehmet was right about the conference.

"I love you," she told her dad and hoped he wasn't the target. A moderate helping hold together a country as much in the crossroads of history as Egypt, Mehmet was always at risk. Was his addition to the conference new or had he just not mentioned it before? He could be evasive that way, in part because dad liked to maximize his schedule and would happily cancel one thing for another he preferred.

Emine heard someone coming up from behind and jumped. She turned and saw a mid-height slim brown haired man dressed in a charcoal pinstripe suit walking toward her, engaged on his Blackberry. As if sensing her sudden attention he glanced up from his phone and smiled. She felt something akin to a kick in the stomach, an attraction, and realized she'd need to finally break up with Ed. While the realization was a bit random it followed that quirk of reality which dictated that decisions often ultimately come from seemingly unrelated events triggering long suppressed memories. The stranger in the suit had the same shoulders as Piers, wide, tapering, yet slim, and she still hadn't moved on from the memories of her ex-fiances' body. Perhaps next year.

But life goes on.

She started dialing George, hoping she didn't get his voicemail yet again but did. Damn. She stood up and began striding toward the UN building, pondering the implictions of her father's words and forthcoming arrival. Could the answer be so simple? Then again, people so often complicate things such that they no longer work. Suddenly her phone rang and she pulled it back out of her pocket, wondering if Mehmet had thought of something new.

The caller id showed George and she scrambled to answer it.

Timing

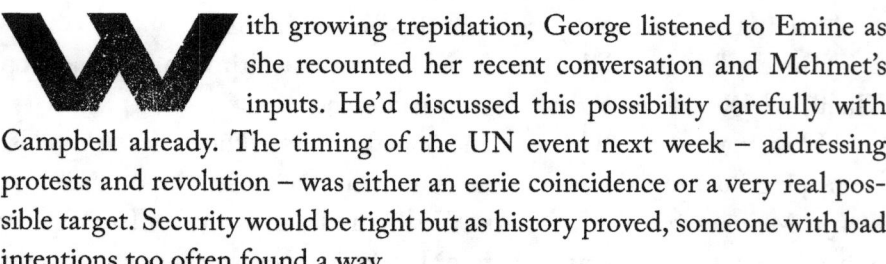ith growing trepidation, George listened to Emine as she recounted her recent conversation and Mehmet's inputs. He'd discussed this possibility carefully with Campbell already. The timing of the UN event next week – addressing protests and revolution – was either an eerie coincidence or a very real possible target. Security would be tight but as history proved, someone with bad intentions too often found a way.

Emine was animated so he let her continue her monologue as she detailed one possibility after another, with the best of intentions and thankfully not the only one so idealistically motivated. Who seriously did this for a living otherwise? The bad guys just kept rearming and coming at them with bigger and better guns.

Shooting a Saudi? Well, Al Qaeda liked to re-visit their old adversaries until they succeeded, as with the WTC and, yes, the house of Saud. But

George wasn't happy with that answer as it lacked Khalil's drama. Khalil wanted credit for his success, not a more subtle implication that another was to blame, in this case Iran.

Earlier, Campbell had confirmed some very imprecise information from a just captured detainee about an assassination plot targeting the conference but had barely squeezed clearance to tell George and he wasn't sharing in turn with Emine. He could guide her without betraying a confidence.

"A young man will shoot but our source didn't know from where or at whom," Campbell had repeated, broadening the scope of the danger while also narrowing it by tying the assassination attempt to an event. While in a movie such complications would play out in a dramatic chase scene across the city landscape in real life it just meant more windows from which the snout of a rifle could peak, hidden and virtually impossible to spot. Assassinations are hauntingly dramatic, a face sticking in the public memory and with re-sults long cascading. One man is remembered.

"Great," George replied, but only managed that single word before Emine cut him off and he let her. He was still sitting in his living room nursing the cold remnants of his coffee in a Cardinals mug and staring down at the little ants swarming the streets crossing Central Park. Dressed in sweats and unshaven, he'd been on the phone all morning again, barely even finding time to glance at a newspaper. So much for that run.

The room was quiet, with his guard duty keeping themselves busy and Karen was both a silent presence and a memory. The isolation helped him think but still George wished for movement and a resolution to this endless quest. Why couldn't Khalil just get himself killed?

"You don't agree?" Emine asked and George pondered her question. Meanwhile he sipped again at his bitter cold morning leftovers and studied the still green tree tops outside his window.

"No," he finally answered. "But I don't disagree either. We don't have enough facts and ..."

"Oh my God," Emine gasped. George felt a stab of concern but told himself not to panic. She didn't follow up immediately with clarification but he knew that she could handle any contingencies, and probably better than he would.

"It's Khalil," she muttered. "With a younger man. I'm hanging up to take pictures." George heard the click. In a city of millions bumping into your adversary might seem to be a coincidence but for George it confirmed that their suspicions and information had been right and they'd possibly just narrowed the plot down to a number of square blocks. Any terrorist stalking his prey needs to return over and over again to the target site. Studying it, knowing it and obsessing over it are more effective in person than in fiction. Was Khalil's friend the younger man they'd been advised might take the shot?

And better that Emine stumbled upon Khalil than George since she was a professional photographer so traveled with a zoom lens and great camera and, even as important, wasn't likely to be recognized. What she wouldn't be able to do was track both Khalil and his companion and hopefully wouldn't even try as doing so might risk drawing their attention. Much as George wanted to nab Khalil now, as soon as possible, he didn't want to alert the man to the fact that he'd been spotted and his accomplice photographed. Sometimes losing a battle really was the only way to win a war.

Solitude can be your closest friend and forced confinement provides a space in which to reflect. George needed such time because he sensed that soon the luxury would be a long forgotten memory now that Khalil's nearby presence had been confirmed. The man might quote philosophers but practically speaking he was all action. A familiar adrenaline rush was building as George's body instinctively kicked into gear: the conference was days away and Khalil was here as the pieces began falling into place faster. The clues were always there in retrospect; meanwhile the hard part was recognizing them in the present.

What was the most productive use of his time, George wondered, as he waited for Emine to call back? Probably digging through the complete list of attendees to the conference at the UN. Now he needed to understand everything about the event and those attending, as Khalil doubtless did. He already knew Khalil better than he knew his own family, intuitively and deeply. This was all starting to make sense and George needed to follow Khalil's example: stay alert, poised and ready for opportunities as they arose for they always did.

On and On

Everything was set to go.

Khalil felt Jennifer's lush body as she curled closer. Her soft, flushed skin was glistening with sweat and she smelled of him, her breath still coming quickly. They were both exhausted after hours of enjoying each other in the fading afternoon sun, time that both passed quickly and seemed to go on forever. His tears blended with the sweat on her back as he held her close, the covers crunched at the foot of the bed and air coming only from a small window high above.

His plan was perfect so far.

"Please be strong," he whispered, half hoping she wouldn't hear.

"What," Jennifer said, and did what women always did – pushed him away so she could see his eyes when she confronted him.

A spider crawled just past her shoulder on the pillow and then up the wall, its legs moving so fast and efficient. Khalil tried to ignore it but wondered at the warning, for his code name was the "Spider".

Jennifer's eyes were on him but she said nothing, perhaps just waiting for his answer; that was a change. Her glance cast across him and she had to notice his tears and probably red eyes. He couldn't remember the last time he'd cried, no longer sure if he'd done so at his mother's deathbed months before. Emotions were suddenly swarming through him and he no longer knew how to regain control.

"The plan is perfect," was all Khalil could muster.

"I don't want to hear about it," Jennifer's eyes hardened as she spoke.

For a passing instant he felt unappreciated and unloved, as a burst of anger intruded on his sentiments and uncertainty. He was, after all, one of the best at his profession, a tough and dangerous one where few survived as he had. Why couldn't she appreciate that he risked his life for his beliefs unlike lesser men who preached but rarely followed through on their convictions? And he knew she'd had lesser men. Plenty of them, to be precise.

"Why are you so angry?" Khalil stammered, feeling more a boy than a man as he watched her temper twist those normally pretty features. How did she do it, that rapid jump from sweet to Medusa? Sweat was building on his forehead and he willed away the warmth of the room. The air conditioner was broken again.

Jennifer continued to stare but the hardness in her eyes began to soften as her palm reached out, then she brushed her fingertips across his beaded sweat. He felt the tears well up again. What was wrong with him?

"Khalil," she began, her voice barely above a whisper, "You left me. You continue to leave me. You kill people."

"But don't you love me?" Khalil responded, instead of pointing out that she had taken him back, sensing that the latter would draw her ire again. People don't like to be reminded that they compromise their principles regularly. Women in particular were weak which was why the Koran was harsh in its guidance on dealing with them. Still, he was glad to feel her hand take his unexpectedly as touch seemed important at that instant. Perhaps he couldn't stand to have her reject him physically as she criticized the core of his existence

"Of course I love you," her eyes were heated now and her words coming faster. Khalil willed Jennifer not to lose her temper completely. Would that lack of emotional control be the death of them both? She bent down and drew the covers up from the bed's foot and wrapped the fabric around their bodies.

"Khalil, listen to me," her hand was stroking his, her fingers so sure in their motion. "I've given everything up to be with you. What more proof do you need that I love you?"

What more proof indeed? Was there proof enough in the world to fill the void that had substituted for what should have been his soul? The spider was back, crawling an inch from her shoulder and Khalil finally brushed it away. Meanwhile, Jennifer kept her blue eyes focused on his, unflinching. Trust, indeed. He could have killed her at any moment and she couldn't stop him yet he couldn't hold her gaze and watched a scampering spider instead.

"I...," and that's all he could reply.

"Don't do it," Jennifer yanked at his hands, forcing him to look at her. One hand broke away from the other and held his chin steady. "You don't need to do it."

"But what would I do instead?" and for a second Khalil felt a new confusion, a different one as if there was no end to the emotion's variations. Not do it? The plan was perfect. It was in place ready to unroll within a few days unless he decided to take advantage of KK's early arrival and lighter security to shoot the man himself before. This assassination was his job.

"Stop it from happening," Jennifer sounded calm but Khalil couldn't trust her stability, fully aware of her volatility just moments before. He wanted to ask for whom she was working but knew that she'd never confess any betrayal. Damn actress, like most women.

"I'm not begging you to stop the assassination because you love me. I won't be that manipulative." She paused, her breath coming faster, and teardrops glistening on her lashes now. "Stop it because he shouldn't die and if he does so many others will also."

Wait, how did Jennifer know about an "assassination"? He hadn't told her. He slapped her across the mouth. She had to be a spy.

"Either way so many will die," Khalil said, regaining his emotional footing, miraculously, and wondering if he should kill the false-hearted bitch. Best not to leave evidence behind and she was starting to become a liability. Then again, Khalil still loved Jennifer even as her sapphire eyes flashed their challenge. "Death won't stop because one man lives," he said, more to buy time for a decision than for any other reason.

"Bullshit and you know it," replied Jennifer, still shockingly calm and out of character. How long had she been planning this confrontation? She, who usually got ridiculously emotional during fights, must have been steeling herself for this one. "Don't lie. Not at this point in our relationship," she begged and he let himself believe for a few more seconds that their relationship could survive this confrontation. But could any relationship withstand an honest airing out of skeletons?

"But all I do is lie," Khalil said, finally stating the obvious.

"I know and I've decided to love you anyway but I'm asking you not to do this." Jennifer, to her credit, asked for little more, if Khalil was honest with himself. He pulled her close and felt himself harden then entered her fiercely, sensing her body yield as she sighed. And, lucky for her, she kept her mouth shut for a while.

How much did she know and from where did she get her information?

"Do you speak Arabic?" he asked her, in Arabic and she mumbled "yes" and kissed his shoulder. So that was the key. She should have mentioned it earlier. Khalil didn't want to kill her but might end up with no other option. And how much time did he have to make a decision before it was too late? Coming quickly he knew that he needed a cigarette and walk in the moderately fresh air of the packed and frenetic city.

Partners

Emine wondered at following them, Khalil and his new addition. The other man appeared to be in his early to mid twenties, heavy set but still graceful, exuding confidence but a restrained version as if he hadn't yet overcome youthful doubts. Dressed almost like a native with a too large t-shirt and baggy cotton pants in deference to the heat he'd also added a backward baseball cap, which was trying too hard for this part of town.

Aiming to stay discrete, and glad that even in her bright pink she usually managed to fade, a personality disorder of a sort, Emine considered her options, follow them or not? She'd hung up on George without asking him to send support. Did she have time to call back and for help to arrive before these two disappeared into the crowd? Probably not, but at least she had taken a number of great shots. She'd seen the pictures George had sketched after his escape and, while George was a talented artist, a photo was always better. And now they had a picture of a likely accomplice!

Emine studied Khalil through her lens, the way she liked to frame people then clicked. The boundaries and focus helped her catch little details that a broader portrait wouldn't. Fascinated, she watched the man responsible for so many deaths, including very nearly George's. Does a murderer carry any sign labeling him for what he is? Thus far, Emine had noted little to so distinguish the group and had met enough not to expect one.

Khalil was slight, but moved powerfully, seemingly so confident and natural. He was clearly a man who knew his body's strengths and weaknesses and could correct for the latter. Far away, she could still study his face through her zoom lens. He had intense eyes, not large but almost girly with thick lashes, and the lips were distinctive below a sculptured nose. Emine tried to see the plastic surgeon's path but noted only that his facial structure seemed softer than his lean body. Dressed simply, he clearly didn't care about his external appearance. She got the impression of intense energy and speed.

The pair separated without a goodbye gesture and Emine let them go, lingering next to a wall and sheltered from the sun. She started emailing pictures one by one to George and wondered at giving Bright a scoop. Then again, she had to be careful and wasn't in the mood to fuck around with any government security matters. Not worth it. Feeling paranoid she glanced around but only saw the busy streets of a crowded city. The more people around the less likely that any one of them would notice her.

If this plot really was moving forward what was her best angle? Clearly she wanted to stop it but then what? Did she still want a book with George or one on her own? Well, she couldn't decide now as so much seemed poised to still happen

She glanced at her phone and noticed that George had sent her an email response.

"Great photos. Can you come to my apartment?" he asked and had added his address in his Central Park location, near a Trump Hotel and before both the Upper East and Upper West sides of the city

She'd walk the distance and while it might take her over twenty minutes she really needed the time to think. Smelling yeast and coffee she noticed a pretzel seller and felt suddenly hungry so made her way to him. Black, she heard an odd accent as he addressed her, and one she didn't like.

"Pretzel, miss?"

"Somali?" she asked.

The young man was lovely, with high deep cheekbones, large round eyes and smooth dusky skin. But he seemingly didn't know how to smile and just nodded.

"Your name?" she asked.

"Aaban," he replied and she noted a lilt in his voice which seemed so oddly appropriate with the accent. He still wasn't smiling when she handed him money.

"Have you been in New York long?" she asked, wondering if he was still traumatized from the brutal civil war (not officially declared but understood) in his failed state homeland.

"No," he replied and turned his back on her, spitting at the pavement. Damn misogynistic pig, probably judging her for her clothes and thinking she was a whore. Such men were all alike in their ignorance. She threw her pretzel at his back and walked away. Had she turned around she would have seen him watching her, staring with an intensity that noted more than a woman in a sheer blouse. But she didn't turn back, heading instead to her rendezvous with George.

Shots

George studied the photos Emine had sent on his 27-inch computer screen. The camera had been high pixel but the computer screen wasn't, at least not enough to capture all the details. Thus the men were grainy, with softer lines and those bleeding edges that don't happen in life. The pictures were much clearer than the grainy ones of Khalil in the desert that George had seen a few days earlier. But the taller man was clearly Khalil though George had never seen his heavier and younger companion. Perhaps in his early twenties, he likely wasn't yet on any terrorist watch lists and had been chosen due in part to that fact. Well that reality would change. US based or imported? Campbell was doing the checks, running the images through those massive global government databases. Pictures were getting increasingly easy to identify, with time being the biggest variable. No one enters America easily without a passport or photo id, and it's hard to live here without building a database of records.

Lunchtime was drawing near and George considered ordering food but didn't feel like much. Along with Emine his guards were also here and lingering, protective though Khalil hadn't been noticed nearby again. Since they had no idea of Khalil's precise location until Emine's encounter today, George wasn't fully reassured that Khalil wouldn't return to the streets below his apartment. Moreover, George was increasingly convinced that he himself wasn't the target. And Khalil had now been spotted by the UN headquarters and not Columbus Circle, George's immediate neighborhood. But that presence had been just a passing moment of time, and Khalil could be anywhere by now.

What to do about lunch? He should just order something for everyone, right? But how could he focus on food when much more important issues were at risk!

The UN conference was starting in five days but already numerous dignitaries were arriving, families in tow, to do shopping and pre-meetings. Security was tight but that was perhaps an oxymoron. When the world's stability hinged on a few men wielding protective guns how could it ever be careful enough?

He called Campbell and got through immediately.

"We're analyzing the list of attendees based on region," Campbell said. "I think we're making progress."

Without me, of course, and I'm here and know Khalil best and more, George felt like saying but kept his mouth shut. Of course he wanted to run the show but there had to be no me in this mission, especially with so much at stake and a potentially short timetable. It was all about thwarting Khalil. Hearing Emine enter George made a quick judgment call.

"I'm putting it on speaker phone and having Emine participate."

Campbell paused; George let him. This wasn't an argument and the girl was either on their team or not. Moreover, he couldn't trust the information she gleaned from her very important father, an attendee at the conference in question, unless he let her in. She was too smart to let herself be blatantly and coldly used, and too sophisticated for her inputs not to be analyzed carefully. A journalist and politician's daughter, she could keep secrets when doing so was important.

"Fine," Campbell finally snapped and George waved at Emine. She smiled, wanly, and plopped on an overstuffed – beige – chair. Her shirt was a flimsy, scarf-y thing that left little to his imagination, especially as her bra was likewise gauzy and cream lace. Too snug jeans and runners made her look about fifteen and he had to smile. Easy to underestimate a girl like this one but she was smart as a whip, even if she dressed like a punk. That camera was merciless.

"We're discussing the attendee list and who should get shot. We think it's most certainly an assassination attempt. The security will make a bomb tough to pull off."

"Unless Khalil has bought off the right people and some can always be bought," she stated and George gave her a harsh look. She shifted in her chair, crossing one leg over the other and leaning back but she met his gaze.

"People can always be bought," Campbell's voice echoed before changing the conversation's focus, "but most of these diplomats also have their own security detail while bombs haven't been succeeding domestically, in case you haven't noticed." Touchy due to the stressful situation?

Campbell regularly played the intermediary among government agencies and offices so was thus poised to best understand the complexities of both law enforcement and succeeding in a terrorist plot. Bombs just didn't go off on a regular basis in American cities irrespective of corruption. Emine shrugged at what had been a rebuke.

George watched Emine study his living room, her eyes scanning like the professional observer she was, lingering rarely. He knew what the usual response would be, that he lived an expensive and ordered life, which he did. But she was from a truly rich family and would be thus oblivious to his lesser wealth. If their situations were reversed, and he was hoping to write about the owner of this apartment, he'd focus on what personal objects had been displayed, or not. It was those choices, calculated or inadvertent, which betrayed a person's values or the façade they'd built.

Mostly this room was littered with family photos and books, though Karen had added ones with the President and a spattering of celebrities. True to her fiction, she'd put all of those on the piano.

Campbell was painstakingly going through a list of names over the phone line, reading one off then explaining recent analysis on related risk factors and repercussions from an untimely death. George listening impatiently as his voice droned on.

"Saud," Emine said, interrupting, her voice calm and firm. She suddenly seemed to develop a presence and George could see her surprising interviewees when the nice girl morphed into a verbal bulldozer. He let her talk. "That's what my dad said. Perhaps Iran or Egypt, even Pakistan or India thus endangering the least stable border in the world, and a nuclear one."

"We just don't know," George whispered.

He gave Emine and the phone a half smile and let them all talk, just listening and thinking. A few other analysts had joined the conference call and were sharing their thoughts and theories. Someone pointed out that Khalil had just been working with the Iranians; would he fuck them over so soon after they delivered George? To stage a kidnapping in the Middle East was a joke; some of the most highly trained experts in such matters worked those streets. But they had sold their prize to Khalil.

So Saud? No, George didn't agree with Mehmet as Iran wasn't likely to risk another US based confrontation and so making a set up look believable would be tough. And both Saudi Arabia and Iran funded organizations sympathetic to Khalil's so they weren't the obvious choice; not that he had to go with obvious.

Algeria didn't matter, not even to Khalil. He was working on a global war now.

Egypt was a strong possibility, being such a key state in the region with an important election looming. As was Turkey, which Emine must realize?

Israel. And the long but brilliant outliers India or Pakistan: a potentially even uglier mess. Asia was a no and Europe was easier to attack there than here.

Which American politicians attending made sense?

Listening to the conversation, George's mind drifted back to his Cairo prison as he struggled to remember every word Khalil had said. He'd talked of love and now it seemed that Jennifer was back and in his life. Could they find Jennifer, an American citizen but disappeared in her own country? What impact would her presence have on Khalil's choices?

These people keep disappearing in a wisp of smoke, like genies going back into their bottles! They would eventually turn up, not being imaginary creatures with otherworldly powers. Hopefully, it would be on time.

"We need to find Jennifer," he said, not caring that he interrupted and bringing the conversation back from theory and into action. Then he glanced to Emine and asked, "Should we order lunch?"

"I'm starved," was her response.

Ice Cream

Aban was squirming and Khalil didn't like what he heard or saw. Such a lovely boy, so fair and symmetrical, with exquisite features and delicate bones. Yet strong and utterly dishonest. Khalil hated him. Aaban had been assigned to this project so Khalil would need to at least pretend to mentor. Mentally, he listed all the Somali's faults. Too self-serving and always looking to better himself not his mission. Greedy when the food came, he ate faster than the others thus got more. Dishonest. Realistically, Aaban had been raised in a failed state so who could expect better? Khalil did. He had a mission that must succeed and these boys must rise to the occasion; heaven comes easily for no man but at least they were being given a chance to reach it.

"The girl was taking pictures of you and Radwan," Aaban stated, unwilling to look Khalil directly in the eye, with his dark ones rooted firmly to the ground. Khalil really had bigger items on his checklist than this coy silliness. The boy just looked like a liar. Meanwhile, the tails had been real and continuing; pictures would be potentially catastrophic. And anything that compromised the security of his mission was critically important. "I sold her a pretzel. She's small."

"And her camera?" Khalil asked the obvious.

They were in a small Pinkberry frozen yogurt shop near George's apartment. George didn't eat frozen yogurt; Khalil had checked on his habits and this dessert wasn't one of them. George preferred coffee shops and black coffee with an occasional frosted sugar cookie.

The location was mostly white with a few flavors of tart yogurt on offer. Khalil liked the plain, with a variety of fruit piled on top. The mix reminded him of the many tart yogurts he'd tasted over the years, but cooler and more refreshing. America did that: it took a good thing, made it better and multiplied the price.

They were sitting at a white plastic table, in white plastic chairs, eating from white paper cups and Aaban was wearing a white shirt, highlighting the whites and the darks of his eyes. Aaban was also gulping down his chocolate yogurt with cookie crumb topping.

Khalil mixed his raspberries and blueberries into his milky white base, watching the colors blend. The American flag or just purple juice? He was studying fruit but trying to decide what to do. When we learn something we don't want to know the first emotion is denial. No, this can't be happening. Then we get mad. Then we accept. His current mission was so corrupted and likely by multiple parties. Hiding in the digital world had gotten so very much harder and Khalil wasn't happy with his current related success, even with Osman's brilliant help. This mission was an open book, or at least open enough that it should be scrapped.

He gave Aaban a half smile and watched as he continued gobbling down his rapidly diminishing chocolate yogurt. The speed with which this one could eat! "Slow down," he barked at his charge and hated the flash of anger he got in response. He yanked the cup: never break the discipline.

"What kind of camera?" Khalil asked again. Like a mad dog the boy's eyes never left the yogurt cup as Khalil dangled it.

"I don't know but it was huge," he responded. Not good. Khalil handed the yogurt back and Aaban grabbed.

The shop was crowded, and night had fallen long ago. A line of affluent Americans filtered out the doorway, chattering and happy. The shop had no odor whatsoever. He should blow the place up.

When you're compromised you need to cut your losses but Khalil wasn't deserting this mission; he'd do it himself. Standing up, he waved at Aaban and walked out. The cabbie in the first car that stopped almost pulled away when he saw Khalil's dark skin but then decided otherwise and even turned down his radio talk show. An older man with a scruffy beard, he seemingly liked Fox Radio. Khalil didn't care as he was too busy creating history to listen to it.

Radwan's building was hard to identify and close by Times Square. They'd tried to cluster in the same area of New York, Aaban being the exception. An apartment instead of a hotel, he'd be less noticed even than those who paid for daily lodgings.

Khalil dug through his wallet, a crumbling brown leather stuffed to bursting with bills. He didn't shop much. The currencies inside were diverse but everyone recognized a dollar. He tipped just well enough. Did he care if he was remembered? Would the driver even risk saying anything when he didn't want trouble? Khalil scanned the inside of the cab with its fare warnings and local ads but didn't see anything that looked like a camera.

Exiting the cab he heard the car door slam behind him and waded through the evening foot traffic, like a treadmill across the sidewalk, to the buzzer. One word and Radwan let him in.

Khalil took the tiny elevator. Located in a cheap and older building it also didn't have a camera. America was so dollar oriented and only spent on things that had a return or catered to a rich crowd.

Radwan was waiting and let him into the studio apartment. With a futon, television and mini kitchen it had enough and more luxury than he'd likely grown up expecting. The television was on and Khalil smelled marinara sauce. He turned to see the wide brown eyes of his charge and shot him repeatedly in the chest. The boy tumbled into a heap; his limbs sprawled in all directions. Blood bubbled between his lips and his eyes faded from bright to that milky glassiness of death. Seasoned enough to know that checking for a pulse was time wasted Khalil headed back to the elevator. The silencer would keep the building occupants quiet, perhaps for days. Only Aaban would check but would he say anything or just walk away and protect his own ass? Eventually, the body would smell.

A spider cleaned up his messes. This plot had to be perfect and there was no going back now, when Khalil was so close to glory. Mission corrupted, he was on his own.

Khalil entered the night, the air was slightly stuffy but cleaner and lighter. Where would he head next? Was it time for him to face and fix the Jennifer problem now that he was in cleanup mode? Bullets were a clean solution but if he shot her would the bullet penetrate straight through his own heart and kill him as well?

Eyes

mine was just watching now. George had moved into another realm and left her long behind but she was okay with it and learning just by observing. Even the way he could phrase a question made her conceptualize their challenges differently. May was ending and the days were rapidly hotter and stuffier. Noticeably. And the stress was building.

None of this was about her.

Tomorrow her father would arrive and she had mixed feelings about seeing him in person again. Playing geopolitics is easier when no one you love is involved. Throw in a family member or a friend and the motivations shift, sand mixes with water and fire with ice. A news story is always someone else's blood.

So she took notes and avoided thinking about her personal issues. They hadn't found Khalil. They hadn't found the boy with him. How could it be so easy to disappear?

Mostly Emine studied the physical evidence she had before her. George was so controlled, and she'd never observed anyone quite like him. Ever calm and always displaying an energy nonetheless, she noted how much he held back, listening, quiet. So much was missing in his interactions yet others just let it go and he guided the dialogue almost without participating.

Mehmet would...? He would factor George's style into his responses and pretend not to notice. Mehmet never got distracted by others and stayed focused on their mutual objective, or just his own objective.

Emine had dictated that they finally order food, after the call and a follow up conversation with just Campbell. No, she didn't eat much but loved the ritual of pulling out silverware and laying out a spread of options. Her personal tastes ran to a little rice, salad and meat, which could be a challenge to find in this overly complex society. This time she got her desire with a few honey pastries on the side.

Still, when it arrived, she wandered with a glass of George's scotch onto the balcony to study trees. And they were lovely, still green and vibrant, the summer heat not yet wilting their vibrant chlorophyll.

Life was complex. She was so blessed to be sitting in her seat of comfort, watching these crises rise and fall. Her own country was far from stable but she'd deserted it long ago, decamping to the arrondissements of Paris. Blessed with rich parents she was able to flit through life as she saw fit, understanding that not everyone had such a luxury.

The scenery was so vibrant and marred by little contrary news.

And that really was her day.

Egypt

eorge was seeing a pattern and he increasingly believed that Khalil was going after someone from Egypt – why else had he been in Cairo? Of course, no one agreed because they all wanted to clutter up the analysis with overly confusing insights into hidden motives and geo-something-or-others. Khalil was pretty simple in his complexity.

He liked clean plots that were more likely to work. Webs could weave on forever but they always follow a pattern. In that, if little else, Khalil was predictable.

But then the narrative would have to follow a waterfall of likely decisions and if George headed too quickly down one stream he might wander down the wrong one. (Leading to likely utter disaster: not a little bit of pressure!). If George were Khalil, what would he want? What would his bosses want?

Intellectually, George grasped the elegance of an assassination on American soil. This apartment was starting to feel uncomfortable and stifling, as any captivity, chosen or not, ended up being. George didn't much desire braving the streets with Khalil at large but the realities might lead him outside regardless. His work had been mostly intellectual thus far but nothing replaced actually physically chasing down the clues left by his adversary. Conclusions never came from the mind alone.

Emine was curled up near the phone on an overstuffed chair, raptly listening but speaking only rarely. The speakerphone was a constant, still, and the guards had called in a grilled chicken order on a cell phone. As the voice droned on, one replacing another with theories and facts intermingling into guesses, George left his velvet couch and went to the window, scanning the park below. We fit so many people into cities, all hoping for a better life and enriching themselves with culture and opportunities. The small cafes and diverse stores promised a more interesting world but increasingly proved a vapid answer to what ailed mankind. Unrest kept spreading. People wanted to believe in something bigger yet as media globalized and digitized the messages kept getting thinner and shallower. Would someone emerge to fill that gap, and perhaps could democracy be the best religion, replacing the more traditional God-based ideologies of suffering and sin? A religion in its simplest form is essentially a guide to living life.

"We've identified the boy," George heard Campbell say in that grumbling tone he adopted when under excessive pressure. Snapping back to attention George left the scurrying ants below him and got closer to the phone so he could hear the details.

"Algerian, no history of trouble but left Algeria two years ago for India then disappeared, probably into the training camps of Pakistan or Afghanistan. Not much else. Typical family background and two years of higher education," Campbell continued and George heard his disappointment. The facts were slim.

"A sacrificial lamb?" Emine whispered. "If Khalil risked coming to America, even after plastic surgery, something huge is at stake. He can't trust a mere novice?" George made a steeple with his two forefingers and touched them to his lips. Emine's glistening amber eyes followed his every movement. She looked thoughtful and was clearly pondering every word.

Campbell continued his update.

"The Aswan plot has lead to many arrests and too many confessions. Still, we got interesting intelligence from it...," Campbell said but George just laughed. When would these "experts" realize that the torture used by our allies (if the Egyptians were even classified as such any more) didn't always result in reliable intelligence? Men would say anything to stop pain; the Egyptian army was likely only sharing information that made them look good, especially with an important election pending. After all, it was Khalil's phone call that might have saved their country and they'd missed the entire setup as it happened.

"Bullshit," George said.

"George!" Campbell exclaimed, sounding angry. "You're attitude isn't helpful. Listen, this report quotes a detainee who claimed that the dam wasn't meant to blow but rather an assassination was the real plan and this plot was meant as a mere distraction."

Which made sense and was consistent with other intelligence. The theory also provided a plausible reason for Khalil to betray the plot and signified that perhaps someone else within his organization had wanted the dam to blow even if contrary to the original goal. After all, the plot had come uncomfortably close to succeeding. Al Qaeda typically worked in small cells with minimal information shared but a plot this big would need to include a larger circle. Discerning the tensions within that group was a guess at this early stage of information. His understanding of Khalil was their best advantage so far as the man was clearly a central hub in whatever was going on.

Assassination?

"Kill who?" Emine asked the obvious question and George was curious to hear Campbell's answer.

"The report doesn't say," Campbell said, sounding dejected again. George heard the buzzer from the doorman and assumed that their lunch must have finally arrived, which was welcome as they were now reaching mid-afternoon.

Things were happening behind walls that none of them could see. So close but not yet transparent enough. Our best guesses often provide the answer to a problem cloaked in disorder and obscurity as our unconscious makes connections impossible for our conscious mind to grasp.

"The blind sheik served with Khalil in Afghanistan," George said.

Endings

Desire. Khalil felt the helplessness of an emotion he couldn't control and which lingered even when he was apart from Jennifer. Years of discipline and sacrifice had apparently left him with little willpower when confronted with love. That was the counter effect no one warned you about. Helplessness in the face of newly emergent emotions, stifled such that they had you unprepared when they finally surfaced.

Jennifer was asleep on their bed and he'd abandoned her – momentarily – to sit on the window ledge, opening it wide and into the warm Manhattan air, to smoke a cigarette. Well, actually, he was now on his third. But she was still peacefully sleeping, her breath coming in an easy motion, predictable and steady.

They'd fought earlier, after she'd heard him on the phone. He'd been speaking in Arabic yet cryptically and in code, a language he now knew she spoke. He'd watched her eyes shift with his tone and recognized that she understood, or at least thought she did, which was just as bad. To her credit, she stayed quiet until he'd ended the call and returned the phone to his pocket. They'd been about to leave for dinner, that little Italian place just down the block and on a corner and he still hadn't figured a solution to the conflicts she presented. Was she with or against him? He loved her.

"Don't do it," she'd said, her eyes angry but her face still. She was wearing a white sundress, with a green ribbon tied around her waste. He was tired.

"What are you talking about?" he'd responded and pulled his faded red t-shirt on, pretending to ignore her concerns.

"You were discussing a mission," she'd hissed at him, so sure that he'd put up with this crap. Well, he wouldn't.

"Jennifer," he'd cooed back, never fight directly at first. Soothe, deflect and calm. Then go in for the kill.

"Fuck you," she spat at him, displaying her unpredictable temper. This woman was so weak and sure in her opinions but who cared what she thought? Thoughts and words were so cheap in this world, as many found out. The only thing that ultimately mattered was action, and successful ones at that. She'd applied a rose pink lipstick and he watched her lips, willing himself calm.

"You know my beliefs and you know what I do," he stated and faced her wrath head on. The room was small but being located in an old building had high ceilings thus looked more spacious. The light bulbs were pink, softening Jennifer's features in a flattering way.

"I thought you'd change," she replied and he watched her anger deflate into defeat. "Who's going to die and when?" she asked. He studied her, gauging.

"Thursday," was all he said in response, lying and giving her a date two days late. She didn't move for a second then crumpled onto the bed, her dress bunched up on the mass of blue pillows and stripped comforter, new linens brought that morning. He held himself back from reaching out but all he could think about was the soft wetness between her legs and those butterfly kisses. The way her wavy hair caressed his cheek when he fell asleep. And the lilting tones of her voice as she teased him in the morning.

But he was a warrior. What had happened to him?

"I'll bring back dinner," he'd said, needing to escape but still returning with the promised food. She'd found a vanilla travel candle and lighted it on the coffee table, scenting the room like a Madagascar plantation. Then she curled up into hard couch cushions and watched. On the table he'd laid out chicken picatta, a salad, some penne pasta and three cannoli. All her favorites as he hated Italian food. She'd had a glass or so of wine while he was gone and poured herself another one for dinner. He stayed quiet but prayed quietly to Allah for her deliverance.

"Thursday," she said, repeating his comment and choosing not to gracefully ignore their earlier conversation. "As assassination?" she asked and he knew that by not answering he'd confirmed her suspicion. The flicker in her eyes proved it.

He'd grabbed her shortly thereafter and ripped the light dress from her body, satiating his appetites and she seemed to enjoy their passion as much, her body melting into his. But he knew that while his appetite would return too quickly his trust had been resolutely broken.

For a while he held her, feeling the softness of her body as she breathed against him. But then he'd left the warmth of their bed and headed to the distance of the window frame and his cigarettes. Let her dream for a little while longer.

Mentally he was dying and not so slowly. The desire he felt was an emotion he couldn't figure out how to control. The pain and deprivation of his years had left him confident that he understood how to overcome emotion and that discipline was why he was alive and so many of his brothers weren't. Why had he recovered from the trauma of his brother dying in his arms but not from this woman, with her sun stained face and softening flesh? His mind and body just kept returning to her. Khalil stared at Jennifer, asleep in their bed and lighted by the full brilliance of Manhattan, not needing a moon. So light and blonde, comfortable and belonging. This was her country and not his.

Should he kill her and clean up this loose end or let her live? "Allah," he whispered, "what should I do?" Would the divine provide an answer or was even asking for such intervention a sacrilege? Confusion shouldn't be a sign of weak faith but rather an acceptance that only the divine knew clarity of vision. Man is weak.

She lay on the bed, peaceful and glowing in the night's lights. He heard her sigh deeply, as if she was answering his desperate plea, and succumbing to his decision.

Khalil stubbed out his cigarette and left Jennifer again, closing the door behind him. He'd pay for the week before he left. After that, he'd survive the desire or not but he wasn't taking her with him.

The Morning After

Jennifer woke and knew that Khalil was gone. Nothing in the room was touched but they'd reached that point, hadn't they? She'd dated enough; trust was gone, and on both sides. Sitting up in bed, she pulled the covers around her warm but empty body. Why did she feel so old and beaten? The feelings just coursed through her and yet, she'd have to take the next steps even if painfully.

Before doing more she gave herself a few minutes to mourn. Moving would have broken her; only stillness could keep the pain from seeping too quickly and overwhelming her fragile emotions. She pictured the way Khalil's hard muscles curved at his shoulder and remembered the warmth of his firm chest, lightly sprinkled with wiry dark hair. She saw his eyes as they looked into hers and questioned without asking. How they'd spoken without needing words. She let herself recall how he'd held her the morning before, sunlight hitting his bare back. His scents. He made her smile; intense, he nonetheless projected a lightness that he tried to escape, as if acknowledging it would sully his brother's memory. She'd hoped to reach that depth and reconnect him to happiness and hope. She'd failed.

Then she shook it off. Memories would have to fade quickly because Khalil wasn't coming back this time.

Searching for her phone Jennifer felt a stab in her abdomen that shattered her attempts at concentration. But she willed her way past it and dialed the number that was saved in her phone, more out of guilt than obligation.

"Hello," the man's voice said.

"Thursday," she responded, feeling the sun hitting her eyes and wishing for coffee.

"Who is this?" was the response, though the voice was calm. Jennifer heard garbage trucks below and then a loud car horn blowing. She felt a little hung over but mostly she'd be all right.

"Jennifer," she responded. "Khalil said Thursday but that's all I know. An assassination." She pulled the covers tighter and liked their soft scratchiness, the existence of which proved she was still alive.

"Why are you telling me this?" George asked.

"I'm a lawyer and have to. It's the right thing to do," she said as she faded into pillows. Shouldn't she have ordered coffee first?

Hearing her own words she caught the clichés: all the smart women, foolish choices bullshit or perhaps the excitement he'd brought into her tired world. Khalil had livened things up but she hadn't been happy with that change and could see how she'd driven him away and needed him to go. So what was the real issue? Tired of being left by the same man?

No, much as Jennifer loved Khalil he'd made choices she couldn't support and she wouldn't be a part of the related consequences. So she'd told George everything she knew, which wasn't much. The she headed for the bathroom and threw up. Coffee and breakfast were already ordered when she checked her pregnancy test and saw it was positive. Would Khalil have made different decisions had he seen the results? Jennifer threw the plastic in the trash and headed back to bed. What's gone is already lost and the facts matter much less after a door closes.

And so she thought about the baby. Was she making amends for the one she'd aborted before and correcting the decision, which had haunted her childless years? That baby would have been an adult now, already having met its father, only to see him likely still leave. Well Khalil was lost but she'd at least tried to set the past right. He really had always been willing to sacrifice her for his stupid jihad yet his faith was an integral component in why she loved him. Few people truly believe in anything with such passion and sacrifice but he was willing to fight windmills.

A chill ran through her as she passingly wondered if Khalil would live to meet his child. But the doorbell rang so she let the concept drift, guessing it was room service. She'd need to eat then shower quickly for as George had promised some government agents were on their way with numerous questions. While she believed her information was sparse and cared little, the world wasn't understanding and the agents had questions. For a moment she pictured Khalil's eyes and smelled what essence of him was left on her sheets. The world was moving but no one could make her go at its speed.

Peering through the door's peephole Jennifer saw a man in uniform holding a tray with coffee and an omelet, as she'd ordered. Tentatively, she opened the door, wondering if this was a trick or not. Then she wondered at how she'd ended up in such a position: over forty, pregnant and unmarried, frightened about men delivering eggs and a lawyer to boot. But we never anticipate the twists our life will take, do we?

Khalil was a past with which she'd only fleetingly dealt and accepting this resolution, brutal as it was, would take time to assimilate.

She opened the door and let the man and his food into the room. The smell of coffee made her want to greedily grab but she held back. Never content, was she? Always grasping for those fictions that could never be realities, how she'd fallen into the novel that was Khalil's life.

Most people are never truly content? Other's mental states were irrelevant to her happiness and by comparing she only fell deeper into confusion. She was going to be a mother now thus had to find her footing in a world that never made getting grounded especially easy.

The waiter was busily laying her breakfast out on the coffee table and Jennifer just watched. He'd brought milk, sugar and Equal for her coffee; catsup for her potatoes, nestled next to her eggs. Perusing her check she saw it was correct, with tip and tax included so she signed. Watching him leave she sunk into the hard couch pillows as soon as the door shut. Life would go on and this baby would be born. She'd finish her omelet first then begin rebuilding her life.

Betrayal hadn't come easily but he'd left and left her no choice.

Death

They found the boy. A paranoid, probably racist neighbor watching a shifty looking Arab guy leave the building too quickly. Turned out, this woman's windows faced the street and she knew who came and went regularly and how long each visitor stayed. Since 9/11 she'd been poised for the next attack on Manhattan and practiced her own forms of racial profiling and sleuthing. George and Emine had rushed down to the building to help question - not interrogate - her.

"Skinny, taller than you'd think," the woman had boasted, knowing her tip had led to the discovery of a dead foreigner but not realizing that the people interviewing her handled national security not homicide. She was a short woman, on the round side, with that nervous habit of justifying what she said. Around fifty, and fussily dressed with impeccable nails, long and red, she clearly put time into the activities she valued. Being female in an airbrushed society is difficult.

But she was their eyes and ears into the last few days of Radwan's life. She'd watched the boy closely, his dark skin and foreign accent catching her laser lens. She'd even kept orderly notes in a spiral notebook, favoring black pen with an occasional red underline.

The building was older, which meant it had the clean lines of the earlier city planners who designed based on an overall aesthetic for their urban vision. Inside it was a mess of wallpapers, or so it appeared to George, more used to Karen's clean if bland tastes. Others seemingly liked a more rococo world, with swirls and splashes or flowers clustered tightly together.

"He moved in about ten days ago," Clara said, and puffed on a cigarette, the smoke being something to which his California palate hadn't yet adjusted. George stopped his fingers from rubbing his nostrils, knowing the gesture would be insulting and alienating. He already struggled with his over-intellectualized and too proper appearance. Women like her always saw some ex-boyfriend who'd married above them.

"And I never liked him," Clara continued and George watched Emine put her arm around the woman's shoulders, then nod at her. The girl was good projecting empathy and Clara blinked away a tear. All those years of watching, now she finally had a story and rapt audience. He stayed quiet and let the women bond.

"He wasn't considerate and acted like no one else mattered. He pushed me once just to get his mail. As if his time mattered more than mine and he couldn't wait while I skimmed mine. Really!" She puffed again and George asked himself if she'd be able to provide much relevant information. Really, what could Clara know except possibly what the visitor looked like? The murderer. Radwan's apartment had already been searched, the requisite computer found and it was now being scanned. George would hear once they found anything important.

"What did his visitor look like?" George asked, interrupting. He'd confirm what he already knew then Emine could keep the conversation going should she so desire. Clara began her description and George' world got hazy when she confirmed that, yes indeed, Khalil had cold bloodedly killed his ward, co-conspirator, charge, or whatever. And for a second he marveled at still breathing. Khalil knew how to kill and had held George's own fate between his fingertips and let it flitter free. Twice.

Surprisingly, Emine followed George and left the witness to the other questioners when he walked away. They headed into the streets and Emine stayed quite. Wisely waiting, to hear what he'd say? That locution would take a minute.

"I'm hungry," she said flirtatiously and flashed a smile. Trying to divert him? "I'm getting a pretzel. You?" she asked. He nodded and they headed toward a pretzel vendor about twenty yards away.

"Shit," she exclaimed and stopped. Turning back to him he saw her eyes opened wide, perhaps registering fear for the first time since they'd met. "I know him," she whispered. "The pretzel vendor. He sold me a pretzel after I got the photos of Khalil and this boy. I threw it at him; he was rude. A Somali based on the accent."

George didn't know how to respond. This pretzel vendor did seemingly find himself in the unlikeliest of places. Before George could answer he watched Emine fearlessly stride up to the man, long and lean, a rich cocoa color, and stunningly attractive. Wisely or not, George was curious at the outcome.

He didn't fear for Emine's safety though in retrospect, later, he'd wonder at why his instincts consistently failed him in moments of peril. Like the deer in headlights cliché of many bad novels he'd seemingly stand and wait for the car to hit him, or Emine in this instance.

Emine started out strong and he watched her quietly question the slim man, in his loose, low jeans and simple New York T-shirt. She looked petite next to her interviewee but calm and perhaps even reasonable, her hand gestures kept to a minimum and her eyes shaded by lavender lense-d silver aviator glasses.

The first sign of a conversation going bad was when the vendor pushed Emine, hard, and she fell. George should have leapt forward to help but was rigid and transfixed instead. She tumbled into the street and George saw a taxi bearing down on her quickly. New York taxi drivers are known for their aggressive and even erratic driving and he braced for the worst, watching the girl as she tried to roll away but not really having time to stand and run from the moving wheels.

Tall buildings and dense, slow moving traffic formed the backdrop, like an eerie Hollywood soundstage, more camp than reality in the starkness of an early summer sun. Hitting so much glass, the light reflected blindingly around them and George felt his old nausea return.

He heard a bang then saw a concentrated flash, or whirl, or ghost. Something, and then the dark boy fell, crimson spreading across his shirt and obliterating the red letters of New York in a field of color. Falling out of his limp fingers was a black gun and George heard it clatter before he saw the body collapse on top. He turned and saw that one of their police escorts had luckily not watched Emine's fall but rather her aggressor as he pulled the gun and seemingly pointed it her way.

Where to scan next? Oh, yes, Emine; George seemed unable to focus on the ring with the most compelling act. She was standing now so evidently the taxi had stopped in time and then sped away, off on another fare. She was brushing her clothes, those slim fatigue pants and loose blouse, nothing seemed obviously torn or even out of place. She waved but he wasn't ready to wave back. Loud sirens got closer and an ambulance pulled up to commandeer the wounded man. George couldn't see much as police and medics swarmed the body but he forced himself to go over to the man. Alive and speaking? If so, George had a few questions to ask before medical care was administered.

And he still had to address the implications of Jennifer's call. Could this pretzel vendor shed any further light on Khalil's plans?

Freedom?

Khalil was free now and felt the lightness. He was in Brooklyn and walking along the water, glad to be outside the dense city proper but still a part of it. His team was dropping, but he himself was a valuable weapon and could execute alone, perhaps preferred to execute alone.

While his larger organization was deep enough to fill the now empty slots he felt little need for a team. In retrospect, Radwan wasn't ever going to be the one who assassinated KK. He'd at best have been a decoy, meant to draw the authorities one way while Khalil took the shot from another. Aaban, his lookout, would hopefully have gotten shot without a weapon leading to mayhem as the authorities frantically tried to catch KK's killer. No one wants to take blame for a foreign VIP getting assassinated on their watch; worse was not catching the perpetrator. Would Khalil's original plan have worked? Little matter now as Radwan was dead and Aaban either captured or likewise departed, since he'd gone MIA. Or, had Aaban deserted, Khalil would send a tracker in pursuit to shoot him dead for good.

First, the task at hand!

Assassination by gun is a precise but dying art. Most great assassins were trained during the delicate dance of the cold war, with its ever menacing threat of nuclear bombs and utter destruction. A lone assassin provides a clean solution, leaving few attributable trails and a kiss of death. Today, in contrast, solutions were mostly bombs and the related mess of dead bystanders. No one is innocent.

Never was anything great achieved without danger

So said Machiavelli and so it was in life. In death, Allah prevailed. Khalil quickly muttered his prayers, not washing or bending in supplication but assuming that Allah would understand. Sometimes victory was so difficult to achieve, and turned into a constant grind of one hopeful action followed by numerous others. Khalil felt past everyday life and prepared himself for greatness. Only on himself and his God could he rely.

KK had already arrived in the city and was checked in at the Four Seasons, room 458. Khalil's original plan had been seemingly perfect yet had gone awry in about every possible way, not so dissimilar from the insanity of daily life. And Jennifer was...just gone...while George was still around and alive. Was the last a huge mistake and yet another loose end he'd need to tie up?

But first, KK must be assassinated so he couldn't win Egypt's looming presidential election. Khalil had originally planned the shot for the morning of the main dinner, most likely during the candidate's transport from the hotel to the assembly but kept in reserve the later evening should that backup prove necessary. It was perfect,;risky but clean. The simpler the better! But now his mission had been compromised, so he'd adapt to the missing participants and KK's early presence in Manhattan. So how?

Luckily global terrorism was big business, funded by despots, rich businessmen, drugs, prostitution, gambling and simple commerce (or even taxation) and could afford the change in plans. Typically, during a mission, smaller hotels were chosen because they were safer, with less caring eyes, not because Khalil couldn't afford better. Now he was checking in at the Four Seasons.

Khalil had to begin moving faster. He'd told Jennifer Thursday while his original target day had been Tuesday. It was Sunday. Well, he should move today or tomorrow though realistically today wasn't likely. Osman had sent KK's tentative (hacked) schedule so better to play it safe and focus on tomorrow, during which he had some predictability from his target. Bribes got you close but schedules were invaluable, even if they changed at the last minute sometimes.

Khalil repeated his mantra, that simplicity was always the key, and which he'd keep repeating until the plot reached its fruition. Too much clutter and numerous things could and did go wrong. For now he had no overhead, calls to be interrupted or minions to mess up – excepting Osman who was perfect.

Studying at the schedule one clear option struck his fancy: KK was an ex-professional football player and exercised every morning, no matter how early. We're all vulnerable to our habits and they are the strength that kills us. With the excellent Four Seasons work out room KK wouldn't be able to resist and could have free range of weight machines and his favored stationary bikes. But Khalil should check in early if he was to have time to vet the room beforehand.

The security at the Four Seasons was minimal to someone with Khalil's background. A luxury hotel, they didn't have metal detectors and just assumed that their guests weren't packing guns with murderous intent. But he'd need the right passport and luggage to sail through their smell test during a local diplomatic pow wow and their normal high standards. If he could get a reservation.

They would also have cameras everywhere, monitored.

Last minute changes in plans complicate matters considerably but he had to stay opportunistic and get past the roadblocks. Khalil dug through his passports, what nationality, what picture, would work? All fake, but expertly crafted, these documents wouldn't be the problem.

He paced, his new room was even smaller than the last but he'd wanted to suffer some and feel the penance of loneliness. In emotional agony for having left the woman he loved finally and forever, he wanted his outside surroundings to match his inner barrenness. What if they'd had that baby twenty years ago? Would he be here now or rather advising his son on summer jobs? A scar was itching and his stomach growled.

Still despite his distractions, the answer came and today it had to be either Saud or Kuwait and he'd go for the latter.

"I need a suite, please. Tonight. For Sheik Abdullah al'Asmani. Cost is no object. We need the best."

"Sir, my apologies, but they're all taken," was the response so Khalil humbly negotiated, begged and pleaded. A last minute addition and he needed this hotel and a suite. Management finally found a small one and would remove all alcohol as per request. The fictional plane was in the air so Khalil hung up and ran out the door. Was Vuitton open on Sundays? Something, even a high-end department store, would be willing to sell him what he needed. New York was one of the commercial capitals of the world so Khalil could purchase away to meet his arrival time. As a traveler he'd only need to be presentable with that added polish. The clerks at the lobby desk evaluated but with a forgiving eye as their guests were paying a fortune to occupy the pristine rooms.

Khalil had so much to do and hoped to be installed in his suite by early evening. He'd then have time for a quick trial run to the gym before the morrow. Afterwards, he'd be poring over his briefing papers covering all and everything there was to know about KK. He might not succeed in the gym at dawn's light, as with any plot. But the many unexpected variables that could work against you also destabilized the enemy and in chaos came opportunity.

Life surprised but blessedly gave an occasional forewarning. Khalil finally felt comfortable with his course and hoped those emotions signified eventual success.

What did one wear to work out in a high-end hotel gym in America? Undoubtedly, some salesperson could tell him. A Nike store perhaps? Khalil always felt more comfortable when he could blend.

He headed for the door and into the city. For now, he was all mission focused. This time he really wanted to die, having not much reason to live.

Dirt

Quite a day! Emine picked herself up out of the gutter and watched the stopped cab start up again and weave its way around her. The pretzel vender was down and George was headed in his direction, not hers. Her father should be landing at JFK about now. She meanwhile had landed on her right hip and it hurt. Thankfully, the policeman, her rescuer, had been a good shot because she was mere yards away from the bleeding man, mumbling in his foreign language and invoking Allah who had clearly wanted him shot in the first place. Fuck with people then pray to Allah when he strikes you down....

Another cabbie swore at her through his open window but she couldn't hear his exact words. Excuse me for almost dying and causing you to slow down. Now what? Always the trooper, Emine headed to the medical technicians who ignored her for the bleeding terrorist, clearly not practicing racial profiling. She spoke not a word of Somali but recognized the vibrant cadences. She scanned his body, trying to get a sense of the wound because where he'd been shot would determine his chance of living and they needed his information.

George blinked at her, looking briefly before turning back to the bloodied boy. She felt his hand on her elbow, finding it without eyes to act as a guide and sensing it there. She gave him a half smile and looked down at the chaos of emergency care and the patient. Having spent too many hours on the battlefield she didn't like the look of the wound, with too much blood too fast. Out in the field that reality upped the pressure on a medic; he could count down the seconds before a hemorrhage drained too quickly. With a bullet wound came a lot of luck and a millimeter could make the difference between an artery and a muscle.

Glancing at her phone, a distraction, she saw a text stating that her dad had landed and was headed to the Four Seasons. They'd meet there in a few hours for dinner and she'd need to clean up first. Looking up, she saw that George had backed away from the trauma scene and was shaking his head.

"They had to take a clean shot but I need this boy alive," George looked angry as he spoke.

"He probably doesn't know much," she consoled him, "The cells are pretty tight and they don't share much information."

"He'll know something and I'd take just about anything right now."

"You have Thursday, right?" she asked.

"No, Jennifer said Thursday but Khalil wouldn't be honest with her so at least I know that one day isn't it. So I now have a murderous killer unhinged on the streets of Manhattan with numerous foreign dignitaries and know that he's likely to strike before Thursday."

"Today is Sunday," she replied and watched for a response. He radiated such a sense of control that she loved to watch his energy mixed with hesitation. George thought faster than she did but missed emotions on his path to results. Like how that bleeding man might feel as white foreigners stuck him full of needles and tubes.

George was quiet so she continued. "My dad arrived. We're having dinner with him at 7:00 and...". Emine stopped. She really needed to explain Mehmet who sometimes seemed almost simple minded only to strike with a scorpion's insight. He liked luring people into letting their guard down with a mind like a trap that missed nothing, always weighing and evaluating. At least, like them, he wanted peace.

George rubbed his eyes and Emine noticed the deep circles for the first time. His eyes were also reddened from the scotch she'd been watching him down nightly, not that she wasn't joining him. How else do we deal with stress when there were so few other escapes? Oh, whom was she kidding? She just drank too much, and what excuses really justified finding oblivion in a bottle day by day? Could she do better?

What did the bleeding boy regret as his blood seeped into foreign soil?

Emine studied George, who wasn't seemingly the quickest in an emergency. She should get him back on television and off the front lines. Sure, the world was a better place for the fieldwork he did but George wouldn't last long on the streets where you had to be merciless, like her father who'd be on top of that boy and ignoring the medics. If he only had a few minutes left why cater to the life givers?

So she left George, as he pulled out his cell phone, doubtless to call his boss to see if they could get background information on the murderous pretzel vender. Can't violate rights in the USA.

Grabbing her camera she flashed a smile at the man seemingly in charge of life saving, his uniform blood spattered. He'd complain but only as procedure. Realistically, after someone tries to kill you a lot of leeway attaches when you come to ask why.

The shot was clean through the chest but the man was still breathing, a lumbering throaty movement. Amazing what modern medicine could do if help arrived fast enough; she wasn't sure he'd make it anyway. Small bother as the world would be a better place with one less terrorist and Emine was willing to judge the bastard who tried to kill her. The sun was in his eyes, glistening off the grey steel and glass lean buildings around them. The buzz of the city wasn't deafening but it was uncomfortable, with horns and chattering pedestrians. She spat in his face and he glared back while his helpers looked away.

She spoke slowly in Arabic, hoping he spoke the language also. "When is Khalil shooting?" Silently she said a prayer. A man with his coloring didn't drain into whiteness but this one came as close to that vision as was possible. Please let him answer while she still had time. Please, oh God, please. "I'll make sure you get the best medical care. A car."

His wide and still lovely eyes flickered, delicate as a butterfly, dark as granite and glistening with a like glitter. Most of us, facing death, don't want to become its subject in the foreseeable future, if ever. Take the bait, she prayed, and held his gaze.

"Tuesday," he choked. "But the plans changed." Emine could see his strength dissipating with each word and waited to see if he would say more. Feeling the increased pressure from his caregivers she decided to back off. Hearing a monitor start beeping she acceded to that American caution, that all lives should be preserved and mulled the few words he'd lisped.

Oh, of course she'd watch to ensure he got the best medical care but if Khalil's plot was days away how long did she really need him alive? At his age he'd have only been trusted with the barest minimum of information so, along with the dead boy in the apartment, did he really have much to offer in return for his life?

This boy looked like cannon fodder, and just another young hopeful believing lies of jihad and glory only to die on foreign soil and in hostile arms.

She walked away in disgust, to grab George with her new information. No one moved a plot farther out when exposed: they sped it up.

Free Will

George was angry. Not at Emine and only some at Campbell, but very much so at the world and perhaps even God. Luckily, his God allowed for anger and argued with men often in the Old Testament. Fuck free will.

Campbell had yelled at him for letting this bleeding terrorist, Aaban, get shot. As if pulling a gun on Emine after throwing her in the street wasn't enough justification. There really did sometimes exist one law for those in power and the rest - who were just toys arbitrarily assigned.

Aaban's father was an important warlord currently trying to help the United States negotiate the release of a citizen held by some Somali warlords. One of many kids, he wasn't even noted to be out of the chaotic excuse for a country, Campbell nonetheless seemed to think that force was overdone. Easy to judge while seated in a government office with job security, a pension plan and heavy security. George had hung up on him, even though he knew it wasn't Campbell's fault: he'd only been passing on a message. The hands of government weren't working together.

The gunslinger was getting loaded into an ambulance with a dutiful surrounding cluster. Emine was silent but visibly waiting for George's attention. He noticed now that her slim pants had a slight tear, right on the hip where she'd fallen, or seemingly skid. What a mess the day had been. He wanted to go home and nurse his thoughts for a while, trying to decipher a way through the new information. In retrospect, piecing together life's puzzle is remarkably easy but the challenges facing us in real time are generally insurmountable. The mind shelters so many blind spots and illusions thus hiding behind their curtains is easier than heading into an unprotected reality. When he'd had patients, many years ago, challenging them to do otherwise had been a rare and tricky risk; better to leave them sane and protected.

"Tuesday was D-day but it's changed now," Emine said, and George noticed that soft flecks of blood speckled her shirt, or what she wore as one.

"So it'll be sooner," he stated and she nodded. They both knew the drill. "Who?" he asked her and watched as her face drew a blank.

"I missed the question!" she exclaimed. "I focused on when but not who. Oh, we must go to the hospital before dinner." He studied her. She sounded like the heroine in a dime novel from fifty years past, but was that more his mood than her reality? He was in charge so what did he want to do?

"Go home, shower," he decided. "We'll meet at your dad's suite later. He still wants to dine there, with room service, for the privacy, right? And you'll call me with the room number...don't text!"

"Call when you arrive at the hotel," she replied. "We'll send someone down. I'm doing the same for security reasons." She wiped an ever there sprig of hair from her eyes and looked back trustingly. That brush with the street and edge of a tire had obviously scared her and Emine was less visibly confident. Now only 4:30 George had time to ride with the lieutenant to the hospital and see how this wayward Aaban was faring. Until then he'd ponder that they were heading into Sunday evening, Khalil's mysterious plot had been confirmed and they had a world full of dignitaries in attendance but no idea whom to protect.

George hailed a cab for Emine, stepping into the street. Never fully comfortable with the rituals of this city, he was mostly a west coaster but did his best. Emine dutifully got in the car and headed to her hotel. Why wasn't she staying at the same one as her father? He knew better then to ask as families are rarely logical.

Grabbing a ride to the hospital in a patrol car and wondering where national security was (lurking), George hoped for a real break. All he needed was one: a name. The date was clear enough: ASAP.

They'd actually been lucky so far in this plot, thanks to Khalil, who wasn't living up to his past professionalism. Terrorism and hiding were both increasingly harder to sustain and Khalil seemed to be - not surprisingly - on the run. Technology decimated security and governments, even bankrupt ones, still had more inclusive resources. Importantly, Khalil had also lost his emotional edge whether due to his mother's death, conflicted relationship with Jennifer or as the result of his earlier captivity. Perhaps those surgically softened features made him vulnerable.

George was not happy to see the ambulance heading to Harlem's trauma center and not Bellevue's. Because Aaban was black or had no insurance? Both excellent hospitals in their own right, the demographics weren't the same, which lead to differences, ultimately, in available resources. Then again, in Manhattan sometimes you made decisions based on traffic patterns, especially when your patient was trying to die quickly. Maybe George was the one with prejudice on the mind. Harlem certainly knew a lot about gunshot wounds, as did most urban hospitals.

Walking into an emergency room with police escort gets you past barriers fast. Arrogance falls when bypassing life and death for survival. Indeed, George was starting to feel above the law himself so he willed himself into reality; too many close calls yet someone was likely about to die. Thus they rushed to Aaban's room, with the touchingly thin body delicate and attached to numerous machines in the intensive care unit. That police officer was a damned good shot.

George walked up the youth, scared to even touch him and not wanting to set off the many alarms systems. A respirator covered his mouth and his chest rose softly, only to collapse without a breath, which filtered through the mask. The blue hospital gown was a thin veil covering small bones and lean muscles, making the boy look slighter without his street clothes.

George whispered to the boy but got no response, his police guard and nurse watching grim faced. Tough shit, such was the reality of national security and world peace. Crouching carefully, George leaned into the bed, all frames and metal, and lined with respirators wrapped in plastic and poised for emergency. George felt a shadow as a young but intense Indian man walked in, looking like a doctor wearing scrubs and authority. "He's in a coma. Maybe in the morning," the doctor said, not introducing himself and frowning with disapproval. Flashing through George's mind were the melodramatic idioms of a soap opera that dramatized the severity of the situation. Not today and not ever. "We need to talk to him," was all he said and the doctor stared him down, dark eyes not blinking nor reflecting uncertainty.

Everyone in the tiny and altogether neon bright, white and sterile room stared at George, except the patient, whose vital signs stayed constant, blips on screens.

Well if he's in a coma.…

"Doesn't sound like talking to him would help anyway," George backed down politely. He handed the doctor and nurse both a business card. "Will you please call me if he wakes up?"

"It concerns a murder," the police officer said, but he hadn't been briefed on the whole situation. This boy had to do with so much more than a murder. Fighting his way through the clichés he could add to the situation George decided on, "This man is involved in much more and it's very important that we speak to him as soon as possible. I can't tell you how much is at stake so please." We all beg sometimes.

Feeling slimy (who crouched over the hospital bed of a possibly dying man?), George left the doctor and nurse behind to patch up whatever they could. George decided to head home for a quick change then would rush to meet Emine's father at the hotel for dinner.

He felt vulnerable, disjointed and disadvantaged. The air was heavy with humidity and night hadn't yet begun to darken the buildings' shadows. Still in the early grips of summer, the light would linger for a while longer before dropping suddenly into darkness. Khalil might be close to wrecking havoc on George's adopted city but he himself was grappling in a swampy darkness, taking more steps backwards than forward, or so it seemed. Like a desperate girl, waiting to hear back from the boy she'd impulsively slept with the night before, George imagined Khalil briefly and hoped that he, at least, really would call.

Exiting the hospital, George found himself in a less than pristine neighborhood with young men loitering, aimless and watching. Not so many taxis, he noted, even outside the hospital itself, so he headed to the subway and took the stairs underground.

White

Khalil settled into his room, a tasteful gold and off white starkly decorated beauty, with a dramatic view of the city, trees, buildings and lights. Scarcely like the dumpy room he'd left Jennifer in, this one had a spacious marble bathroom littered with deluxe shampoos and other cleansing products, a tub, shower and magazines fanned on his coffee table. The bedroom was its own separate room and he had flat screen televisions there and in the living room.

The lobby was a blur. Graceful grey pillars and soft lighting, he'd been more focused on check in, hoping that his fake ID would live up to its promised "no one will be able to tell" and he'd be taken to the elevator not into handcuffs and a prison. The girl behind the counter had looked at him oddly, to be expected by any Arab man in Manhattan still. People have long memories when it comes to airplanes flying into local buildings. He'd smiled nicely and said nothing. Jabber and talk demonstrated nervousness.

"Do you want to use the credit card on file," she asked with a smile. He nodded and handed one over, removing it from an alligator wallet he'd picked up earlier. An African vendor had sold it to him off Central Park, promising that he'd killed the alligator himself in one of the many waterways in his home country of Congo. By Khalil's guess it was stolen but such a rich brown he'd decided to buy it and build his persona for the hotel staff's benefit. Who was he to judge?

The man was an infidel and damned no matter what thus if he wasn't going to devote himself to Allah no reason for him not to rob, even kill. The net result would be the same.

The clerk, Anne, had stared at the wallet for a nanosecond, and then moved faster and more politely after that. The same African had sold him some impressive looking credit cards as well. He wouldn't use those as they'd likely been reported, unless their owner was dead, but no one in America snatched your wallet to verify the status of your credit. He'd shred them upstairs after he passed check in.

Her violet eyes, flecked with a deep blue, scarcely glanced at him thereafter and he'd evidently passed her shallow inspection.

"Two keys or one?" she asked with a smile, as she patiently keyed in the requisite information to get him his access. To Khalil the process couldn't go fast enough. He'd rarely visited hotels this luxurious and watching the other patrons, in their equally expensive clothes and mannerisms, he felt the rough country boy that he was. Taking a boy out of the desert and giving him a large bank account and too many guns had little impact on whether the boy belonged in a high end hotel or not. Everyone wanted the best for themselves, but not all were comfortable with the sophistication of these worlds. It took a special hubris or even narcissism for a man like him to pretend he was a George, with his polish and way of wording everything. Khalil felt more like the Libyan soldier he'd seen sitting awkwardly on Qaddafi's old bed in a video, too rough for the silk and feathers.

And the arrogance. Why did some get forty dollar main courses and mini-shampoos while others watched their children starve to death, in the dusty plains of a less fortunate country? Better to create greater equity but God in this country was too willing to seemingly sell a worldly salvation.

Khalil reluctantly turned off his television; he'd been flipping among news channels and laughing at the anchors with their twisted realities. Ridiculous what passed for news in this country. He watched a story on a naked woman with big breasts who seemed to do nothing but go to parties. No wonder this country was losing its super power status so quickly. He was here to nudge it that one step further of the ledge.

He quickly changed into his new Nike outfit, purchased from a massive Nike store on 57th, right near his hotel. He's chosen black shorts and shoes with white and neon yellow stripes. Then, he's opted for a white shirt made of a light, gossamer fabric that apparently absorbed sweat and odor better than cotton. He'd purchased a like outfit for tomorrow, but with a black shirt. He was planning on using a knife to kill KK in the morning, after much reflection. The logistics of this plan were terrible. He'd bring a gun with silencer in the gym bag he'd also purchased but pulling it out might get tricky and would delay his shot time such that a quick witted body guard or fitness buff might dive for him, save KK and get Khalil arrested. With a knife, he'd have to get close but so few people were observant no one would likely notice until he'd planted it in one of KK's arteries. He'd try to time the plunge when no one was obstructing his path to the gym door. Black doesn't show blood.

For now he was leaving his extra gear in the hotel room, going only to scope out his stage, so that he could spend the rest of the night perfecting his plan and compensating for likely risk factors – like other exercisers. He'd also do a quick workout while he was in the room, and try the various machines to see how much noise they emitted.

Khalil slipped out of his suite, key card in hand. The exercise facility was open from 6:30 a.m. to 9:00 p.m. daily, the first variable he needed to consider. How many people arrived at opening? Tomorrow would be Monday and with the city drawing global business travelers he'd expect a smattering of those who'd arrived today for first of the week meetings. With time differences factored in, the gym would likely be busy when it opened. The fit west coasters would perhaps sleep in but European and east coasters would be up and ready, if perhaps less committed.

Waiting for his elevator, Khalil shifted back and forth from one heel to the other. He thought of his mother rarely but now that Jennifer was gone, leaving a painful and gaping emptiness, he found his mind more often wandering to Miriam and her glowing dark eyes, hidden behind folds of Muslim cloth. She'd warned him, repeatedly as he grew from a small and trusting child to a willful teenager that he'd never wanted to face reality.

"You dream that what you envision will happen. Dreams only come true for the rich in this country. Don't fight the government but leave and find a better place. The system is always stronger than the citizens," she'd said, hugging him close and he recommended the wetness of her teardrops on his neck.

"The system is changing, mom," he whispered to the empty space of the luxurious hotel. "Too bad you didn't live to see it happen." As he continued staring ahead the elevator finally opened and he headed to the gym floor. Walking out into the new hallway, which looked exactly like the one from earlier, Khalil saw the glass doors with the requisite gym sign. He ambled over, not wanting to look as alert as he felt. Scoping out his target? Or coming to realize that his plan veered from ambitious to unwise? He had to succeed!

As Khalil reached his keycard forward, the door began moving out to hit him. He looked up at the glass door and saw KK pushing it open to let him in. Khalil froze, then scanned in a periphery around them, used to responding quickly and rationally regardless of what unpredictable force hit him smack in the face. The only constant in life is surprise and the separator of those who survive fate's twists is the ability to act wisely in the midst of ongoing change.

"Good evening," KK said with his mega-watt smile, ever the celebrity and always on. He was dressed like Khalil, with brand named black shorts and shirts, but his sported the Adidas logo. Khalil, who knew about as much about KK as there was to know, knew that the brand had sponsored the soccer player for years, using his image in ads throughout the Muslim world, focusing on the popular player's many charitable efforts and causes. He was a populist's dream, emerging from a sandy back water team to becoming one of the world's best players, and charitable to boot.

Khalil smiled back and nodded gently, feeling the presence closer than all of his surveillance. And that charisma did radiate. Arrogant and rumored to be a narcissist in the first degree, KK's dark eyes, wide with long fluttering lashes, radiated warmth and charm, swooping the energy from the corridor with a flash of white teeth and red lips.

"Good evening," Khalil responded, scanning KK's thickening middle-aged body, not a threat, and the stiff way he walked, favoring the injured right knee that had ended his career and never fully healed. Then Khalil improvised.

"The elections scare me," he stated and waited for a response. Behind KK was a long room, massive indeed and more impressive and complex than Khalil had imagined in his hours of plot perfecting. Shit. But he'd deal with that reality later; right now KK was the focus, for as long as he could hold the man's attention. Important people always called the shots. Always. That's why the rest of the world vacillated between worshiping and hating them.

"Chaos threatens civil war before the election but the old leader must go," KK responded and stepped through the doorframe, gesturing for Khalil to do the same, but entering as opposed to leaving. Khalil did as beckoned and continued to study his target. "The past power structure shouldn't have been blocked from participating. They're the only ones who know how to rule the country, as we're learning."

"You're a moderate," Khalil responded.

"But you knew that," KK whispered with a smile and turned to walk away, no body guard trailing behind. Khalil let him go, studying the tall, stocky body and its movement. A thought crossed his mind that he should grab the man from behind and crack his throat. KK was strong, but a retired athlete and not a trained warrior. Khalil could kill him easily, especially from behind. He didn't do it.

Instead, he turned back to the massive room he'd already entered and looked across the wood – teak? – and machine laden monstrosity that held more possibilities for getting lost than for control. KK was off schedule, the room was too large and so cleanly cluttered. Who knew if KK would work out in the morning if he'd done so tonight. Moreover, the spacious room was packed. A kill would lead to certain capture...that reality looked inevitable.

Row upon row of treadmills, stationary bikes and elliptical trainers hogged the room's center, while weight machines lined its windows. Towels neatly rested on every machine and a bowl of apples sat next to a water contraption, much too expensive for him to have seen before. Bodies, lithe and heavy, diligently moved forward in an alternate reality of television screens and manufactured effort. Khalil picked out a bike with a view and pondered what to do next.

He sat on the bike, fixed the many electronic settings, only some of which he understood, and began to pedal. How he hated last minute plans. Increasingly, he was getting a sinking feeling that this one wasn't going to succeed. Chaos could work in the battlefield because so few men reacted well to its sudden appearance. In a larger plot, where so many variables had to go right, winging it typically led to disaster.

He'd likely need to revert to his original plan for Tuesday. Luck might pay another visit in the morning but Khalil couldn't help but acknowledge that he'd just met his opportunity in the hallway and let it take an elevator to safety. So, to maximize the good from his bad judgment he'd need to use the new information from KK and turn it into larger success.

The man needed to die. No moderation would save Egypt from falling into failed nation status and events had proceeded too fast and too far. The only salvation was through Allah and his mercy and only a God could fix what men so carelessly broke.

Khalil noted that his heart rate was starting to rise as he clutched tightly at the bike's handles. Slowing his speed just enough to keep his heart safe he focused on the details of Tuesday. Where and when, how and how not. The inevitability of capture or death, the latter being likely at this point. He'd spent his time on earth and just given up its only worldly pleasure so lingering longer held little appeal. Most men were hindered by the fear of their own self-protection.

Sure, he'd try in the morning to cut one of KK's arteries. If that didn't work, a quick well-placed shot on Tuesday would do the job.

Makeup and Masks

mine had showered the dirty gutter off, actually put on makeup and a dress, then called for a car. The commute between her hotel and her father's was an easy walking distance but he'd be annoyed

that she'd done the walk and not acted more like a respectable girl and called for a ride. Sure the farce was a hollow one but they both kept up their end.

Sitting in front of her mirror she'd even contemplated doing something nice with her hair then stuffed it into a sleek pony tail instead, sophisticated but simple.

Her hotel was modern, workable and nice. Her dad's was stylish and sophisticated, a confection of pillars and stone. Indeed, this had been her home for a night before accompanying George to Cairo not long ago. She'd announced herself to the concierge and was whisked up to his suit via private elevator. Cheese, wine and some cute little crab cakes had been set out on the central coffee table. Emine grabbed one of the latter, whisked it through what appeared to be chili mayonnaise and scarf-ed it down. Had she eaten earlier today? Neither her dad nor George appeared to be around so she fixed herself a plate of food, with a few types of cheese, a cluster of grapes and more of the delicious crab cakes.

"Would you like something to drink?" a waiter asked and she smiled at the question. Would she ever? A quick vodka tonic in room had cut the edge off her attempted murder but a glass of wine could only help.

"Burgundy?" she requested and noted his happy smile. Dad must be planning to spend on this dinner, not that doing so was unusual for him. Digging her fork through the red mayonnaise she wondered at how to handle the evening. What did she want to get out of her father? Out of George?

The crab cake was rich and flavorful, moist with crab meat and whatever else went into the recipe. Breadcrumbs? Certainly cayenne. Pushing it around her plate, she switched to the Brie and dragged a cracker across the bumpy top, picking up a light dusting of cheese. She heard commotion and gulped from her wine glass, preparing for whatever drama Mehmet would provide. He'd been the center of attention for too long, and competing with generals (10 percent of whom were now in prison thanks to the current government) and elected officials, attentions seekers par excellence. The ego needed to be fed and validated.

Emine stood, straight, smoothing her fitted black dress around her hips. She'd started eating more recently and it clung to the curves she'd added.

Her shoes were her favorite sky high Jimmy Choos, with black laces that wound around her ankle. She'd deserted her food but clutched her wine tightly. Mehmet didn't mind her drinking but he'd lecture if she ate too much. Perhaps that was why both she and Liz were skinny drunks.

Distinctly a woman's laughter rang its way through the hallway and slapped Emine in the face. She gulped more wine. It would be this sort of night, where she'd pretend that his new "assistant" wasn't also sleeping with him instead of Liz. While her mother just bought jewelry at any hints of infidelity, and found her own lovers, Emine didn't handle it so coolly. But her family never admitted anything openly, nor did they take responsibility, so she'd just have to ignore the tramp (takes one to know one) and direct an occasional well-placed barb. Shockingly, they were all surprised when she did so, as if they didn't realize that she'd been around for a long time and wasn't going anywhere. Much as Mehmet might tell them how special they were, each girl was just another string in a chain of pretty ones.

Mehmet walked into the room first and Emine saw humor flashing in his unexceptional brown eyes. Looks wise he was perhaps, on a good day, a five. Five ten or so, with a dense middle and thankfully broad shoulders he got away with looking more like a bull than a hippo, but the line was a fine one and he barely made it. His clothes were impeccable however, and his valets – for there were more than one – kept him exquisitely dressed. Today he was in soft grey pants, a loose silk polo shirt and enough crocodile to depopulate a river.

The girl was the opposite. Younger than Emine and perhaps just reaching twenty she was graceful and very thin. Emine perceived the moves of a dancer and her too wide charcoal eyes watched Mehmet's every move, mesmerized. Dressed in an almost dress of yellow strips, exposing a flat stomach and so much more, she fluttered around him. Long, dense cascades of chocolate hair reached to her waist and spun as she moved. The hair hid more than did the dress.

Emine rolled her eyes but smiled brightly when her father's eyes caught hers.

"My fiancé," he introduced, knocking the wind out of Emine's lungs. Usually, the girls like this one were called "assistant" and lasted a trip. This confection was indeed sporting a ring the size of the couch into which Emine found herself sinking. As if an attempt on her life wasn't enough for the day.

"Mom?" she asked, though honestly she was more concerned with her own feelings at that moment. Why couldn't he just behave respectfully? Why did all politicians need to put a sex scandal in their closet?

"She knows and approves. I moved out," Mehmet was watching and she could see that he knew of her fury and didn't care. Well fuck him. For a moment only she hoped that Khalil was aiming for her father then felt ashamed for even allowing that thought to cross her mind.

Meanwhile, fiancé had crossed over to Emine and threw arms around her. Luckily, she didn't try a word like "daughter" so Emine didn't bother batting her away. "I'm Juliet," she peeped.

"Of course you are," was all that Emine could respond, staring up from her pillows into a mass of fake breasts, more buoyant than feathers. Pretty, yes, but usually a distraction for her father and he'd always gone back to Liz, even as they must have continued growing apart. Emine just kept drinking her wine and noted how her father coolly ordered for him and Juliet, ignoring his daughter's glare and rapidly dwindling glass. Well, this was going well, wasn't it?

The doorbell rang and Emine watched staff answer it. She gestured to a waiter that she wanted more wine, which he brought while another waiter poured her dad and his bride to be from "their" likely more expensive bottle without offering her any. She gulped again and watched her dinner partners toast. The crab cakes threatened to revisit and she willed them down. Her parents blamed her for not being around more and used it as an excuse to do whatever the fuck they wanted. What a joke.

George walked in and Emine stepped out of her crazy family dynamics to greet him. The suite was lovely and so very large, with floor length windows and a glistening view of Central Park and tall city skyscrapers. Designed in soft earth tones with luxurious fabrics and deep pillows, Emine felt like she was in yet another of the empty rooms that made up her childhood. Rage at dad? Absolutely. He'd given her everything that money could buy and little else. But right now she needed to focus not on her dysfunctional, selfish parents but on the impending assassination, perhaps of Mehmet. So she detached. Her parents could fuck up their lives on their own time; she'd given up on any illusions of that "family" utopia.

George made his introductions and Emine watched, sipping slower now. Waiting. They had an investigation and she'd let her partner guide events, nudging him as need be since she knew Mehmet and how to elicit his help. Should she be angry with him for finding his comforts where he did, not so different from many of her actions? Was she being selfish? No, her parents used anything and anyone as an excuse and she, and Selim, had been the casualties. Still, no point in not trying to keep the pretense going as they were the only parents she'd ever have.

George took over, seeming to have an agenda but thus far managing not to divulge details. Tonight he was more intense and less polished, raw in his urgency to get answers, aware of the tight clock and the possible risks of failing. Hot spots were always bubbling with risk and these men were often tasked with fixing such tensions. Could they learn from each other or would they clash in a war of egos?

"You know better," George said, deferring to Mehmet, and at that point Emine knew they'd cooperate.

So she watched, alert but quiet. The room was huge, echoing at moments, usually when her dad got demonstrative making a point. The light had faded with the sunset and the room's ambience favored a soft effect heading into nighttime. Its delicate beiges and cool greys felt as controlled as they were tasteful. George pressed Mehmet with numerous detailed questions and Emine let him, focusing on food for a change and actually tasting her cheese. Her father liked to talk and George was an avid listener, something Emine could only handle for so long when re-hearing her father's often-repeated stories.

"Help me with an assessment of the attendees," George asked and Mehmet enthusiastically obliged, ticking through each one meticulously, describing the merits and geopolitical implications of each possible killing.

Juliet had wandered away, trailing *People* magazine and Violet Blonde in her wake. For all Emine knew this surprise fiancé could be a rocket scientist but she suspected instead that her dad had stayed true to type and chosen a dumb girl willing to adore.

So she just listened until dinner was called. By now the room was rich with the scents of meat and spices and she felt her stomach cry out in protest. Not used to eating much, she'd stretched its limits with the cheese and crab cakes. The two men were vibrant and engaged. They'd switched to scotch and were animatedly playing one faction against another, all sketched on napkins and laid out on a pine coffee table. And they'd settled on a few highly probable assassination candidates.

Emine stood up and led them to the dinner table, set with glistening expensive crystal, silver and china. She sipped her heavy wine, rich with coffee and cherry notes, and let her father hold her chair as she sat. Sitting, she played the silent female, as she did when with her parents always.

"Emine, you were listening?" George asked respectfully but Mehmet ignored him, resuming his ruminations on one dignitary he clearly didn't like. His eyes were bloodshot from alcohol and jetlag but his shirt collar was still straight.

"We've decided on the nations at risk...those that house individuals whose death would create chaos or further enable the religious extremists." Mehmet guzzled his scotch and Emine saw where she'd picked up the motion.

"Turkey and your father being high on the list," George added, and Emine watched him sip his water with stern eyes. George was wearing a white, button down collared shirt and khaki pants but managed not to look conservative or predicable. His eyes held the calm of seasoned men about to enter battle, expecting something bad to happen but resigned to defeating it at any cost, including themselves. She feared that the night was veering into melodrama and they'd all be lost in patriotism and good will before the clock struck twelve. These two were hitting it off almost too well.

"Turkey, yes!" her father bellowed. "Iran, Pakistan, Egypt, Saudi Arabia, Israel, Syria, Jordan, Iraq, India, Pakistan and Israel. Pick from those.

Perhaps Indonesia but no one cares today about Asia or South America so I'd go with Iran or Egypt."

"Why those two as your final picks?" George asked as he picked at a Caesar salad and noting that Saud wasn't one of those two choices any longer. Mehmet wasn't eating as he never let food get in the way of a speech. Emine slipped away, muttering, "bathroom" before heading onto the suite's balcony.

In front of her sprawled the city, its lights beginning to sprinkle the tall buildings as the summer sun gasped its last breath. The parks trees were still green, only by August would they likely lose that freshness but since Emine didn't live here she could only speculate at the play of passing seasons. There were few stars in a city this size and the smoky, bitter air filled her nostrils.

She needed comfort and George couldn't get her there; he had his own agenda and she was merely along for his ride. For less than a second Ed flitted through her mind but she didn't bother doing the math to figure out the time in Paris. Instead, Emine dialed Capetown and after five rings Bud picked up. For some reason she'd been imagining the curve of his firm abdominals all night, that deep rich color and sparkling of soft brown hair. With him around she was never alone. Hadn't he promised to do anything for her, anytime? And hadn't Bud correspondingly always delivered when so asked? What's in our past remains present.

"Emine, what are you doing?" he asked, in his familiar deep tone, with music and mayhem in the background. His voice echoed no concern or impatience, unlike so many men when they sensed no immediate gain from a conversation. She crept back to him always because he never judged, and there was so much to accept, on both sides. She kept hearing voices on his end but he seemingly ignored them.

She summed up her situation as best she could without betraying too many confidences.

"Egypt," was his simple response. "Now you figure out exactly who. And weren't we just dealing with a crisis at Aswan? You're ignoring the nose on your face."

And she was. And she did. Including him. At least slowly Emine was beginning to emerge from the clouds of her own mistaken thoughts to face what she'd known to be true but ignored anyway. No big plans yet, but she could feel God speaking and knew that through Bud he'd just highlighted her way. No path is easy, neither straight nor narrow, but stay on it and eventually you arrive. So while her father and George talked she listed to Bud as he made her laugh and explained why he'd be leaving South Africa soon for Bangkok to discuss importing jewels and shrimp won ton bowls into Africa. We all react to our own realities.

"I'll stay at the Oriental Hotel and drink Martinis from my balcony overlooking the river, boats cascading madly in all directions," Bud said. She had her own view and watched the bright traffic bustling below her in the evening's lights.

"You're invited to join me," he added but she could only whisper no, both to the night and to her long distance friend. She had to help catch Khalil before she could jet off into her own sunset.

Egypt? The elections were coming to replace the newest false prophet and broken promises, finally after the army had delayed them repeatedly, nominally to ensure stability but more likely to retain power and the Islamists had fought back. The Islamists were surging in popularity, both through the Muslim Brotherhood and a more conservative newer party. KK, the more moderate favorite, was less well established politically and while many western governments hoped for his victory that likelihood was still hard to gauge. As with all elections the biggest risk thus far had been stability.

Some movements and people speak to our hearts as they articulate hidden hopes for the world that we hadn't dared imagine but knew could exist, one day. Mostly these visionaries reflect our dreams and desires but offer a path to making them a workable reality. Illusions fall away and the world evolves to meet this new paradigm; change is possible.

Bud brought Emine back to reality as he said, "My friend KK, the presidential candidate, is staying in the same hotel as your dad, so call him. Not only is he the best source on the country and its politics but he also seems a solid bet for assassination." Bud laughed but Emine heard his forced bravado.

"How do you know him?" she whispered.

"My dad was a college classmate for a year and a friend," he answered. "Oxford, where he was on scholarship but it didn't last long. They both flunked out so had much in common. He spent a lot of summers with us drinking on dad's boat." Emine had visited said "boat" and knew that it was anything but, more like a yacht. The pampered worlds of the global elite were perhaps worth a discussion another time but for now she had an assassination to stop.

"KK is a perfect target if someone wants to destabilize Egypt. He's popular and favors both democracy and women's rights, not exactly the platform your terrorist is likely supporting. Still, don't narrow your focus too much as nothing seems certain based on the limited information you have. But you're a smart girl and know that much." Emine grasped her cell phone tightly and felt an evening chill. Her dress was diaphanous and she didn't feel like going inside yet. She liked talking to Bud!

Yet she should say goodbye and rejoin the other conversation, of endless debate and countless conspiracy theories. She felt like telling Bud she loved him but why did she get sentimental at the oddest moments? Perhaps because in her line of work she saw daily how precarious life truly is, balanced delicately between today and tomorrow, shedding promises at whim. She herself had been a target earlier, something she'd neglected to mention to her father, and so no wonder she was feeling fragile.

She stayed mute.

And worried. Right now was not the time to fall apart! It was Sunday night and Khalil's plot was set to unravel by Thursday, or Tuesday. A jihadist unleashed on a mission disrupted was both dangerous and unpredictable.

Talking to Bud had been calming, after her scare, and hopefully had redirected her onto the right path. Emine silently kissed the phone line, hung up and headed back to the dining table, thanking God that he provided kids abandoned in boarding school with an extended family of loyal other virtual orphans. Arriving to a clearing of plates, hers included, Emine snagged an olive roll before it too disappeared. Juliet was still mercifully absent.

"I eat too, dad," she said, but smiled to appear less rebellious, a trick he never fell for but a game they played regardless. He ignored her and continued his subdued conversation with George. They were at the Zs, meaning Zimbabwe, who wasn't represented at the conference. Emine just listened and was glad the men hid their fears.

Lecture

eorge was calm. Listening and discussing geopolitical realities with Emine's dad, a 21st century Turkish Henry Kissinger and master of the political game of diplomacy, was a pleasure even under the circumstances. Nothing he said could be relied on 100 percent but much had at least an element of truth, forming the kernel upon which George could build a theory. Awed? Absolutely! Mehmet had survived military rule, terrorism, Islamists and neighbors Iraq, Iran and Syria.

Emine came and went but mostly she just listened and picked at her food. Mehmet was very different, though they shared coloring, including those sparkling flecked amber eyes. Mehmet exuded presence and strength, while she tried to disappear into the background, muting her intelligence and capabilities. He was almost a parody of a developing country politician, not that Turkey could really be called developing anymore, and larger than life. His phrasing was bombastic, though his words cascaded multiple meanings as George listened carefully. Their conversation was helping George understand politics and the regions around Ankara from a different perspective but mostly he was noting what a true loss Mehmet would be to his country should this man be the target.

Assassinations could be harsher and uglier than less targeted bombs. While the latter generally wounded more they rarely triggered war or instability the way killing the wrong man did. A bullet could and did change history, leaving a long string of what ifs. Rarely contemplated was that the loss actually might have made the world better in some odd butterfly effect way. Ambiguity mostly hurt in these cases.

"Now if it were me," Mehmet started dramatically and George noted Emine's attention focused for the first time that evening. Oddly enough, he'd heard no talk between father and daughter about Emine's close call with a taxi wheel and black Glock. Should he mention it? No, that was Emine's domain. So George merely nodded to Mehmet, signaling his willingness to hear what he'd do, given a haywire murderer on a mission for Allah, some weapons and a key Manhattan location.

"Only one plot makes any sense. "

Mehmet paused dramatically, then slugged down his port and pushed a fork around his chocolate soufflé. The dusky pudding spread easily across the plate and a streak of whipped cream slid across the top, following the fork's tines.

"The best shot to take is at an American. Isn't the Vice President attending part of the conference?" Mehmet let the question settle but not long enough to allow for an answer. "So elegant; it would perhaps even rouse a mob."

George stifled his first response, which was that the mood on these streets wasn't so close to hysteria but then wondered. One doesn't always see a revolution when in its middle, and change can creep up until it overwhelms. As a psychologist he knew that mob insanity was always bubbling closer to the surface then civilized men imagined. Mehmet might be right.

Emine, in her sleek black dress and ponytail, was still just staring at her dad, quiet. She was a very pretty girl but wasn't radiating that reality right now. Her eyes were too focused and intense and George noted how like her father she could look, if only for a passing moment. Their eyes alone gave them away as desperately driven people. "I'd kill you," she said and Mehmet laughed but George didn't like the look in his eyes. "Turkey is as much on the brink as America and sways back and forth between the east and west," she continued, challenging

"True, we didn't support the Americans as they bombed Iraq," Mehmet began, holding her eyes. "Understatement!" she replied and George decided to interrupt if only to break the tension.

"The protesters here have mostly been peaceful economic activists and they hardly advocate chaos and violence. Our society allows people to speak out and have a voice which underlies the strength of the system."

"Bullshit," Emine responded, surprising George and he noted a nasty smile cross Mehmet's lips. They must agree on the issue

"Your own fruit seller will set himself on fire, mark my words," Mehmet continued, supporting his daughter. George let them bicker for a minute over the likely timing – soon or sooner – so said the fatalists as his phone buzzed with a text. Campbell wanted him but didn't say why. George felt tired and pushed his own fork around his dessert. They, or at least he, needed to leave. With more work to do and the conversation helpful but essentially over, time continued to tick its merciless way forward. The ultimate truth in catching or preventing any intelligence disaster was unfortunately luck. So much skated below the surfaces of our complex societies for any man or government to monitor and understand the chatter they did catch, let alone act on it effectively. George was still worried that luck wasn't on his side right now. He studied his port glass and contemplated taking another sip but felt to weak to make the motion. So he got more ambitious and stood instead.

"Sir, very nice to meet you. I much appreciate your time," he started and Mehmet nodded his head in acknowledgement. Then they both turned to Emine, who stared back with her glittering jewel eyes, not responding. "Emine, I need to leave. " George continued. Her eyes flitted between the men. George felt a slight alcohol buzz but was glad that it went no further. Discipline was one of his good qualities; calling his wife was not.

"History always favors the victor," she finally whispered.

"Oh, Emine, I could have stayed at the Waldorf but the President stays there so I think it must be too stuffy," Mehmet responded, deflecting her comment and changing the subject. "This hotel has a sleeker, more modern feel and better for my image. Don't you think?"

Emine nodded, then got up from the table, going to the other side and hugging her dad with a peck on the cheek and a genuinely warm smile. Mehmet gazed back, unfathomable as always and George realized that for all his skills he couldn't read the man.

"Don't tell your mother about Juliet," Mehmet said quietly and George saw a moment of vulnerability flash across the man's features. Emine patted his back and said, "Of course not. I need to work, dad."

"A lot is at stake," he responded.

"We're all trying to save the world," she said and then left him, joining George and heading to the elevators, handlers showing them the way every few meters. The lighting was now luxurious, as only the best experts can create, with rich yellow light bulbs and the right number of skylights and windows allowing in the city's illuminating show.

"Bud gave me the phone number to KK, the Egyptian presidential candidate and high risk execution fodder. His cell. We should call him; he's staying here so maybe we can drop by now."

George laughed. She was so intense and they were standing in a long hallway where anyone could hear. Her black dress was nicely hugging what curves she had and the look was a far cry from her usual boots, jeans and t-shirts. The hallway reflected the hour and was serenely quiet. But it was late and he needed to call Campbell.

"Emine, it's 10:30 and KK must be jet lagged. Let's leave a message with the concierge to be delivered under his door. He'll call us when he's up and rested.

"Politicians never call: it seems to be an unwritten law. Even when they want something; especially when they want something," she responded, glaring. The alcohol was obvious and she looked tired, nice dress notwithstanding. "I'll get you cab," he told her. "After you write out that message."

She smiled back and once in his own cab he dialed Campbell.

"The boy died," was all his boss said. And so did that lead.

Luxuries

Khalil sat on his amazingly soft and impossibly pillow-covered bed, his room service tray, demolished, nearby. The food had been so delicious he'd eaten every last scrap, from a simple salad to elaborately baked sea bass. The entire contents of the breadbasket. He had half a mind to order another dessert, but had bigger problems right now and should refocus his attention resolving them.

He'd blown it, and he couldn't deny that he'd blown it. Life crashes rapidly forward thus we must always be prepared for opportunity, which strikes quickly and passes by even faster. Khalil had KK, without a doubt, but he'd let the moment pass. He berated himself, that the pieces of every plot were so complex, and almost impossible to line up correctly, thus such opportunities couldn't be so easily wasted. A fine line separates success and failure

Drifting in and out of sleep through a very long night Khalil found that unfortunately Jennifer was more in his mind than KK. But she was long gone and KK was his immediate reality. Life was so hard sometimes as it crushed out any hope and joy, leaving you huddled up on a warm bed wishing for mercy. His risks were immeasurable, and he was making no progress. Seemed like his plot was a pointless exercise when faced in a no bullshit dream. Finally, waking to a bright morning sun Khalil instead confronted his reality. He'd committed to this assassination and this life.

After prayer Khalil quickly showered. Cleansing himself as he headed to his jihad he also used the toilet.

"Allahu Akbar," he whispered to himself in the mirror. Donning black shorts and slim black t-shirt in sweat wicking fabric Khalil sipped at his tea and watched CNN. It was a slow news day, not at the politician kissing babies level but rather at the bridge collapse and political office recall variety. He nibbled at toast and had a bite of an omelet. Somehow he'd ordered breakfast en route to a workout room but also not knowing if he'd be arrested there. If so, when would he eat next? One had to plan for such contingencies as it was too often the basic physical realities that broke people.

Amazing how valuable a currency basic human bodily functions could be when denied.

The knife was difficult to conceal in his skimpy and form fitting clothes. Khalil had seen a few cameras in the hallways, this was a lux hotel after all, but they wouldn't capture discrete bulges. An exceptional bodyguard wouldn't miss such protrusions but those were few and far in between. Really, an assassin's best ally was that most people ignored what went on around them, being more focused on themselves. As Britain, with the IRA strikes of years past, and Israel, with their ongoing fight to exist, had learned - combating terror strikes required a well-trained, actively engaged populace.

Finished tying his trainer laces, he grabbed the bag containing a gun and another larger knife. Hopefully, he wouldn't need them but they were there as insurance. The caffeine from his tea was making him jittery but death by knife required less precision than a sniper's shot. He'd go for the carotid artery; a favorite target as it was easy to slice, being just a quick grab and then a sliver of skin. Men knocked off their feet responded slowly.

Feeling more like a ghost than human, after surviving so many brushes with death, Khalil once more prostrated his forehead on the floor. Sinners couldn't be too devout. He made his way to the door and out into the well furbished hallway, with its dense carpeting and clean walls, then to that elevator bank with a bowl of apples.

Khalil descended to the gym's floor. KK was typically a morning exerciser though he'd deviated the day before, which hadn't been flight related. Disrupted by a morning meeting? A girlfriend who'd stayed over Saturday night? One part of Khalil wanted to know but the other didn't care.

His step faltering, Khalil knew that he only fought himself not anything or anyone outside his head. He'd left that insane alternate reality years ago, people all believing that their crazy views had any bearing on the actual world. No, he battled himself - then life just threw in its twists.

Would KK be here and would Khalil succeed? The knife's blade dug into his side, brushing ribs but never pushing harder, skin against blade. Long and very sharp, he'd go gloveless since doing so was less obvious and just risk the prints. He'd be lucky to escape alive.

The hall was shortening and Khalil removed his keycard from his hidden key pocket, tucked inside the waistband of his shorts. He slid it into the entry panel and pushed the door open. Walking into the room he noted quickly that at least half of the numerous machines were filled with avid exercisers, sweating and monitoring their heart rates. The hum of the machines masked the chatter of the few people trying to talk. Most were either watching news channels on personal video screens or reading morning papers. Khalil scanned the room then slowly made his way around the perimeter looking for his adversary. The room was more than spacious, and his quest took more time than he would have anticipated.

At one point he saw a broad back and slight paunch with dark black hair pedaling on a high tech stationary bike and tightened his grip on his knife. Still holding his workout bag he'd drop it should he go for the kill as its bulk would slow him down otherwise. But the bicyclist was only a false alarm and Khalil had to decide what to do next. KK wasn't there but might come later. Khalil had waited fifteen minutes after the open, giving KK that arrival cushion but expecting that later meetings in New York would force an early workout, as per KK's stolen schedule.

Khalil settled on an elliptical trainer until the knife started digging too deeply into his own flesh, at which point he moved to a reclining bike, sweat pouring into his eyes. Numbly he pedaled and watched more CNN as it repeated the same stories he'd seen earlier in his room. Switching to Fox would probably only get him televised attacks on freedom fighters such as himself while the local channels would be covering car crashes and beauty pageants.

KK never showed up so Khalil decided to check out of this wonderful hotel before he got caught. Then he'd take Radwan's shot on Tuesday, tomorrow. But first he'd order one more round of room service. Their pancakes with real Canadian maple syrup had caught his eye.

Dejected and sweaty from doing a full forty minutes on the bike, Khalil toweled off his machine and headed to the elevator in defeat. Things weren't going well and he'd have to turn the momentum of his movements back to positive. Entering the lift he turned back in time to see KK down the hall exiting the spa with its massages and beauty treatments. Wearing a bathrobe and flanked by at least five men he clearly wasn't heading to the gym but rather toward Khalil. But even had Khalil exited the elevator and lunged at his target, judging by the size of KK's companions and the long distance between them, he wouldn't get far. His elevator doors closed before he reached the gun in his bag. Was Allah against him on this one? No, his own impatience and insecurity were messing up these easy opportunities. Khalil really was his own worst enemy. He had until tomorrow to get over that flaw.

Dialing Jennifer's cell he got voicemail and cursed once again. Leaving her wasn't as simple as he'd imagined or as easy as leaving had been in the past. A deep crushing emptiness had entered his mood, haunting his thoughts and distracting him when he should be working. Until now Khalil was alone in an elevator and not sure where he should wait out KK or whether he should order pancakes first. Jennifer had stolen his mind.

Worms

mine plain passed out and her evening was filled with nightmares. In dreams she visualized big buildings blowing straight to heaven her dad being shot and that Somali bastard as he threw her into the street. She woke to the sound of garbage trucks and one piercing car alarm. Grabbing a Coke from the mini bar she took it into the shower, ignoring all forms of electronics beforehand, knowing for sure that someone, somewhere had been trying to reach her. They always did.

Dressing, back into jeans and a tee, with sandals to combat the increasing heat as summer continued its takeover, Emine finally checked messages. The first voicemail was from KK's assistant requesting a breakfast meeting with her and George. From a political family in which appearances mattered, she scrambled to pull on a decent dress and heels, did the ponytail thing and dialed George as she ran for the door.

"I left you a message. You didn't get it?" he asked.

She ignored the question and said, "Wait for me in the lobby, I'm only a few blocks away," and she ran. Past the Body Shop, the bagel and coffee guy, the newsstand, the commuters and a million other distractions until she entered the pristine Four Seasons to walk with George to KK at the Garden Restaurant with its soaring Acacia trees and pristine service.

KK was gregarious and immediately likable, his smile lit up the room and she grinned back as he kissed her cheek, pausing to catch her passing glance. KK was dressed formally, in a charcoal suit, white shirt and yellow tie. His large watch was gaudy, masculine and ridiculously expensive, intermingling diamonds amidst chrome.

He was already seated at a large round table with a few companions and they'd all been drinking tea. He gestured for her and George to sit.

"Bud said I should talk to you," she said softly, as befit the sophisticated room.

"You think I might get assassinated?" KK asked with his megawatt smile and too practiced voice. Emine immediately noted the pattern in the act and knew she was dealing with a mega bullshitter and super slick operative. Arrogance mixed with polish but no nervousness.

So she decided to push him for real answers now, while she had a chance, and knew George wouldn't stop her. They could listen to the fluffy clichéd press release version when he got impatient with her more probing questions.

"Who really backs you?

But KK just smiled, not rattled by her bluntness. "My country is in dire straights at this point," he stated, then sipped his black tea and buttered a piece of toast. Emine felt like applauding his self-control and dedication to his story line; she'd shake him off it.

"I can't die," he continued, toast poised between two fingers. "For you see, no one else can partner my celebrity with a will to fix what's broken and no need to curry political favors." He sipped again. "I'm only running because I can't ignore the desperation of my countrymen when they've been so good to me. We need change."

Campaign speech.

George took over by starting an earnest conversation much like his one of the night before with Mehmet. Meanwhile, Emine smelled a rat and she ignored them as she pondered what was making her so uncomfortable. KK clearly wasn't the type who did things purely out of his heart's goodness, or at least had a limited history of doing so. He walked with an entourage, was stylishly attired in Gucci and diamond watch and he talked in platitudes not issues. A beautiful and charismatic figurehead much loved for photos with the poor and making large public donations, he was a wonderful asset for the people of Egypt and she didn't want to discount that part of his persona. But he didn't seem to possess the depth to wade into the turmoil of a nation at risk; his life was too comfortable and he seemed to enjoy that perch.

Thus someone must have put him up to his Presidential run, maybe with a promise of figurehead status but little real risk or responsibility. A rock star candidate with a back office of worker bees guiding their puppet king? So who was his source of support? And who didn't want them to win? Khalil?

And who was financing him? Sports stars, even with Adidas as their sponsor, only made so much in his part of the world. Well, anyone willing to stick their neck (and life) out to further a political cause always found a bank roll supplied by the more cautious, who often had vaster financial resources thus more to lose.

She watched him as he spoke to George, animated but always holding back, as befit a hero and sports star. He'd grown up poor, she recalled, playing football in the back streets of Cairo. In high school he'd already started becoming famous, the street kid who moved faster than the ball, and he was recruited professionally early, dropping out of school and touring Europe. Oxford had been a brief fling at respectability which he dropped when Adidas turned up.

The girls. Settling down, and now the election and the ultimate stab at becoming the establishment.

"I love my people, they've given me everything," he responded to one of George's questions and she believed his answer. But the careful words also made for a wonderful sound bite to be reprinted and repeated.

Much as the homegrown Occupy Wall Street protestors had been surprisingly legally savvy as to where they could protest and how far they could push the authorities, experts who'd charted out an ambitious course had clearly briefed KK. His words had the glossy sheen of an ideologue and she noted few practical details which could be attacked. And she and George weren't even voting but rather trying to get information to ensure he stayed alive! Clearly KK was a slave to his public message, which had to be maintained at all costs.

Thus George wasn't wasting time asking KK for truths; Emine could hear that decision in his questions. Politicians never strayed from message, even when their words sounded impromptu and genuine. George had interviewed enough to know that they weren't much different from his terrorist, all of them hiding behind an ideological gloss with little basis in actual reality. People never wanted to hear unpleasant truths but rather a simplistic reflection of their personal idea of reality.

Still, a mad jihadist was loose in the city and he wasn't scared of shooting at key political figures from the world's hot spots including KK, of the big white teeth and movie star looks. Did this man even understand the potential risk to his life or did he think that his fame and success had granted him immunity? Well, with an ego like the one he was radiating, Emine knew that this big man wasn't ready to die.

Games

George probed, curious and alert.

KK was both smarter and less aware than he'd suspected before this interview. Canny, he had a survivor's sense of finding the right answer before providing it.

"Whom would you shoot?" George asked, still not settled on a final answer so looking for help in getting it. KK's eyes went suddenly cold and George saw the backbone that had propelled the boy out of the ghetto. The entourage waited, watching and quiet. One man, with a hooked nose and tiny intense eyes seemed to almost speak but changed his mind and waited. Dressed in a business suit, this man now caught George's attention and he could see the signs of an expert handler. All candidates had them; the important question was how much they actually took over and what they left untouched for the candidate to address.

"I don't think about killing people. Are you sure that an assassination is planned?" KK dodged; fine.

"It's real, the plot," KK's handler with the hooked nose confirmed. A look passed between the men but KK didn't respond verbally. George could have asked for background on his confirmatory evidence but decided not to take the handler head on. He stuck out his hand for a shake instead, "George Harris," he introduced himself.

"General Abdul," was the response, along with a return handshake and knowing half smile. KK watched shrewdly. "Nothing happens in Egypt these days without a little support from the army," KK said, and smiled defiantly at his handler, who remained expressionless at the snipe.

Shit.

The military was running its own candidate, well, not officially, of course, and KK was it or not? George couldn't tell. Didn't this balanced loyalty complicate KK's candidacy, especially having a general as senior advisor? He was supposed to be the more liberal, reform and anti-establishment candidate! George weighed his options. What did he need to get out of this meeting?

Well, it was opportunistic. As with Emine's father, he'd gotten a chance to weigh perspectives with political experts actually attending the conference during which evidence suggested there would be a high level assassination. By Khalil. They were his eyes and ears into a world they lived daily but he just read about.

One concern weighed on George and he intended to complain later to Campbell. Their government seemingly wasn't warning the pool of attendees and, George suspected, the United Nations organization itself. Instead, domestic national security was handling the threat and as part of national security he knew that they were still missing key information.

What George really needed was one man, at one agency, who was in charge of security for terrorist threats. Then, instead of calling Campbell who'd try to wend his way through the various halls of assorted agencies to make something happen, a quick decision would be possible. Until then, his efforts were subject to this chaos and later related finger pointing when, not surprisingly, uncoordinated efforts didn't work effectively. Or was George just being demanding and impatient again?

The counter argument was that panicking global delegates and seeming unable to handle an unconfirmed domestic assassination looked weak, especially for a global super power. Indeed some politicians attending faced similar threats daily and stayed alive. Look at the global litter of leaders with brave voices ringing out from podiums and demanding freedom who were succeeding, despite battling despots.

A waiter brought their food and began handing out plates of eggs and George's plain oatmeal with sliced strawberries. No one began eating immediately. KK was whispering something to his General so George had another moment to think through his next questions. Meanwhile, he poured some nonfat milk on his cereal.

How best to understand the instability of Egypt's election and its importance to his own country? The United States was similarly dealing with deepening unrest based on unbalanced income distribution, the lack of jobs and opportunity and limited common sense about economics and finance. George had studied human beings enough to accept that too often they heard and believed what they wanted. Not everyone was prepared to participate in democracy, and therefore too many relied on sound bites to form their opinions. And perhaps the country was in decline, with those years of prosperity and a chicken in every pot a rapidly disappearing memory.

KK was facing worse, a country with an estimated 30% illiterate, yet the most populous in the Middle East and the third most populous in Africa. Their population bulge of unemployed youths, a mere threat in America, was a huge factor behind the country's social unrest, though ultimately only one among many. Likewise, the mostly peaceful protests in the United States had been milder than the Egyptian versions, which toppled a dictator then turned murderous and violent when reforms didn't come fast enough. *Vive le Revolution!*

Studying KK, now meticulously eating an omelet, George acknowledged the candidate's complexity, and how he was being used for his star power and celebrity. Karen had urged George to run for US President; had she meant that his celebrity draw could also be so utilized?

But first he had to deconstruct Khalil and his plot. The dining room was filling up thus George was glad their table was tucked in a corner where other guests couldn't hear their words.

Emine had taken over questioning KK and appeared to be flattering his ego. He visibly warmed talking to an attractive young woman, which his reputation would have predicted. But his answers held little depth and even less insight. A talking shirt.

"Jihadists are everywhere," KK laughed as he spoke, visibly relaxed but his handlers tense. His eyes were focused on Emine's, and she winked flirtatiously back. "Why, I saw one at the gym last night; he was lurking around this morning as well."

"But with a bag today," the general added, coolly correcting. "Any dark Arab is always a suspected jihadist, including us," the general finished and George noted his sharp tone.

KK's eyes hardened as they met his advisor's. "And sometimes the charge is true." While they traded private, silent messages, Emine and George did the same. A dark man lurking? "Please describe the man," George asked, so KK did with some comments interspersed by his guards, who'd duly noted that a dark man had returned to the orbit of their charge. Khalil wouldn't be so bold?

Of course he would. He'd escaped before in the middle of a raid on his jihadist colleague in Los Angeles, despite an army and arsenal surrounding him. Khalil would do anything to succeed and seemed to fear nothing. Had they somehow lucked into their target? Stranger things happened daily and indeed, in intelligence, it was these lucky breaks which ultimately trumped the detective work.

Now if George's hunch was right could Khalil possibly still be in the hotel and would Campbell get authorization to lock it down for a search in time? Sitting in the Four Season's restaurant, George couldn't help an uncomfortable scan of the room. He wasn't in much of a mood to get shot again.

Anger

Khalil was furious with himself, with life and at KK for, now of all times, deviating from his routine. The man operated on the clock, disciplined like the athlete he once was, a factor they'd considered when choosing him as their target. It wasn't like panoply of other states weren't close to failing and would with just one carefully directed bullet.

Still KK was the best choice: while driven by handlers and career politicians he actually meant to effect monumental change in Egypt. His platform was dominated by women's rights, democracy, modernization and education at the expense of Sharia. Having chosen his ideologues poorly he now had to die.

Khalil had left his room at the Four Seasons immediately after his recent non-encounter with KK, checking out on his plasma television and deciding to skip the pancakes. The hotel was strewn with video cameras, the land mines of his profession, waiting to get you from the wrong angle, doing something you shouldn't be doing. If anyone was suspicious, and people always were, they might wonder at an Arab wandering the expensive hallways before an important conference, at an upscale hotel so close and favored by a sizable percentage of the elite attendees.

Entering the early morning streets from 57th Street, Khalil headed to the bowels of mid-town and pondered going back to his cheaper hotel room, not the one he'd shared with Jennifer but rather the after affair. He hadn't given it up, not knowing if he'd need a quick place to hide before escaping the country and also wanting to leave his other passports and ids in a less vigilant hotel. The staff wasn't the sort to bother monitoring their guests. For now, Khalil needed to collect himself and re-focus on his next steps.

He stopped at a coffee vendor, a silver cart under an umbrella and another dark man, not so different than himself. Only this one had chosen a stable and probably boring life, away from the promises of glory and eternal paradise like his jihad. Who'd made the better choice?

"One black coffee, a bagel...," he requested and handed over a five dollar bill.

"Visiting from out of town?" the man asked, proving that New Yorkers were actually surprisingly polite much of the time. Khalil heard the Middle East in his voice and would have guessed Jordan but didn't want to appear so obvious and knowledgeable.

"Yes, visiting family," Khalil replied, knowing that he didn't have to explain but that by doing so he'd more easily be able to avoid further questions and could slink away. He sipped at the coffee as the man got distracted by another patron and headed further south, getting closer to his dingy room. The streets were already humming with pedestrians and cars, horns blowing and all moving as fast as the crowded space would permit. The buildings in this part of town towered above like trees, too new yet somehow showing a graceful aging wearing on their city facades.

Khalil continued sipping, still in his workout clothes. The coffee was hot and bitter. He'd left the fancy luggage and suits behind in his Four Seasons closet. Sure, they'd note the oddity but by the time anyone connected his fake identification with his actual location he'd either be out of the country or dead. Nothing moved quickly unless you got very unlucky; if you did get so unlucky nothing much could save you. He'd seen smart men hit by falling rockets because who could accurately predict where they'd land?

Up ahead he saw his hotel, a small sign on the side of a towering, steel building, with a laundry on the ground floor. He entered the lobby, with its disinterested guard sitting at a console of controls and large desk. "Hotel," Khalil mumbled and was waived in. He took an elevator up to the flat of rooms that matched his key card and was soon inside.

The maid had visited and he noted a pile of fresh towels and a carefully made bed. The comforter was spread tightly across the queen frame and two slim, hard pillows carefully set against the walnut headboard. The room was starkly plain, to a noticeable extreme, with no personalization, let alone artwork or magazines. The mood was thus a far cry from the similarly plain but luxurious and opulent starkness of the Four Seasons, with its rich fabrics, woods and stone. He'd crossed from a world of fantasy to one of reality.

Sitting on the hard bed, Khalil rearranged his pillows into the semblance of a headrest and leaned back into them, his shoulders still feeling wood. He had decisions to make and not much time to sort out the related implications. At the simplest level he could leave New York and any assassination attempt behind but would probably need to go into hiding as his bosses wouldn't understand his cowardice. In support of that option, Khalil had learned over the years that once a plot starts going bad salvaging it was difficult and numerous dead bodies typically resulted. The latter was already a side effect of this "attempt". And, his bosses might be more understanding than Khalil was anticipating as their organization was feeling the repercussions of multiple well-targeted drones and arrests. Seasoned leaders were in increasingly short supply so Khalil was worth arguably more alive than dead.

Or, since Khalil wasn't a quitter and was already in this cursed country he might as well at least try something, even if less bold. He could still follow through on his original plan of getting KK before the forthcoming assembly dinner Tuesday night or earlier that morning. Were the authorities alerted, with Aaban's mistakes and Radwan's death? Perhaps. But alerted to what exactly? Neither knew how to find Khalil in this urban metropolis and Radwan, the keeper of the keys, was dead. Had he discussed the details with Aaban then Khalil might have a problem but Khalil doubted Radwan would disobey to that degree and have made such disclosures.

Last, Khalil could go for a more ambitious plan and shoot an American. The country's Vice President would be speaking at the dinner and Khalil had little to lose in aiming for a larger target. Sure, security would be tight but even at the White House a well-dressed couple had been able to sneak in and shake the American President's hand before security responded to the lapse. Imagine, if one of the two had been a trained assassin the job would be done with a quick snap of the neck before the Secret Service could even respond. Weapons were an aid not a necessity and so many vantage points for taking a shot existed in a large and chaotic city.

Except Khalil didn't have details on the Vice President's itinerary like he did with KK's. Could Osman help?

Khalil sensed he was at the pinnacle of his career. He's escaped captivity, snuck back into the United States and was now close to succeeding at an assassination. They'd kept the plot simple to increase the probability that it did indeed reach fruition and he'd be the one now to take that shot. If Khalil failed his life would be over and he'd be on the run. Death seemed a preferable course to always trying to find a place to hide from himself.

If he died in jihad he'd find himself in heaven pretty quickly. Better than this shit hole of a city, or world.

So what was his internal struggle?

Khalil broke open the bag with his bagel and began to eat. He bit into the chewy dough, cream cheese nestled in the middle. Dense, yet crusty, with a sweet yeasty taste, the meal was distinctive to this city. The water used to make the bagels? Unique flour? Khalil had no idea. Taking another bite, he focused on his body, starting with his limbs and working his thoughts around the full spectrum of its confines. How strong was he? Mentally? His decisions must be based in reality and what he believed he could accomplish. As was always the case, this analysis had to consider his main weapon, himself. Khalil's current concern was his mental dispersion;

his mind was running in every which direction while not finding a foundation. He typically didn't struggle with such issues.

Continuing on as his own worst enemy, Khalil questioned whether if opportunity struck again, as it did when he bumped into KK at the fitness center, would he freeze or act? One never knew for sure in advance. Those who froze not only didn't succeed but also in his line of work too often died.

Khalil thought back to a decoy he'd chosen to distract some American soldiers at a roadblock in Iraq. The boy had been a seemingly solid young Saudi but out of his home country for the first time. He'd been on a stop over en route to university in Frankfurt to spend three weeks training at a desert camp. The day had been hot and the checkpoint but one of many scattered in a seemingly random patterns across the occupied country.

Khalil and the boy had both been sweating. Dressed in western style clothes, the norm in Baghdad, they'd discussed the requisite steps the boy would take to create a distraction but not get shot.

"Walk up and ask if they need a translator. Use your English and speak slowly, respectfully," Khalil instructed.

"They won't shoot?"

"No, not it you hold your hands up in the air. They must always see your hands or will get scared."

"But they have guns and I don't," the boy had replied. So he wasn't a complete idiot. It was dusty, and the small particles were mixing with sweat on Khalil's face and turning into a sticky paste. The boy's complexion was turning red and his forehead puckered with worry.

"Now, go," Khalil had finally commanded, becoming impatient. They were on a schedule and the bomb-laden car would be pulling up in sixty seconds. He watched the boy walk slowly, which was good, with his hands in his pockets, which was very bad to soldiers clustered around Humvees at a checkpoint. The shouts were expected and while Khalil guessed they were orders to put hands in plain site his charge didn't obey and gunshots rang out, loud and clear. The boy's body crumbled into the hot dust as had those of many like boys over the years.

In lock down the soldiers also stopped the bomb laded suicide bomber in his Toyota. The bomber detonated anyway, and killed a local family of five but no military.

One needed to keep presence of mind to succeed at these plots and Khalil had to question whether he'd lost his. And if not, how far was he willing to go to achieve the ultimate martyrdom?

Chewing on his bagel Khalil felt bored with his life. This was the best it had to offer, sitting alone in a cheap hotel room chewing bread? If he'd stayed in Algeria he very likely would be doing much the same, and the risks to his safety would have been roughly comparable though improving much as they declined on his present path. The desert was a harsh master but it teaches survival. Colonization by the French, civil wars and the climate itself had toughened the Algerian people, but infused them with a fatalistic romanticism. Man had the tools to create the future and Allah supported those efforts much as so many fought that determinism.

How could Khalil best serve both his God and his mission? As Machiavelli had stated, *God is not willing to do everything, and thus take away our free will and that share of glory which belongs to us.*

Khalil played with his new disposable phone and considered calling Jennifer, just to see how she was doing. He wouldn't. She'd never accept him fully and he knew that now. His past, their past, would always come between them.

His recollections of her were becoming predictably pat, and starting to verge on parody. The softness of her skin, the sharp cry when he entered her, those sapphire eyes that glittered like jewels, her deep laugh when she was happy, and it just went on. But perhaps by confirming for the second time that their relationship couldn't work he'd finally accepted that it wouldn't and part of him was relieved to have achieved such certainty. Ultimately, she was just a woman and evidently not the right one.

He needed someone who believed in his mission and in him. He'd served his whole life pursuing the return of a Muslim Umma, that promised holy community serving Allah's will and at his mercy. A deceptive illusion or admirable goal was of little matter at this stage of his life as false promises reveal themselves over time. But it was his life and she wasn't.

So, with that over, what would be his glory?

Walking

Emine actually liked her assignment. She was out in the streets and doing something while once again George was stuck on the phone dealing with bureaucracy. Walking the possible paths between the Four Seasons and UN Headquarters she was hoping to get lucky and run into Khalil. Sure it was a long shot but by now they'd seemingly narrowed his activities to about 40 or so square blocks in Manhattan. While that might not sound like a lot of real estate in a dense city of about 8 million, with Manhattan being the densest part, it was a lot of skyscraper stories.

Accompanying her was one of George's goons, Fred. The name didn't fit the person, being a bit old fashioned for the former Navy Seal with biceps that curved voluptuously and who stunningly towered above. Really, what girl wanted more in life than a bodyguard with a hard body so perfectly sculpted? In reality, they were both too distracted with the task at hand to flirt. Fred was on board with how dangerous Khalil could be.

They were dressed for battle, albeit a chic urban version. Emine was in sleek black capris, black converse Jack Purcell's and a little black and white stripped tee, black being the fashion color of the city. Fred was in Levis, black Nikes and a very unfitted mustard yellow tee that managed to fall in all the right places. Too bad she couldn't enjoy his view more.

The city streets were crowded and hot, and pulsing with movement from people to cars to bikes. The mid-day sun was beating down and the lunch rush was in mid swoon, disgorging people from buildings as they rushed off for food or an errand. Emine and Fred had both decided that a hot dog, unhealthy though Fred pointed out it was, made sense given that they could eat it walking and preparation took less than 30 seconds from an efficient vendor.

Would they find Khalil this way, just walking? Likely not but without a better lead it was their best chance. Had the government been willing to search every building in the city they perhaps would have succeeded but doing so wasn't practical given American civil rights and their time constraints.

She smiled deeply at Fred, wishing she had cute dimples. Why not? There was always tomorrow or even next week. But then she felt guilty as she'd continued delaying the breakup with Ed and he'd left so many messages. And she should call Liz though her mother had left no messages whatsoever.

"Where should we go next?" she asked, deflecting from her personal responsibilities to more worldly ones and willing to defer to his instincts. Fred was so much better trained for this task and she felt safer with him around. While she could interview and write she'd never tried to foil a plot before. He pointed east so they walked in that direction, eyes scanning the crowds. Periodically, she called George but he was always on the phone. They were tasked with three hopeful hours of this blind prospecting.

"I'm frustrated," she told Fred and stopped to call her dad. She repeated the same phrase to her father when he answered.

"And here I was hoping you had the mystery solved," Mehmet said cheerily but sounding worried. Did he know something that he wasn't telling? Emine was paranoid, of course, but she also knew that each party with an interest in foiling this assassination reported to a different master and thus held their cards closely. Still, she was now getting ahead of herself and projecting her fears on a skilled man, her father, who was here to help.

She'd ask.

"Dad, what are you worried about?"

A long pause of silence greeted her question and she played the game of not speaking first, lest she lose the related battle of wills. A cute teenage girl on a scooter whizzed by carrying a massive pizza and trailing blonde hair. Then came a group of businessmen, one of whom was smoking and suddenly Emine wanted a cigarette too.

"No one came from Iran," Mehmet finally said. "But they were supposed to send a representative. Emine, why would they make a decision change like that with no forewarning?" he asked, and she heard fear in his voice. Why indeed?

"I don't know," she said softly. "What are your thoughts?" She felt nervous and noticed beads of sweat congealing on her forehead. It was a remarkably hot and muggy day but she'd been so intently scanning the crowds that the reality struck her completely until now. And her feet were even hotter, the soles burning from the asphalt through thin rubber. Glancing at Fred he looked warm but not hot. His eyes hidden behind reflecting shades, she could still sense him still scanning the crowd, watching as she spoke with her father.

"Not to show at the last minute is a very aggressive position," Mehmet said, and brought her back to his reality of daily politics. "It's a good pre-signal to a military raid that starts a war. That, or internal repression. A crack down."

Emine felt her deep breathe as it happened, she certainly didn't create it. Someone was chattering as they walked past as she tried to block the noise. The bright sun also shifted so it burned into her eyes and she felt anger rise. War? Repression? Iran? Shit.

"Would they do that?" she asked.

"I hope not," was the response. "I'm going to start calling some of my contacts. Perhaps the Mullah's just want to up the drama." Emine could see Mehmet in his penthouse suite, sitting on that plush beige couch with Juliet massaging his shoulders as he dialed around the world pursuing an answer on Iran. It was a lonely and dismal picture.

"Emine, if I can die without a third world war having started I'll die fulfilled, regardless of the mistakes I've made," he stated before hanging up. Emine felt grudging respect. He was a cold and calculating bastard but his redeeming quality, and it might be his only one, was that he wanted to make the world a safer and better place. She stared down at her phone, shining in the sun.

The red star for a text message was lighted. Who chose a red star, anyway? The Chinese? She checked her texts. *Come back to my apartment*, George had messaged her. So she gestured to Fred and they did, no idea why.

Control

George was tied up with Campbell on the phone again. He had half a mind to hang up and go walk the streets around the UN Building with Emine instead. These conversations were helping? Waiting for lightening to strike was making him impatient and he hated the loss of control. Somehow he didn't feel that Khalil was moving in whatever direction he was headed any slower so George could waste time on the phone.

It was now 2:30 on Monday afternoon and they'd all spent the morning digging through the hotel videos, which showed Khalil, clearly in George's opinion. They also highlighted Khalil leaving with a workout bag, but not his luggage, after he'd checked out. The luggage and related artifacts were a dead end; as was the identity that of a Kuwaiti who'd died of a heart attack in Prague the year prior.

He'd sent Emine with one of his bodyguards to walk the streets between the Four Seasons and the UN building, around a mile or so, knowing that their likelihood of bumping into Khalil was small but not non-existent. How complicated could this situation be? Still, all of their evidence was circumstantial and, if KK had been the target, according to hotel video footage Khalil had been confronted with a clear opportunity to kill him and had done nothing. Even George had to admit missing such an easy opportunity didn't sound like the Khalil he knew.

"Explain it again?" Campbell's tone was almost patient but George could hear the tension. They were all feeling the same hopeless frustration with the close encounter and rapidly ticking clock. So George did. Covering in painstaking detail every last event that happened, from the security cameras to the input from KK and his handlers.

"I need something concrete," Campbell responded and George felt his eyes roll of their own volition. He was too tired for sarcasm. And it wasn't that he didn't sympathize with Campbell's complicated position, as a government naturally couldn't act without reasonable cause. Still, this gridlock was ridiculous. Major terrorist caught on film with leading Egyptian presidential candidate in luxurious Manhattan hotel. And KK wasn't the only foreign dignitary checked in at the Four Seasons with Khalil, now MIA.

And the bureaucrats in Washington DC were stalling.

"I'll call you back. My boss just walked in," Campbell stated and George was suddenly, inexplicably reminded of the insanity that accompanied his last official mission, into Westwood with Khalil to defuse his bombs. That response had been similarly riddled with conflict and politics, as each related department sought to accomplish their individual objectives regardless of the eventual outcome (cover their ass and protect their pensions?).

He stood up, studied his books and scotch but knew both would need to wait. The apartment was so quiet and his other guard was busy monitoring the hallways and other vulnerable areas as George himself dealt with the more mundane and less predictable, the government. At least he could guess with certainty that the government would never work as well as he'd like it to.

Studying Central Park, expansive, still green and glistening in the early summer sun, George decided to finally call his wife. Poor woman, what she suffered through; no, what he'd put her through and she'd reluctantly accepted. Karen likely just wanted a normal husband and she'd ended up with him.

They'd once been more alike.

He dialed the number, heard it ring, and then left a message at the tone. Well, those few muttered endearments were better than nothing and hopefully he'd at least brought a smile to her slender lips. He could picture Karen now, with those delicate features and soft voice, probably digging through a book, curious and insatiable when it came to plot lines. She liked to read when not working and had recently undertaken a Proust re-reading, which would take quite sometime to complete, with its thousands of detailed pages. Wearing her Stanford Cardinal sweats, always a believer in their school, she'd curl up by a window and sip chamomile tea. Once, he would have sat next to her. Now, she was in hiding thanks to his work and he didn't even know where for her own safety.

George picked up the iced tea that he'd left hours earlier on one of the numerous coasters inhabiting his large coffee table. It was mostly melted ice now but had a slight aftertaste of tea. After a few deep gulps he grabbed his government issued cell phone and saw that he'd accumulated a few new messages. The first couple were from Emine just checking in. The next one was from Khalil, no number identified, but his distinct tones loud and clear on the recording.

"I want to turn myself in but want to negotiate conditions first. I'll call you at 4:30 later today."

George was willing to label himself a skeptic: Khalil just wasn't the type to surrender. Moreover, much as George puzzled through the possible outcomes of surrender – from Khalil's viewpoint since the bastard seemingly didn't care about anyone else – all roads led to a bad end. At least free the wily snake seemed to be okay and, well, what the fuck George didn't have a clue. Jennifer had turned on him so he wasn't reforming to salvage that relationship.

When something doesn't logically make sense you must re-assess your key assumptions because one of them is wrong. What was George getting wrong?

More importantly what did Khalil know that George didn't?

He studied the scotch again and figured that there was no quicker way of ensuring his own death. Numbing his intellect and reflexes while waiting for a terrorist's call would be stupid.

Start from zero and think your way up from there.

Terrorists don't look for the physical result of their actions. Rather, it was the counter response by a government to their actions that was the goal. Aiming for psychological impact and a resulting over reaction from those harmed, they had others create the larger impact or change. It was that fear, or terror, that was their ultimate objective. So by turning himself in Khalil effectively killed his own cause yet he risked little by staying at large.

The bastard must be fucking with him, distracting everyone from the streets of Manhattan to focus on a little phone line that might ring, or not. Reluctantly, George knew he'd have to report this message to Campbell because doing so was his job, even if he thought it was utter bullshit. They probably had his cell bugged anyway since they'd given him the stupid phone. Impressive. Khalil had the number and George's landline was listed in the city directory. Had the FBI added his cell as well? George wouldn't put it past them.

Terrorists were also like magicians, distracting you with their right hand while they fucked up some poor bus with the other. This message stunk of a stunt, which did seem in character for Khalil, drama king. But would the resources and time they'd spend following up on this newest "threat" distract them from something possibly more important about to happen in the streets below? And why had Khalil started calling George?

Picturing his adversary again, George found a sketchpad and charcoal pencil. Sometimes he needed to collect himself before making that next call, stilling his mind so he could ponder his next words. And the best way for him to get inside Khalil's head was to draw it; somehow remembering the physical details helped him to better re-assess the non-physical.

His kohl charcoal hit the thick, white sketch paper quickly and George tried to draw from memory. The eyes and butterfly wing eyelashes were easy, as were the stark, harsh edges of his chin. But George couldn't remember the lines of the new nose or the subtle tweaks to the cheekbones and eyebrows. The thick hair was also different and George struggled to remember how it flowed.

If he couldn't remember the physical evolutions of his adversary how could he hope to analyze the psychological ones? George struggled with the sketch and watched fifteen minutes pass to only limited positive effect. Still, even that small clarifying effort made the time worthwhile and George felt a new clarity and resolve as he stared into his reproductions of Khalil's eyes. "I'm going to get you," he whispered to his picture like a crazy man talking to any other inanimate object.

Then he picked up his phone and did the responsible thing by calling Campbell. He explained the curt message and empty promise.

"Shit, I hate negotiating with that bastard. He always has so many tricks up his sleeve," Campbell said.

"That he does," George responded. He sent Emine a text asking her to return to his apartment, which if Khalil did blow up this building would just put her at risk but what else could he do? One can't live scared, even with a lunatic stalking you. And if Khalil was using the cell line he couldn't be asking for 4:30 just to track George for such an explosion since the cell was portable and not tied to the building.

"It's got to be a trick," Campbell concurred with George's first hunch. "But he'll know that we can't ignore it and must re-allocate resources. Call you back."

"Sounds good," George responded, without the energy to find humor or even hope in the situation. He let the receiver fall into its cradle and walked to his panorama windows to study the busy park below, with its tall green trees and mini lake. It was 3:15 and the park was crowded with people criss-crossing the city or just strolling amidst the pristine setting. So now Khalil had George holed up in his apartment for an hour and fifteen minutes in case he called the landline not cell. George still half expected the building to blow up during that time period. Who knew, with Khalil involved stranger things had happened and bombs were nothing new.

George continued pondering Khalil's twisted psyche. Before he'd wanted to escape (and had) but now he wanted to turn himself in? No, impossible. His adversary must want time to complete something specific and had realized that the net was tightening around him, especially after losing two colleagues and a girlfriend. How best to lighten the heat? By offering his surrender Khalil would buy at least twelve hours of distraction; look at George, who was now neutered and trapped waiting for his call. If George was right about these guesses then their time to stop Khalil was quickly running out.

Assassinate whom? When and to accomplish what?

Khalil's group wanted to rule the world, as they themselves had proclaimed, but doing so required a political foothold upon which to base a greater movement. Egypt? George recalled his political science readings: to build a universal political movement that can work on a local level, where motivations vary expansively, a group must find a locus outside their movement or country. The Islamists had chosen anti-Americanism, damning the imperial power who supported, sometimes clandestinely, rulers in their countries of influence. This outward focus deflected from the varying support they would have built otherwise as they called for Muslims globally to unite and protect their religion from an outsider. Thus an emotional political community hung together, in spite of the bloodshed and bombs. The angry malleable crowd was channeled through faith or ideology while progress, such as jobs and human rights, continued to be trampled.

Only the mobs weren't staying quiet anymore, not abroad or here. Indeed, the Occupy Wall Street protestors, who came and went with the winds, were currently starting to congregate again outside the United Nations headquarters, causing mayhem just where George wanted it to be deserted. What if Khalil was actually planning a bomb there? And if he succeeded detonating one would anyone believe it was Al Qaeda and not the American authorities after the tear gas and press-free raids?

Texting

irst, Khalil sent Osman a text. *Come.* He'd housed the boy in a small Queens hostel, across the river and much closer to John F. Kennedy International Airport, their gateway out of this sacrilegious cesspool. Somehow, the boy had found a secretive Internet Café, untraceable and mostly anonymous in that so many people used it daily and no sign in was required if you paid cash.

Osman had seemingly spent his time there and at numerous local pizza shops, the small kind where they sold pizza a slice at a time. While his passion for the triangles didn't quite match that for electronics it came close and occasionally, on a late night call, Osman would gush about his newest discovery. He usually favored mushroom pies, with extra cheese when available.

Khalil was more a McDonalds devotee and thinking of Osman's passion decided he'd have his favorite Big Mac for dinner this evening; he might be dead before the next dinner hour arrived. The sandwich was salty, a little light on the stomach so he could eat two and probably not healthy. But the special sauce set off the cheese and lettuce perfectly, being a masterful foil for the ground beef patty. And that bun! Tonight, in celebration of his decision and plan, or in advance of his plan, he'd add French fries and a strawberry milkshake to the order.

For Khalil had decided what to do. Lounging on his bed and feeling the stress of too many options and not enough time he'd reached a breaking point. And a plan materialized. That was how events came to pass when you perfected your craft and trusted Allah to intercede when the problem got to large for one man.

As the Quran said, *"Think not of those who are slain in Allah's way as dead. Nay, they live, finding their sustenance from their Lord. They rejoice in the Bounty provided by Allah...the (Martyrs) glory in the fact that on them is no fear, nor have they (cause to) grieve. They rejoice in the Grace and the Bounty from Allah, and in the fact that Allah suffereth not the reward of the Faithful to be lost (in the least)."*

Khalil wanted Osman to help him create a martyr's video, that last spoken statement filmed before undertaking a suicide mission. But first would come his Salah, his prayer, one of his five daily, to honor Allah. This would be the Maghrib, his sunset prayer, as the day was winding down in Manhattan. His call to prayer would be the heavenly one, a softening of the light and the first hints of orange in the blue sky.

Outside his small third floor window, not far from the street, Khalil watched the ever-changing colors of early evening as the shadows began to collect in corners and grew longer. New York was always busy and this Monday evening was no different with people rushing in every which direction as if arriving anywhere really mattered. They'd just rush back the opposite way the next morning.

Time for a martyr's prayer? Khalil really wasn't sure. If it were to be a true martyr's mission he'd follow the distinctive rituals and enter paradise pure. But Khalil had more faith in himself and expected to survive the next twenty-four plus hours. He liked the idea of creating a video just in case....

Martyrdom would be a reward in and of itself but he wanted to share his glory with the world and create a broader reach for his sacrifices. Don't we all want to create history and be remembered for doing so? Well, he was at the crossroads of fate and wanted to be honored for his actions.

Indeed, the video would be even more powerful should he live and escape from the brink yet again. Having already slipped from American captivity, to succeed again on their shores and escape a suicide mission would create a legend. All political revolutions need their leader as a platform, from Lenin, to Che, to Robespierre, to the founding fathers. In this new media age, where all was sound bites and lies but broadcast to millions, he'd stand out from his competitors, many of whom had spent their lives in caves and dusty training camps.

With fame came opportunity.

What if he brought the last super power to its feet?

Osman was taking the subway and would be here in less than thirty minutes, depending upon whether he dawdled or not. The boy worked hard but he could get lost in whatever device he happened to be carrying so until then, Khalil would pray. Standing before his god he could thank him and ask for guidance along the Straight Path. Deferring to Allah's will, he would also be thankful for his blessings.

Khalil washed in ritual ablution, and was wearing clean clothes, in a somewhat clean place.

O you who believe! when you rise up to prayer, wash your faces and your hands as far as the elbows, and wipe your heads and your feet to the ankles; and if you are under an obligation to perform a total ablution, then wash (yourselves) and if you are sick or on a journey, or one of you come from the privy, or you have touched the women, and you cannot find water, betake yourselves to pure earth and wipe your faces and your hands therewith, Allah does not desire to put on you any difficulty, but He wishes to purify you and that He may complete His favor on you, so that you may be grateful.

He followed his raka'ah, or repeated cycle, being extra vigilant in his piety as he was preparing for a big day tomorrow. The cycle flowed, from standing, to bowing, then stopping, prostration, sitting, a second prostration and then a second sitting. He felt a rush of peace enter him and finally felt still. What a day he'd had. What a month. But certainty returned and he knew his course was the right one. Allah was answering his prayers and he'd enter tomorrow rightly cleansed and prepared for whatever outcome was ordained.

Khalil continued his cycle, forehead hitting floor then starting over again. Until the door bell came and Osman was there. One can cleanse a soul.

The boy was frightfully young but Musa had raised a solid boy. He'd grown in the last month. Sixteen and in that spurt of adolescence, he had a grace rare among young men his age. The boy was so quiet and handy, able to do anything online or off if it had a plug, battery, wifi, satellite or other high tech element.

"Khalil?" was all he said, not wrecking the calm aesthetic of the room.

"You will help me shoot a video," he responded, knowing that Osman would do it well and distribute a perfect finished product should that be necessary, but only then. The boy smiled and pulled a Canon camera from his pocket.

Khalil was ready to explain his forthcoming actions and how they would benefit the Umma, his Muslim community. The days of Saladin, the great Islamic general who'd saved Islam during the Crusades, were upon the world again and Khalil himself would be the tipping point.

Khalil watched Osman as the boy confidently shot the video. They'd do a quick edit, adding in music and pictures pulled from around the Internet. Osman would post it at just the right moment, on all of the carefully culled chat sites. Al Jazeera? If he hit his target. YouTube? Absolutely!

Looking at the initial raw footage Khalil was impressed at how good his new features looked on video. In person he felt they were too feminine, softened to the point of blandness. On camera he looked handsome, as he never had previously. Meanwhile, his deep voice and calm mannerisms played like those of a well polished newscaster. Once you've lived lies long enough your performance flows like the professional you've become.

"You should add a joke or two so your audience likes you," Osman suggested. "They need to connect with you emotionally and the jihad message, while good, is too deep to hold a mass audience's attention." Khalil was about to protest, even counter that a joke might be sacraligious, but realized that Osman was right. Most martyr videos were too musty and intense, holding only the attention of family and friends and thus helped recruit only among a narrow demographic. His message was global. Thus Khalil took Osman's guidance and shot the extra footage, speaking clearly. The boy was a new media whiz kid.

"Yes," was his simple answer, deferring to his much younger charge, as a good leader would when in the presence of someone more talented at performing the task at hand. Too many leaders refused to relinquish such control, preferring to march everyone off a bridge rather than cede authority.

Khalil started to speak once Osman indicated with his fingers that the camera was running.

"Today the world begins anew......," was the beginning. How would it end?

Cleaning....Messes....

It was a mess, and a potential bloody mess. Literally. Emine had noted the gradual buildup of protestors gathering outside the UN Headquarters as she wandered numerous streets with Fred, hoping that luck would propel Khalil into their path. The people were coming in tens at a time, or so it seemed and dressed to reflect varying lifestyles. Most carried placards and their mood was exhuberant as they clustered in smaller groups.

She was being passive, as we all must sometimes, and letting fate strike as it chose. Realistically, Emine had few options and right now their best ally was luck. Her religion, Islam, would be fine with this sitting duck role, just waiting for Khalil. So would most religions, all of whom served the basic purpose of keeping people passive when fate turned its back and fucked them over. Such was God's, or Allah's, will.

Her task at hand was increasingly frustrating, but Emine was used to waiting around for a story and leaping in the fray of conflict when the right moment finally arrived. Khalil was unpredictable and continued to puzzle her and haunt George as they could only guess at his intended plans. From George she'd heard stories of this ruthlessness and amorality and wondered at how they'd find an answer in time. Most people had limits and you could at least anticipate their next move. This man was dangerously bold, and terrorism was an attention game so he seemed made for the role.

For now she just watched the massing crowds as she pondered their dilema and missing target.

"Down with international finance," a guy with blonde dreadlocks and a ripped yellow t-shirt shouted, almost in her ear. Emine just sighed. What did these people want? Did they not understand that they might be protesting in the midst of the next 9/11? The situation was too absurd, and security obviously hadn't been warned to clear the area.

"Down," was echoed and Emine laughed.

The chamraderie of the crowd was evident, and people were joking, laughing and smiling in the dimming sunshine. American protests were mostly peaceful though the authorities occassionally resorted to tear gas and rubber bullets. In contrast with some of the global protests these more priviledged rebels seemed much closer to reaching their ultimate objectives. A Starbucks in every cup and free chance for all?

Not that she'd read much about their complaints being more focused on her job and the lands she visited on its behalf. George had been her only reason to visit the States, and now Khalil. She was also luckily protected from the realities of the less fortunate. Life never promises to be fair.

Clouds were increasingly gathering in the sky and Emine could feel the heaviness of an impending summer storm. The rains would cool the pavement and cut the heavy moisture, washing away the grime of modern city life. Would they also cleanse the heavy bitterness and anger of the protestors?

She heard a chant; something about banks then Fred pulled her close, enough so that she could smell his clove cologne and feel his warmth. His arms were a shelter and she yielded to his promise. "George wants us," he said and she rolled her eyes. Again? This back and forth, meaning that they kept getting pulled to the apartment only to hit a wall and get told to return to the streets.

From the corner of her eye she saw a man that looked like Khalil and felt her head whip in his direction. Dressed in a simple black t-shirt and jeans she could only see his back now, the face being left to mystery. He carried a sign which read:

Equity, not for banks but for people

But the way he walked and the set of his shoulders convinced Emine that the man had to be Khalil. Our bodies, at least at a distance, betray us more than our faces. The latter can be hidden so many ways while our form keeps its shape and movements. Hats, scarves, jackets and layers, we still walk with the same gait, strides constant and our arms swinging just so.

"Ignore George," she said, gesturing. "That's Khalil and we must follow him. Fast!" Fred actually stopped in the street, staring at her, not the disappearing figure of Khalil and Emine yanked at him. She could see him weighing his orders from George with her assertion and deciding. She was relieved when he took a step in her direction and they headed off in pursuit of their terror target.

The man ducked between a few taxis and Emine saw his placard, with its bold black letters, clatter to the ground. He didn't so much see them, since he never looked back, as sense their presence. Emine knew because his gait changed, tensing, and he walked faster, as did they, weaving amongst the other pedestrians. He was heading up town and soon crossed to 5th Avenue with its fancy shops and dressed up patrons.

Manhattan was amazing and fabulous but mostly it was just shallow and crowded with poorly dressed pigeons amidst the peacocks. But that density made tracking Khalil difficult and confusing. Passing one designer store after another Emine got a flash back of her shopping days and willed them away, like a bad video. She was a serious journalist now, chasing a wanted murder, except he was gone.

They were on 57th Street and so close to the Four Seasons, except, shit, Khalil had probably just led them right by the building from which he planned to take his prospective shot and they had no idea which one it was. Fred had a downcast look in his eyes though as yet he'd said nothing but they both silently acknowledged a lost opportunity. He looked away, not needing the question in her eye.

Meanwhile, people thronged around, buzzing and moving, a swarm that overwhelmed, but harmlessly. Emine could still hear the chants from the protesters cutting across the horns of traffic, not quite a symphony. She started laughing at the insanity of their situation, its helplessness and gravity mixing with her own frustration and hysteria. Fred didn't join in.

Finally, he spoke. "Khalil is turning himself in according to George's message." No way, Emine thought but kept it to herself. She wanted to call her dad but delayed, deciding she'd call from the hallway of George's apartment.

A taxi and elevator ride later she held back, "I need to make a quick call," was all it took and Fred left her alone.

Mehmet laughed when he heard her question.

"Terrorists provoke a response. What's yours? A refocus of efforts, right? You're leaving the city open for him to take a shot whenever he damn well likes. I'm starting to respect him but just hope that gun isn't pointed in my direction because it looks like he just might succeed." With that he hung up.

Emine braced herself to enter George's apartment. She agreed with Mehmet but would anyone else? Most people wanted life to be easy, pat and come with little effort while the reality was that it just didn't behave that way seemed to barely impact perceptions and desires. People would always hope for a fairy tale ending no matter how many times one never materializes. Blame the story books.

"The bastard is playing with us. Am I the only one who sees that!?" George was saying as she entered his luxurious but sleek living room. Well, he now had one more ally - her - but who exactly was on the other side of their alliance? The US government?

Ring

George felt calm and controlled though no one else seemed to be, as they all followed different tangents of disjointed thoughts.

"Keep him on the line so we can trace the call." Duh.

"Fail fast. If he won't surrender immediately tell him no deal." Double duh.

Khalil would be calling in five minutes. He'd be bugged (as if he wouldn't see that coming), tracked (ditto) and analyzed (yawn). Meanwhile, he kept getting question "suggestions" yet George knew Khalil would stick to message.

The apartment was increasingly crowded. Did they keep these agents on call, like understudies, for whenever disaster, or opportunity, struck? There were wires and phones and just bodies sticking out from the oddest places.

Then the main phone line rang, a harsh echoing in the beige, tasteful apartment with the wall length windows overlooking the park and too many people overlooking George. He let the phone ring a second time and watched too many eyes focused on him. Looking desperate is never good so they'd all have to wait, including Khalil. George was still more focused on stopping an assassination and didn't think this plan got him there. Label him a skeptic.

He picked up. "Hello," he said, to fit the cliché, and watched the crowd around him jump on cue, to fit another cliché. He couldn't help but smile, to a lot of obvious chagrin as they seemingly took Khalil seriously. Then, George realized more somberly, that he once had as well. Lessons learned, right? Khalil used people's weaknesses against them, pretending to give them what they wanted so that he could get his own desires met.

But in life, the best strategy is often unpredictability so George waited for Khalil to take the lead, vowing to say no to every request, no matter how trivial. The man clearly had a plan and George's only option was to scuttle it, then deal with his boss' inevitable wrath. The rock never rolled uphill so he'd have to be the one to do the heavy lifting or Khalil would find a way to roll over them all.

"Hello, George," was Khalil's minimalist response. So George was supposed to break and speak first? They were playing that juvenile game? Well, George benefited by keeping Khalil on the phone so the spooks could track his location, a fact Khalil would know down to the seconds required. But Khalil also had ownership of the relevant information and could dribble it out should he so desire. In reality, for this call only, Khalil held all the cards and knew it. And he could always call back or assassinate someone if he didn't get what he wanted.

George decided to jab at Khalil in the little time likely offered and expected Khalil would guess as much. They were like a married, or divorced, couple, moving in tandem until they didn't. Then the fights would begin if he didn't take the high road but George knew better than to let the situation reach that level of tension. He wanted a lot right now and wasn't inclined to risk anything, especially with a petulant and explosive adversary.

"What do you want Khalil?" he asked, going the direct route to maximize his ticking clock but also ignoring Khalil's earlier offer to turn himself in. A bullshit bargain. Khalil just laughed.

George felt the eyes around him as they all focused on his face and the phone. Luckily, he was used to performing for a classrooms or audience, so could ignore the distractions provided by so many. The late afternoon light outside his windows was still bright and only showing the first signs of fading into evening. One or two clouds cluttered up the deep blue of the sky and the heavens only existed in imagination. The quick afternoon showers had cleared the air and it looked cleaner from his perch, less murky as the day wore on. His life for the moment was all about the here and now and the practical reality of nabbing his terrorist so he took a deep breath.

Khalil still hadn't answered.

So George stood up and took his cordless phone to the table that housed his decanter of scotch, pouring himself a healthy finger. "I'm getting a drink," he told his teetotaler conversationalist, knowing if nothing else he was doing the unexpected and Khalil would hear the verifying movements through the phone line. Always counter a rough move with the least expected response. Anyone who struck out aggressively wanted the emotional charge of a counterpunch so they could up the aggression back. Sick, but predictable. Some people just like drama and you needed to head in the opposite direction, responding with as little conflict as possible. Stated differently, never give a tantrum-ing child what they want as rewarding bad behavior only leads to more.

Offering to turn himself in had been aggressive on Khalil's part. George would take the call but wouldn't play into the mirage.

"Drinking will land you in hell, George," Khalil responded and George ignored the panic in the room. These people didn't know Khalil as he did so he willed himself to continue without their support. Only Emine smiled and George tipped his glass to her before downing a healthy slug of scotch. Then he waited. Khalil was wasting his time, and on purpose. But he wouldn't give the bastard the satisfaction of hearing the frustration in his voice.

"Yes. See you there."

The silence fell deeper and George saw one of his experts signal that they'd tracked Khalil's location. George was sure there would be some trick; Khalil was too smart for such an obvious error. The alcohol had settled and he felt himself relaxing.

"I'm done. Can you get me a deal?"

Wasn't this a replay? Hadn't the last deal ended…

"Last time I got you a deal you shot me," George responded. Khalil laughed.

"Think about it. I'll call you at 9:00 a.m. tomorrow morning to hear the details. I want to get married and plan on handing myself over Wednesday morning if you can make it happen. After that, all bets are off. Don't touch her or I'll kill you."

So the deal terms were on the table. Now the ball was in his court, along with the mobs and throngs that had taken over his tasteful apartment. Weren't they playing around with an earlier date.

"Great," was all George replied and heard Khalil hanging up. Mostly the exchange reminded him of his interviews, a scripted and precise few moments of sound bites and story lines. He really needed to escape the pretense of his life where no one was ever honest, including him. And the stress of constantly acting was starting to weigh too heavily.

At least the scotch was true and ever so real.

His mob started chattering and the cell phones went wild. Meanwhile, George swigged down more alcohol musing about the exchange. If Khalil did blow up the building he'd take along half the FBI but George himself would be well anesthetized. Then his phone rang. Again?

"Hello."

"George," was the soft voiced response. Karen. His wife. She had to call now? He poured himself more scotch and lied. "I miss you, Karen."

He heard her deep in-breath and didn't really care how she responded. Yes, he could be a bastard but given the gravity of his current position, and that of the city, didn't he deserve at least that much leeway?

"I'm coming home," was all she said and then hung up. One more risk factor. Perfect. Hopefully, she'd done more than worry about him while she was gone and had maybe even begun writing her book.

Then the phone rang once again and George saw a DC number. Campbell.

"We got a location. He was on a cell phone in a moving vehicle and the phone was ditched after he hung up. But he is Manhattan."

Now it was George's turn to laugh.

Smoke

Khalil didn't have a restful night. Had he bothered to consider it, he would have realized that George wouldn't either, nor would anyone around him. Really, a major terrorist would rarely surrender regardless of his plight, knowing that there would be little mercy at the other end of the gesture. Khalil was anything but naïve and he could imagine the back and forth as all those security experts tried to figure out their plan. But anything to keep them busy and distracted elsewhere as the net around him was tightening too fast. A successful strike always looked like a perfectly orchestrated concerto and it was, along with a lot of luck. He needed one shot; his aim was that good.

But who would he decide to shoot?

Osman had been hacking into calendar programs trying to find the Vice President's exact schedule. Thus far, Patterson seemed to be flying in late afternoon tomorrow, Tuesday, then driving from the airport to hear the end of the day's program at the UN Headquarters. Thereafter, he would keynote the dinner, his speech starting roughly forty-five minutes after the salads were served. What Osman couldn't find was information that zeroed in on his expected accommodations, but the indication was that Patterson was staying with friends, which meant shooting him after the dinner was likely a fool's mission and close to impossible.

Joseph Patterson was an acceptable Vice President, but mostly because he was kept tightly hidden and thus generated little talk, positive or negative. The former Michigan governor had once been a firebrand, angering vast swaths of his constituents, delighting both their opponents and the press. Labeled a leader, he'd been the action oriented running mate the incumbent president had added to ensure his re-election, ditching his more traditional and ineffectual first time VP. The President seemingly was a master politician, who ruled with an iron fist, sharing little power and emerging from the related slugfests seemingly little harmed or impacted. Patterson had been promptly sidelined after the re-election win and took action no more. A good candidate for the next presidential election? Who knew? Still controversial, Khalil didn't understand American politics well enough to know if that image helped Patterson's chances or hurt them.

Seemingly, the Americans just liked to fight, and they justified it by adding some flimsy argument based on democracy and equality. Knowledge on issues wasn't a prerequisite for having an opinion and a vote thus the related debates often sounded to him like dialogue from George's *Alice* book, which Khalil was still carrying around and ocassionally skimming.

No wonder the Americans couldn't keep their hands off other people's countries. They likewise assumed that they had such right of divine intervention globally.

Who to shoot?

Khalil stared up at the ceiling. Its white wasn't so grey, let alone black, because the room never got very dark due to the density of the lights in the neighborhood. Khalil thought he heard a train and suddenly realized how close his room was to Grand Central Station. He never noticed during the daytime, when the streets were ever so much louder and he was busier.

For hours he'd been lighting one cigarette after another and the nicotine obviously wasn't helping him doze off. But Khalil was used to relentless insomnia and wasn't needed until the afternoon anyway so could sleep in.

Who to shoot? Winging it was a good attitude but not a workable mission. When opportunity struck you couldn't be too fixated on a set course but rather needed the flexibility to respond to Allah's will. But going into his mission Khalil still needed a plan to define his desired outcome and guide his related actions. Follow the original and shoot KK or take a greater risk and chance the Vice President of the United States? Oh, the initial impact of the latter would be devistating, and the American government would overreact to keep its citizens reassured; but how much did one man in a stable country ultimately really matter? Protests and growing unhappiness in this first world superpower were both building but essentially the revolution wasn't even close to coming. Adding a common cause and external enemy, should the VP get assassinated, might backfire by pulling the country closer together thus delaying that inevitable collapse. No one, no country, stayed on top forever and this country was now fat, lazy and arrogant. How could it be otherwise when the food was all so good!

KK's death however was an entirely different paradigm.

Khalil lit another cigarette, striking a wooden match and then holding flame to tobacco. The smell of sulfur lingered, mingling with the tangy burning tobacco of his Marlboro Reds, which were quickly heading from habit to addiction. He enjoyed the distraction and the feel of acrid smoke against the back of his throat. A wisp of smoke blurred the red lights of a sign outside his window and he wondered at the tricks of fate that ditched him alone in New York.

Jennifer should be asleep right now as it was almost 2:00 a.m. She'd be curled up in that homely comforter of their cheap room unless she'd already abandoned it and any hope of him returning. Back to San Diego? To her little tract house and public policy lawyer job? Where she'd meet some equally pedantic professional and buy more flowers to plant in front of their white house in a cul de sac. Wasn't that how Americans prettified their lives, by spending money on cosmetic adornments? Her new boyfriend would lift away the entwined comforter and spread her legs, as Khalil himself had done. He'd stroke that soft white skin, with an indentation from muscles built over many long miles of running. And she'd sigh with a half smile and let him have his way, begging for it deeper if he started to slow down.

But none of that mattered, did it? Nor did Jennifer, with her hugs, warm smiles, and fondness for Italian food, especially anything parmessan. Khalil had an important job to complete in the morning, or later in the day if it wore on, from lilacs to blues to the oranges of the hours burning off. Jennifer was perfect until she wasn't and the wound of her continued to burn. They'd bonded more deeply afer this reunion, two people who'd never replaced each other as time passed and they both continued facing it alone. Yet Khalil had also finally accepted that loss. Jennifer's beliefs were too different from his lifestyle and she couldn't see past their limitations to the better life Khalil was offering. Bickering about intangibles and ideologies would only drive them apart until their love turned to emptiness. Such passion not only wouldn't combust, it would die an absent and ignored death.

But forever he'd carry the memory of her soft creamy skin and curving rounded belly into his nightly dreams. We never lose our vision of heaven once tasted and Allah would reward him with its return someday; perhaps even tomorrow.

But oh how deeply he wanted that woman now.

Khalil stubbed out his butt in the paper cup he'd gotten from a street coffee vendor. He'd drained the cup almost dry and the used cigarettes were clustering in a barely damp pile on the bottom in his hazy room.

He wanted to sleep, so desperately and yearned for that drop into sense-lessness. For Khalil was so tired, each joint aching but the tension from his muscles rebelling. He could at least enjoy the soft bed and warm blankets which created a cocoon and a temporary respite. Life is a rapidly passing illusion and this was his for the moment.

He willed his discipline back and lit another Marlboro, sitting up and staring outside at the now almost empty street. He considered getting a piece of paper upon which he could write and explore his options but didn't want to create evidence. Just one other detail he'd have to tie up.

And the options were simple. Kill KK in the morning on his way to the UN conference or after the dinner on his way home. Kill Patterson entering the UN headquarters right before the evening progeam. All tomorrow; oh, no, wait, today. Then Khalil would be either be dead or headed out of the country fast.

Logically, Khalil should probably take a shot at KK first thing in the morning, in which case he should be leaving his apartment soon for the empty office they'd rented across from the Four Seasons. He could sleep later and the adrenaline, nicotine and some added coffee would hype him up enough to get a clear shot. Marksmanship required a clear head more than a steady hand, or so Khalil believed. Some snipers were purists and wouldn't touch substances such as coffee. Then they found themselves in a real battle and realized that fear could clear out your system immediately.

If the shot proved impossible for any reason, he'd still be able to take another later in the day. And sleep.

Khalil snubbed out his cigarette and began to pray. Ultimately, he'd ask Allah for guidance, knowing that an answer would come as it always had in the past. His job required such solitude and introspection he'd learned that only a God could ultimately provide a guiding hand in the depths of night.

If only Jennifer had been more supportive and quieter she'd be here as well. Khalil touched his forehead and felt ground. And he muttered his devotion to Allah, adding a side request for guidance and divine will.

I can't afford her....

Light

Emine woke early. Sleep had come easily since she'd learned long ago to leave other people's battlegrounds where they belonged, with other people. Her job was all about observing the unacceptable and painful then letting it unfold before her and on camera. Life wasn't always pretty but she still needed her sleep, especially if she was going to stay sharp for the surprises tomorrow inevitably always brought. Her battles with insomnia were totally the fault of her own internal demons and needed little support from the world's insanity.

And at 4:00 a.m., much later in Paris and Cairo, respectively (the other time zones to which she was half acclimated) she rolled out of bed and into the shower. Luckily, her room had one of those brew your own coffee with a pod machines so she doubled up and chugged her two servings down.

Emine wasn't crazy exactly, or at least no more than the average person, but this situation was rapidly driving her in that direction. Really, a bunch of goons (George's term) clustered on the phone strategizing and planning and getting approval while a killer was stalking their prestigious geopolitical conference unhindered by procedure and focused only on results. Damn fault with the world was that people liked to talk, or even brag, but when time came to take the action that would get results they were all debating or on another line.

Emine finished a quick dry of her hair then did a scan of her clothes, mostly still jumbled up in her suitcase and a mess. What did one wear to stalk Manhattan's pre-dawn streets? She wasn't in the mood for jeans as they were too constraining and the temperatures were rising daily. So she added some distressed khakis, loose and with a low rise, then her trainers and a navy t-shirt. She grabbed her card key, camera and passport plus a twenty. What else could she need? Yes! Her phone, full of text messages from those overnighters who wanted to appear to have been working maniacally all night and taking the situation seriously.

She noted that George wasn't one of them and hoped that he'd been sleeping. But no one was leaving George alone and she feared that he'd been up most of the night deflecting and then ultimately deciding when no one else wanted the role. He was clearly smart enough to drive their stategy but she worried that in government decision making typically carried later blame.

And so she headed down the elevator bare-faced, leaving her make-up and social conventions behind. Time was ticking and Emine wanted to see the streets empty so she could put herself in Khalil's shoes.

The walk to the Four Seasons was a mere few blocks and she stood outside the hotel, studying and trying to view it through another's eyes. Tall, regal and grey, the building looked like many others but currently might host the world's security. Her father was also inside, likely on the phone with someone at their country's capital discussing policy and what should happen across the day's span. The Iranian's no show had numerous capital buildings astir, none more than Turkey's. Their neighbor was a complicated one and rumors of a cross border raid were lighting up the Internet. The actual border to be invaded was mere speculation, as was often the case with rumors, though major event did typically now break online first thus whispered fears could prove true.

The morning clock's hand hadn't yet touched 5:00 a.m. while the summer air was still cool. Even this early taxis were rushing in every direction and the occasional pedestrian passed by quickly. The city that never sleeps, according to Frank Sinatra, seemed determined not to dishonor that title. Darkness was cut more by city lights than the sun and Emine could study the area with ease. She began a steady pass back and forth between the hotel and the UN building but saw little of interest and no man with a stride like Khalil's. Was she looking for a needle in a haystack? Probably. But the best way not to find it was to stay in her hotel room and join a conference call.

Emine stopped at a Starbucks to get more coffee and also because she was starting to feel dejected. They seemed almost at a pivotal point of clarity yet weren't catching any substantive breaks. Their team even knew the block across from the hotel where Khalil most likely had rented a place to perhaps take a shot. But how many rooms might he have rented, in how many locations, and would there even be a shot? And how much time could they have left? Only George's mood seemed unaffected.

"Eme," she heard a barrister call and jumped to get her mocha latte, a much needed surge of energy and calories. Her stomach was too distracted for food so might as well fill up with liquid calories. She took her paper cup outside and sat on a cement step, puzzling possibilities while she slurped. After a few minutes her phone rang. The sun was beginning to warm the streets and she wondered if now was the time to start taking pictures. The world looked so different through a lens.

But she had to get the phone first and did, to hear George's voice. She quickly told him what she was doing and why.

"I've been stuck on calls...," he started.

"Khalil," she shouted, spilling her drink and hopping up, holding the phone but fumbling with her camera. And she got the shot.

"Emine?" George was asking as she re-directed her energy back to the phone. Why had she shouted Khalil's name? Surprise, for when Khalil turned to look directly at her before rushing off she hadn't know what to do next but instinct dictated she take a picture. It had happened too fast.

"I just saw him!" she exclaimed into the phone. "I'll call you back." She hung up and began to run after Khalil, hoping that she was running where he was headed and not where he'd been. She'd had too many distractions to react faster and kicked herself. That hesitation was exactly how people ended up dead and some might now due to her delayed response. Damn.

The only good news was that not only were their efforts like pushing a stone up a hill, with a little luck matched by some quirky error or major disaster, Khalil was seemingly having the same bad run of luck. And in life, once something starts going against you that momentum only increases, while turning it around gets progresively harder. She might not be getting much right but Khalil was doing worse since they'd narrowed down his location and haunting grounds: now, in front of the Four Seasons near the same buildings she'd seen him only yesterday Her possibilities were narrowing, as were his. Whose options would run out first?

She grabbed her phone and called George back. He needed to commandeer some agents and increased security here immediately.

Karma

George heard what Emine said and it made perfect sense. Being a psychology professor he had great respect for instinct and the subconscious mind. Less willing to accept terms like physic, channeling of energy and even the third eye he nonetheless respected the concepts behind those more adventurous ideas. Emine had clearly somehow formed an instinctive (second) sense for Khalil and thus kept bumping into him. People worked that way; attuned to someone else they'd keep finding them as if propelled by an invisible hand.

But Emine hung up on him. He knew she'd call back, unless Khalil harmed her, so that she could get support and resources directed to whatever information she'd find or discern from following Khalil. But he'd have to wait meanwhile as seemed to be his life's rhythm. George had waited to drive, to marry, to get tenure, to finally quit his cushy teaching job and try something new and now he just spent a lot of time waiting for Khalil. As if Khalil was the only terrorist on the planet instead of an especially dangerous one that George seemingly couldn't escape.

Terrorism never died though its name changed.

George poured himself more coffee. A deep dank brown, it was still warm from the machine's heating pad. He dug through the freezer looking for frozen cookies he could re-heat in the microwave. Usually he favored the heavily frosted sugar cookies but right now he was more in the mood for peanut butter. Karen was pretty neat and the freezer was organized by food group. She'd had a grocer send him some extra frozen food when she'd been whisked off to safety however and one of his guards had shoved the food into their double-doored Sub Zero haphazardly.

Eventually he found some chocolate chip cookies, not his goal but close enough to his desire. About to stick one in the microwave he heard his phone ring and jumped for it, cookie and coffee carried along for the ride. Normally, he didn't eat to deal with stress but normally wasn't never and he would gnaw at a frozen cookie for now if need be. He'd been on the phone since before dawn, everyone asking and probing, as if he knew what the bastard was going to do and just wouldn't tell them. Now he remembered why he'd taken that television job where people actually seemed to listen to what he said. Sure, they might be on the verge of a new national crisis but weren't his bosses the ones with hundreds of millions of dollars worth of high tech gadgets and scores of agents? All they'd given him was a cell phone and two guards.

"George," Emine sounded breathless as she spoke, but she had that way about her. He bit into his hard cookie and chewed as he listened. The room was light enough, though he only had one small lamp on. He still really wanted a peanut butter cookie.

"I lost him," she continued. Again. The man was an eel. Or what was it that was visible for a second then disappeared into thin air? A genie? An avatar?

"He was on the same block, across from the Four Seasons, in front of their main lobby entrance," she continued. So there it was, he'd been planning a shot at someone leaving or arriving from the hotel? Did she see the evidence of a gun?

George glanced at his clock and saw that the time was well after 8:00, the start of the day's program at the UN. Had Khalil missed his morning window when Emine saw him and yelled? He grinned at her babble. She had so many ideas regarding what to do but he could barely process them all. So what would they do? Good ideas notwithstanding, he'd have to see what Campbell could pull together.

"What are you doing now?" he asked, still gnawing on his cookie. The texture was growing on him and he especially liked how the frozen chips warmed then melted in his mouth. In the hallway one of his bodyguards was on his cell and arguing about something but George couldn't hear the actual words. Still, George just didn't want to know as he already had enough other problems.

The coffee was now cold but did its job of washing down the last wet crumbs.

"I'm going to walk to the UN Building. I want to see it once more but through his eyes this time. I need to sense what the progression would be. Oh George! He moves so fast yet never in a straight line."

"The zig zags and odd dashes to the side make him harder to shoot. He's well trained, never forget that." George was well trained too and thus was helping her fill in the blanks. "You'll be back here soon?" he asked. But finally Khalil's actions were making sense and George had an idea of his plan and why it wasn't progressing faster.

In fact, Khalil's mental state was also crystallizing and George could see his emotionally weakened but still determined enemy. KK most likely had been the target - they were right - but Khalil had arrived in Manhattan as backup and boss not meaning to take the shot himself. One of the two dead youths had been the trigger boy and the other had perhaps been a lookout or alternate shooter. Khalil might be the only one left to take the assassin's shot.

If George was right then Khalil seemed to be tightening in for the kill. And if he wasn't....?

KK had surprised Khalil twice, God bless him. Both men played by no rules beyond that of always doing the unexpected to keep others guessing and had thus excelled on field and in war, two not disimillar battlefields. KK was currently playing at politician but still had that street boy edge, just like Khalil. Faced with different opportunities they'd both followed ambitious paths leading them to this seemingly inevitable standoff. George was actually betting on KK; Khalil was too disturbed emotionally as of late and folding under pressure.

But back to stopping Khalil who'd lost his minions and was only questionably following his original plot. George doubted it. By checking into the Four Seasons Khalil had shown a willingness to take bold steps which he couldn't expect others to dare. Because of Jennifer?

They'd all tried to find Jennifer but she seemingly had disappeared again. Khalil must have given her a new identity and spirited her away, outplaying them. Quite frankly, even if they found her she might not know very much as George doubted Khalil would have risked her lawyer's caution with the truth. Her calls were as unpredictable and sporadic as her boyfriends.

"Yes...," Emine said but as she drew out the word George realized he'd forgotten what they'd been discussing. He needed her where? For a moment he puzzled through his options and game plans again. She should be on the streets as Emine seemed to sense Khalil, or had at least gotten lucky bumping into him often enough to narrow his perimeter.

"Keep looking for him but mind your phone!" he let her drop off and then pondered his next step. Some would say that it was wisest to act quickly on new and important information. They were wrong. Unless you knew of some actual imminent and precise threat a better decision was to take a few minutes to evaluate what you'd learned, mixing it in with what you already knew, and then deciding on the right outcome. Only upon reaching such a conclusion did you push for that eventuality ruthlessly and with every bone in your body.

George shoved aside his half melted cookie and cold coffee. He wished then that he had a dog, like his childhood Golden retriever sidekick Buddy, with whom he could share his thoughts. The dog would hear him out, never doubting or slowing his train of thought with a question or insight of his own. Alas, he was alone now with a few hired thugs whose job was simply to keep him alive.

Suddenly, a lights went on inside as the information swirling in his head made sense, a perfect fusion of the impossible. Tonight was the big UN dinner at the headquarters, for which the whole building had been turned upside down. What better an event to stage an assassination and embarrass the United States? Some station most likely already had the Vice President's opening speech scheduled for live cable viewing. Inside the building, security would be too tight to count on taking a shot and even a suicide knifing as the Assassins of centuries ago wouldn't be a guarantee.

But arrivals and departures opened up the risks of the chaotic and dense metropolis, which no security could completely offset. No one was immune to the inconveniences of modern transport and crowded cities. So what insights was George missing?

KK should be the target. Khalil had just left Egypt and he clearly hadn't been there to blow up the Aswan Dam since he himself had foiled that plot. Revenge? He'd been tortured there two years ago and had gained custody of George, so revenge was a concept in his mind. But, Khalil was more outwardly destructive than vindictive. Meanwhile, if Egypt became a failed state the Islamists would fill more of the related void, being the most organized group other than the Egyptian military, their allies.

But, Khalil apparently was taking the shot now. He'd been too present, physically, these past few days, risking his own life. So why not up the ante and aim for the American Vice President or Emine's dad? Killing the VP on American soil? Catastrophic. The country would go nuts and shoot first, consequences be damned.

George scratched at his knee then realized he couldn't remember the last time he'd worked out. Well, little matter. His health didn't seem like the biggest priority at that moment and he had a lot of calls to make.

Then he heard his cell phone ring and saw that an unknown caller was trying to reach him. One could only hope.

Confusion

Khalil heard his name and knew better than to turn around to see who'd shouted. The voice was female but it wasn't Jennifer's. He'd only been in this country under other identities so that real name shouldn't have been known by any woman other than his. With his surgeries the number of people who would have been able to recognize him was nominal.

Turning would have acknowledged the cry, and that he was indeed Khalil. It also would have slowed him down. He was on a narrow tiny island which was part of a bigger island hence constantly at risk. All around him was closing in, the time window, and the space to do the assassination, the people and the weapons. He actually liked this part of the plot when all that planning evolved into action. Tight and crisp, the tension built adrenaline and focus. He knew every aspect of every detail, contingencies and possible roadblocks and like the spider he was named for, was now just weaving delicately to keep everything perfectly in proportion, neither too tight nor too loose and dense but with enough air.

The sun was brightening now but not to the point of glare. The woman's reinforcements, if she had any, would take at least ten minutes and Khalil wanted to study the UN building before making a final decision. He'd originally been heading in the opposite direction, to the empty office he'd rented across from the Four Seasons, planning to take a shot at KK as he left the hotel's lobby. That way, if something interfered with shot one Khalil would still have the option to come back later and get him in the dark, after the dinner.

But now something had again gone wrong so Khalil turned quickly away from the voice and headed across densely populated pavement in the opposite direction. Walking south he turned left and onto 47th street, passing the Dag Hammarskjöld Plaza but ignoring its modernistic statues. The bronze human like blobs scattered around and even seated on park benches were an abomination against Allah who forbid such idolatry of human images. The plaza's trees were vibrantly green and the branches sheltered cascades of red poppies in protected flowerbeds.

Reaching First Street, Khalil approached the compound from its right, starting with the large General Assembly Building, then working his way to the row of flags that lined up at attention across the circular entrance way. A large gun, its muzzle twisted into a knot, was a signature key anti-violence symbol that held court among other reminders of the building's purpose and implied gravitas. To him it was just one more tall building in a city too filled with symbolic sculpture. The river backdrop was a nice touch.

Indeed, as Khalil studied the massive landscaped sculpture he knew he'd likely only take a shot here in desperation. Which didn't rule it out; desperation was rapidly setting in and he'd rather die than fail at this mission, for so many reasons. He'd originally told Radwan to arrange a boat and essentially was now picking up after his failed minion who was dead because he fucked up. Shooting someone is easy if you keep the plan clean but Radwan had wanted the drama of being a hero. Clue: heroes often end up dead or at least gravely imperiled with the consolation prize being a title or, even more insulting, a medal. Success was what mattered, with safety being a key element of that superior designation, and a smart man realized as much. The best escape was by boat but arranging that option now would be too difficult.

Or would it? Khalil had two choices. He could go back to his shoddy hotel and sleep or he could figure out whether he could finagle an escape boat so he could successfully flee after shooting the Vice President of the United States. He scanned the area again, looking for any distinguishing advantages he could utilize. Radwan had also rented an office across from this building but looking from the outside at the shot he'd have to take Khalil didn't like the odds. The expanse was workable but far and the arrival of the Vice President would be crowded, making a clear shot unlikely.

Not allowed to spend the night, the city's protesters had begun gathering before dawn and provided both cover for a gun shot and also a potential fall guy. Indolent with little else to do than notice any guy with a gun, they also might succeed in disarming him. If one of his decoy boys was still alive Khalil could have thrown him into the unwashed crowd with a rifle and taken the real shot from a window, letting the new face of America take the blame for killing their Vice President. That plan, alas, wasn't practical anymore.

Should Khalil have deduced these complications before as he'd been guiding Radwan? Perhaps. But he'd been planning that the boy would be on a suicide mission, not him. And, honestly, Khalil had been too distracted by Jennifer thus happily offloaded the risk and responsibility. Things just hadn't gone as planned and now he was the trigger man.

A part of him wanted to call Jennifer, to hear her voice and escape if only for a minute into her reality. But escape was a dangerous concept because it implied a safe place to which you could run and hide. The world allowed for no place or no one that ultimately was really such a haven, as he'd learned the hard way. She was but blood and tissue, divine only within his mind. And his mind was unpredictable.

The streets were slowly getting more crowded though the summer day was still early and each minute that passed, each person who arrived, increased the likelihood that he'd be spotted. While the Four Seasons was an expected given for tracking him as Khalil was on their security cameras the UN was a jump but not too far. A number of related dignitaries had chosen the hotel and Khalil was an internationally wanted terrorist bent on impacting politics. George would figure out the connection even if no one else did.

Staring at the entrance he saw a man emerge from a black town car or limousine or whatever they were called and recognized KK. The large head set off against broad shoulders, the way he walked with that distinctive limp and the arrogant set of his neck. KK was alive for another hour as Khalil had retreated earlier, responding to the woman who called his name, and was now too far away to take this shot at a new location. What else would the day bring?

Khalil hailed a taxi and then paused before telling the obviously African driver whether to take him someplace where he could charter a boat or to his hotel to sleep. The cab was fragrant with spices, cloves and cinnamon being the most prevelent. A deep blue throw had been carefully placed over the seats and the cabin was meticulously clean. The driver's personality was evident in these details and Khalil felt immediately confident that this man would do his best to accommodate any requests, especially if a large tip was attached. Hard workers who took pride in their tasks were consistently so, a simple management reality. In contrast, Radwan's sloppiness was now costing Khalil dearly. Too bad he hadn't recruited this driver instead, but his cross, hanging from a large loop chain, testified to his likely reluctance where militant Islam was involved.

"I'd like to drive around the city a bit. You have time?" Khalil asked. The driver nodded yes and Khalil picked up his cell phone, an expensive iPhone for a change. He dialed a number he'd memorized during many sleepless nights and was his current lifeline when he needed help. Osman was exceptionally talented at hacking into government data bases so what else could he find out about the day's schedule?

Khalil was feeling hunted and wary as he sensed opportunity slipping away repeatedly. Something didn't feel right and he always trusted his instincts since they were what had kept him alive this long. When something works the best rule is not to question it; when something doesn't you need to approach the problem from a new angle. But did he have one?

Solitude in the Sun

mine felt pretty much alone. This reconnaissance work was bullshit and Khalil had vanished into thin air - again. Their process was like tracking a fly in a very large hotel...it just sort of didn't happen.

And she felt famished! It was now after 9:00 a.m. but you'd think she hadn't eaten in days. Oh, had dinner last night been liquid or actual food? Yesterday felt so long ago now but she did recall having been so tense that food had lost all appeal. Today she'd been up early and attempting the coffee thing. Glancing around she found a few options but mostly quick breakfast take-out while suddenly she wanted heavy, real food. Perhaps eggs and toast or pancakes with maple syrup. Except she was in a hurry. Well, this was Manhattan and could do anything fast.

And she hadn't heard from George whether or not Khalil had called as promised.

She dialed George as she started walking in the direction of his apartment, her eyes still glancing every which way looking for just the right restaurant. Today was a work day so the streets were mostly full of people heading off to jobs spiffily dressed in suits and carrying work bags. Her heart yearned for Paris, currently home, which had a more intimate feel than this glass and steel metropolis. Both cities were examples of urban planning but with a much different time and place footprint.

George didn't answer so she left a message.

"Heading to your place. Updates? I'm starved so what do you want to eat?" He'd get the message someday. Until then, she'd make the food decisions and find the dense food she craved. Her stomach grumbled and she regretted knocking over her mocha latte earlier when she'd chased after Khalil.

Walking, Emine saw numerous bagel options and then finally stumbled on a crowded deli with a broad storefront windows and a line out the door. Rude and impatient, a waiter nonetheless agreed to take her order amidst the tumultous noise and crowded tables.

She listed whatever she could imagine: pancakes, omelets, scrambled eggs and bacon and a smoked fish platter with those omnipresent bagels. "Oh, and a fruit bowl," she added, trying to be virtuous but only scoring a nasty look.

The waiter rushed away and she surveyed the crowded rows of tables and red checked table clothes. This reality was so different than her own. People seemed comfortable, settled and chattering away, as if someone might not be about to die and their certainties to implode. Emine had come so far out into the world but had she lost herself chasing other peoples lives and even their dreams?

She picked up a copy of *The New York Times* and started reading an article on the Euro until her phone rang. Well, George was just too late to add anything to the order, not that there was much to add since she'd already ordered more than she might be able to carry.

"Allo," she said.

"You sound like me," came Mehmet's response, strong and clear. She smiled at the thought that her dad was close by for a change. She pulled at her khakis and realized she was glad she'd worn baggy pants as the day was warming up fast.

"I don't have good news for you, Emine," he said and she heard the edge he got in his voice when he was angry. She braced herself. Her mother.

"I'm at the airport and heading out of the United States. I learned that the Iranians didn't show for the conference because your Al Qaeda friends haven't been quiet about the planned assassination and the Iranians want to be far away when the shot is taken. More importantly, I was or am a potential target." Emine could hear planes in the background not that she would have needed confirmation of his intentions. She struggled with the logic of it all and wondered if what he was saying made sense.

Better to ask and look like a fool for five minutes than to be a fool as the day wore on. "Because…?"

"The best thing for Al Qaeda would be to blame the United States for destabalizing the Middle East and surrounding areas. They could then join vulnerable populations against the aggressive west and assert their own agenda. The US resources and attention would be diverted; Iran is vulnerable due to the failed plot to kill the Saudi Ambassedor on US soil for which the Americans have blamed them."

"You?" Emine asked, as two huge bags of food were handed to her. She put them on the corner of a long table and ignored the hostile look of the waiter. She turned her back on him and sensed as he moved away. The smells were overpowering and her stomach responded with yearning. She could almost taste the bacon and eggs, even as they sat ignored.

"My death would be destabalizing but I have no obligation to stick around and play my luck. As long as I stay in power I defuse the true evil aim of people like your Khalil for a return to the Islam of the middle ages. The fight isn't really over religion but rather power. But Emine, my leaving doesn't solve your entire problem as I wasn't the only target on the list."

She took a deep in breath and reminded herself to think first before speaking, even to her father. He could be so cold and Machiavellian when he wanted and even when he didn't. No one survived for long in politics without a solid slug of ruthlessness in their character. Meanwhile, she still had another life to save.

"Who dad?" she asked and suddenly felt her hunger lift as her new worries took hold.

"I don't know. My source only warned me to leave the city as quickly as possible."

"And if there's a bomb planted on your plane?" she asked.

"Decisions are never easy, Emine. The higher you rise in influence the more difficult they get," was his response. Suddenly, Emine realized that in seeing him this time three of her other shadows really had faded into utter darkness and their disappearances hadn't been her imagination. Obviously, she'd been bad about calling, the whole foiling a terrorist threat on a short timetable thing, but she still couldn't recall her last calls from Liz, Ed or Bright. That was unlike all of them, except perhaps Liz who'd likely heard rumors about Juliet and wanted to avoid any potential related conversations.

But Ed, who said he loved her.

Bright, who always chased a story relentlessly and knew there was one.

Bud was still calling, but he always did just mostly when she least expected it. Basically, her line had gotten quiet outside of George and the chase for Khalil.

And those other two? Well, perhaps they'd both finally gotten bored with her inability to open up and trust. She did get flighty and then clingy and then crazy. Honestly, she had to admit that she'd miss neither. Bright must have another angle while maybe Ed had met another girl.

"My flight is getting ready to take off. Good luck Emine."

"I love you dad," she replied but he'd already hung up. Life gives us no easy answers and he'd just left her with another big gaping hole to fill. She grabbed the heavy, fragrant bags and then found a taxi. No way would she walk with all this food.

Buzzed into George's apartment Emine only laughed when the guards told her that they'd get no back up until the Washington bureaucracy got around to approving it. George was on the phone and Khalil hadn't called at 9:00 as promised. Another red herring. So they spread out the food and Emine poured cold coffee, pushing the buttons to make a new pot. With George's guards she ate a full buffet of breakfast foods, starting with a pancake and then attacking a large ham and cheese omelet. The hot food was grounding as the earth was falling from under her feet otherwise. Emine wasn't completely comfortable in George's apartment and wondered at how he could stay calm with a terrorist calling him periodically and sometimes staring up from the park below.

While George stayed huddled over whatever call he was on his guards filled her in and none of the news was good. Well, she also had a lot to tell him, but would need to wait.

Her father's words ket bothering her and she wondered if anyother country representatives were clearing out of Manhattan before the Vice President spoke this evening.

Perhaps she should bring George some food and get a sense for how long his call would take. While the bodyguards had given her valuable updated information she knew that George kept a lot close to home and was learning more likely as she was just eating away. Similar to everyone in the intelligence community his level of trust was pretty limited and he shared things more in discussion than as a briefing. One slip of the right information to the wrong person was potentially catastrophic.

She started piling a plate high, using his daily dishes, white with swirling pastel yellow flowers and deep vibrantly green leaves. The omelet was good, so she started with a large wedge, rich with ham and dripping orange cheese.

Security?

eorge was shocked. "No extra security at all!?" he asked Campbell, who sounded apologetic, a little, but mostly at his whit's end. About how George was feeling but without the fury. He took another long gulp of cold coffee and stared at the park. No one gave a shit sometimes, did they?

"It's gone to both the heads of Homeland Security and the FBI," Campbell explained.

"NYPD?" George asked and heard the answer in Campbell's silence.

"Doesn't Emine have a photo of Khalil from her sighting this morning?" Campbell asked hesitantly. "That would help. A lot."

"You don't believe her?" George heard himself take a cheap shot at his ex-boss. Well, one could hardly expect perfect behavior when he didn't have the proper authorization or resources to track a known killer in Manhattan, who'd been wandering close to the conference instead of calling as promised.

But Campbell ignored his swipe and played the bigger person. Thankfully, that role was wide open.

"George, I'm fighting this roadblock as best I can. Washington hasn't speeded up since you left as one of our finest interrogators."

George felt like telling Campbell to cut the bullshit and that the stress was showing but didn't have the heart. They were all struggling and, frankly, Emine's lead was a flimsy one since Khalil had just disappeared again. They'd already known he was in Manhattan so she'd merely verified that he hadn't left. Reluctantly, George accepted that their information was rapidly drying up. Did they know much more than they did yesterday? Well, actually yes but not enough to fix the problem and catch their wayward murderer.

Still, the most reassuring aspect of their stumbling was how close they kept coming to Khalil's path. Campbell was prattling on about something but George had stopped listening long ago. The apartment smelled like a Jewish deli and there was a flurry of activity, or so it sounded, coming from his kitchen.

"And we found Jennifer," Campbell was saying, which whipped George's attention back to where he'd left it. His brain was buzzing with stress and the sheer frustration of the situation but now he had a new focus and that somehow helped. Hope?

"Where? San Diego? Aruba?"

"Ha," Campbell responded, not even attempting to radiate real humor. Poor guy in the midst of bureaucratic hell. Though he'd done it to himself and probably had a killer pension when he inevitably lost his job for pushing past what was acceptable in his rule based offices.

"And she'll only talk to you. On the phone," Campbell answered the question he wanted to answer and delivered only as much information as he wanted George to know.

"You should run for office," George responded. Campbell ignored his comment.

"Here's the number and can you call her now, please?" George just shook his head. Part of him wanted to make a joke about whether or not he had security clearance to do so, etc, but there was something off about Campbell just reading him a 212 area code number, local, and not sending a squad to "protect/arrest" her so he let it go. We all do the best we can, he kept reminding himself.

Hanging up the phone he saw Emine coming at him, grim faced and brandishing half a bagel with lox and a big plate of food which he waved away. She took a bite and he noted how rarely she actually ate, usually preferring to push her food around her plate much like his wife. That was how these women stayed so thin. Emine was dressed in a baggy outfit of drapey khakis and a dark t-shirt but she looked so together and even elegent. A filmy bone silk scarf was wrapped around her shoulders and tiny earrings hung like bells. With almost no makeup she still had lashes that were so long and dark as to be just short of fake. Most women couldn't pull off a look that effortless while still seeming sophisticated. Perhaps her chic was in her DNA, that history of Riviera yachts and luxury. Then she smiled and George saw a flash of fear that she dropped into a flurry of words. They both knew that they were losing but neither was the type to acknowledge it.

"I was hungry," she started. "So I ordered one of everything, most of it hideously fattening," and there she left the fears and insecurities. He loved women who didn't nag or force but rather accepted that sometimes a man had priorities beyond them. Like the city. He let Emine head back to the kitchen, with her bagel and baggy pants, and only then did he dial Jennifer.

"Hello," a soft voice responded after the second ring. Like Emine she was a woman who could mostly pull off an act but was vulnerable enough to let her weaknesses show. He heard no fear or conflict in her voice though knew she must be going through a kaleidoscope of emotions. She'd left her life for Khalil and now seemingly she'd left Khalil. The love of her life? Well, she was a lawyer so he knew she'd have a story and some information to barter.

"Hi, Jennifer. It's George."

He still smelled Emine's food which reminded him that he'd bothered little with such mundane pleasures as of late. Well, the spread would have to wait as this woman might hold his fate, along with that of many others, nestled in her palms. What would she have to say? It was already 11:00 a.m. and time seemed to be speeding up just when he wanted it to slow down.

"Hello George," she replied then paused, seemingly waiting for something. Reassurance? He'd spent countless hours as a therapist and knew how not to prod, or scare away a hesitant confessor. She'd been so upset the last time he saw her, long blonde hair flying and mascara running down her lovely cheeks, that he especially didn't want to seem intimidating. Before, he'd tried to use her against Khalil and was now perhaps the weapon of her destruction or at least hopefully of Khalil's. Opening her Pandora's Box he'd seemingly swept Jennifer away into a world of high drama and great risk. Well, he hadn't forced her to go back to Khalil, just reintroduced them thus she'd have to own the consequences of that self destructive decision. People are all so fucked up at the end of the day. It kept him in business because sometimes they wanted to understand why or fix their neurosis. What did this woman want?"

"I learned Arabic, after he left the first time," she said, but hesitantly.

He still waited, letting her take whatever time she needed. He'd actually studied Catholic priests in confession to learn their secrets. The church had spent decades perfecting the art of drawing out incriminating information and manipulating the sinful. Mostly, people wanted to tell you, as if that confession absolved them of their guilt.

"He didn't realize at first so spoke freely on his phone," Jennifer's voice was slow, and he could hear her breath, a fluttering echo across the telephone line. Imagining her, the tense frame curled up to confess, he could hear her position in her tones. People don't realize that their voice reflects their pose; hunched up air would be constricted, and the voice would have a muffled, higher pitch.

His coffee was cold but he sipped it anyway, knowing she would hear him and be reassured that he was waiting patiently and thus she needn't feel a time pressure. He felt the clock however, but knew how to outwardly control his tension. In times of stress or fear people, like all mammals, resort to subtle physical signals and their response is based on how they evaluate that feedback. Subconscious, the response is often dependent as much on their own insecurities, which magnifies or minimizes their inputs and leads to a response. Someone trained in crisis situations, like Emine and Khalil, would know how to ignore their irrational responses yet draw on their more often correct instinctive feelings. And if trained correctly, their instincts would have been reinforced by sensing similarities and patterns from past crisis and thus staying alive, again. Jennifer wouldn't be so trained and would more likely be responding to his cues based on her emotions not her wiser subconscious gut feelings. He needed to guide her gently otherwise she'd be likely to either bolt or give him misguided information that she was incapable of evaluating correctly. She had to be traumatized somehow; otherwise, she'd still be with Khalil. George's time pressures weren't hers and he couldn't force them on her delicate psyche.

Whoever thought his job was easy was crazy. Subtle symbols are often the only indicator between truth and lies, and human lives rested on his ability to discern those differences. One wandering glance or missed verbal cue and he could blow a chance to figure out a terrorist plot. Jennifer's role thus far was a mystery and George knew that Campbell was giving him the first shot at interrogating her before the masses got involved. And the number involved down the road, ripping her privacy and life to shreds, would directly flow from whether or not he pulled the necessary information from her to stop Khalil, whatever the bastard was doing.

The fastest way someplace is often not a straight line. So George sucked down more coffee and ignored the smells wafting from his kitchen. He was wearing sheepskin slippers and the air conditioning was blasting, spreading a chill in the air. Americans were so used to controlling their environment that they confused such power in the broader world, where men were more often subject to a seemingly greater random plan. Jennifer had likely thought she could control Khalil but once you enter the cage of a tiger you relinquish reason to the blood thirsty instincts of a wild animal. Doubtless she'd learned that painful lesson by now as he himself knew its sting.

Jennifer's breathing was getting more labored and rapid and foretold tears by an instant. George noted movement and saw Emine delivering a new bigger plate of food. He gave her a warm smile and part of him felt fake and always "on" while another part was glad for that polish so she couldn't see his absolute terror at how fast time was moving independent of progress. He was relieved that she seemingly understood he was on an important call and didn't try to chat. He took a bite of the food so Jennifer could hear, then waded into her tears.

"I want to tell you a quick fable, Jennifer," he said the words softly to sound comforting, and used her name. He paused as if for a timid deer, first holding his hand out and letting her step forward before doing the same.

"Yes," she sobbed, after a brief hesitation, as expected. He took another bite of food to let her hear that he wasn't rushing forward. "A man walked up to a river and saw that the bridge had been washed away. He despaired as he needed to get to the market and sell some goods and the market only came once a week." George stopped.

"It's okay," Jennifer said. "You can continue." Her sobs had lightened but were still audible over the phone line. Poor foolish crazy woman.

"A crocodile swam up the bank and offered to give the man a ride across the river. The man protested, saying that the crocodile would eat him. The crocodile insisted that he wouldn't and only wanted to be paid a small sum for his efforts. So the man climbed on his back and as the crocodile started to eat him mid-point across the river protested that the crocodile had lied. 'But I'm a crocodile" was the response. 'Why did you think I would change my nature for a small coin?'"

George heard Jennifer's almost laugh; a chuckle mixed with a sob and knew that he'd reached her. Step one accomplished. Today was going to be a long one.

Confusion

halil could barely see through the foggy haze that stung his eyes. Tear gas was being sprayed on the massive number of protestors in front of the UN. The people had begun assembling early and, as always in the midst of a growing angry crowd, he'd been able to blend in. Camaraderie was more important than introductions and a background check. By noon the swarm was chanting and Khalil slipped away for a nap, returning with a few wet bandanas by 4:00. The Vice President should be arriving fairly soon and Khalil knew that the security guards wouldn't be happy to see this small army of disgruntled citizens. If they pulled out tear gas or pepper spray his sunglasses and a few well placed wet bandanas would dull the effect.

His rifle was at home but he'd brought a high powered hand gun, a black Austrian Glock, tucked into the waist of his pants and hidden under his loose t-shirt. While he would prefer to be tucked safely in the office they'd rented at the building across the street, with a scope and better chance of escape, once Khalil had seen the people begin to gather he'd known that plan wouldn't work.

The confusion would be intense, with the Vice President slipping in quickly and being dropped as close to the entrance as possible to avoid the masses. Politicians always did that when confronted with angry constituents. And the Americans were angry these days. The signs and placards would be further variables blocking a clean and successful shot.

So Khalil had come with a smaller but still powerful gun and would try to get close to the man himself as he slunk from limousine to assembly hall. Then he'd try to disappear into the crowd before getting killed in turn by a body guard or security officer. Somehow he doubted that his fellow protestors would shelter him from the repercussions of his shot. In this country the demonstrations were still peaceful but as in all such situations that line was a fine one to cross. Violence gives little fair warning and he couldn't predict their response to his actions.

The ideal outcome would be for the security detail to fire into the crowd in hot or irrational pursuit. And he was, after all, assassinating the man one step away from a presidency.

Khalil pulled his wet bandana tighter across his mouth and nose. Seeing a young whore in ripped jean shorts choking he handed her one and gestured at putting it over her face. She did so and waved at him, a friendly American whore who was now at least respectfully covering her face if not her legs. The world was a dangerous place and women should be more careful before entering into it so freely.

"Watch out, they're getting ready to spray more tear gas," a young man with a megaphone shouted out, standing on a bench. He was tall and lean, but built powerfully. Even from a distance, Khalil could make out his vivid green eyes tinged with red from the gas and he was waving a white towel, in surrender or defiance. Like most young people there he was dressed casually which on him was loose jeans and a charcoal t-shirt.

Khalil watched the police who appeared poised to attack the protestors again. Signs decried corruption, bankers and the rich. But mostly they were solution free and just expressed anger. The scene was clearly more peaceful than Cairo with the crowd smaller and no tanks in sight. Much of the world was simply furious and willing to shout out that rage. Meanwhile, he was happy to exploit it and instability could only help his cause. One thing Islamists weren't was visibly rich. No, they espoused old values and piety, mixed with moderation in all things, including wealth.

While not sleeping, Khalil had pondered the situation here in the States versus that in Cairo and had numerous thoughts as to why these people weren't happy. He was tempted to start some conversations and probe his theories but unfortunately couldn't spare the time or attention and was mentally on edge waiting. For, Osman, miraculous Osman, hadn't been able to find out the Vice President's exact arrival time. His charge had been able to track the Vice President's plane by hacking into the air traffic controllers' frequency thus Khalil had an educated guess but no certainty. He'd added in traffic and a range of other variables then arrived early to wait.

Khalil also didn't want to be remembered so he kept to himself.

Was America over? These people around him, shouting at the world, seemed to believe so. A corrupt system in which the rich exploited the rest of society? He'd been saying that for years and now finally it seemed at least some Americans were listening. Such was always the point of power, to grab more by those who could, so why should the masses blame the elite for doing so? Once a man begins chosing money over God there was never enough to quench his greed.

Khalil had grown up in a corrupt country and knew the feelings of a child in poverty with no hope of creating a better life. The hopelessness had driven some friends to jihad and often martyrdom. Most had lived lives of quiet desperation instead, becoming old men before forty and speaking softly so they weren't overheard. One had become a police officer after his father bought the rare spot through a bribe. That friend was rich now and part of the system that kept looting Algeria. Khalil's own father had bought him little and expected undying gratitude for whatever scraps he threw at his ex-wife and ex-children, preferring to spend on his girlfriends instead. Scum.

So he'd learned, like these people shouting around him, that the only hope for a poor man was to take fate into his own hands and fight back. During the French Revolution the aristocrats had gone to the guillotine rather than repent their corrupt ways and share what they'd stolen from the peasants. History repeats, endlessly. Now he just needed to wait for the Vice President and link this protest with a real revolutionary act, an assassination. They'd thank him one day.

The air was clearing and Khalil could see much better without tear gas. The half circular driveway to the complex was off limits to the protestors but they could go up to the edge of the pavement. Khalil moved closer; the shot wouldn't be easy but he was skilled enough to make it. Disciplining his mind, he scanned the area, noting the location of every guard and police officer. It seemed they had stopped spraying tear gas which could be a sign that the VP was close. Khalil watched as the guards emptied out a cluster of people by sending them to the emergency room, making the protests look smaller. Then they let the air clear to hide their culpability. Governments were the same everywhere, even those who loudly trumpeted human rights. As with the slaves on these shores a hundred years ago most people preferred to look the other way.

"Hi, come here often?" a soft, husky voice asked and Khalil turned, deliberately slowly, so appraise who was speaking. It was the girl to whom he'd given the wet bandana and she was both smiling and waving. He grinned back, knowing to act so as not to look suspicious. This new face seemed to attract American whores much as thankfully he'd seemingly lost his tails on these golden shores. Finally.

"First time," he responded and saw how pretty she was, with wide hazel eyes and freckles scattered across her nose. Young and probably in her early twenties she had bright teeth and a little top barely hiding her flat stomach.

"It's a great crowd. They all care so much about the future of this country," she replied and gave him a sideways wink. He never understood these women, flirtatious and so bold! Not like in his homeland where the girls wouldn't respond to a stranger let alone go up to one on the street and begin a conversation. Well, who knew what happened in Algiers these days but his memories harked back to another time.

"What do you care about?" he asked and saw another smile. In another context he'd like the attention but not today. She really was a very lovely thing and utterly without shame.

"Buy me dinner and I'll tell you," she responded and her little belly moved with her words and the soft in out of her breath. It was so flat and he could see blonde fuzz, lightly sprinkled but still perceptible across lean muscles.

During school Khalil had read about it all, the power and powerful, the games and the bargaining. Life was about the survival of the fittest. Normally, he'd take this girl up on her offer and see how far she'd be willing to go after dinner. He could imagine pulling up her shirt and sucking on one of those small nipples visible through thin cotton. But tonight he had to kill someone and wasn't much interested in the evolution of life.

"I can't," he replied. "I already have plans." And he turned away, gazing back at the entry way to the United Nations looking for his evening date. Hopefully, she'd wander off and leave him alone. Then again, if she stayed around he could use her as a shield. Women never seemed to understand when it was better to just let a man call the shots. Luckily this one took the blow-off for what it was and stalked off to find other prey. Khalil was glad; she was a cute little thing and he didn't want to have to kill her.

Breakfast....Food....

mine had learned a lot talking to Fred and his partner Jose over eggs and a full spread of accompaniments. George had been on the phone since early morning. The government was worried, didn't have enough information and was looking for someone to blame. Increasingly, George was becoming that person.

In life, volunteering was the quickest way to get shot when something went wrong. It was also the best way to ensure that something important got done since the bigger the risk the less likely it was that someone else would volunteer.

Thus she was on George's side. So were Fred and Jose (being men of action themselves they were natural supporters for George's brave willingness to wade into high level national security even when he wasn't getting paid to do so).

"So what do we do?" Emine asked.

"Find Khalil. Arrest him. Preferably before someone dies," Fred replied. He was the friendlier one which meant he actually answered questions. Jose mostly just frowned and nodded, holding back and careful as befit his role. A large and powerfully built man, Emine could picture Jose in whatever Special Forces had trained him, perhaps only letting down his guard with friends and family. His looks were classic Latin, with full lips and dusky dark eyes. His smile was vibrant though she'd only glimpsed it once.

Jose typically wore jeans and a button down shirt while Fred preferred baggy t-shirts and crisp jeans or khakis. Both were the ultimate polite professionals and Emine respected them for their ever vigilent dedication to protecting George and helping her. Now however she was thrilled when they let their guard slip and she enjoyed how the two, who obviously knew each other well, joked and smiled. Their situation needed all the levity it could get. Jose was loosening up as they talked over the spread of food. You took what you could get in life.

Speaking of which, Bud had been texting her all day. He'd stopped in Cairo en route to his greater travels and met with Bright to get her an update.

The violence continued to build in Egypt and the country was rapidly spiraling into total uncertainty as the people waited, tense, for the upcoming elections. Food shortages had become rampant and expectations for a new President were running high. Bright hadn't been allowed to print a story on his Aswan experiences but other journalists hadn't displayed such scruples and, thanks to their reports combined with his earlier broadcast video, the whole world knew that the dam had almost blown. That disclosure had only made the chaos worse.

"I love you," Bud kept texting, but Emine just joked back. He'd said it so many times over the years only to ignore her for months on end. Then there were all those other girls! Sure, men expressed love differently than women did but come on!

Still, he seemed lonely today as he went from meeting to meeting and kept her phone busy with his stream of consciousness and rants of devotion and love. Emine had first met Bud when she was twelve and he was thirteen, and she could still picture the boy he was before the phone and job. Both attending the same Swiss boarding school, deserted and high up on a steep mountain clustered amidst tall trees. He made her smile. The school had been the type to which parents send their kids when they wanted them far away.

Bud had been her brother Selim's best friend, which meant he was up for any and all trouble though somehow he'd managed to survive seemingly unscathed. They both almost got expelled a number of times but kept their school slots through continual large parental donations. Sending rich children off alone with big allowances and strict supervision only teaches them devious ways of avoiding the law. Little outside love means that while the atmosphere can resemble the *Lord of the Flies*, kids also develop deep familial bonds amongst themselves. Emine had stood lookout for the boys many a time, when they drank, smoked and then got into drugs.

Bud also apparently didn't have the addictive personality which seemed to run in her family.

Taller, and strong, he'd seemed like a vision from another planet when she first evaluated him, sporting tanned skin from a summer outside and utter self confidence. He'd told her then, at their first meeting, that he loved her and always would. The game had initially been confusing until it lost all meaning and she barely heard his proclamations anymore. Occasionally he even proposed but usually he'd been drinking. Today he was being overbearing which probably meant he was very bored or had just dumped another girlfriend. Commitment issues.

"Run away with me" he texted.

"I need to work," she responded.

Words and empty promises were just a distraction and she was in crisis mode. Still, his updates on Cairo were better than what she'd find in the newspapers or online and for those she was greatful. If KK was the target then his death would be an utter disaster for Egypt. Impatient for a resolution she wondered why things wouldn't move faster and could barely wait to hear an update from George, the pulse of information.

So she kept listening to his guards and hoping to learn something new. George walked into the kitchen surprising them all.

He looked rested, though she could see a faint darkness of shadows under his eyes. George was the type who obviously thrived when the shit hit the fan. A few people do and she'd studied the phenomena once, in an attempt to understand her warlord interviewees. They seemed to love the mayhem of battle and kept the tension up even in their camps. She suspected that this predelection came from trauma and a lack of stability or predictability in childhood. Essentially, most people are soothed by reminders of the constancy of their youth; in contrast these other sorts only felt comforted when thrown into chaos (as in their childhood). It was why some societies had such a hard time returning to stability; their population couldn't cope and subconciously did their best to wreck that calm and return to anarchy.

"What was your childhood like, George?" she asked and saw all three men whip their eyes toward her in astonishment. Then George laughed.

"You want to discuss that now?" he asked, his eyes twinkling. She noted that he didn't answer her question.

"I guess we're in charge of defusing the bomb that is Khalil," George responded, deflecting, casually and with smooth grace. So why did he lose his head in battle if he was the master of self control? Someday she'd make him open up about the forces that had shaped him, but they didn't have time today. No, bigger issues were commandeering their time and attention.

But first she had another pancake drowning in syrup to enjoy as she watched George walk out again and back to his telephone, juggling another piece of omelet and some rye toast.

Careers

"George, I may lose my job for telling you this but I'm willing to take that risk. Of all the crazy things I've seen over the years your current predicament stands alone," Campbell's tone sounded different and George struggled to figure out how. He'd phoned Campbell to discuss his conversation with Jennifer and pass on her insights, a mix of the mundane and the shocking. He'd paused briefly, after she hung up, taking his plate of food and exuberant mood back to his green couch for contemplation. She was willing to help them! Who knew how effective her input would be but after getting dejected with the lack of progress, George was hoping that his luck was now changing.

Emine had been waiting in the steel room, all chrome and a little marble, another one of Karen's impeccably tasteful creations. She'd been chatting with his guards and they'd all looked surprisingly relaxed. Then again, no one had yet mentioned that their back up support was stuck in bureaucratic hell. George ate with the group for a minute, tried to joke, and then poured himself a coffee refill. Someone had thankfully made more as it tasted fresh, though he hadn't noticed the beans' loud grinding in his machine. He sipped the hot liquid greedily, suddenly losing interest in his food and enjoying the caffeine surge.

"I need to call HQ," he said and ventured a smile. Emine was perched on his sleek counter, next to the double-door sub zero and looking worried. She was such an enigma one moment and then so evident another.

He ignored her and headed back to his bear's den with its velvet couch and well-worn phone.

Now Campbell seemed ready to throw yet another loop, as if the day wasn't tough enough. George just gulped down more coffee, stretched out his legs and wondered what principle was important enough for Campbell to risk his job.

"They're thinking of taking you into detention," Campbell said and George choked, the hot coffee spilling up through his nostrils and on his yellow polo shirt. Detention! He didn't reply but waited for his ex-boss to continue. The government had Karen. Was she now no longer in a witness protection program but rather in detention too? And his kids! Poor Nicolas and Natalie.

"You know that since the Defense Appropriations Bill voted it into law last year we can take any suspected terrorist, even citizens, into indefinite custody?"

"With no due process," George responded curtly. "I know."

"Well, there's concern that you and Khalil seem too tight and with too many related coincidences. Couple that with the work you're doing with Emine, an old friend of Khalil's now dead suicide bomber buddy, and the government has started getting concerned. They think Khalil tipped you off about Aswan to bolster your credibility but it increased suspicions instead."

"I used to work for the government until Khalil shot me!"

"But you lived; he could have shot better being a trained killer who knows how to aim a bullet. Additionally, you helped to set up the conditions that led to his escape. Then, no sooner do you arrive in Cairo but you're holed up with Khalil."

"I was his prisoner!"

"But again he doesn't kill you even when rescuers storm the building. Now you're one of the few who can identify his new face and he just walked away from that house without putting up any fight. He even sends you coffee in Manhattan! Risky for a smart guy like that."

"You're saying that he has a reason to keep me alive?"

"And to talk to you."

"Well, it could just be a Stockholm syndrome thing; prisoners often bond with their wardens. I'm probably the only one who didn't torture him and he's lonely now that he broke up with his girlfriend," George said, trying to keep the sarcasm from his voice but knowing he hadn't.

"I've told you before the US government doesn't torture prisoners," Campbell responded mechanically. "But we can't be responsible for what our allies do, though we exert all reasonable efforts to ensure that they honor the Geneva Convention."

"Bullshit. He was in Egyptian custody before we took him, and tortured. No wonder he doesn't like their old government."

George looked at his food but by now had lost all appetite so he pushed it away and nursed his black, still warm coffee.

"George, let's not argue about Khalil right now. Your safety is my concern. You're now a suspected terrorist conspirer. I don't believe it but others do."

George had to admit that Campbell's narrative made sense in a very odd and dysfunctional way. He scratched his chin. Yes, Campbell might lose his job for sharing this information since it bordered on treason if George really was a double agent. Yet Campbell had obviously seen the insanity behind the logic and had decided to follow his moral compass and not a set of generic rules. Today, sometimes in government, it was hard to get credit for doing the right thing but Campbell was proof that some people tried. George had seemingly bumbled into indefinite detention for himself, and God forbid, his family. What to do?

Ask Campbell.

"Serious?"

"Very." Hmm. Campbell was the epitome of reason under pressure and an expert at channeling hysteria. Indeed, sometimes the latter function seemed to be his main job responsibility. George burrowed deeper into his plush couch and glanced around the room. He wondered if this would be his last view for a while. Well, no bother, he'd never much liked this apartment anyway. Karen's floating island but never his, though on the run hadn't been how he'd envisioned leaving.

411

"What do I do?" he asked his savior, deferring to his boss' more complex understanding of the situation. But how much did he trust Campbell? George, ever paranoid about the motives of other men, what with his lines of work, found that he couldn't answer his own question.

"Do you have cash?" Campbell asked.

"Yes."

"Then I'd go for a walk and look for Khalil. Take only Emine and not your guards but only if you trust her. She seems to have a nose for that bastard. Find him, stop him and then go back home. I don't envy you; I'll try to stall your arrest."

George heard Campbell hang up and wondered how long the call had really lasted. Feeling like forever, as with any moment you hear something that drastically changes your life for the worse as time takes on a new meaning. Suddenly no longer a friend, your mind must adjust to the clock's new more ominous ticks and tocks. Once, George had felt invincible as success and a stable life can encourage. After being the first in his family to attend college he'd thrived in his ivory tower. Then he'd gone out into the bigger world and had taken on the sorts of problems that people get killed trying to resolve. Perhaps he should have stayed in that aerie and not listened to the siren calling him into battle.

But he had and wasn't the type to get reflective when he had important actions to take. He'd deal with the related emotions in therapy after defusing Khalil. First, he needed to leave fast. Cash. Yes, credit cards were too track-able, but so was his government issued cell phone. He studied it, a glistening screen against the deep wood table. He'd like to be able to stay in touch but it would betray his location and perhaps lead him straight into a jail cell. Well, he could always come back to the apartment if he really needed the cell.

George stood up and took a step toward his bedroom with the safe holding stacks of cash and a clean shirt. Stopping as quickly as he'd started he wondered at Emine. Could he trust her? She'd been Omar's friend, the boy who was Khalil's last known suicide bomber. George took a deep in-breathe and then exhaled, willing his heart to slow down so he could reason more clearly. He was now going to be operating almost entirely on instinct and judgment. Did he trust her?

Picturing Emine's tiger's eyes and that reluctant smile he remembered her hesitation and control while sitting with her father. In life, she could have turned anti-establishment with a strongly political and controlling parent like that. But instead she reminded him of Mehmet, manipulative and able to pull the quieter levers of power, staying calm while dealing with crisis. Someone with those connections and that level of self-discipline didn't need to lob bombs from behind a mask.

He'd have to trust her. George needed help and had no one else while she had an uncanny ability to find Khalil. They were so close with a little luck they'd get Khalil in time as the noose was now around his neck and tightening. If they could find its rope they'd pull the loop tight.

Suddenly George remembered that Campbell hadn't asked him to discuss all of Jennifer's information. Had his boss done so on purpose, or had time to get George moving been limited? So for now Jennifer's insights were his alone unless their earlier call had been bugged.

George took money and grabbed a sweater for evening even though the day already looked hot outside his air-conditioned apartment. Better to be prepared. Emine was still in the kitchen chatting with Fred over coffee while the other guard was back in his hallway nook. George gestured to her and she followed him out the door.

"Where?" she asked, looking curious but not concerned. He just shook his head, unsure if the elevator was bugged. Once in the street he stopped her.

"The government wants to arrest me instead of sending reinforcements. We need to find Khalil ourselves and stop him."

She just gaped at him.

"I'm going to do it. Are you coming?" He asked her roughly, knowing that if she wasn't tough enough for the days to come he'd be better off leaving her now. But she nodded and followed when he headed down the street toward downtown.

Luckily she didn't ask what his plan was since he didn't have one.

Security

Security was standing taller now, and they were clustering around the entrance, their eyes more focused. The Vice President's car must be getting closer. The crowds had been forced into the circular driveway, and Khalil was next to the fountain, which formed the whole of the concrete donut hole. He'd assumed that the protestors would be forced off the main street or traffic would have been shut down. Nope. As the demonstration was peaceful right now, the troublemakers having been removed, the police were letting it happen mostly unhindered. Khalil had worried at the difficulty of the shot earlier, and wondered if he'd even get that chance. Now it looked like a certainty.

What he hadn't decided was how close to thrust forward: any distance made success less likely but escape easier. He fondled the Glock, tucked up against his hard belly with its safety on. Warm now from his body, it was his one partner left. Osman he'd left at home and the others were dead. Bullets are more reliable than people.

The cheers and jeers got louder as the protestors seemingly sensed the arrival of someone important. Most arrivals had been in the morning but Khalil could now see that a dark town car was turning into the driveway. Two men waving signs stepped out in front of the car, blocking it. They were a wonderful distraction and had the windows of the car not been shaded Khalil would have headed in their direction and started shooting while the car was stopped.

One sign said, *Fight Corruption of the Elite*. The other said, *End Wall Street*. The men were shouting and waving at the crowd to join them in blocking what was presumably the Vice President's car. They probably didn't realize whom the auto was ferrying, being more concerned with being heard than in identifying who heard and whether they cared.

Khalil surveyed the crowd, trying to sense its mood. Always be aware of your surroundings, especially when taking a big risk. The day was hot and the air humid. A human smell had built during the day, from sweat and detergent, perfumes and whatever people had eaten. Most were lightly dressed to accommodate the temperature. More male than female, both sexes were still well represented in the 250 or so people who'd been stewing under the sun and waiting for something to happen. And isn't that how most people behave?

Too bad he didn't have matches. A small fire would be a wonderful precursor to the big event and would draw eyes away from his gun. But Khalil didn't seem to be thinking of these great possibilities until the last minute lately. Bad.

He tucked himself closer to the grey fountain as he surveyed his surroundings once again. The cement was warm through his pant leg and he felt a soft dusting of water, little drops that touched him ever so gently.

The people here were waiting and full of anticipation but they weren't seemingly desperate in mood. Few of them were as hungry physically, while their souls were more lost. He sensed a desire for change but a lack of mission. It was this exact moment in the crowds that he loved the best. If time and place were different he'd try to lead them, demonstrating the actual steps needed to make a revolution work. Only when the powers that be see that a crowd will use violence do they take them seriously, hence something must burn or blowup or an important man must die.

So perhaps Khalil was indeed leading a new American revolution forward. One could only hope. He saw the girl who'd spoken to him earlier climbing onto the town car, her legs lean and the muscles visible with the effort. She was knocked off by a police officer and her crowd members shouted in protest. A photographer with a large camera, probably a professional, was taking numerous pictures. The car was inching toward the entryway to the building, not knocking people over but letting their natural caution keep them just far enough away so that the vehicle could make its slow progress.

Khalil inched closer and grasped the gun handle, sliding his hand up his shirt and feeling the hard pistol, warm from his own body heat. He felt the adrenaline rush that he'd learned from past experience, the world around him moving slower and with more clarity, yet as if in a dream. The protestors were following the car in and closer to the main entrance, where Khalil would expect the Vice President to head. The crowd must have had some sort of leak with respect to the black car's occupant; either that or the mob just had an instinctive blood lust lying in wait for an officious appearance.

Distance and time were closing in and Khalil was increasingly concerned with the crowd as it contracted around the car. Extra bodies were okay as long as they didn't block a clear shot. His aim was one man and any related deaths were mere additional unbelievers sacrificed on Allah's alter.

The town car slowed and then came to a stop at the UN's main entrance, as Khalil had predicted. Quickly clustering around the passenger side door a bevy of large bulky men formed a wall, but it wasn't dense enough to stop someone with Khalil's prowess. He'd just take out anyone blocking him. As long as he was quick with successive shots only the best-trained guards with impeccable instincts could take any defensive actions.

Khalil began to remove his gun but felt a fleeting doubt. Trusting his instincts he did a quick scan around, figuring he had exactly five seconds to spot a threat before he'd need to take his shots and deal with the results.

And he saw her. The girl with the amber eyes, glowing in the sunlight as if she was lighted from within. Next to her was George. For a brief second he wondered if he should just shoot at them; the girl was seemingly doing a better job of tracking him than the professionals, though perhaps she was a professional as she was with George. That television show cover seemed too pat to be true anyway.

No.

He looked back in time to see the Vice President disappear inside the UN Headquarters, his hair a silvery glimmer in the sunlight, and dense men making up his rear guard. Shit! Khalil was hesitating and losing each and every chance. To be fair, he was improvising and hadn't been meant to be the gunman in the first place. Nonetheless, Khalil wondered whether he'd lost his edge. A hesitant man is a dead man. So he watched George and the girl wander away, as if they'd just been passing by on the way elsewhere. This city was too small for both Khalil and George so how was he going to resolve that conflict?

Water or Fluidity

mine was wandering the streets of New York in a daze, and following George as if he knew where he was going. All the coffee in the world hadn't been enough. George now a wanted man? For consorting with Khalil? Should she even entertain the possibility that the government was right? He did seem to have the oddest relationship with his stalker-ex-prisoner. George seemed to be a good man with the best intentions but the greatest double agents usually did.

Now they were going to see Jennifer who was an ex-girlfriend-ex? These relationships were so convoluted they reminded Emine of her own love life. Vaguely she sensed that her eyes were missing something obvious but her mind was too muddled to make sense of the gut feeling.

Walking past the crowded UN Headquarters, Emine felt her eyes drawn to the river. It was used so little in terror campaigns, unlike in wars where it became a decisive battlefield. She could smell the people and their rhythmic chanting seemed more reminiscent of a sermon than a protest. The collective mood of a crowd always veered off eventually into a religious unity of purpose. Who knew ultimately what these Americans really wanted but it was likely a mix of reason and crazy hope

"Let's get through this quickly before Jennifer changes her mind and no longer wants to help us," George said, interrupting her thoughts.

"God put it on our route so perhaps we're meant to be here?" Emine replied, surprising even herself. Sure she was a believer but at a very tenuous level and had certainly never felt God spoke to her. Then again, Turkey was both mystical and superstitious as are most ancient places. Too much had happened over the centuries to attribute it merely to man and reason. Indeed, even younger Manhattan had its Gods.

George stopped and stared. Emine gave him a half smile then turned away to survey the crowd. Nothing. She took out her phone and snapped a few pictures. The American Vice President was getting out of a black town car and the crowd was chanting hateful things. Then she grabbed her camera with the telephoto lens and got a few shots of the crowd threatening the car. After a few pictures she faced George again.

"What are we going to do?" she asked. George still looked so cool and calm, in the hot sun and not knowing if he was to soon be arrested or if his family was safe. His sky blue t-shirt and khakis were pristine and he'd slipped on aviator sunglasses with murky blue lenses. He watched her and she felt judgment, which made sense in that George would realize he couldn't afford any weak links.

"Let's go," was his only response and so Emine hurried to keep up with George's fast strides, his legs cutting through the crowds and grey of the cement. Clear action requires little explanation? No, not really but what the fuck, right? She didn't have any other plans and as long as George (or Khalil) didn't kill her she could always write a book about this day.

Emine pulled her eyes from the UN and scampered after George through the crowded streets. Even in the hot summer sun Manhattan-ites were sheathed in black and business suits. Still, here and there were the bright flowery sundresses and even shorts that signaled the season. Emine's eye's followed a sleek blonde who was striding purposefully through the concrete jungle in stilettos with shorts, cute yet not so practical. Emine felt the utility of her work clothes and realized that they were more suited to the Arab Spring than New York. Once a war journalist always a Chanel refugee.

Not that she didn't have bigger issues to address.

George stopped in front of a plain-faced building with a small hotel sign and two stars next to the name. Why he'd chosen to walk instead of grabbing a cab she couldn't begin to guess. As much as she was in a fog he seemed to be in a cool haze. The feeling of being fugitives was proving a far cry removed from how they'd woken, as the pursuers.

More cabs drove by, and people passed. The loud sirens of the city mixed with a jackhammer and Emine smelled hot pretzels, reminding her of too much. She coughed as a man walked by waving his cigarette and discussing the Fed with a bevy of younger suited boys. "They need to get more involved again and hopefully the Fed will surprise us with more intervention soon!". George checked his Blackberry and ignored everything, including her.

Then he looked up and she saw his peaceful smile.

"Ready?" he asked. Emine nodded, not wanting to answer because then she'd either have to lie or say no.

"I *won't back down. You can stand me up at the gates of hell but I won't back down*," George said and she saw humor in his eyes. She shrugged in bewilderment.

"Tom Petty," he said. "A singer." Emine just nodded.

"No," she finally said and tried to smile. George grabbed her wrist and a woman walking by swiveled to evaluate for danger. Big cities. Emine waved her away.

"We'll figure it out," he told her and staring into his clear grey eyes she believed him. A phone began to ring and Emine watched George as he pulled his out of a pocket. "Campbell," he said and took the call. She pulled out her own phone and started looking through the photos, listening all the while.

"I'm taking care of a few things." Pause. "I know." Pause. "Yes." Then she saw it: with the American next in line as a backdrop Khalil stared in the foreground straight at her. She glanced briefly up at George, still on his phone and looking annoyed. Instantly she knew what she needed to do. George helping Khalil? Bullshit. He was a good man putting himself and his family at risk. Growing up with a half crazy father who shared the same idealistic bent she knew the destructive choices such men left in their wake. You can't try to save the world and care for your family at the same time. She was a byproduct of that refuse pile.

So she quickly typed a message explaining the photograph and emailed it to Bright. He'd know how to get the right spotlight for that terrorist bastard to lose any possible hiding places. The Vice President! Thankfully Khalil hadn't done anything. Just as when she'd missed in real life what had happened in front of her eyes as George was kidnapped she'd now caught Khalil too close to an important man. Again, after KK and the Four Seasons' cameras found him lurking there. Technology's eyes catch what human ones miss.

Would Bright mis-use the information? Perhaps. But if he helped pull the rope closer around Khalil's neck she could live with the repercussions.

Emine felt sweat streaming down her back and was glad to see that George was off his call and heading into what was hopefully an air-conditioned building.

Behind them a siren screamed, getting closer quickly and Emine jumped. She turned to see an ambulance drive by, slowly attempting to make its way past a traffic signal. Thankfully, it wasn't the police looking for George. She glanced over but he'd ignored the whole spectacle.

The waited for an elevator, still not speaking, in the shabby lobby. The lift came quickly and Emine could only stare at the cream and burgundy patterned wallpaper as George pressed the button for the fifth floor. The silence was comfortable mainly because they both had a lot of information to process so perhaps she was merely distracted. Should they be discussing the limited facts and reasoning out a strategy for this interview? Suddenly a thought hit Emine.

"Khalil was in a photo at the UN, with the Vice President getting out of his car in the background." George's eyes flew open as she spoke, his eyelids rising. To his credit he calmly asked, "Can I see the photo?"

Emine pulled out her phone and handed it to him. The creaks of the elevator were slowing and she was glad they were alone. Too much to hide or explain otherwise to people not authorized to hear anything. George studied the picture.

"I sent it to Bright," she continued, timid but certain. He'd approve? And George just nodded, handing it back as the elevator doors opened with a bell signaling arrival. She stepped into a hallway with cheap paint and a "Hotel" sign outside an open door. A man greeted them and Emine let George do the talking as he asked for Jennifer.

"Room 505," was the response and Emine watched the man puff his cigarette, wispy trails of his smoke floating around his black hair. Small and compact, he barely mustered words and certainly didn't aspire to emotions. In the background he was watching a South American soccer match and a black and spotty brown dog was curled at his feet. The man gazed up and down her body and Emine felt the judgment but turned her back on his black eyes and mottled skin. As if she cared.

George headed back into the hallway, which wasn't secured through the hotel office but rather open to all, thus providing extra privacy for the occupants. If Khalil had once stayed here with Jennifer Emine could see the allure of the careless security as being watched could work in two directions.

Oh dear, Emine almost tripped on a rip in the carpet. Jennifer opened the door surprisingly quickly when George knocked and Emine saw her for the first time. Sleek, but not sophisticated, she looked like a rounder Barbie doll with big sapphire eyes. Her smile was hesitant and she'd clearly been crying. Jennifer just stared at George, ignoring Emine. Then again, she'd met him before and he was the crux of this investigation.

"It's KK," Jennifer whispered. "I thought Thursday but now I just don't know." The tears started anew and Emine watched as Jennifer shoved a stack of loose papers at George.

"I can't help anymore. Please?"

George took the papers and nodded. Then he turned and guided Emine out the door. She'd missed their earlier phone conversation so decided to trust that he knew what he was doing. After all, they did have more information now than even moments before. Her hands ached to dig through the papers but she controlled her impulses and continued mirroring his, expecting they'd pore through the sheaves once outside.

The mutt barked when they re-entered the creaky elevator but Emine ignored its yapping. She checked her email on the way down and saw that Bright had posted the picture of Khalil with the Vice President on the front page of all his newspaper and channel web sites. Or so he claimed in an email response to her.

The shit was hitting the fan all around them. What next?

Names

urned out George hadn't been able to leave his cell at his apartment much as it also acted as a tracking device. Wise or not, he'd face arrest before he lost control of his communications. He'd

now spent time in the streets on the phone, free still, so thus far his risky bet seemed to be paying off. Campbell had promised George he'd work to get government attention focused away from George and back onto Khalil or at least to stall George's detention, seemingly a prudent course of action since one was trying to kill while the other was trying to stop him. Taking George into custody at this stage of affairs seemed insane but perfectly consistent with how bureaucracies work: find someone to blame instead of solving the real problem.

But at least Jennifer had given them a name: KK, though she was less sure of date and knew little about where and how. "A lot of possibilities were discussed. Khalil left me before the final decision was made," she'd muttered. Seemed a lot of truth in the aphorism that hell has no fury like a woman scorned. For an instant George wondered at what his own wife was up to, hidden away in government custody, and hoped she was all right.

George glanced over at Emine, sipping at a bottle of cold water and tapping on her phone maniacally in the blazing sun. She'd reconnected with the no longer eerily silent Bright and they were planning a media blitz on Khalil. George liked the more active side of his still actual boss, one of the two masters to whom he was currently reporting, not trusting any alpha male who went silent for too long. Realistically George knew his government contacts would likely be furious but in this case he was siding with the media. Annoying at times, prying and quick to conclusion when it suited them, the free press was also able to apply public pressure to expose what someone, anyone, was trying to hide. And Bright had a lot of smart lawyers on staff helping him walk that delicate line. Someone needed to alert the public that a lethal terrorist with a gun was on the loose in Manhattan; based on the inconsequential number of NYPD at the UN building George was increasingly convinced that DC was keeping information tight to the capital and, predictably, not alerting the local mayor or police chief.

George started paging through the papers Jennifer had handed him and saw that she'd kept meticulous notes based on the calls of Khalil's she'd overheard. Amazing! And lucky her boyfriend hadn't caught her. He glanced at Emine but she was still conspiring with Bright so he didn't give her a stack but rather scanned them alone. If only he'd had these papers days or even weeks ago. The plot unfolded before him but it was all predicated on the boy who Khalil had likely killed taking the shot. Then the notes ended in uncertainty. He'd have to hand them over to someone who had the leisure to read in detail and draw more nuanced conclusions or theories since he himself didn't have time now. For the shot was supposed to occur at the dinner, about to start tonight, and not Thursday. Jennifer just hadn't known the date of the dinner so hadn't realized that she had the answer all along, instead originally believed Khalil's statements about timing. Once a crocodile...

George wasn't sure how to handle this mess and glanced over at Emine. Was she his only support? He could see further suspicion falling on him if he "miraculously" got hold of Jennifer's notes right now, if that's what the government wanted to believe. Or, they could realize that their theory about him working with Khalil was crazy and provide the backup support he needed. Which risk was George prepared to take?

Emine was holding up well. Used to roughing it she was quite a trooper and her smile was more ready than it had been before they'd recently gotten closer. The day was stifling and soft sweat dusted her face. Otherwise no stress was visible as she chatted on her white phone and sipped slowly, legs spread out in front of their bench, and all of it shaded by a tree. They had nowhere else to go. Yet. Not until Campbell solved the multiple problems of getting back up support in New York and persuading whomever it was that wanted to call George in for questioning that their timing was very bad indeed.

Jennifer hadn't looked so well. Stress was etched in her every line and the pastiness of her complexion. He'd noted red webbing in the white of her eyes and deep shadows underneath them. Her blonde hair was stringy and she'd pulled it into a loose ponytail, achieving sloppiness not nonchalance. The hotel had been just clean, barely, with threadbare furnishings and cheap doors. People who romanticized life on the run would benefit from a thorough study of those who did it. Any hotel that didn't ask basic questions of its patrons wasn't running the place for lifestyle reasons or comforts.

George looked down at his hands and noted overgrown nails and deep creased lines. He hadn't spent much time studying his own reflection but suspected that he'd fall closer to Jennifer than Emine. At his age hiding stress, and not letting it kill you, was increasingly more of a chore. But he'd chosen to start interrogations realizing some of his detainees would prove to be more than that, with the resulting implications implicit in getting to know a terrorist.

"Now what?" Emine asked, suddenly alert to him and not her phone. He didn't have an answer but as the "leader" of this mission from hell he couldn't admit that. *Fuck if I know* wasn't an answer that inspired confidence.

"We're waiting to hear back from Campbell. You heard; I told him KK was the one and he's trying to get a team out here so we aren't the only ones actively trying to stop the bastard." George smiled, recognizing the anger in his words and the futility of fighting. Except he planned on continuing to fight, with every last breath. Bitterness could come later, if he didn't stop Khalil. With Jennifer's information there was now a set target and potential time so no one could later say they weren't forewarned. The name, time and place made the information concrete and he'd texted it to Campbell a few minutes ago, not wanting to speak or mention Jennifer's papers.

"So let's head back to the UN building where KK should be. No point in waiting for Khalil to show up here visiting the woman he ditched."

"Again!" Emine said brightly and he saw her effort. Yes, this situation had gotten wearing for them both and honestly George wanted more than a bottle of water sold by a street vendor. "Let's find some caffeine en route," he said, standing.

The city looked the same but he was thinking differently, more determined after Jennifer's inputs. Here, the tall buildings and wide grey avenues were bursting with activity and cascading colors. People moved with purpose, intent on getting somewhere, if only to the next corner. Yellow taxis flashed by while everyone seemed so busy, and safe, if he had anything to do with it.

George and Emine were at 38th Street and Broadway so they just needed to head north and then east to the water. They'd pass convenience stores and more than a few street vendors, some with coffee. There would be an electronics store, perhaps cupcakes and a drug store. That was what made New York work so well: everything rolled out before you in a short block. You paid for the convenience in rents and a lack of privacy but a lot of people were obviously willing to make that trade. The downside for him now was that, as in most big cities, no one was looking and alert to danger. So George tried to maintain his vigilance, hoping that an epiphany would hit and Khalil would fill in for his charge, not altering their original plan thus better enabling his own capture. One side of George realized that Khalil already had deviated by showing up at the Four Seasons but perhaps with that apparent failure he'd default back to the original logistics.

Also unclear was the spot and actual time Khalil planned to take the shot, though his choices were limited.

George breathed in deeply, trying to clear his mind but being conscious of soot instead. George liked New York, much as he missed the wide-open green spaces of northern California, the ideal he'd left for this sophisticated, dense metropolis.

Emine was much shorter but her strides matched his as they kept a steady beat moving toward the UN. What they'd do once they arrived George could only wonder. Hopefully life and fate together would provide an answer as the variables were so unpredictable he couldn't begin to guess at the eventual outcome of Khalil's plot.

Remarkably they made the distance quickly only to find the area awash with uniformed NYPD, vans and patrol cars. Campbell must have made some progress (assuming that they weren't swarming in search of George!). He paused to think through the implications of the police and glanced over at Emine. Right now was when he needed to decide whether or not to trust her; Khalil was fearless and wouldn't back down upon seeing this circus. Until now he'd kept Emine at an arms length, as he did with most people, ever wary with all options open. Perhaps he'd never learned to trust fully, using his studies in people to keep them a distance away. Now, George needed help and she might be his best ally. Could he open up enough to let this girl help him?

She gazed back and held his stare. Then her arm fanned, waving at the police production, and she laughed. "They listened to you," she whispered. So he looked again, and watched numerous cars and the mob being pushed back. The uniformed officers lined up, looking like they controlled the circle in front of the UN building.

George felt no relief as his perfectionistic side took over. "We need to keep looking for Khalil because none of this will scare him and will only make him more determined. Think; you seem to sense him." Somehow, much as George felt more in control of events the magnitude of the threat was only just hitting. That's what denial does.

Now?

Khalil was in the office building across the street from the UN Headquarters, where he'd spent the afternoon since he saw George. Osman had brought food and a rifle. They'd spent time snacking on cold pizza triangles and diet Coke, with an occasional chocolate bar thrown in. Osman was still learning about being holed up in a location and his refreshment choices had been marginal. Next time. The boy was promising and should be allowed his mistakes.

The office was small and striped bare. The last tenants had left torn beige carpet and a multitude of cords but little else. Khalil had added a small table by the vast and floor length windows, second story, upon which he could set his rifle, a way of holding it steady. The shot to the UN was easy.

Should he have tried at the Four Seasons instead? Perhaps, but he doubted it. For Khalil knew that KK was still in the UN building while the increasing swarms of police made him suspicious that the bitch with George, or George himself, had seen him thus his risks would only increase with time. He also had already been on the Four Season cameras so they might have greatly increased security or moved KK and the other visiting dignitaries to other hotels. This plot still wasn't going well.

But Khalil was free and ready to take a shot. He didn't need to succeed but wanted to, then could go on the next plot and the next person. His war was evaluated by his successes and the times he got caught (or killed), while no one needed to know when he didn't take a shot, disappearing into the night instead.

Osman was scanning the crowds and security apparatus out another window, using binoculars as appropriate. He was an imperfect lookout but anyone who'd confronted life knew how rarely the ideal presented itself. No guts, no glory. If you didn't take the opportunity, no matter how limited and dangerous it proved to be, no plan would ever succeed.

The boy was proving to be his last supporting leg in this winding mess, and a shockingly reliable one. Thankfully. He'd grown physically in the short time they'd been together, reaching what Khalil guessed to be about 5'9, his own height. Lean from his upbringing, leaving his family and being on his own mostly had resulted in a continuing weight loss, much as the boy had taken to the local pizza with an unexplainable zeal. Still, he was only a youth and his growth spurt was obviously directing his nutrition up and not out. Meanwhile, Osman's technological prowess had proven to literally be a lifesaver and the main reason - likely - Khalil was still free.

But what Khalil liked best about Osman was his utter stillness and calm. It was a quality the desert cultivated, and most people who grew up in a city were never able to develop that same quiet steadiness. Only by thus focusing energy could you see what was plain before you to find the correct course of action or decision. Analysis was far simpler than many assumed. Man just got in the way with his cluttered mind and undisciplined thinking.

The boy was looking, scanning and focusing at the action below.

"How old are you now, Osman?" Khalil asked.

"Seventeen, last week," the boy replied but his eyes only momentarily glanced in Khalil's direction and away from the street. What a work ethic! Too bad Radwan hadn't been more like this boy. Then Khalil wouldn't be here at all as he'd have let his trained sniper take the shot. What a waste.

A flurry of activity caught Khalil's eyes and he focused on viewing the building's entrance, across that circular driveway with its row of flags lined up in front, waving barely in the lackluster wind. And in the dusk he saw that large head with its shock of thick hair, its owner making his way to a car. Security was dense and one officer had KK's arm in his own, propelling the candidate quickly to a waiting town car. The protesters had been pushed back and no longer blocked Khalil's crystal clear shot. Indeed, Khalil could watch the path laid out for KK and saw that in four seconds he would have a perfect shot. His rifle was ready and Khalil watched through the scope, finger poised on trigger. As early evening had settled in the light was less bright than earlier in the day, casting a shadow on the scene before him.

Four, three, two...

A blast, loud and piercing.

The gun was blown away below him and Khalil saw his own blood spout from his upper right arm. The flash of pain was intense but didn't shock him as much as the thick red spurting fluid, dropping in clumps on the now rifle-less table. His eyes scanned, evaluating, not yet ready to decide on an action. In danger, it's usually better to move out of target but not so when you didn't know who was shooting.

Outside all was calm and no window glass was broken so the shot hadn't come from a sniper out in the street. KK had disappeared and his car was pulling away from the curb. Meanwhile, the police and security were mobilizing, but not in response to an assassination, rather looking over at this building for they must have heard the gun shot and recognized the sound. The door to the office hadn't opened. So?

Khalil turned to see Osman pointing his own Glock at him. The lean black gun was raised and aimed straight at Khalil. The boy's eyes were cold and dark, unwavering and showing no fear. He'd been raised by a tribal elder and thus was likely as cold blooded as his father. Tribal justice is harsh and unforgiving. Khalil didn't move, but understood that the boy might shoot again. He himself would.

"Why?" he asked the silent boy.

"We don't want KK dead. We want Egypt to be stable," was the unwavering response and Khalil saw an utter calm that scared him. Emotion could be exploited to escape. This resolve was tougher to beat. The boy, a mere seventeen, was displaying no fear of Khalil's retaliation, which had to come, unless he killed Khalil first.

"Your father sent you to stop me; you knew it might mean your death."

"We had no one else who could build the right trust and be trusted in turn. The Internet...". Khalil's arm was throbbing and he noted with surprise how much blood was pooling. Osman had luckily not hit an artery but his arm still wasn't very mobile and he was right handed. His gun was lying off to the side and he'd never reach it before Osman shot him dead. In a hand-to-hand battle Khalil always won, but likely wouldn't with a useless right arm even against a boy. He had no other weapon on him, wanting to keep light when taking his shot and trusting Osman with the rest. Not a good situation.

And pretty soon someone would be at the door to investigate the gunshot. Before, Khalil had felt safe knowing that even if George had seen him earlier the government would have a hard time getting a warrant to search this whole building in time, if they could even figure out where he might be hiding. The gunshot across the street from an international conference attended by the US Vice President would require no warrant for a search. Khalil had little time to escape and Osman with his gun stood in the way.

Shot

uck. Emine heard a gunshot from the building right above. They hadn't even made it back to the UN headquarters itself yet, being across the street a block away and already everything had gone haywire. Really? She glanced at George, who looked implacable, much as his eyes were scanning all directions and evaluating the scene. He was like a calm man in the middle of a typhoon: it made no sense but it was and you were trying to stay alive so you let the oddity go.

One of Bright's news vans was twenty feet ahead and she saw Bright himself stick his head out a window. A marvel. Worth over a billion dollars he still couldn't stay away from the action, like a big kid who just wouldn't miss any story. Indeed, that's how he'd made that billion in the first place; by always being where the hotspot was and making sure his reporters got the story. Too many bosses weren't willing to take the risks.

The police were visibly tensing, but thankfully they were there along with other security forces she couldn't name. Someone, somewhere had listened to George and brought in heavy reinforcements both on the waterfront and lining the street. A man was being bundled into a town car and Emine thought she recognized KK, with that flash of dense black hair. Evacuating him? Well, he looked okay and alive. The day wasn't going badly after all. But what about that gunshot they'd both just heard? Now that Emine knew, as per Jennifer, that KK was the designated target she had to wonder if someone had taken a shot and missed or if someone had been shot trying to take that shot. Time would reveal the answer. She followed George, who was moving faster now, his phone in hand. It was ringing again. Of course.

And she saw him wave at a man across the street who had to be Campbell, George's other boss. She'd seen a photo once, a long time ago. The man had tousled, thick brown hair, brown eyes and a professional look, with predictably creased trousers and pressed shirt. Government might often seem a mess but when realities necessitated it, they always pulled themselves together. And, as if on cue, Emine heard the helicopters and sirens from the patrol cars. KK thankfully rolled away in his town car slowly but with only one patrol car (and no medics) in attendance. Khalil must be pissed because in her estimation they were taking the likely future President of Egypt to an airport and military plane ride home for his election. Khalil had failed unless he had something pretty unexpected and spectacular still planned. He was most likely more worried about escape at this point.

"George," the booming voice came and Emine just watched the mutual shock.

"I didn't expect you," George replied. "Does this mean I'll be arrested or I won't be?"

"You're a free man," Campbell answered and introduced himself to Emine. She shook his hand back. "Nice to meet you," she said. His eyes were so cold, but she sensed decency, as if he'd tucked it deep behind the role he was obligated to play. Campbell immediately shifted his attention back to George. "How do we find this bastard? We've got agents combing that building floor to floor," he finished gesturing to the one from which the bullet had seemingly come. No cover except perhaps from a hidden sniper or two protected them from Khalil's wrath but the skies were free of bullets. She decided to head over to Bright and his van to hear his version of events. Since most of his information was unofficial, bought or even stolen it typically diverged from the official version.

"Excuse me," she said before heading off in the direction of the news van and leaving them to their likely confidential conversation.

"Hi," she said, but skipping the smile as she walked up to the vehicle. Bright peered out his window but didn't say anything. The sun was softer now but strong enough that she had a disadvantage as it was setting such that the glare hit her eyes. She decided to play with and not against it. Squinting and defenseless, she asked. "What am I missing?"

And Bright smiled, happy to assume the dominant and controlling role. "You missed it all, baby," was his chipper response. "Washington hit the fan when they saw your terrorist trolling around Manhattan and their fucking UN conference. The troops came in aerially ASAP and they got their gunshot. I think I'm the only press who was here to catch the story as it unfolded." His smile was enough to light the city. Who'd ever keep him muzzled?

"Now what?" she asked, more to hear his thoughts on the matter than because she expected to believe them.

"I've got my cameras and we'll see," he responded. "But that shot was eerie and I'm expecting the day to only get more interesting." Prosperous, happy and plump, he was dressed in loose ripped jeans and a ridiculously expensive silk shirt. She knew quality and saw it also in his supple loafers. Bright was the master at crafting images and now he'd try to assert utter control over this story. He was the only major news source with the inside scoop being lucky enough to follow her, and secondarily George, around. She'd been the one to tip him off and send him those photos indirectly leading to his presence here at ground zero. She'd remind him later, when his next threat was dangled with a promised opportunity for the story of a lifetime. Until then she had some questions.

"Where's Khalil?"

"I have guys trying to figure that out." Of course, but his answer was also utter bullshit and meant he had no idea. "You'll tell me when you find out?" she asked and watched him look down at those priceless loafers. Asshole.

"Who else is helping you?" was her next question. She'd sent him the picture of Khalil but hadn't told him about the UN Building or conference specifically.

"Buck," was his response. Her not a boyfriend but still a friend.

"Bud," she corrected and wondered at what else yet another man in her life wasn't telling. Why did she keep hanging out with men for whom the words honesty and disclosure held little meaning? A daddy fixation? And then Emine heard another gunshot puncture the chaos. Everyone stood suddenly taller.

Direction

George was ready to end this mess but it wasn't taking direction. The good news was that KK was safe and apparently out of harm's way; he'd be on a plane back to Cairo very soon, no longer a glaring American concern. And now they knew that KK really had been the target and Khalil had failed. Personally satisfying for George was that troops had been brought in and security was at a red level while Khalil was likely still close, focused on escape but only succeeding if lucky. He breathed in the exhaust filled air and felt relief for the first time since he'd left the city almost a month earlier. Oh, sure, Khalil could be directly above and pointing a gun at his heart but nothing new in that risk. Yet George had somehow, unwittingly, foiled this plot more effectively than the last, in which a number of people had died, though not as many as Khalil had hoped to kill.

Times change and we get better at dealing with those difficult people in our lives. We learn.

George scanned the skies and saw nothing unusual. Would Khalil call Jennifer? Should George? For some reason his mind was muddled and again George felt uncertain. He was missing an important piece of information while events were passing before him faster than his mind could process these unrealities. Circumstances weren't supposed to unfold this way. Who fired the shots and why?

The street was a stream of activity, and George saw that the UN building was in lock-down. They'd evacuated the Vice President through a side door, along with the most important international delegates, efficiently and probably safe now. Bright was still the only major news channel with camera vans nearby so he must be in heaven (no new traffic allowed in, even reporters, since the gunshots and Bright had already been in place).

So George decided to take a seat on a doorstep to shut out the chaos, as he needed to think clearly and find some answers that would lead him to Khalil. What would Khalil do after missing his target? Well, really the answer depended upon why the shot didn't hit KK. Regardless, Khalil would try to escape and hopefully wasn't loaded up with explosives.

Disguised, he'd have a better chance so George could assume he'd thought of that contingency. By now the exits from Manhattan would likely be shut and the airports on high alert. Khalil would have to hope there were no pictures of his new face available to law enforcement but wouldn't be able to count on it. Thus he'd need a safe house because he wasn't leaving the area immediately as trying would be too risky. And he'd need to leave the towering building from which the shot had rung if he was still in it.

So should George call Jennifer?

Logically, yes. She'd already turned on her boyfriend and knew more about him than anyone so might have some guesses as to where Khalil would go. But George sensed he shouldn't make that call. A woman's heart was so fragile and she'd looked unstable when they last met. That path could go untended for now.

Suddenly, George decided on his next steps. First, he'd go into the building as soon as Campbell let him. There must be evidence scattered inside detailing what Khalil had been planning and why he got derailed. The more information George had the better he'd be able to track his adversary. It was almost over, if they could catch Khalil. So the second thing he'd do was just that.

Changes

"Not my problem anymore," Khalil whispered to himself. "I control this outcome – not them, or him." He crouched, staying far from the windows so he couldn't be seen from outside. They'd be looking now, and while the windows were tinted, allowing for a clear view out but none in, one could never be too careful. A gunshot would have been recognized and he didn't need to glance outside to know that the security at the UN would be mobilizing, along with the NYPD and many others. For now, his focus was on what he could control and here inside this office. Osman.

They had three exits: two windows and one door. But there were likely sharpshooters pointed at the building by now and any unusual window activity would only give away their exact location, which no one outside could pinpoint otherwise since the gunshot hadn't pierced the building's shell or gone external. However, a general location would be easy to guess by the trained men outside thus Khalil had perhaps 90 seconds left to make it past Osman and out the door. And Khalil wasn't in the mood to take any more risks. *No guts, no glory* was bullshit and mostly used to send dumb people to their deaths. The only thing that mattered was survival, when all came down to the end.

He'd kill the boy in a second if that was what it took to exit that one door in the next 60 seconds, before the building was swarmed, making escape more difficult. It might already be too late.

But men can only get across the street and up two stories so fast. Would they need formal orders or just run for it? Khalil couldn't waste time or energy looking out the window to check. All that mattered was focusing his attention on getting the hell away from here.

Osman could have killed him already but hadn't done so, focused on stopping the assassination instead. The boy might still shoot him, but Khalil guessed he'd rather follow him on the way out and escape either life in prison or the death penalty. He was only seventeen and no one might believe that the boy had single-handedly just saved KK's life. They weren't on the same side anymore but they did have the same enemy for now.

"Follow me, we need to get out of here," Khalil stated the words confidently suddenly realizing that if Osman shot him dead he might actually be considered a hero. Khalil could be identified and Osman might be able to make a strong case that he'd just foiled a high level assassination. Or not.

"We can't get caught. We maybe have thirty seconds left. Do you trust that they will believe you tried to stop me?"

The boy's eyes didn't waver. "I did stop you," he replied, his gun still aloft. But he gestured Khalil to the door. Too young to handle the realities of what happened if he did need to stop Khalil, as per his father's orders, this boy still wanted a commanding officer. The fire escape was in the back, an advantage Khalil had noted before renting the place. They were moving fast enough that no one from across the street could beat them to the exit, even if they knew where it was; doubtful. Any emergency vehicles, especially with the traffic in this city, were still at least five minutes away. Khalil led the way, hoping Osman didn't shoot him in the back but not having another option. Fighting the boy would slow them down and he didn't have those precious seconds, if he even won given his useless arm and the boy's gun. They moved fast, and no alarm rang when he opened the door to the sleek steel staircase of the fire escape, warm air hitting his face. The sun was softer now and it was just light enough that people could see them exiting. Moving slowly, so as not to look suspicious, Khalil knew few civilians would be certain that it had indeed been a gunshot they'd heard and less would be willing to risk their own lives under such unclear suspicions.

Radwan had tucked away his gun but Khalil couldn't do anything about him now, in public. Too many people were around, the swarms that existed throughout the city. He noted the river but realized a taxi was a better option.

A fierce pain stabbed his arm and briefly he worried. Still so much blood, which would attract attention. He needed medical care. Every step of any plot had to be perfectly planned because something inevitably went wrong. In this case, a lot had gone wrong and the plot had failed. But he had planned the escape part perfectly and now was reaping the related benefits. Unfortunately, the blood needed to be staunched so he could make it to his safe house and a doctor.

Briefly Khalil wondered if he'd failed due to attachment, in this case a woman. Well, that guess might be true but he'd have to question himself later, once he was safe.

"The promise given was a necessity of the past; the word broken is a necessity of the present, as Machiavelli said," he told Osman, and waved as he walked away from the boy. Who knew if he'd be okay alone in the big city? Having turned on Khalil the boy's fate was no longer a variable Khalil needed to consider. The youth stood there for a brief second and then headed in the opposite direction, his stride long and firm. As Khalil suspected, his father had given orders to stop the assassination but not to align with the Americans. He likely had his own safe house in which to hide and unlike Khalil had no record with any law enforcement. While Khalil would need to hide out for a while, all exits being closed for him, Osman could board a plane for Cairo this evening.

For a second, Khalil envied his former charge but that was all the time he could spare and seeing an empty cab hailed it. He only needed to make about ten blocks without being recognized. The cabbie was surprisingly a woman and she looked like she wanted no trouble. Khalil could hear sirens and knew they were headed here but it was likely too soon for her to suspect so. Indeed, nothing technically had happened, Osman had assured that.

The follow up by the authorities had to be based more on suspicion than clarity. Besides, this city always had a siren going for some reason or another and it was the perfect place to get lost with the ever-present anonymity of the crowd.

"The Arrow," he directed, a small hotel with a discreet lobby.

She nodded and Khalil studied her back, with short reddish hair and a thick neck. The driver appeared to be in her late 50s, and she'd probably had a tough life to be driving a cab in this dangerous town. Khalil covered his arm with the charcoal sweater he'd brought along, in case. Well, in case had happened and the dark color was the best he had to hide the blood. He didn't need to camouflage it long.

The streets were crowded and the cab stopped for a red light. Khalil felt the sweat as his heart pounded too quickly. This part was the most dangerous. If he survived the initial hour of his escape he'd likely be okay. The light turned green but they had to wait to let a throng of LAPD cars pass, headed for the UN. The cabbie didn't comment nor did Khalil. He was starting to like her; she was smart enough to mind her own business, knowing that not doing so was always the best way to get in trouble. Briefly he wondered if he should kill her but with no weapon and a limp arm doing so wouldn't be easy, thus adding additional risks. And, how could he find a hidden place for her to stop the car when there was no private street for miles? He'd give her an extra large tip instead and maybe that would keep her quiet.

He also memorized her name and car number. You never knew whether that information might come in handy.

Thankful when he pulled up at the hotel, he paid the driver and entered the softly lit lobby. White marble and a patterned wall gave it an antique but gracious feel. The clerk at the front desk conveniently had his back to the door and the room was otherwise empty. Khalil snuck into the private bathroom on the ground floor. She was there with his supplies so he dumped the last of his pre-paid phones into the trash, no longer needing to text anyone.

Jennifer looked terrible and Khalil felt a stab of guilt at seeing her so, with messy hair and reddish eyes. But no matter, if she was strong she'd survive; if not he'd never be able to save her as life was just too hard.

Rummaging through the bag she'd brought he quickly applied makeup, changing his skin tone. Wordlessly, he slipped out of his clothes, wincing at the pains that shot through his right arm. He slipped new pants on, some loose dark jeans. Used to seeing wounds he coldly studied his. The bullet hadn't exited cleanly and the wound looked raw. The blood was slowly congealing but not as quickly as Khalil would have liked. Khalil turned to Jennifer and noted her white face and horrified expression. Welcome to the jihad; this was nothing. But she was merely a woman and an American one at that so what could she possibly understand of war?

He pulled her close with his good arm, still shirtless and felt her soft flesh through the thin t-shirt. He wanted nothing more than to make love to her on the floor here in this bathroom. That wasn't going to happen so he kissed her softly again.

"It will be all right," he told her and looked deeply into her eyes. She returned the gaze. "I'll be done here in a minute. Help bandage my arm, go back to San Diego and I'll call you when it's safe."

Jennifer returned his gaze but her eyes were now sprouting new tears and she looked even worse. He'd brought her into this mess and regretted it. Not much of a life for a gentle woman like her with those lofty ideals and expectations that the story always had a happy ending. Then again, had she been stronger she never would have let him back into her life.

"Will that time ever come?" she asked, and he knew enough to lie.

"Yes, of course. Here, the bandage," he said and held out his arm. She wrapped it silently and helped him into a long sleeve t-shirt, also baggy. He'd be hot but at least his wound would be hidden. The bathroom was a large, single unit meant for handicapped people so it had extra railings around the toilet. Mostly white and chrome, it looked ultra modern unlike the hotel itself, probably the result of some re-model to meet newer city sanitation regulations. The wastebasket was mostly empty and he decided to dump his old clothes, the bag and other paraphernalia there. No point in him or Jennifer taking an extra risk trying to dump it someplace less conspicuous. The both donned wigs.

"You slip out first," he told her, allowing her the safer position.

"Your picture is posted all over the Internet," she said, looking at him sadly.

"Thank you for telling me. It doesn't matter anymore, not with the disguise you brought me." And it didn't. The make-up and wig would be enough for now; he'd have surgery later. So he kissed her one more time and opened the door to let her out. He ignored any misgivings he might feel as life was too short for regrets.

This hotel would perhaps be the last place to which he was traced. He liked its lack of cameras, discrete and sympathetic staff and very busy street location. Khalil had managed to disappear into a public black hole and by now his risks were dropping fast. His safe house was a subway ride away. And heading into rush hour he'd be even harder to find on the busy transportation system. He'd hide in a borough until the heat died down, which would be pretty quickly since his plot had failed. Then Khalil would head to Rio de Janeiro and a plastic surgeon. After that, who knew?

Khalil left the bathroom and saw no one in the hotel lobby. So he exited into the massive rush hour chaos of 63rd Street. Dusk was beginning to fall faster.

Questions

What had happened? That was the question of the day.

Emine and George had arrived just in time to watch a lot of men (and one woman officer) rush across the street into the apartment building from which the gunshot had boomed. Others went into the UN building to secure the safety of the country's Vice-President who was shuttled away quickly by helicopter. And then a measured sort of chaos descended, with numerous local residents having seen nothing of true value, if they could even remember seeing anything.

"They found blood and a sniper rifle in an almost empty office on the second floor," George said, finally detaching himself from Campbell. Mostly, George was the center of operations again, whatever suspicion that had been casting a pall apparently lifted. He'd been huddled in the group of commanding men and Emine had snuck a few snapshots, always carrying her camera and no one stopped her. What was the law here? If she was standing in a public street could she just take whatever pictures she wanted? In most of the places she worked the law wasn't the defining principle but rather the men with big guns.

George looked worried.

"Khalil?"

"They'll test the blood. But, the rifle looks as if it tumbled to the ground when someone disarmed the sniper. And based on what we can piece together it looks like someone was meaning to take a shot at KK. All circumstantial evidence but...", and George paused.

"It looks pretty clear?"

"Yes. My guess is Khalil had a companion, a helper perhaps, who shot him. I can't see Khalil being sloppy enough to make access to him right before a kill so easy otherwise," George was looking tired, and worried. Usually unflappable, the wear and tear was starting to show and his silver hair glistened from the lights illuminating early evening. The day had been long and difficult. With the sun well down for the night, none of them had eaten or had water for hours. Both buildings had been evacuated long ago but their lights intermingled with those of the fluorescent city and dark seemed more like a relative term than an absolute.

"Reports of him anywhere?" she asked.

"None. Though someone noted a dark man leave here in a taxi, separating from a much younger man who melted into the crowd. It isn't credible information."

"Not much to go on?" Emine asked and George gave her a wan smile. "He's a pro. He found a building in a crucial location that provided an easy escape. But he's likely wounded; we'll know for sure after the blood test comes back. We have his DNA from when he was in American custody."

"But we have no idea how badly?"

"We don't know anything," was George's response. Emine heard the frustration.

"But he was going to take a shot? At KK?" she asked.

"That does appear to be the case," George answered, looking reflective. The traffic swirled around them, mixing horns and that soft hum of a modern car. The world looked as it had hours earlier but everything was different, and not just the arrival of evening. KK, a man likely important for the world's future, had seemingly survived an almost assassination attempt and no one knew who stepped in to save him. Their angel of mercy was a vague description of a much younger man, dark but inconspicuous.

"But why didn't Khalil take KK out earlier? He could have avoided this last minute fiasco if he'd killed KK at the Four Seasons." George muttered, seemingly to Emine but really invoking the higher authority to which his conscience reported.

Her stomach grumbled and she realized the intensity of her hunger and how much she craved a drink.

"Is he softening, losing his nerve or just getting tired?" she responded, more to be helpful than because she cared at this point.

"Maybe he's in love?" George asked then shook his head no. "Once a terrorist, always a terrorist." George turned and stared at the deserted UN building. Bright had been picked up via limousine hours ago and was likely supervising story after related story at his headquarters. Emine would read his output when she got to a computer, later, she suspected, glad that he hadn't been bugging her for a story.

George turned back and she saw a misty, sad look in his eyes but still didn't know him well enough to understand why. "Do you want to get dinner?" he asked. His faint silvery five o'clock shadow glistened under the neon lights and her feet hurt.

"Sure. You pick the place," she responded and tried to give him a reassuring smile. She could sense his perfectionism; that he'd failed because Khalil got away even though so did KK and the Vice President. No wonder George was so driven: he didn't seem to accept that bad things happened around people who were trying to cause problems. Khalil was likely still hoping that the Americans would crack down harshly and harm themselves in response to his failed plot. A threat can be worse than a success because people fear the unknown and their imaginations can run amuck with secret unrealized scenarios. Perhaps George was pondering those risks, still hanging above them.

"Sushi? With Campbell?" George suggested, breaking her reverie.

"Okay," she said and smiled again, trying. He wasn't going to save the world but deserved a little kindness for his continuing if naïve attempts. Sushi and a night of discussing Khalil. What more could a girl want?

She checked her phone Internet while George went to fetch Campbell. There it was:

International Terrorist Threat Diffused at UN Headquarters New York

Bless free speech, sort of. She'd neglect to mention Bright's headline over dinner as George and Campbell would be in a bad enough mood with Khalil having given them the slip again. He certainly was an amazing agent; too bad he worked for the wrong side.

How had that man just disappeared? Emine hoped one day to interview him. Stranger things had happened.

ESCAPE

George

The phone clicked into voicemail after the first ring. Almost a week had passed and Jennifer still wouldn't answer her phone. George pondered his dilemma. He'd left a message after the assassination that didn't happen. She'd be understandably conflicted and he was no longer a government insider. Now, being an online "personality" dumped him into the media bucket. He'd love an on camera interview with her, who in his position wouldn't? The girl friend of the notorious terrorist.

But he'd called out of human decency and not to get an interview.

George nursed his scotch. The amber fluid was filled more than a little too high in the cut crystal glass but he'd earned the indiscretion. Who knew what Karen had paid for it and for the room too? While she'd probably paid too much he was still glad to be back in his apartment with its view of Central Park and the glistening nightlights of Manhattan. He was thankful for the plush green velvet couch, the dimmed lights and the soft music that came out of Bose speakers.

So he'd left a message for Jennifer that first night but hadn't said much. Straddling a fine line between press and government, with numerous ties to old bosses and the related conflicting loyalties, he was still trying to cover all bases and do his best. Bright had yelled, "Get interviews!" and so had Campbell. Carrots and sticks, offers of promotions and even a boat had been dangled. George didn't want a boat and felt bad for Jennifer. She must have loved Khalil even if she turned on him; she'd done the right thing.

Mostly though, George had just wanted information. Anything that might help him catch Khalil before he slipped away into an endless void would have been so welcome.

Authorized to say little beyond what the papers reported George still had little idea what had really happened in the room between Khalil and the boy. Seemingly a mere teenager from the limited witness information they'd gathered, the boy likewise had disappeared as thoroughly as Khalil. Why had he betrayed Khalil when he'd seemingly been a protégée (for that assumption seemed a solid bet)? No one knew, but George wanted to thank the boy for doing everyone's job on this one. Not surprisingly, the building in question had no security cameras.

So George had left a message for Jennifer but she never called him back. Had his government buddies found her by now? They weren't saying. Of course, they probably had and were asking her questions upon question but hadn't brought him in to participate. No, he'd gone back to his television job instead of government.

And he was more worried about Jennifer emotionally than physically. She had bad taste in men. But she was also a lawyer who'd turned her criminal boyfriend in to the authorities and Khalil wouldn't be happy should he find out. Technically, she only had to do so if she knew he was planning to harm someone; otherwise as a lawyer she could claim to be representing him and all related communications would have been confidential. She was an American citizen, knew her rights and could fight for them. But emotionally, she had to be a wreck.

Gulping at his drink, George could hear Karen tinkering around in the kitchen. Cooking a nice dinner or ordering? The scotch soothed him and he was thankful to relax for a while without her chatter. They were back at playing good spouses, smiling and relaxing into their predictability and privilege. And he was again appreciative for his wife much as she had her insanities. After all, he was a difficult man and selfish spouse, and while sometimes she got mad mostly she tolerated him. For that devotion he was finally developing gratitude.

Clicking his remote he switched from whatever bullshit classical music Karen had put on. Wasn't it time to admit that he'd never be cultured but rather liked a life stirred and not shaken or some such bullshit? Nicolas had some equally awful CD of music he'd heard in the clubs of Europe and George chose that instead. He hated it all too, perhaps music wasn't his thing but he missed his son acutely and cherished any tie. Nicolas had spent the last six months learning French and Arabic and was now working at the IMF in Brussels. Impressive kid...but how had George helped create that?

Khalil was?

Hopefully, dead. George knew that such wishful thinking was a coping mechanism and expected that someday he'd get another related call. All bets were off with respect to whom it would be from or what new trouble Khalil would brew.

He'd texted Khalil's old cell number and asked for an interview, as a what the fuck why not attempt. Keep your enemies close. Would the number still work? It hadn't. Not a surprise.

Gulping more scotch as he heard Karen approaching, George braced himself for what his evening would bring. He was considering quitting the prestigious job and going back into the trenches working for Campbell again. They'd need to discuss his decision at some point so was tonight the night? Was he fair to plead her love and ask for understanding? Would George do it without her approval and support? Probably.

George recognized now that they did really love each other and deeply. They'd become parts of a whole over the many years, even if they often clashed, both being head strong and determined. Their visions of life weren't aligned and he refused to compromise, forcing her to, over and over again. Where would that clash and difference in vision take them this time? So far it was to a beautiful apartment, wonderful kids, professional success and a great social life. He was the continuing problem....that wanting to save the world thing.

"Hi love," Karen said, as she entered the room. Her smile was real and the diamonds Bright had sent glistened, even in the dim lighting. He smiled back.

But really, he was now fully engaged in his scotch, stack of books and deep green velvet couch. A loner. With bare feet on expensive wood table and unapologetically unwashed grey sweat pants and navy t-shirt he was not quite ready for a deep conversation.

She hugged him and he kissed her cheek.

The world is a dangerous place but it has its own odd sanity in spite of the horrible things that could happen and sometimes didn't. Then tomorrow he'd be back on Bright's fancy interview show, as if none of the unpleasantness had occurred, and interviewing some famous person. George was a lucky man indeed but still not satisfied.

Perhaps he should get a dog. Or move back to northern California. Or perhaps he should just stay put for a while and be a husband for a change. George slugged back a shot of his scotch and felt it burn its way down his throat. Karen snuggled closer, having forgiven him for putting the family in danger. Then again, she never (thankfully) had all of the facts. No one did.

He ignored *Wuthering Heights*, his novel of choice this evening and one of her favorites. There was hopefully tomorrow and perhaps for just this one night he could focus on his wife.

"George," she said and smiled, hesitantly but familiarly. He could only stare back at her, slight and lovely, soft and welcoming. Her hair was tied back in one of those high ponytails she liked and her clothes were all beige, from the slim jeans to t-shirt to Todds on her delicate feet. Her make-up was minimal though she'd added a blue eye pencil that made her look younger. And prettier. As always, she was spotless, like little else in his life. Composed, she gazed at him as if waiting but for what he didn't know. Graciously, she didn't seem mad and had come back. Would he have shown such understanding and forgiveness? Probably not. He was so hard on her, as he was with himself but she didn't have to play life by his rules so why did he keep demanding that she did?

The apartment lighting was muted, as he liked it to be, hating bright lights. Another quirk she'd accepted. He took her right hand in both of his and kissed it, pulling the palm to his neck. Then he kissed her, deeply. "I love you," he said and recognized, mental professional that he was, how much he really did. She'd married a tortured and demanding man. While he might kid himself otherwise, she was really just along for his ride and thus far she'd mostly followed along, adapting with minimal complaint. So let her be shallow once and a while and shine under the glow his increased celebrity illuminated around them both.

"I love you too," she replied, her voice husky and sweet. He poured her some scotch, and then pulled her shoulder closer. She picked up his book and opened it to page one before taking a sip from her glass and gazing deeply into his eyes. Had they been in their twenties or even thirties the night would have ended with sex but for now he wanted to sit together, legs touching, and feel blessed at their mutual fortune. She needed him and really, no one else in this world did.

Tomorrow would bring its inevitable reality. Khalil was loose, in Manhattan or places undetermined. He'd likely be looking to harm someone again or blow up a monument. People didn't readily change, for good or bad. But someday Khalil would be gone, replaced by another man and a new threat. Someone always wanted to fight stability and a good life for all.

For now George just wanted to sit with his wife and enjoy their view of Central Park. They'd read and order dinner in. Perhaps if they felt romantic later they'd do something about it but until then they'd just revel in their safety and sanity. As George ran his hands through his wife's fine hair, wrecking her prim ponytail, he was happy. Perhaps tomorrow he'd find another windmill, or the same one, to attack with a rusty sword. For now he'd just pick a different book and let Karen read *Wuthering Heights*:

1801 – I have just returned from a visit to my landlord, the solitary neighbor that I shall be troubled with. This is certainly a beautiful country!

And George indeed did seem to be troubled with a certain solitary neighbor who abutted his life at the oddest moments, and in frustrating ways. Man's future is determined by his past. For this moment, with Karen in his arms and an air-conditioned, well-stocked apartment George was happy just to relax knowing his past would catch up with him eventually but not likely this evening.

Khalil

The sun in the Southern Hemisphere can be harsh in its glare. Khalil was swaddled in new bandages in a small apartment overlooking Ipanema Beach, Rio de Janeiro at its glorious best. He wasn't bed bound thus was poring through the towering stack of papers and magazines he bought daily from the newsstands of an international hotel a few blocks away. George's *Alice* peaked out from behind the *Financial Times*.

His arm had healed quickly, luckily and thankfully, as a disabled right arm would have wrecked his career. He'd then gone to a local plastic surgeon to hide the scar and change his face once again. The last visage had been plastered all over the Internet and so now law enforcement thought they knew his appearance, which they had but no longer did. He'd also highlighted his hair, creating a mix of colors dramatically different from his monotone black.

The food here was healthy and Khalil had spent time relaxing, albeit in a turmoil of frustration at his continued failure. KK's assassination should have been easy and he'd botched it repeatedly. Was he losing his touch? Seemingly, he really was and that new challenge created numerous questions with respect to his future. Terror is a young man's game and in this technology driven word hiding had become a laborious chore once you'd been caught, scanned, fingerprinted and whatever else they kept adding.

"More tea?" his maid queried but Khalil just nodded then shoed her away. At fifty and still spunky she drove him nuts. But her cooking was divine and she handled everything so he didn't need to leave the apartment until his new face healed. Thus he tolerated her overwhelming energy and paid well enough so she didn't ask questions.

The cover of the new *Economist* magazine had KK proudly displayed, with his large teeth and broader smile. That familiar shock of black hair. He was also on the local paper, the *Herald Tribune* and, honestly, just about every news source. That's what winning the Egyptian presidency did for a man already famous for his sports career. KK's acceptance speech had advocated unity, equity and jobs but that glow would fade fast as the realities of the country's massive foreign debt and internal instability hit his administration. George had interviewed him a few weeks ago and the resulting warm interplay had been broadcast everywhere. The gratitude interview, as expected, though all should be thanking Osman, or killing him, less so George.

Moha had apologized. Liar. His boy Osman was safe and hidden away from the likes of Khalil. Mad, he actually did still respect the boy. Someday that boy would rule Egypt. Tough kid, the turncoat.

What next?

Most likely Khalil would go into politics himself, which seemed the safest option for a warrior losing his edge as he aged. Their organization was still reeling from the recent death of its supreme leader to an American bullet. Khalil could be like the American Ike who fought a war and presided over its aftermath. Of course, Khalil's war wasn't won yet but all things in due time. The continuing global sporadic revolutions and related disorder worked in his favor and he was still hopeful that America would eventually fall to its exotic allure. KK's win was just a delay of the inevitable.

Khalil sipped at his iced tea. Sprigs of mint intermingled with the crushed ice and he'd asked for condensed milk as well, giving the beverage a muddy color but sweet taste. The beach below him was among the loveliest in the world, with its vast expanse of white sand meeting sapphire sea. The color of Jennifer's eyes.

The coastal area was crowded, with tourists flocking the wide, vibrant streets with their cameras and multitudes of languages. Watching over the city was a giant statue of Christ, standing boldly on one of the sheltering hills, and Khalil was getting tired of that eyesore. The favelas full of poor people likewise stared down at the wealthier flat dwellers with their large fences topped with crushed glass and barbed wire.

Eventually Khalil would have much to do but not today. For now he was just reading and had picked up *On War* by Carl von Clausewitz. Really, he shouldn't be perusing this tome but rather books on diplomacy and taking over a political organization. There was always tomorrow.

He adjusted himself on the rattan chaise, his shorts showing off pale but hairy legs. His shirt was breezy and soft, a blue only a few shades lighter than the ocean. He sipped more tea and enjoyed the combination of bitter and sweet.

Suddenly, Khalil heard a woman's voice, light and lilting as it flowed through the airy apartment. She was back and Khalil felt his heart jump.

Emine

mine cried out as she felt him enter her, hard and thrusting, with the confidence of a skilled lover. Oh, how she loved the familiar sensations and erotic allure. His burnished skin was even darker from his recent trip to Phuket's beaches and the contrast of the outside lights. He pushed harder and harder, driving her wild, and she screamed out as an orgasm rocked her body, sending shivers up and down her length. His skin was soft but the muscles underneath were anything but. She felt his tongue dig into her mouth and responded, savoring every aspect of his smell, touch and taste. Oh he was good.

Ed wouldn't approve but he was on the way out and she'd needed a good fuck to remind her that alternatives existed. Their downward spiral had started with the word "love" but then "marriage" had been the final straw. What about commitment phobia did he not get?

Bud thrust deeper. "Cunt, you cunt," he shouted as his body jerked and Emine could feel him come inside her, condom notwithstanding. He stayed inside for a moment, as he liked.

Emine liked wars, not ladies luncheons and charity balls, which rather belonged in Liz's domain. Tomorrow Emine was heading to the Sudan where fighting had picked up yet again and she didn't want to miss the action. She'd call Ed when she landed and be honest finally. She wasn't ready to love for real again. Not yet. Each night she still saw those same hazel green eyes and missed Piers whether as an excuse or a reason not to move on. People aren't so easily replaceable no matter how hard we try.

Bud rolled off her tingling body, his sun kissed skin contrasting with her lighter ivory expanse. He grabbed his pack of cigarettes from the bedside table and offered her one. She took it and watched as he did the same then switched the plastic package with his diamond crusted lighter. Silently, he lit both cigarettes and pulled her tightly as they smoked in silence. She knew he'd drop ashes in the bed just like he'd dropped his champagne glass into the bathroom sink only to watch it splinter.

"God, Eme, we need to fuck more often," he whispered into her ear, blowing smoke into the canyons of her neck. "Will you stop in Capetown while you're in Africa?" he asked, his tone deep and his accent that same mottled mess as her own. Bud was a hang over vice and she couldn't resist the temptations he dangled. Over years their bond had never faded and they could always revert to conversations about their mutual past with its rootless jadedness. Or they could just fuck when they ran out of words.

Emine caressed his familiar shoulders and massaged a knot in his neck. Bud groaned and kissed her wrist.

"I'm breaking up with my boyfriend after this. He wants to get married," she told him and waited for his counsel. Bud loved her like a brother. Confident, wealthy, good looking and treated like a God when he went home he'd give her honest advice as he had little to lose.

The ever-present sirens of Manhattan exploded and Emine took another puff on her cigarette. She waited, knowing that she didn't need to hurry Bud. He'd answer her. She loved how big his body felt next to her own more delicate one. Scared to leave Ed, dependent because she was weak, she also knew he wasn't the right one and certainly not to marry. Emine couldn't be a good match for a corporate lawyer and would only wreck his perfect life.

"What's he like?" Bud asked?

"Perfect," the word popped into her head again. It was always the word that came to mind when she thought of or described Ed. And she was so thoroughly fucked up; a mess with the reporting and alcohol and nameless men she'd screwed in dirty hotels. The palace on the hill overlooking the Bosporus was only part of her past and the rest she kept shoving under various carpets.

And if you don't feel loveable how can you trust someone who says they love you?

If Emine married Ed she'd look at him daily knowing that she'd betray him and eventually would see the disillusionment in his eyes, accusing and angry. Her past, present and future all combined to make her impossible of better behavior. Did she even value doing better? Bud expected her betrayal and she expected his so their relationship was inherently more honest in its hidden allusions and unanswered questions. They were like siblings who'd learned to love past the bad behavior and countless mistakes. Their loyalty was absolute and she had no one else who accepted all her flaws and selfish decisions. They'd shared so much.

But to explain Ed.

"Blonde, educated, Brahmin..." she continued and watched as Bud got out of bed, crushing his cigarette into the hotel's cherry wood night table. He was laughing now and opened the minibar, studying its contents. Grabbing a cognac he threw her a handful of little bottles. Always the gentlemen, she knew he'd pick up the tab.

She laughed with him, and then nuzzled deeply into his chest when he rejoined her. She could feel a new erection pressing into her leg, throbbing and almost violent. He was always ready for more and she braced herself. Sometimes, as the night wore on, he got rough.

"I liked that doctor," he said. "The Belgian." Bud's hands were on her now and she felt him expertly massage the deep knots in her back, cooing as her pent up emotions were released under his expert pressure.

"He died," she responded, then cried out as his fingers seemingly dislodged some deeper tension in her shoulder.

"I want to make you pregnant, Eme," he whispered, and kissed her tenderly on the lips. "Marry me instead." Bud exhaled and she smelled the alcohol but knew he wasn't drunk. He rubbed his firm body into hers and she could smell his familiar, pungent sweat. She drew him closer but looked deeply into his eyes to discern his emotions. The blackness of his pupils contrasted with the white that surrounded them. He smiled at her.

"You didn't say you love me," she replied. "I'm not living in Capetown."

"I'll get you an apartment somewhere else. Visit once a year."

She studied him.

"People like us are too broken to love easily, Eme. Don't marry someone who won't understand you. I do."

"Aren't you a warlord?" she asked, more curious than anything else. His father was among the wiliest and best connected in Africa, a mining baron with a presence in countless countries. The interviews he could get her... She'd just been too timid to ask before. Nothing comes for free.

"What a romantic notion," Bud replied, not really answering her direct question. Then again, did the answer really matter when the definition of warlord varied with the defining body?

He laughed and entered her quickly, condom-less this time. Against their rules! Who knew what he fucked when she wasn't around, which was most of the time. "I'll buy you the biggest diamond at Harry Winston and we'll elope," he promised and she tried to push him off but he just kissed her and she felt him come, so fast, inside her.

"I hope that makes a baby," he exclaimed with a chuckle. And she laughed back. Bastard. He was so used to getting his way. If she hadn't known him for so long and trusted him so deeply she would have killed him. But culturally, she was used to strong men used to dominating women.

Bud's eyes sparkled in the dark light, illuminated by the cityscape outside floor length windows, and he kept her nuzzled tightly.

"You love tough men, Eme," he said. "Marry me and I'll make you happy. I promise. We'll name our first boy after your doctor. He's in your heart and head still, but can't be in your bed so let him go."

She curled into him, not resisting, and pulled the white sheet across their bodies. Why did he keep the air conditioning so high? The suite was massive but they were off in the largest bedroom, glistening high above the rest of the city and its less protected residents. Bud was as flawed as she was; perhaps even more so.

Maybe?

"Okay," she answered, not sure but starting with a tentative move in his direction. He was her rock and she was addicted to him, indeed kept running back to his open arms in times of desperation or need. Emine loved everything about Bud from his smell to those broad shoulders and hard muscles, his voice and that always tanned skin, smooth like marble but so much warmer. For tonight she'd let him be her home, then perhaps also in the morning. But no babies!

Emine curled closer into the pillows; feeling the hardness of smooth muscles as well, lean, against her skin. She was glowing from the sex and her heart warmed as she contemplated whether she really should commit to this man. They were both so rootless, yanked from their native soil too young and tossed into globalization, parents jet setting and busy with their own lives. Ed, in contrast, had feet planted in firm soil. He might wander for a few years in Paris or perhaps even a place more exotic but he'd always end up back home, protected and sheltered by a society in which he belonged.

Dispossessed, she knew that she belonged, at least for now, with her own kind. And Emine also wanted to venture deeper into the chaos of Africa, beyond the Sudanese refuge camps and bloody Mogadishu streets of her past work. Bud was the perfect man to take her into that world and perhaps eventually they would find a place to plant mutual roots. Egypt had been a gateway that hinted at the mysteries of delving deeper into the continent's mysteries, Arabic turning to Nubian, and then the labyrinth of tribal dialects and identities (4 major languages). What was Africa, really, today? Vast and increasingly mega-cities and not safaris, she knew only of corruption, beads, drums and disease. Forests, rivers, mountains and valleys were all expansive so what better landscape for her camera lens and multitude of questions existed?

Emine was one who could only move forward if she had a mission and questions to ask. Those distractions kept her from the forced self-analysis staying put can encourage. Bud let her live thus and as she desired.

Tripping in life or even falling doesn't matter; rather what makes the difference is whether you get up again. Emine and Bud both took chances so they'd stumble around plenty more before finding their right destinations, but she vowed to keep getting up from her tumbles and falls, regardless of how much they hurt. No need to walk that path alone when she had a hot man willing to take those risks alongside.

"Cigarette?" she asked Bud and he took one, lighting hers before his own with his diamond lighter, and their intermingled smoke floated up to the ceiling before disbursing.

The End